BY LOVE ENCHANTED

"I had to come," Eirik murmured softly, his voice sounding like water moving tranquilly through a brook.

"Why?" Alysa inquired just above a whisper.

As if dazed, he confessed. "You have bewitched me, my beautiful enchantress. I know it is perilous to tempt fate, but I cannot help myself. I need you, Alysa, more than air or food or victory."

Alysa engulfed him with her loving gaze. It had been many weeks since she had lain with Gavin Crisdean, and it seemed to be her husband—her lost love—whom she was seeing tonight, hearing this very moment, reaching out to her . . .

JANELLE TAYLOR

THE LAST VIKING QUEEN

PINNACLE BOOKS
WINDSOR PUBLISHING CORP.

PINNACLE BOOKS are published by

Windsor Publishing Corp.
475 Park Avenue South
New York, NY 10016

First Printing: February, 1994

Printed in the United States of America

Britain 430 A.D.

STRATHCLYDE

ALBANY

CAILEAN

BRIAC

CUMBRIA

BARDWYN

CAMBRIA

LOGRIS

VORTIGERN

FERGUS

JUTE

DAMNONIA

ORIN

HORSA

JUTE

KEEGAN

TEAGUE

HENGIST

WEYLIN

ALYSA/GAVIN

* King's castles   # Stonehenge
● Feudal lord's castles
× Enemy strongholds   □ Treasures

One

"Dark days are ahead, my beloved princess," warned Trosdan, powerful wizard and a High Priest of the Druid sect, which had been outlawed and dispersed by the conquering Romans many years ago. "Days of treachery, peril, and evil lie before us. All must be conquered before peace can rule your land once more. You are the key to turn back the forces of Darkness. Only you can reopen the Door to Light and Good which is being rapidly closed and locked. Only you can halt this madness which threatens us."

Trosdan's voice lowered as he warned, "But the price you must pay is great and the perils you must face are terrible."

A smile warmed the old man's clear blue eyes and deepened the countless wrinkles on his face; he did not want to panic or discourage this girl whom he loved and respected. The sacred Runes had told him what he, what *they,* must do to obtain victory and survival. No matter his personal thoughts, feelings, and desires, he must obey the Runes' messages and be true to his calling of High Priest, Guardian of the Ancient Laws and Master of the Great Mysteries. "You can bring your people back from the edge of destruction, but you must endure many torments to save all you love and rule. I will guide you and protect you during those dark moments, but you must follow my advice no matter

7

your doubts, fears, and pains. You must use all of your wits, and your courage to battle these savage invaders. And, you also must depend on your special powers to aid your cause."

In an age when people believed in superstition, sorcery, and the supernatural, she understood Trosdan's meaning. It was alleged that her grandmother Giselde possessed potent skills of magic and the gifts of insight and healing, as Alysa's mother Catriona had before her death ten years ago. Princess Alysa Malvern Crisdean had witnessed many inexplicable things, but doubted her inherited ability in such mysteries of life. The ruler of the principality of Damnonia, which belonged to the kingdom of Cambria, refuted gently, "But I have no special powers, Wise One."

"Yea, but you do, my beloved princess. You will summon them and use them well when the time comes to battle Evil. There is a magical glow about you which Evil cannot extinguish, though it will try for a second time to do so. You must not fail in your awesome task, for victory and survival are controlled by your grasp alone. Even I can do little against such powerful forces."

Alysa moved a few steps away from Trosdan in the large cave where he lived and practiced his wizardry. As the Celts still believed in and practiced the "Old Ways," especially since the Roman withdrawal, his words were both frightening and stimulating to Alysa. Her heart beat faster as she recalled the first time "Evil" had tried to destroy her. Victory had been won six weeks past with the deaths of her evil stepmother and half brother and with the defeat of their wicked brigands. Isobail and Moran had tried to steal her land and enslave her people. But a handsome warrior from another kingdom had arrived to claim her heart and to help gain victory. Six weeks past, they had wed, and now ruled Damnonia side by side. Prince Alric, her father and son of King Bardwyn of Cambria, had been slain during those previous dark days; now, she listened to Trosdan warn of more

8

dark days ahead. The Vikings were greedy and vicious invaders; each day they were becoming stronger and attacking closer. She wondered if her land would ever know true and lasting peace again. She wanted to think of nothing except ruling her people, loving her husband, and bearing his children. Grief over her father's death had been soothed by the fact he had suffered greatly and had welcomed release from his pain and anguish. He was united with his parents in the happy afterworld, so she must not mourn his loss. Since birth, she had been schooled to become this land's ruler, a task she was carrying out with skill. Her people loved and admired her and obeyed her commands. Why did more trouble—

Trosdan interrupted her thoughts. "I have prepared for this wicked time, but I cannot reveal such plans to you today. Soon you will learn and do all expected of you, as did your ancestors Connal, Rurik, and Astrid. Their bloods run within you and make you stronger and wiser than other rulers. Your destiny is at hand, Alysa; you must accept it and follow it. To refuse it brings disaster."

Alysa could not forget that Connal, her great-grandfather from Albany, had been captured and carried away by Vikings. He had escaped and brought Astrid—his Viking love—to his homeland. Enraged, the Norsemen had attacked again and as they again searched for the treacherous couple whom their *attiba*—wizard—had vowed would be the cause of all future defeats on this mighty island. During one of those raids, a royal Viking warrior had fallen in love with her grandmother, causing Rurik to take sides with the Albanians. He and Giselde, daughter of Connal and Astrid, had given birth to Catriona, Alysa's mother. *How strange,* Alysa mused, *that my family's blood is always mingling with that of our fiercest enemies.* Stranger still, and an alarming threat, was the fact Alysa was alleged to be the Last Viking Queen of royal birth, a prize for any Viking to capture.

Alysa did not like that thought, so she dismissed it from her mind. "Tell me more, Wise One," the young princess urged.

"Soon," he responded mysteriously. Trosdan's watchful gaze eyed the lovely young woman before him. Her medium-brown hair tumbled down her back and halted near her waist. Her sea-blue eyes were bright with intrigue, and her beauty could be denied by no one. At nineteen, she was one of the youngest rulers of this mighty island of Britain. The old man knew what loomed before her, for his hand controlled her fate. "You must return home. As we speak, your first challenge approaches. Throughout the ages, each time Evil strikes at Good, the Great Beings provide us with a champion to battle their dark forces. Remember," he cautioned, *"you* are the ruler here, the one chosen by the gods to save all. Let nothing and no one mislead, halt, or discourage you. No one," he stressed, his expression grim.

"What is your meaning, Wise One?" she questioned the man with white hair and soft and snowy beard which fell below his heart. Never had she met anyone who was kinder or gentler or wiser, or more trustworthy. There was a reverent air and magnetic mystery about Trosdan, and all heeded his words. His skills were said to be matchless, and many feared disobeying or angering him. His insight and magic had guided them through their last battle with Evil, and he was offering his help once more. No one knew the enemy better than Trosdan, as he was a Viking by birth and a Briton by choice. He had loved and served her grandmother Giselde for years, but a wizard never wed if he wished to keep his powers. To save and to help those he loved, it was imperative for Trosdan to retain his strengths and talents, to remain unblemished by surrender to worldly desires.

"You must be strong, Alysa. You must put your destiny and victory above your own desires and dreams. Soon you

10

will travel a narrow path, a dangerous one. Do not let anguish halt your journey, or all is lost—for you, for your land, for your people, and for Good. Many have suffered and died already. If you battle your fate, many more will do so. Others will draw from your abundant courage and prowess; they will follow your lead, even into death's jaws."

The High Priest's words revealed an awesome responsibility. She asked, "What if courage deserts me or the knights refuse to follow a woman into fierce battle against our invaders? It is easier for a female to rule a peaceful kingdom than to persuade men to allow her to lead a battle charge. Will the gods prepare their hearts and minds to accept me as this chosen one?"

Trosdan caressed her cheek and smiled again. His eyes twinkled with the knowledge he possessed. "Before the new moon shines on this land, you will have proven yourself to all." Trosdan lifted her left hand and touched her wedding ring with a gnarled finger. "You shall become a legendary warrior queen who even this powerful ring of desire cannot restrain or defeat. Go, for a great adventure with many sacrifices and challenges awaits you. When the time is right, I will come to you and set your feet upon the path you must travel."

Alysa wondered where her husband fit into the events confronting her, as Trosdan had not mentioned Gavin. The elderly man had made it sound as if she were going to face those perils alone. She recalled how Trosdan and Giselde had foretold the truth about Isobail and how those two special people had used their skills to aid Alysa's side. Somehow, she could not resist believing in such powers.

Fear furrowed Alysa's brow. "How can I become a queen without my grandfather dying? Is that your meaning, Wise One? Do you say King Bardwyn will soon pass into another world?" she inquired, worried and sad as she anticipated his answer.

11

"That was not my meaning, Princess, but I can tell you no more today. Hearts do not accept difficult words until they have been prepared to receive them. You are not ready to begin your journey."

Although he clearly had ended their conversation, Alysa persisted. "When will I be ready, Trosdan? What will prepare me?"

Trosdan smiled. "Your mind runs in many directions like a wild horse. Tether it until you understand the secrets in my words today. Then, I will come to you. There will be no need to summon me, for I will know when the time is here."

Trosdan gave Alysa a final warning, a tormenting one. Her face paled and she trembled. As she stared at him in disbelief, she began to shake her head. "Nay, Trosdan, you have misread the Runes."

His sea-blue eyes exposed honesty and sympathy. "The will of the gods cannot be denied, my beloved princess. But there is hope," he added, and explained his meaning. "Go now. I will come to you soon."

Knowing the Druid leader would tell her nothing more, Alysa embraced him and departed. Mounting Calliope, she rode for home with mixed emotions. Perhaps, she sadly decided, Trosdan had gotten old and his mind and eyes were playing tricks on him. Surely he could not be right about . . . She reached Malvern Castle only minutes before her "first challenge" arrived, just as Trosdan had predicted.

Sir Teague and his wife Thisbe dismounted hurriedly and joined the alert princess, who had halted on the castle steps to speak with a servant. Their faces shone with perspiration, and Alysa knew from their expressions that something was terribly wrong. Trosdan's words flooded her mind, and her heart pounded in dread. She ordered water to wet their throats, which most certainly were parched. "Rest a moment and drink, Sir Teague, then reveal your bad news."

Thisbe, who had been Alysa's handmaiden until her marriage, collapsed on the steps in exhaustion. Alysa commanded her servants to carry the young woman to a visitor's chamber to recover. Alysa was anxious to hear the news, but did not press the fatigued man, a past squire at this castle and a longtime friend. She wondered why her husband, Prince Gavin Crisdean, had not joined them. Surely he was aware of the commotion in the inner courtyard. Before she could send for him, the prince galloped through the castle gates with several of his knights.

Alysa's sea-blue eyes washed over Gavin's handsome face and virile body. From their attire and gear, it was obvious her husband had been hunting with a few of the knights. She watched his eyes take in his curious surroundings as he dismounted and came forward. In spite of the dark episode in progress, she could not help but seal her loving gaze to his probing green one. "We have trouble, my husband, but Sir Teague must catch his wind before he reveals it."

The Prince of Cumbria and Damnonia observed the red-haired knight who was still laboring to breathe normally after his swift and lengthy ride. Teague's sorry state of appearance alerted the ruler to trouble. "Let us go into the Great Hall where we can sit and drink while we talk," Gavin invited. He extended his hand to Alysa to escort her inside. He felt her tremblings and knew she was gravely concerned over this apparently grim situation. He, too, was worried. Under the guise of a hunting trip, he and several knights had been scouting the countryside for any signs of peril and foe, but had found none. Yet Gavin realized it was only a matter of time before the persistent invaders reached Damnonia and created the same havoc here they were causing in the neighboring kingdom of Logris.

After a short rest and a cup of inspiriting ale, Sir Teague revealed his grisly news. "The Vikings crossed our border,

Your Highness, and raided our castle. They slew, burned, and pillaged. Lady Gweneth and her two daughters were captured with other slaves and carried off after the attack. There was nothing we could do to halt them; they were many and strong. They raided with a blood-lust which I have never witnessed before." The weary knight's voice was hoarse from his dusty journey. He drank more ale before continuing. "At my guard's insistence, Thisbe and I were concealed in a secret room just before the Norsemen broke down the inner gates. We were forced to remain hidden while they plundered my home and lands. After they left, we escaped to a nearby village to procure two horses and rode here with much haste. I have dishonored myself, my country, my rulers, and my rank with such cowardice."

Alysa watched the red-haired knight lower his head in shame. The scars from his capture and beatings by Isobail and Moran were still visible on his face and arms. Only four weeks past he had been knighted, wed, and placed in control of Lord Daron's estate near the Logris border. Alysa grasped his hand and said comfortingly, "Do not punish yourself, Teague. There was nothing you and your men could do against such odds. You have served us well and you will continue to do so. We have been friends since childhood, and I love you as a brother and Thisbe as a sister. Do not burden yourself with undeserved blame. I have no knight with more courage and honor than you possess."

Prince Gavin added, "If you had not concealed yourself, you would not have survived to bring us this news or to battle our enemies on another day. You are not responsible for your defeat. Lift your head and shoulders, for your honor is still intact."

Teague did as he was commanded, but his gaze exposed the anguish within him. He felt it was his duty to protect the property and people his rulers had entrusted to him. Shame would plague him until revenge was obtained. "We were taken by surprise and had no time to prepare a defense. If you will provide me with warriors, I will ride after the raiders and rescue Lord Daron's family and the others."

The tawny haired ruler said, "First, we must gather our forces and plan wisely. I will send for our lords and knights. We cannot strike at our foes until we set up defenses for our land. It will require many days to track them and attack. We cannot leave our homes and families unprotected during our absence. To do so would invite the raiders to swoop down on them. We must be patient and cunning."

"Prince Gavin is right," Princess Alysa remarked. "To venture into Logris will be a long and difficult journey. We must be well prepared. How many raiders attacked you and who was their leader?"

"It was a giant of a man called Rolf with hair the color of the sun. From the parapet I saw him battle several men at once. He has great prowess. His followers numbered more than fifty—fierce men who clearly enjoy killing and destroying. Our victory will be a hard and bloody one."

While the men talked, Alysa called to mind Trosdan's warnings and wondered how she could lead a defeat of this would-be conqueror. What, she fretted, were the "price" and "perils" which the old man had mentioned? How could she alone lead her people to victory over such awesome forces? Gavin loved her. He had proven so by remaining here in Damnonia to live and rule at her side, even though he seemed bored and restless with his quiet existence. When the time came for him to become King of Cumbria and she Queen of both Cambria and Damnonia, they would decide together how to carry out their duties in three different lands. Trosdan had to be mistaken about them taking separate paths. Nay, Gavin would never betray or desert her!

"We need courageous and daring spies, my husband, to bring us news of their numbers and locations. If one band of raiders counts more than fifty, there must be *hundreds* of Vikings in Logris. We must do as you did before—separate and conquer them a band at a time. If they are allowed to join forces against us . . ." Alysa shuddered and did not finish her distressing statement.

To relax his anxious wife, Gavin suggested, "Let us wait for our retainers to arrive before we talk more on this depressing matter. There is nothing we can do or decide today. Teague needs rest and nourishment." He summoned Piaras, the trainer of castle knights, and ordered the man to send for their vassals. Leitis, Piaras's wife and head castle servant, was called to prepare food and lodgings for Teague.

Alysa and Gavin were left alone when Teague excused himself to check on Thisbe his wife and Piaras departed to carry out his ruler's command. Gavin slipped his arms around his wife and whispered, "Do not be afraid, m'love. I will allow no harm to come to you."

Alysa looked up into his smiling face and witnessed his love and desire for her. Their bond was a powerful one and nothing could destroy it. Easing to her tiptoes, she sealed their lips in a heady kiss. As always, passion's flames and tingles swept over her and she clung to him, refusing to think of any intrusion by fate or a visitor. She felt his arms tighten about her slender frame and perceived his possessive grip on her heart and body.

As his lips roamed her flushed face, he disclosed ardently, "While I am gone, I will make certain you are guarded and protected. When I return victoriously, we shall have a large feast to celebrate."

Alysa tensed in his embrace. She leaned back to gaze into his eyes. "Nay, my husband, I cannot remain here while you battle our foes. I must ride with you and the others. Piaras has trained me well, so I can fight beside any man. A ruler always rides into combat with his knights and warriors. I can do no less because I am a woman. Did I not prove myself a skilled fighter only weeks ago?"

16

"This is different," Gavin protested in a gentle tone. "In days past, you used your wits and daring. In the battles awaiting us, warrior skills and strengths will be required. You are not strong enough to fight men. You are needed here to hold our people together, to keep them from losing faith. You will be safe at home."

Alysa knew that Gavin—as most men—was raised to think of women as wives and mothers, creatures who were born to please and serve men. Perhaps he had not realized she was different; she was a royal regent. She was a leader, not a follower; she was a commander, not an obeyer. Trosdan's warning flashed through her troubled mind. She had to make her husband understand her position and agree with it. "One day I will be queen of two lands, Gavin. If I cannot protect my people and ride with them into the jaws of peril, I am not a worthy ruler. Being wise and just while sitting in the lap of safety is not enough to hold their allegiance. I must prove I am strong, cunning, and valiant in the midst of danger. My warriors will be filled with greater courage if their regent is riding and fighting with them. To face such odds and perils, they will need this added courage."

Her words did not persuade him. He shook his head and stated firmly, "This is foolhardy, m'love. I cannot let you go."

"I must," she argued just as resolutely. "I am the ruler of this land. I cannot allow a warrior, even a prince, from another kingdom to lead my people in my place. It is my duty."

Gavin was concerned over her determination. He did not wish to be forceful and stern with his gentle wife, but he would do so if necessary to halt her wild plans. He could not permit Princess Alysa to play warrior for *any* reason. How could he and the others concentrate if they were distracted by protecting her? How could he imperil his love? "I am your husband and joint ruler of your lands. My wishes must be honored. You have many talents, m'love, but you are not a soldier. Our enemies will laugh if we go into battle with a delicate woman riding before us. You could be injured or slain. What then of our warriors' courage? What of *their* safety with their thoughts turned on defending their ruler?"

Alysa's gaze roamed the stubborn set of her husband's jaw, the scowl lines on his forehead, and the determination in his green eyes. His dark-blond hair with its sunny streaks rested on his shoulders, shoulders whose size revealed the strength and prowess in his six-foot-four-inch frame. His well-toned and strong body was proof of the practice and exercise he participated in each day with Piaras and the other knights. Yet those steely muscles were covered by smooth flesh of golden brown, flesh which tantalized her when pressed against her silky skin.

Alysa tried another path to reach him. She revealed, "Trosdan has warned me of these dark times before us. He told me of Teague's coming. He has read the Runes which say I am to lead our people into battle. If I do not, all is lost. I cannot yield to your fears for my life."

The prince realized she was serious and not to be swayed easily. Although it was distasteful to him, Gavin knew he had to be slightly dishonest to discourage her from what he considered a wild and dangerous idea. He tenderly chided, "It is only superstition, m'love. Marks upon broken stones cannot foretell the future or control it. The only real magic lies within ourselves, Alysa, within our hearts and minds. Do not allow an old man's dreams and words to misguide you and to cause great trouble and conflict between us and in our land."

Alysa frowned. "You did not feel or speak this way weeks ago when Trosdan and Giselde's predictions came true."

"That was only coincidence, perhaps clever insight or good judgment. Your grandmother is gone now, wed to King

18

Bardwyn and living in Cambria. Forget her curious ways, and those of the old Druid's. Our warriors cannot follow and obey two leaders. Would you have me stand aside while you try to guide them? I am trained and experienced in such matters. You are not. You have only lived nineteen summers and I have lived twenty-seven. You have enjoyed peace here, but I have roamed the world and battled countless dangers. If you insist on leading our forces, they will be confused and disgruntled. Think of what is best for all, Alysa. Do not let your pride destroy us."

"Was it coincidence that my grandmother removed the royal tattoo upon your chest?" Alysa argued, referring to the custom of staining royal symbols on the bodies of high-born men with a woad dye which was supposed to be permanent. Yet Giselde had magically removed Gavin's to conceal his royal rank during their war against Isobail, and that was why Alysa had not guessed his identity during their intimate relationship. Since that day, it had been replaced.

"It was a trick, m'love. Giselde is well acquainted with plants and herbs. I do not deny her skills in nature, but she is not a powerful sorceress. If I was learned in such matters, I am sure I could explain how they perform their spells and deeds. There are many secrets and powers in nature, but that does not make the knower of such things able to do more than use them. It is people's fears or desires which make them believe in such powers and enchanters. Trust me, m'love; Giselde did not perform magic on me, nor on others."

"If I refuse my destiny, we will be conquered."

Gavin caressed her cheek. "Your destiny is to be my obedient and cherished wife, the mother of Britain's future rulers. We have need of several sons to sit upon the thrones of Cambria, Damnonia, and Cumbria. Remain here in safety where my seeds can grow within you and fulfill our true

19

destiny while I go forth to meet this challenge. Is that not enough for you, Alysa?"

Unusual anger suffused her. "I am more than a breeder of future kings and princes. You will become king of Cumbria when your father dies, but I will be queen of Cumbria and Damnonia at Grandfather's death. I will also become queen of your land, but you can become nothing more than my consort. If Fate had wanted a king for my lands, I would have been born a son. I am not just a mere woman, Hawk of Cumbria. A great destiny awaits me as a warrior queen. I must let nothing and no one prevent me from seeking and following it."

"Nothing and no one, Alysa? Not even me or our love or our future?" he questioned. "Do you seek glory more than these precious things? Do an old man's words mean more to you than mine?"

Price you must pay . . . . Put your destiny and victory above your own desires and dreams . . . . Was Trosdan right, would she be called upon to travel her path alone? Could she give up her love to do so? Clearly, Gavin was not going to change his mind. If she believed Trosdan and followed his advice, would her price be Gavin? And if she surrendered to Gavin's wishes, would all be lost as Trosdan predicted? If only she had the Gift of a Seer, she would know what to do.

Gavin released her. "Your silence answers for you."

Alysa grasped his arm and protested, "I love you with all my heart, Gavin Crisdean. Glory means nothing to me. But there is more to consider than our love and desires. My land has been invaded and I have my duty. There are things I as a ruler must do, even if it endangers my life. I beg you, do not force me to choose between my love and my country."

There was an unfamiliar emotion in his eyes and tone as he asserted, "Your choice was made even before we spoke.

ou will do as you wish, no matter my words or feelings.
cannot agree with you, so we waste our breath discussing
iis further. Think more on your decision and we will talk
onight. I must go order spies to the Logris border. We want
o more surprise attacks before we are ready to strike."

Gavin left Alysa standing in the Great Hall. He hoped a
how of anger and coolness would dissaude her. Once she
ealized how impossible it was for her to ride into battle,
e would become himself again. Perhaps a lusty bout of
ovemaking tonight would clear her head—or cloud it with
houghts of only him. He grinned in anticipation of how he
ould master his wayward wife.

Alysa leaned against a towering pillar of stone. Suddenly
he felt weary and dispirited. Trosdan's final warning re-
urned to haunt her:

"The Hawk of Cumbria will not fly with you on this
ated journey. It is a path you must travel alone. Do not
ear, for I will be at your side to aid and protect you. The
rince will not understand or accept what you must do to
in this victory. For a time, he will seek his own fate along
different path and you will rule alone."

Gavin, whose name meant hawk, was dearly loved by
er. Could she risk losing him, after having him only a
hort time? Would he desert her if she refused to bend to
is will? He was so strong and proud yet so gentle. He had
elped her win the last battle to save her land. Why could
e not do so again? He was her husband, but this was her
and. He was practically a stranger here. Surely the Dam-
onians would follow her before following him. Was there
ope?

". . . But there is hope. If you yield to your destiny, he
ill not be lost forever. He is a warrior of great prowess
nd you are a bride of destiny. You have seized the magic
f love which runs undaunted through the ages. Beneath a
onqueror's moon, my warrior queen, you will again bind

21

this man's soul and heart to yours with gyves of love and with this sacred ring of desire. By love enchanted, you shall rule side by side and love forever . . . if you follow your fate. If you do not, even I cannot save you."

Two

Alysa prepared herself for bed without the assistance of her current handmaiden. She had missed Thisbe. The young princess was happy to have Thisbe and Teague back at the castle, but she hated the situation which had driven them here. She and Thisbe had spent many days together—sharing knowledge and secrets, enjoying pleasures, enduring pains, and growing into womanhood. The friendship between princess and servant had been a very close and unique one. Alysa knew that Thisbe could be trusted with all things, even with her life, as could Teague.

In the privy where bathing and other personal tasks were carried out to avoid disorder in the adjoining royal chambers, the blue-eyed princess stepped from the circular wooden tub and dried herself. After slipping into a soft kirtle, she brushed her hair. As she relaxed, her mind wandered to dreamy places. So much had changed since Prince Gavin Crisdean had entered her life several months ago—a mysterious and irresistible warrior. Tonight she must prove her love to her new husband, although it should not be necessary.

She and Gavin needed more time to get to know each other fully. Their romance had been swift and passionate. It had been surrounded by perils and mysteries, and plagued

23

by doubts and fears. Her grandfather, King Bardwyn, had suggested their hasty wedding, and neither she nor Gavin had refused. They had been married for only six weeks, too few days and nights for becoming one person. Before then, separately they had battled the same foe, while meeting secretly in the royal forest to savor intimate moments. During most of their times together, she had not known he was the Prince of Cumbria and he had not known she was Princess Alysa. Both had used secret identities which had caused them much suffering. She had believed him to be a common warrior from a foreign land and he had believed her to be a castle servant, and each had believed neither could wed the other because of their royal ranks. How happy the day had been when each had discovered the other's matching feelings and rank.

Alysa knew there was strong love and powerful desire between them. Yet in many ways, they were strangers to each other. There was so much they did not know about each other, so much to discover. Those first two weeks of feverish marriage had been easy for them, especially with the king present and the thrill of victory still fresh. They had ridden with King Bardwyn to check the countryside and to visit feudal lords and villages. Feasts and weddings had filled their days and devoured their energies. A stimulating joust had been held and many hunts and games had challenged their wits and skills. But the king had departed soon and normal life had resumed in the peaceful land.

A warrior and adventurer by choice, Gavin appeared bored with his existence in the castle. He was unaccustomed to living quietly, to enduring the daily tasks of a ruler, to seeking ways to entertain and exercise himself, to spending his time and passions with one woman. He was a man accustomed to challenges, to constant movement, to rapid changes, to feasting on perils and victories and on life's varied pleasures. Except for lovemaking, there had been little excitement and stimulation for him since the defeat of Isobail, Moran, and the brigands who had been terrorizing her land.

Following the departure of King Bardwyn and Giselde weeks ago, Gavin had placed his friends in control of certain areas and positions which had been left vacant by the deaths of friends and traitors. Dal, their new sheriff, and Lann, his second in command, traveled the principality maintaining law and order. Weylin and Keegan had been made lords of two feudal estates previously owned by Sir Kelton and Sheriff Trahern. Bevan was in love with a farmer's daughter and spent most of his time romancing her. With his friends gone, Gavin had little to do and few diversions. The princess's husband, as joint ruler, could not visit or travel with his friends and leave the castle deserted. Hunting and exercise could only claim so many hours. Gavin was unaccustomed to being alone and to having so much leisure time. He missed the comradeship of his friends and the thrills of their stimulating adventures. Solving the problems of subjects offered no challenge to him. Alysa knew he was bored and restless. But what to do? she wondered. Gavin only saw her as a lover, a woman, his wife. How could she teach him that she was so much more?

During their meeting with Sir Teague this afternoon, she had witnessed the sparkle in Gavin's eyes, the eagerness in his voice, the tension in his body. He had been hearing of the raids in Logris and Albany, presenting a new challenge to occupy his time and wits and to test his prowess, and a reason to call his friends back together. With the challenge of the invasion, he seemed more vital today than he had in weeks. He did not want anything or anyone to prevent this new adventure. Could Alysa allow this peril to destroy all she loved and ruled by yielding to her husband's wishes? Clearly, he was looking forward to battling their enemies, to outwitting clever foes, to pushing invaders out of their land, but without her help or intrusion.

Gavin had anticipated a visit by his father and mother, King Briac and Queen Brenna of Cumbria. But Viking raids in nearby Albany and Logris had postponed their journey, their recent message had claimed. With hopes of learning more about Gavin and providing him with a much needed distraction, Alysa had been eager for his parents' arrival. She was especially eager to meet the man who had been her mother's first love, the neighboring prince who had sacrificed Catriona for his rank and who had once rescued her mother from a Viking raid in Albany. Alysa wanted to see if Gavin was anything like his parents. She wanted to discover what kind of man Briac was, what kind of man chose his royal duty over his true love.

As Alysa brushed her long brown hair, she thought about the two friends who had arrived earlier today. Teague and Thisbe were settled in the visitors' chambers, resting and recovering from their ordeal. She tried to envision the battle at Lord Daron's castle, and could not without remembering how Lord Daron had been slain during Isobail's reign of evil. Sir Teague had been appointed to take care of Daron's feudal lands until Daron's sons—who were squires in training at other castles—came of age to take control of them. Now, Gweneth and her two daughters were captives of the invading Norsemen. What, she wondered sadly, was happening to the Damnonian women? What were their fates? Could they be located and rescued? It was dreadful to think of such offensive captivity.

Alysa tried vainly to put a face to the Viking conqueror whom Teague had described. Strong features, a handsome face, white-blond hair, and a muscular body filled her mind's eye. Would she ever meet this man? Would she be able to defeat him as the old wizard had predicted?

"Trosdan, I need you," she murmured softly.

"Did you speak to me?" Gavin asked as he entered their chamber.

Alysa turned on the wooden bench and fused her gaze to his. "I need you," she murmured, her voice filled with passionate emotion.

Gavin smiled at her as he came forward and pulled her to her feet. "As I need you, m'love," he replied huskily. Pulling her kirtle over her head, he tossed it aside and gazed appreciatively at her naked body. He had been daydreaming about this moment for hours and his thoughts had kindled his body into a smoldering flame. It did not matter that he feasted on her each day, his hunger for her was insatiable.

Without delay, Gavin removed his garments and allowed them to drop to the stone floor. He lifted Alysa and carried her to the bed, where he placed her and stretched out beside her.

Her blue eyes locked with his green ones, and each was mirrored in the other's shiny gaze. The reflections created a dreamy landscape upon which the lovers could explore and savor their emotions. Unspoken messages passed between them. As love conquered their warring hearts and passion invaded their bodies, all other thoughts and feelings were vanquished. All doubts and worries were cast aside, and any cunning guile was forgotten.

Without words, Gavin's hands roamed Alysa's body, and hers did the same on her lover's supple flesh. Again and again their lips touched softly and briefly as they enticed each other to bolder ventures. Gradually the tentative kisses deepened and lengthened. Their tongues danced wildly and playfully together, then feverishly. They took turns nibbling upon each other's lips. Their shared breathing was fast and shallow, and exposed the height of their arousal. The wild, sweet promise of rapturous love awaited them.

Gavin's mouth drifted leisurely down the slender column of Alysa's neck. He pressed his lips to the pulsing vein

27

which told him her heart was pounding in fierce yearning for him. He heard her sigh with pleasure as his lips teased the pliant mounds on her chest before conquering their brown peaks. Soon she was moaning in the bittersweet throes of rising need. He enjoyed giving her pleasure as much as he enjoyed receiving it from her, which he was doing now as her hands skillfully stroked him. For one with such a short span of experience, his wife was a superb lover. He had known no female who could satisfy him more than Alysa, nor a female who kept him ever thirsting for her. He was utterly enchanted, enslaved.

Alysa encouraged Gavin's blissful exploration of her body by writhing and murmuring approval of his skilled attention. He tantalized her with his movements, with his manly smell, with his husky voice and virile physique. As his hard body yielded to her soft touch, she was thrilled by his response to her caresses and kisses. It was wonderful knowing she could send his appetite to such a high level, masterfully make it hover there, then sate it so rapturously.

Gavin's deft hand roved her flat stomach, her silky thighs, and boldly entered her. It took great care to sensuously wander in and out of the moistness of her and over the flaming peak. Her pulsating womanhood burst into flame and she urged him to extinguish it. Gavin moved atop her and guided his soothing member into her.

Their bodies locked together. It was a time of giving, of taking, of sharing. They both quivered with anticipation as their hands and lips continued to heighten their pleasures and desires.

Gavin felt his wife squirming beneath him as she sought to fill herself with him. A white-hot heat burned within him, threatening to consume him with a wildfire.

Alysa was aware only of their swift pace toward the summit of bliss. When she reached love's precipice, she hesitated only a moment before willingly and eagerly throwing herself over its rapturous edge. Powerful waves splashed over her shuddering body. She was carried away by the potent current, so ensnared by its force, she could hardly breathe. Time and time again she briefly surfaced to seize a gasp of air, only to be dragged under the blissful surface once more. She helplessly and joyously rode out the feverish storm until she was cast gently upon the quiet beach of love's paradise.

Gavin rapidly pursued Alysa over passion's beautiful peak, savoring each moment and spasm which heralded his own victory. He was finally carried into a valley of peace with his wife in his arms. Contentment claimed both of them, as did sleep.

When Alysa awakened in the morning, Gavin was not at her side. She wished he were so they could make love again, then talk seriously about their disagreement. Soon the lords and knights would arrive, and the spies would return. Before then, she and her husband needed to reach an understanding about the imminent conflict with the invaders and the role destiny had assigned to her.

She left her bed and dressed, pulling a dark-blue tunic over a clean kirtle. She brushed the tangles from her hair and allowed it to hang down her back free of any restricting band or covering. Making her way down the castle steps, she encountered Leitis. Alysa asked the head servant where Prince Gavin was.

"His Highness rode away at dawn with several knights. He said he would return at dusk," the woman replied.

"Do you know where he was going?"

"Nay, Princess Alysa, but it appeared he was in a hurry."

Alysa was annoyed that Gavin had not waited for her to arise and discuss his intentions for the day. She did not like this new secrecy and distance which she perceived in him.

She was not his underling; she was this land's ruler. Important decisions should include her. True, Gavin was accustomed to doing as he pleased, but things were different now. True, he needed time to adjust to this new situation, as his entire life had changed, but she felt he was not trying to do so. To protect their love, a compromise had to be reached, and soon. She questioned Piaras's new wife about their guests, to learn Thisbe and Teague were eating in the Great Hall. The young ruler went to join them.

Alysa embraced Thisbe, whose brown eyes were damp with tears of joy. The brunette rapidly revealed all the news, good and bad, of the few weeks since the two friends had parted.

Teague waited patiently for his wife and Alysa to take their places at the table. He smiled at both. "You must forgive my wife, Alysa. She has missed you and Malvern Castle. As you can see, she is glad to be home again. I cannot blame her; Lord Daron's estate was not a safe or happy place for a new bride."

"What shall we do, Alysa?" Thisbe asked worriedly. "What if the Vikings strike here next? There are so many of them and they are vicious men. It was a horrible battle to witness."

"Let us speak of other things, dear Thisbe. When my vassals arrive, there will be plenty of war talk. Tell me more of your life at Daron's castle," Alysa encouraged, hoping Teague would dismiss himself if they began a conversation only of interest to Thisbe and herself. She was pleased when he did.

When the two women were alone, Alysa invited Thisbe to her chambers where they could talk privately. They sat on comfortable benches and faced each other. "Be calm, dear friend, but tell me all you observed that day. I am most intrigued by this Viking leader."

"He was a handsome man, but a cruel one," Thisbe said

in an excited voice. "He was taller and larger than the other warriors, and they obeyed him without question. Even in battle, a strangely clad man remained at his side. He wore a black flowing robe with unknown symbols sewn onto it. Many times they talked, and I heard the name of Odin called out."

"Odin is their head god, Thisbe. Perhaps they were invoking his aid in the battle. Odin is claimed to protect warriors. His sign is that of a hanged man. It is said he is a shape-changer, the creator of man, the ruler of heaven and earth. Some say he is a master of the Runes and of magic spells. When a Viking dies, he hopes to be summoned to Valhalla, their paradise. It is all superstition and legend."

Thisbe reasoned, "If such is true, why did they defeat us?"

"Because they were stronger and attacked by surprise. Tell me, did you observe any weakness in this sunny-haired foe?"

"Nay, not once" came the answer Alysa expected but nonetheless dreaded.

Having always confided in Thisbe, Alysa did the same today. When she finished, Thisbe's brown eyes were wide with amazement and fear. No doubt shone within them. Clearly her former handmaiden believed in the Druid High Priest, as Alysa herself did.

"I must go to see Trosdan. Do you wish to ride with me?"

Thisbe laughed nervously and reminded, "You know how I hate riding. While coming here, I feared for my life upon that swift beast."

The princess commanded softly, "Remain here in my chambers until my return. I wish no one to know where I have gone unless it is necessary. Gavin is not to return until dusk. If he does so earlier, tell him not to worry or follow me."

31

"It is dangerous to go alone, Alysa. What if enemy spies or raiders are nearby? If you are captured, all is lost."

"There is nothing to fear," Alysa told her confidently. "I must see if Trosdan knows more about this blond foe and my impending mission. Before I challenge my husband for leadership, I must be certain Trosdan has read the Runes correctly."

"What if Prince Gavin fights you in this matter?"

A great sadness filled Alysa's eyes. "Gavin forgets I am a ruler first and a wife second. If he does not understand what I must do, then I must do it alone as Trosdan warned. I love Gavin with all my heart, Thisbe, but it would be wrong and selfish to put that love above the survival of my people. I was raised to accept my duty and I can do no less even when the price and perils are great."

"What if the wizard is wrong this time?"

"Do you think that is possible?" Alysa asked gravely. Thisbe sighed heavily and shook her head.

As Princess Alysa rode toward the hidden cave, she pondered the curious dream she had experienced last night. She needed Trosdan to interpret it for her. If the old man was right about her powers, it could be a vision of the future. She did not want to wait until it unfolded before she acted upon it.

Alysa searched the cave, but Trosdan was not to be found. She recalled him saying he would come to her when the time was right. She fingered the potions and objects on his work bench, but was afraid to test herself with them. She departed quickly, unaware of the old Druid's eyes upon her from his hiding place.

All afternoon Alysa practiced with Piaras, paying special attention to her accuracy with the spear. He had trained countless squires and knights, and he knew all there was to know about combat and weapons. As she exercised with the men-in-training, she noted with pleasure that none could beat her. She knew the men were surprised and pleased by her expertise and she enjoyed their compliments.

When mealtime came and Gavin's party had not returned, Alysa allowed the food to be served without her husband's presence. She concealed her irritation behind false smiles and gay banter with those in attendance. The meal ended and, when long after dark, a minstrel was entertaining them, Gavin and four of his best friends arrived. Alysa realized Gavin must have gathered them to form his band once more in anticipation of a new adventure. She could not help but envy their tight bond. They had been together for years, sharing times and feelings which had united them as closely as brothers. She understood why Gavin missed this vital part of his life, but things had changed. He was married now; he was a ruler.

Tragan, Dal, Bevan, and Lann—all Cumbrian knights and longtime companions of Prince Gavin Crisdean—sat down at the long eating table. After acknowledging their greetings, Alysa commanded more food and drink be served. Gavin approached her, smiled, and took a seat beside her.

Alysa noted the change in his mood, but knew their passionate lovemaking last night had little to do with it. He was his old self again, the man she had first met—the adventurous, mysterious, vital warrior who was surrounded by his loyal band. That was the existence which Gavin craved and loved, not the tedious and stationary life of a small-country ruler. The conclusion pained her.

Between sips of heady ale, Gavin revealed, "We have been setting up warning camps in all directions. Men with fresh mounts have been positioned every ten miles so that news can reach us quickly if trouble strikes. I have ordered scouts posted along our coast to watch for our enemy's approach. If we allow them a foothold here, they can sneak inland and nibble at the bellies of Cambria and Cumbria."

"At present, only the safety of my people concerns me," Alysa injected, careful to keep her voice light and gentle. "The other kingdoms are larger and stronger than we are. It is we who need their help more than they need ours. We must concentrate on our defense."

As if she had not spoken, Gavin continued. "We will set up weapons along the coast to thwart any landings. A sling full of smoldering coals or a flight of fiery arrows should discourage any Viking ship from nearing shore. They will have no way of knowing how many warriors await them, so they will be slower to challenge us."

"Your idea is cunning," said Dal. Following the recent treachery, defeat, and death of Sheriff Trahern, the Cumbrian knight had been appointed Sheriff of Damnonia by Gavin and he spent most of his time traversing this land to ensure law and order was maintained.

As the men verbally reflected on the strategies of past battles and victories, Alysa silently fumed at her husband's behavior. She felt locked out of the conversation, locked out of his emotions, locked out of her own affairs. This feeling of confinement and insignificance vexed and disappointed her. Gavin had not treated her this way before their marriage. She had participated in defeating Isobail and the brigands, had helped restore peace and prosperity in this domain. Since King Bardwyn's departure, Gavin seemed to have taken over her life and principality. Perhaps she should have objected when he placed his best friends in positions of power in her land. Sir Dal was now sheriff; Sir Lann was his second in command; Sir Bevan was Captain-of-the-Guard; Sir Weylin, now Lord Weylin, had been given control of Trahern's feudal estate; Sir Tragan was in charge of the knights; Sir Keegan, now Lord Keegan, had control of

Kelton Castle at Land's End. Gavin himself was the Prince of Damnonia.

She glanced around the table at the men talking as they dined. In all honesty, she could not think of better replacements for the "foreign" warriors who had saved her land from Isobail's conquest. Yet, it was not right that seven of the ten most powerful men in Damnonia were Cumbrians, or that so many of her people were grumbling.

Alysa had heard the nasty gossip, but did not know how to deal with it without offending her husband and his friends. She had hoped they would grow weary of their dull lives and leave to seek adventure elsewhere. Yet Gavin seemed to be the only member of his old band who was miserable.

If she did not take her rightful place in the upcoming battle, more dissension could be expected in a time when she needed unity. She must show her people that she was in control and not under foreign influence, that she could protect them, that all obeyed her, the heir of Prince Alric and the granddaughter of King Bardwyn, their ruler. How would it appear to the Cambrians, her future subjects, if others always had to fight her battles for her? It was vital for her to establish her rank and power, to pull the people together under her leadership.

Alysa called to mind the three Damnonians who held high ranks: Lord Fergus, whose feudal estate was north of the castle; Lord Orin, whose feudal estate was west of the castle, and who was the father of Teague; and Sir Teague, who was in charge of Daron Castle—if it had not been destroyed—and who could not become a lord until his father died. All were good men, strong and dependable vassals.

But where, she worried, did the Cumbrians' allegiance lie? If it came to full-scale war in all kingdoms, could she depend on them to stay here to fight? If Cumbria was threatened by destruction, what action would Gavin take? Where would his first loyalty lie? Such things had not been mentioned. She hated these doubts and suspicions, but what did she truly know about men who hired out as warriors to any land or cause which caught their interest and filled their purses? Gavin and his band had come here as a favor to King Bardwyn and to seek excitement. They had not planned to stay after their victory. What if their king, Gavin's father, summoned them to Cumbria to help defend their homeland, their friends and families? If fate had not intervened, King Briac could have been her father and Gavin might not have existed! Now, Briac could intrude on her life again.

Perhaps her worries were silly. Gavin's men had done nothing greedy or guileful. They had knelt before her and Gavin and sworn their fealty to them. They were running things smoothly and efficiently. What reason could she give to dismiss them? And replace them with whom?

Alysa let the men talk freely without interruption, until the hour grew late. She noticed that Sir Teague had spoken little during the conversation, and she hoped the Cumbrian warriors did not cause him to feel inferior because of his recent defeat. The princess rose from her chair, the usual signal it was time to end a gathering.

She motioned to them. "Please, sirs, remain and talk longer if you so desire. I am weary and must retire for the night. When my vassals arrive, there is much planning to be done. Think hard, as I will be eager to hear your suggestions for battling these foes before we ride out to challenge them. Good night."

Only she, Teague, and Thisbe departed the Great Hall. Gavin and his friends remained behind. Alysa entered her chambers and dressed for sleep. Without waiting for Gavin, as she sensed he was intentionally avoiding her, she put out the candles and went to bed.

She lay awake a long time, wondering when her husband would join her. Already she had planned to feign slumber to prevent further talk tonight, but it was unnecessary, as she was sleeping deeply before Gavin arrived.

The princess was not surprised when she awoke to find Gavin gone again the next morning. In a way, she was relieved, but saddened nonetheless. Perhaps it was best for them to reveal their feelings about her plan before the others. No doubt Gavin had not changed his mind and had asked his men to speak against her involvement.

Even if Gavin was angry for a while and refused to obey her wishes, their destinies were entwined. The only way to have him and victory was to do as the Runes commanded. Perhaps this battle was necessary to settle their differences and to bind them together for all time. Surely for the good of the many, she could endure a brief separation and quarrel with her beloved.

Once more she rode to the secret cave to speak with Trosdan, to discover him still absent. He had given her advice and warnings, but the decision was hers, and she had made it. No matter Gavin's objections, she was going to accompany her warriors!

It was midafternoon when a rider galloped into the inner ward and dismounted. After handing his reins to a stableboy, he headed for the main section of the castle. Alysa leaned out her window to watch him, but did not call down to him. She smiled as she saw him take the steps two by two and vanish inside the Great Hall beneath her chambers. Quickly she checked her appearance and hurried to meet him.

Lord Weylin, Gavin's closest friend, grinned broadly as he embraced Alysa affectionately. His black hair was damp from his swift ride and the sun's heat. Moist wisps clung to his forehead and mischievously curled here and there.

His warm brown eyes were filled with vitality and intrigue as he asked, "Where is everyone? I came as quickly as I could."

"Gavin and the others are scouting the area. They should return at mealtime. Come, sit, and I will have ale brought to refresh you."

Alysa gave her command to the servant who had appeared upon Weylin's arrival. As they seated themselves, Alysa noted how Weylin's sand-colored tunic did not conceal his muscular build, a virile physique which reached six feet two inches. He was a handsome man, one who ensnared women's eyes and passions. They had met while defeating Isobail and had worked together many times. Of all her husband's friends, she liked and trusted Weylin best. "Tell me how things go at your new home."

"The people work hard and have been loyal to me. It is a beautiful estate, Alysa, and I am proud to run it. Already it is like home to me. Trahern's widow does not seem to mind my presence there, though I see little of her. Unless I summon her, Lady Kordel keeps to her tower even at mealtimes. She is a shy creature and fears others will blame her for her husband's wickedness."

"It was kind of you to allow Lady Kordel to remain in her home. You have a generous heart and nature, Weylin, and I am most grateful you are one of my retainers. I hope you will be with us a long time."

"My father is young and vital. It will be many years before I am called upon to take over his estate in Cumbria."

Alysa teased, "That was not my concern, dear friend. I feared you might find homelife boring and wish to return to your carefree ways."

Weylin chuckled. "I have been a warrior and adventurer for many of my twenty-eight years. I have seen many sights and fought many battles. It is good to settle down and relax, especially on such a lovely domain and as a feudal lord.

This is a new challenge for me, one I shall not fail in. There is much to do and I stay very busy. Worry not, Your Highness, for I am most content and loyal."

Probing cleverly for information, Alysa hinted, "I wish it were so for Gavin. I fear he is restless these days. He rides out at dawn and returns at dusk, only to eat and sleep so he can do so again the next day. He neglects to tell me of his actions and plans, leaving me to worry until his safe return. How can I get to know my husband when he is so secretive and distant? Perhaps he only avoids me because he is angry with me."

Weylin knew of Gavin's love and desire for this enchanting woman, and he was baffled by her grave tone and expression. How could any man, particularly his closest friend, do anything to distress this unique female, to cause her to doubt his love and commitment? Weylin was concerned over the sadness he detected, and more so over the anger and confusion he sensed below her placid surface. As the husband of Princess Alysa Malvern and the joint ruler of this domain, how could Gavin be unhappy and restless, especially so soon after winning them both? It was unlike his friend to be unkind and moody. "Angry with you? How can such be true?" the valiant knight inquired.

Alysa wanted to discover Weylin's feelings on certain matters before he had the chance to speak with her husband. She explained her position, including Trosdan's premonitions, and revealed the disagreement with Gavin. "He forgets I am Damnonia's ruler and have need to know his actions. You have seen me in the jaws of peril. Am I not able to defend myself and others?"

"I have seen few fighters better skilled than you," he replied honestly. "I know little of magic and mysteries, but I cannot deny their existence. I have witnessed things which cannot be explained by mortal man. To dismiss that which we do not understand is rash. I cannot say if the Druid's words are true or if he is a master of the unknown, but you must do your duty for your people. I am a man, and I have no objection to riding behind or beside you into battle. You have proven you have cunning and valor. I am honored to serve you."

"Gavin does not agree with us, Weylin. He will be displeased that you side with me," she warned.

Weylin had observed ill feelings in the villages and towns, in the commoners and highborns and soldiers. He had overheard gossip on his estate, even though his vassals and serfs appeared to like and accept him as one of the "foreigners" who were "taking o'er our land." If discord was to be prevented in this land and with his wife, Gavin had to deal with his personal feelings; and he would tell his friend when Gavin returned home. Another precaution had to be taken soon: Damnonians had to be found and trained to take control of the powerful and prosperous positions which he and his fellow Cumbrians now held.

"It is not that I side with you or against him; I must do what I think is right. In this matter, it is right for you to lead your subjects. Some of your new vassals are from other lands, and many of your people are jealous and discontent. If they are to band together during this dangerous time and fight with all their might, they must see the heir of Alric and Bardwyn standing before them. When we aided your cause before, it was as a separate band and mostly in secret. This time, we will be riding with Damnonians. For the good and safety of all, it is best if the true Damnonian ruler is in charge."

A happy smile brightened Alysa's face, then it faded. "Why cannot Gavin understand and accept this grim matter as you do? It troubles me deeply to see his mind closed and his heart chilled to me."

Weylin realized it was vital that Gavin have his eyes opened to realities which his friend was ignoring. "I will tell Gavin I will ride with you to guard your life. If you agree to stay back out of danger, he should be appeased. We can tell the others that our group rides as reinforcements, that we stay behind to prevent our foe from guessing our strength, and that we guard their rear or flank. This way, you will be present and giving commands, but remain at a safe distance. We cannot allow you to be injured or slain, or your people will lose heart. Gavin loves you and worries over your safety. He knows what it is like to fight a fierce battle with blood-crazed enemies. Once he masters this unfamiliar fear, he will accept your responsibility and rank."

"Will he, Weylin?" she asked doubtfully.

Three

Gavin and his men arrived at the castle late and weary. Alysa had already retired to their chambers, but Weylin was awaiting him in the Great Hall. The six friends greeted one another and chatted for a while. As ordered by the princess, servants were prepared to serve Gavin's group a hot meal upon their return.

Gavin said, "The others should arrive tomorrow for our meeting. This will be a harder battle than we have fought before because these foes number many and are consumed with evil and greed. The worshipers of Odin have no fear of dying, which makes them dangerous and strong. They can show no weakness or dishonor before their gods and followers, nor any mercy. They live for glory in battle and for the riches of plunder. People fear them, with just cause. Yet fear slows a warrior's hands and wits. We must seek early victories to give the people courage, to give them hope for the dark days ahead."

Lann, Tragan, Dal, and Bevan nodded agreement. Weylin asked, "How do you plan to obtain these crucial victories?"

"We must locate their camps and strike each band separately. That is the best way to weaken their strength and to prevent them from joining forces. If we can attack at night while they are sleeping, our task will be easier. I have spies seeking their locations, and lookouts posted along the coast. The moment our invaders are sighted, we will be warned. The lords have been ordered to ready their men, and the knights and soldiers are prepared to move instantly. We must waste no time or energy before repelling them."

The men talked a while longer before all departed except Gavin and Weylin, who asked, "What of Princess Alysa? Why do you exclude her from these preparations?"

"War is a man's affair and duty, Weylin," Gavin replied oddly.

Weylin added, "And the affair and duty of a ruler."

Gavin studied his best friend closely and curiously. "What has she said to you?" he asked, a glint of suspicion in his green eyes.

Weylin watched those green eyes widen, then narrow, as he related his talk with Alysa. "You are a ruler here by marriage only, my friend. If you take control and push her aside, trouble could sprout."

Gavin came back at him almost coldly, "And Alysa could be slain or wounded. She is not a soldier, Weylin; she is a woman, a gentle and fragile creature. We have battled Norsemen in the past; you know their strengths and ways. There is another threat to my wife in this matter," Gavin began nervously as he revealed the Norsemen's desire for the Last Viking Queen. "They will do anything to capture her. The man who does so will become king and leader of all Vikings, a force no land could challenge and defeat. She carries the last royal blood and, by the rule of Odin, must be accepted as queen. Once she is in their possession, we will be unable to rescue her. She must be kept far away from the invaders and that peril."

Weylin told him, "You should explain your fears and love to her. She is doubtful and distressed."

Gavin sighed in fatigue. "If I do so, she will view them as signs of weakness and will press her reckless desires

43

with me. Even if I must hold her captive here, I cannot let her ride with us."

"Her people will not stand for such treatment. Let her go. I will keep her behind with me. I will guard her from all perils."

"If she is sighted by the enemy and your group is attacked, how then will you protect her, my friend, if you are slain?"

"If the invaders get through you and your line of defense, will it matter if she is here or elsewhere? Let her do what she must."

"I beg you, Weylin, do not speak in her favor tomorrow. If it is her destiny to die on the battlefield, do not let it be because you placed her there. This much I ask of you."

Gavin looked down at his sleeping wife. He was tempted to awaken her, to try once more to persuade her against her wild idea. Dreading another quarrel when he was so exhausted, he did not. If only he could believe she was destined to be a great warrior queen . . . If only he could believe that Trosdan had the power to protect her from all harm . . . If only he did not love her and fear losing her.

During his scouting ventures yesterday and today, he had tried to locate the old wizard. Either the man was hiding or was away. He wanted to convince Trosdan not to imperil Alysa by filling her head with reckless dreams and a misguided sense of duty to her people. The Druid's words had begun this conflict between them, and it was too late for him to halt it. The strategy meeting would be held tomorrow, and all he could hope for was that Alysa would change her mind before that hour. If the lords and knights spoke against her going, surely she would not insist. If they did not, how could he stop her?

44

Alysa met privately with Sir Teague the next morning. She placed him in charge of Malvern Castle and all business while they were gone. She explained it had nothing to do with doubting his fighting skills or courage, or with his recent defeat. "I need someone whom I trust above others, dear Teague, someone who knows how to keep things running wisely and smoothly, someone whom the people like and trust. Most of your life has been spent here with me, so you know what is to be done. The people love you and will obey you. Will you stay here and defend the royal lands for me?"

The redhead knew his friend and ruler was being honest with him. "Thisbe and I will remain here and guard these lands with our lives."

Alysa embraced him with affection and gratitude. "Say nothing to the others, even to Gavin, until I have revealed my plans."

Alysa and Gavin sat upon the dais in the Great Hall. Before them were their vassals, the lords and knights of Damnonia. Alysa listened silently and attentively as the conference continued for large-scale, long-range strategy to ensure their survival and victory. Tactics for their first battle were planned, as were defense lines. Men, supplies, and weapons were discussed by the vassals providing them.

During the ardent deliberations, Gavin stood and paced to burn off his excessive tension. He called Sir Beag forward to give his report. The castle knight and temporary spy related news of a Viking camp which had been set up a day's ride from the castle, a camp which looked as if it were waiting to be enlarged before raiding the area.

Gavin ordered fervidly, "Alert all soldiers. We must strike

at them before others land. We will leave at dawn and camp in Trill's Glen. On the next sun, we will attack and destroy them."

Alysa rose gracefully and approached the edge of the dais. All lips fell silent and all eyes focused on her. She had dressed carefully and cleverly for this moment. To stress her rank, upon her head she wore a golden crown with sparkling jewels. She was attired in a flowing dark-blue gown which made her eyes appear as two glimmering sapphires. A golden chain hung low on her hips and dangled down the front of her dress. A matching one around her neck held a golden medallion displaying the royal crest of Damnonia's ruler. Her expression was a mixture of serenity and power. A regal aura surrounded her.

Her voice was calm and stirring as she spoke. "There are dark days ahead for us, my people. We must be strong and cunning. We must not lose hope or yield to fear. We are a victorious people. Do not forget we recently destroyed those who threatened our lives and lands. We will do so again."

Alysa looked at each man as she called his name and made her remarks. "Sir Dal, our sheriff, should remain in this area to prevent common outlaws from creating havoc while we are distracted by foes and battles. Lord Keegan is a powerful and clever warrior. He should return to Land's End to guard against invasion there. All men in that area should report any news to him and he shall be empowered to act upon it. Sir Teague is to remain at Malvern Castle to protect it from any foes and problems. I will allow Lord Orin and Lord Fergus to decide if they can serve us better on their coastal estates or on the battlefield. If we are to hold our people's unity, all must work hard and where best suited. We shall divide our men into two groups," she informed them, then explained the plan Weylin had suggested to her. "Prince Gavin will lead the assault with group one

46

and I will remain with group two. We will join the battle only if necessary. That way, if any foe escapes, he cannot report our strength to others. Sir Beag and Lord Weylin will travel with me as my guards and advisers. I have ordered a great feast for tonight so we can summon our strength before a good night's rest. At dawn we will ride to our glorious destiny."

Lord Keegan and Sheriff Dal, Gavin's friends from Cumbria, nodded acceptance of her commands. Keegan had arrived shortly before the meeting and had not spoken with Gavin. He assumed this order was given with the prince's agreement. As for Dal, he could not argue the woman's wise words about being needed here to control law and order.

Orin and Fergus, Damnonian noblemen and feudal lords, both concluded aloud it would be best if they retained control over their areas. The other knights were happy to see their ruler in command of this situation, and no one protested Alysa's intentions and orders. They were awed by her beauty and confidence, and impressed by her manner.

Observing the effect of his wife's cunning words and daring deed, Gavin knew it was unwise to verbally battle her in public. To do so would cause the discord which Weylin had warned him about last night. No one questioned her plans or looked amused. No one appeared displeased, or afraid to follow her anywhere. He had lost this personal battle, and silently prayed he would lose nothing more.

The castle servants excelled at preparing the food that night. The mood was one of excitement and anticipation, of expectant victory. Minstrels entertained during and after the meal. Visitor chambers and hallways were filled with guests and pallets. The evening passed quickly and soon all were sent their separate ways.

Alysa dressed for bed and joined Gavin in their chambers. For the first time, she felt ill at ease with her husband. She did not know what to say or how to behave toward him

47

tonight. Obviously he felt the same way because he busied himself with his weapons and chores.

She slipped between the covers and reclined, her somber gaze locked on Gavin's broad back. She watched the muscles move in his shoulders and arms as he went about his work silently. His body was without excess fat and displayed a bronze covering which teased at her senses. She wanted to be in those strong arms, to taste those sweet lips, to enjoy his touch. Her eyes wandered over his dark-blond hair and she wondered what he was thinking. They drifted over his virile body and wondered what it was feeling. She hated this new and unusual chill in the air.

Gavin rubbed the greasy rag up and down his blade, conditioning and polishing it for the upcoming battle. When he was finished, he slid it into the protective sheath and put it aside. He checked his lance point to make certain it was sharp and unchipped, then lifted and examined his shield, which was stout enough to repel arrows and deflect swords and lances. Its rim was razor-sharp to slash foes during combat. Carefully, he covered the circular edge with a band of tough leather to avoid cutting himself and his horse by accident. His garments were laid out and ready to don: brown knee boots, a leather warrior's apron similar to the kind which had been popular with the Roman troops and worn over a dark loincloth, and a sturdy cuirass: a leather garment which fit his torso like personally made armor. The apparel was made complete by thick leather armbands which covered his wrists and forearms to protect those vital areas from slashing cuts and to strengthen them while handling a heavy sword for long periods.

Alysa was planning to wear leather knee boots, a *chainse*—a white undertunic of fine linen with long sleeves which was visible at the wrists and hem below the royal-blue *bliaud* she had selected—and the sword which Piaras had made for her. The weapon was of lighter weight than most swords and could be wielded easily.

When Gavin finished his tasks, he removed his garments and joined her. He had doused the candles; the room was almost black. Lying upon his back without their bodies touching, he leashed his warring emotions. They were to leave at dawn and would have little or no privacy on the trail. One or both might not return from this journey. At least she had agreed not to place herself in peril unless necessary. And she was right about the people being glad she would be present. To see that Alysa was unafraid of these fierce Vikings had inspired more courage and confidence in her subjects.

"Alysa, I do not want you to ride with us tomorrow. If I could halt you in any way, I would do so. Since I cannot, I must yield to your rash decision. I pray it will not be your last one. Or that it will cost me my concentration in battle."

Before she spoke a chill passed over her body and she was tempted to change her mind. "When we leave this castle, you must forget I exist until we return. Think only of defending your life and those of our people. As with any battle, you must clear your head of all things except survival and victory. I will be safe with Weylin; I promise you."

"Will Weylin be safe with you, my Viking queen?"

His meaning was clear to her, clear and painful. "If I am their target, Gavin, I would be no safer here than close to you. Do not pile guilt upon my head; I do not deserve it, nor your biting words. I do not wish to try to snatch any glory or authority from you. I only do what I feel I must."

"I care not for who leads our warriors or which of us seizes the victory. I care only for you and our people. Let neither come to harm."

Alysa rolled to her side and put her arms around her husband's neck. "I love you with all my heart, Gavin Crisdean," she murmured hoarsely. "I will not endanger myself or the others. You must trust me." Her lips sought his and she kissed him hungrily before he could reply.

Gavin's arms seized her and held her tightly against his taut frame. His mouth feverishly and urgently responded to hers. He could not bear to lose this woman or to see her harmed. He would give his life to defend hers. He wanted her to be safe and happy, to be his forever. His fingers wandered into her thick hair and pressed her mouth more snugly to his. Gavin's smoldering passions burst into fiery flames and he eagerly relented to them. His hands caressed her silky flesh and he was lost in the wonder of her bewitching presence.

Suddenly, tonight was their only reality, this moment, these urgent desires. Between kisses and caresses, clothes were discarded and pleasures were gathered with raw intensity. There were insatiable hungers to be fed, dreams to be made real, a bond to be reforged.

Quivering limbs were entwined, hands put to enticing labors. Lips were sent on tantalizing quests, desires increased. Pleasures were savored as exquisite delight filled them.

Alysa felt a new kind of tension assail her husband's body and her heart leapt with joy. She felt him surrendering to her. She understood his cravings and she fulfilled them. She teased her fingers over his pleading body and caused him to moan uncontrollably. She enticed him without inhibition, and intoxicated him more thoroughly than any strong liquid could have. She made him writhe with bittersweet yearning. She claimed him with skill and ecstasy.

Gavin's mind whirled madly. His large hands covered her breasts and gently kneaded them. His fingers captured the protruding buds and caressed their hardness. His lips worked lovingly at her ears and down her throat, to join his hands in provoking her to higher need. Soon, his lips and hands were traveling her entire body, savoring stops here and there to drive her wild with mounting desire. Caught up in the sensuous moment, she thrashed upon the bed, but halted none of his stimulating actions. Never was she more in his power than when he made love to her; made love as if all of their energy and emotions had to be spent in one night.

Gavin guided her atop him and slipped within her womanhood. By love enchanted, she rode him wildly and freely. Each time she bent forward to kiss him, her long hair sensuously tickled his unmarred face and tattooed chest. When her release came, she arched her back and let him thrust swiftly to carry her to the end of her blissful journey. His climactic victory was simultaneously obtained, and locked together, they rocked to and fro until they were exhausted and their bodies were slick with perspiration.

Alysa collapsed upon Gavin's body, but her lips continued to mesh with his. Remaining within her, he rolled her over with him and buried his moist face in her tangled locks. His rapid breathing filled her ears, as hers did his. Their hearts pounded, and their spirits glowed. When their bodies stilled, Gavin cradled her in his embrace and held her possessively. This was not the time to speak of anything; it was a time to be gently engulfed by the warmth of love and contentment. They were sated for a time, and drowsy.

Gavin pressed tender kisses upon her forehead and damp hair. His fingers lightly teased up and down her spine. He enjoyed this peaceful aftermath when their bodies were still in contact, when their moods were mellow, when their hearts beat as one.

Alysa felt the same way. She closed her eyes and nestled closer to her love. As if one person, both fell asleep within moments.

Alysa, Gavin, and their large band of Damnonians traveled steadily the next day, halting when necessary to rest themselves and their horses. Scouts rode at a distance on all sides of them to prevent them from being taken by surprise. Most of the way to their camp for the night at Trill's Glen, Alysa rode between Gavin and Weylin.

She could read the tension in her husband's body and expression, and she wished he would stop worrying so deeply about her. He needed his full attention on the impending battle. Because of their pace, little talk was possible. She noticed how each person was silently preparing himself for the life-and-death struggle before them. She prayed—prayed for their victory and survival, and prayed Trosdan was not mistaken.

When they camped, it was dusk. As a precaution, fires were not lit. Food which had been previously prepared was consumed quietly. Horses were tended. Guards were posted. The group spread out makeshift pallets for the night, but all found sleep difficult.

At dawn on the momentous day, the group arose early and readied themselves. They traveled to within a few miles of the enemy camp, and waited while scouts sneaked forward, observed the camp, then returned to report their findings. As planned, they divided into two groups and headed for their assigned positions.

On a treed hill, Alysa and her band were concealed from view as they watched the others carefully and quietly approach the Viking camp. She saw their enemies lazing around many fires, their weapons always nearby. The Norsemen were clad in garments of leather and fur, and their large sizes amazed her. Yet she had practiced enough with hefty knights to know body size did not necessarily mean defeat of a smaller person. Sometimes such a large warrior was stronger but slower.

Alysa realized her heart was pounding with anticipation. She stared at the camp as if mesmerized by it. She rubbed her dry eyes and inhaled deeply several times to slow her rapid breathing and to ease her anxiety. She had not expected such a large number of Vikings to be present or to be so heavily armed. She saw many drinking from wine skins, and she hoped it would dull their wits and slow their movements. Others were playing games with sticks and stones on the ground. From their expressions, all seemed totally relaxed. The princess continuously shifted her gaze from the lazy camp to the stealthy Damnonians who were sneaking toward it. If only her husband and his band could reach the camp before an alarm was sounded . . .

Alysa tensely observed as Gavin directed his men to encircle the camp. Undoubtedly the site had been selected for its favorable defense advantage. When the charge order was given, she lifted herself in her saddle and strained to watch the lethal action. Taken by surprise, her love and her loyal subjects claimed the lead in the fierce conflict.

Soon her eyes grew tired of frantically darting about to follow her husband as he fought for victory. Her heart lurched in pain as Bevan was slain. Instantly, Gavin ran his sword through the killer's body and twisted it with vengeful anguish. He checked to see if Bevan was dead, then bellowed in rage loud enough to be heard on the hill. Men fell on both sides and the vicious combat continued. Alysa wished all of Gavin's friends, valiant knights and powerful warriors, were at his side. But Weylin was guarding her, and Dal and Keegan were miles away. She watched Tragan and Lann fight and knew Gavin's men were more highly skilled and experienced in warfare than her knights and soldiers. She scolded herself for wishing they had returned to Cumbria and for resenting their powerful ranks in her land. These men were risking their lives and deserved their positions.

Alysa glanced at Weylin, whose expression revealed his hunger to be in the midst of the mêlée. She wanted to order him to join the others below, but knew he would not desert her side and his duty. She was tempted to order her band into the camp, but did not want to make Gavin and his band feel or appear incompetent. Until the prearranged signal for help was given, she had to remain where she was. But would Gavin do so and endanger her?

Having overrun the camp before the Norsemen were alerted and armed, the odds were fairly even at this point. Yet so many of her friends and subjects were being slain. If she broke her promise and joined them, could she prevent more and unnecessary bloodshed?

Her heart seemed to jump into her throat and cut off her breathing when Gavin's sword was knocked from his grasp and he engaged in hand-to-hand combat with an enormous foe. She watched her love and his opponent circle each other, slashing out with knives and blows. The two men grappled for the upper hand. She winced in fear and chewed nervously on her lower lip. At any moment her love could be dead.

Another Norseman raced toward the two fighters, lifting a battle-ax in his hand. Alysa suppressed a scream of terror. She felt Weylin seize her hand and squeeze it encouragingly. Trosdan's words flashed through her mind as swiftly as lightning: "The Hawk of Cumbria will not fly with you on this fated journey. It is a path you must travel alone." Had Trosdan avoided her because he had foreseen . . .

Suddenly Gavin grabbed his foe and swung him around just as the second Norseman forcefully brought down his ax, burying the sharp weapon in his friend's back. Rapidly, Gavin recovered his fallen sword and pierced his foe's heart. The man sank to his knees and Gavin yanked the crimson-stained blade from the dying man's chest.

"Look there, Your Highness!" the man beside Alysa shouted.

She followed the point of his finger toward the coast and trembled. A red-and-white striped sail flapped in the breeze.

A towering dragonhead prow made its way toward shore, looking as if it could gobble up ground and man. She estimated the number of men inside the ship. She gauged the distance between the ship and land, the rocky beach and the enemy camp, Viking reinforcements and . . .

Alysa's gaze frantically returned to the battle in the camp. Her side was winning, but the men had to be exhausted. Surely they could not defeat a fresh force. Her keen mind raced with ideas as she hastily studied the landscape between the coast and the camp. "We must attack!" she proclaimed.

Weylin started to protest, but was silenced by the ruler. "Hold your tongue, Lord Weylin, until I finish. See there . . ." She motioned to the rocky boulders and trees to the right of the span between the two raiding parties. "If we hurry, we can conceal our force and ambush them. Before they land, we can be in place. As they pass, I will seize their attention and lead them into your trap. They will pursue me into the rocks where you and the others can pick them off safely from behind. If you work silently and skillfully, we can slay them one by one before they realize what is taking place."

"Why would they follow a lone woman? All of them," one of her soldiers inquired. He eyed her and licked his lips nervously.

Alysa removed her crown from her saddle pouch and placed it on her head. "They will pursue the Damnonia ruler without thought or delay," she responded confidently. She dared not tell the men around her that she had seen this moment in a dream the other night, as they might think her foolish or mad.

She met Weylin's worried gaze. "It will work."

Weylin understood her unspoken meaning and knew she was right, and very clever. The Cumbrian knight nodded and concurred, inspiring the others to do so.

Hurriedly, their cunning strategy was planned and they left to carry it out without the first group's notice. The Dammonians concealed themselves amongst the rocks and trees while Alysa waited at the yawning mouth of the narrow pathway between them. She made sure her sword and dagger were ready to seize. She patted Calliope's neck and talked to the grayish-brown beast who loved and obeyed her.

Alysa calculated the amount of time it would require the Norsemen to unload their ship and to head inland to their camp, which was almost two miles from shore. When she heard their noisy approach, she prepared herself to follow the warnings in her dream.

Alysa prodded Calliope into a position to capture the Viking's attention. When she was sighted, she feigned surprise and fear and hesitation. She saw their eagle eyes fly to her crown, then back to her panicked expression. She pulled on Calliope's reins to make the horse trample the ground and prance nervously before rearing and pawing the air. Although an expert horsewoman, she pretended to have little or no control over the frightened beast. As if terrified, she nudged the animal to turn and head toward the rocky path.

"The queen! We must get her!" a Viking shouted eagerly.

Another yelled, "On horseback? We cannot catch her!"

"On this terrain she cannot ride swiftly. Rolf wants her."

Possessions were discarded and the chase was on. Alysa leisurely guided her dun along the treacherous path to whet the Vikings' appetite by catching another glimpse of her vulnerability. She heard them running and shouting behind her. She kneeded Calliope into a faster walk to keep just ahead of them. She prayed the stragglers were being picked off without notice and delay because the path was a dead end.

Four

Alysa hurried through the section of the area where the path widened and was filled with trees and bushes. She did not want the Vikings to have time to sight her band or for more than a few to move slowly through that guarded spot. She hoped her men were carrying out their assignments of gradually lessening the odds against them.

She glanced over her shoulder and saw several Norsemen scrambling over rocks to cut her off around the next bend. She smiled as she saw one disappear, then another, and knew why. She silently praised her brave men and her cunning plan. Still, there were at least fifteen men eagerly pursuing her. Alysa continued her desperate journey, allowing Calliope to carefully pick the safest path for them.

Within minutes, she sighted the end of the trail. A landslide had blocked the way long ago. She hurried toward a sheltered area and dismounted, knowing she could fight better afoot. She drew her sword and waited for the first man to come into view.

She heard loud shouting and knew Weylin had given the signal for their band to attack in force. Yet two Vikings rounded the last bend and came toward her, their thoughts so intent on capturing her that they ignored or failed to realize their peril. Alysa presented her back to them, concealing her weapon in the folds of her garment. She gripped the hilt securely and called her ears to full alert. She did not have to ask herself if she could slay a foe; she knew what was at stake today. She summoned all her wits, courage, and skills.

The first foe reached her and made a grab for her shoulder. Alysa whirled and sent her blade into his burly body. The man staggered backward, dislodging it himself with his movement. His large hands covered the wound and he watched the blood gush between his fingers. He looked at the beautiful young woman in astonishment, then eyed the stained weapon in her tight grasp. He wavered on his feet before dropping to his knees, still gaping at her in disbelief. As he fell forward, Alysa dodged his body. He weakly made a grab for her ankle, but she snatched it out of his bloody reach. He groaned as he tried to crawl toward her as if he still believed he could capture her. She backed against the rocks and lifted her sword in warning. Her foe's bearded face collapsed to the ground, and she knew he was dead.

The second man attacked, cautiously. A cold sneer claimed his mouth and he locked his watchful eyes on her. She noticed how he seemed to observe her from head to foot without shifting his gaze, the sign of an expert warrior, a dangerous one. Having witnessed her skills, he made no sudden or rash moves. Nor did Alysa. She kept her expression calm and confident and she allowed nothing, not even a quick glance to see if help was approaching, to distract her from the foe and their impending struggle.

Although there was a noisy clash of steel and bodies nearby, it was as if they were alone in the clearing. The Viking drew his sword, a large one. To intimidate her, he waved it playfully before her line of vision, and grinned devilishly as he did so. She read arrogance and cockiness in his gaze, things which always caused fatal mistakes in judgment.

To unnerve the man, Alysa haughtily revealed, "I am Alysa Malvern, daughter of Catriona, daughter of Rurik and Giselde, child of Astrid and Connal. If you dare attack me, Odin will punish you with death and dishonor. I am your queen. I carry the last royal Viking blood, and you dare not spill it. Drop your sword and kneel before me. If you do so, I will spare your life."

The man's expression and stance altered noticeably, as if this revelation was a shocking surprise. She noticed how he gave the matter serious consideration. "Go quickly before the locals entrap you here. Tell Rolf I will come to him when it is safe. It is time for me to take my place as your ruler. Together we will conquer this isle and establish a new Viking kingdom. Hurry before it is too late to flee."

The sturdy Norseman asked skeptically, "If what you say is true, why did you slay Karn?"

She replied guilefully in an even tone, "Because he dared to touch me and attack me. Odin is my defender and guided my hands and wits. He has led my people here to reclaim me and to begin a new land. Hear me well, my countryman, I will rule it all one day."

"Come with me and I will take you to Rolf."

"Odin has made me a Seer. He has shown me the day I am to rejoin my people. I have more work to do here. I must wait until I know the Celts' plans. Then, we can defeat them easily and swiftly."

"We can easily and swiftly defeat them on the battle-ground. They are as ants beneath our boots. One giant stomp will crush them all."

"Do not speak as a fool or refuse to heed Odin's commands!"

"I do not trust you, my tricky siren. You will come with me freely or as my captive," he warned, taking a step toward her.

Alysa laughed and challenged boldly, "No man or force

is strong enough to make me disobey Odin. Many times my spirit has left my body while it slept to train with the Valkyries. You stand no chance to defeat me. Go while you still walk and breathe."

In response to her threat, the man's sword was brought forward to click against hers. With speed and agility, Alysa parried his tentative thrust. The man unhurriedly charged several times, but each stab of his blade was deflected with precision and skill. When he flung his burly body at her to throw her off balance, the nimble princess sidestepped him. Instantly, she whirled and sliced through the back of his leather top, cutting flesh and nicking shoulder bone. He nearly entangled his feet as he hastily confronted her. Alysa's striking features exposed a look of self-assurance and victory mingled with contempt, while her opponent's revealed anger and awe.

The vexed raider forcefully brought up his lowered sword with all his strength in a desperate attempt to knock Alysa's weapon from her hands. The princess leaned right, then ducked, before slashing across the man's stomach. He stumbled over some loose rocks as his body lurched to his left to avoid her next strike. Alysa knew the meaning of his tactic: she was right-handed; to circle or to move toward a combatant's favored side weakened his blows and interfered with his coordination. Attacking from that side was intended to make her right wrist bend backward while striking at him or defending herself. As if dancing gracefully, Alysa moved her feet continuously to keep her body facing his to compel a frontal assault.

The warrior halted and stared at her. Blood was flowing down his back and over his groin. Alysa knew he was waiting for her to become overconfident and lunge at him, but she held her ground. Time was her friend. His wounds would weaken him, and her band would come soon to assist her.

Another voice shouted, "Thorkel, seize her and flee! I will guard your rear and give you time to escape."

Both Alysa and the Viking were distracted by the voice and presence nearby. In a flash, Thorkel grabbed for her, capturing her right arm and causing her to drop her sword. Alysa yanked her bejeweled dagger from the sheath at her waist and stabbed him in the shoulder.

Thorkel howled in pain, released her, and stepped out of her reach as she yanked a second knife from another sheath. He eyed the Damnonian band running toward them and knew they had been defeated. Withdrawing Alysa's knife, he glared at her and fled, working his way between boulders as he sought escape. When he stumbled, his hand reached out to grab a support branch, but passed between trunks and enlightened him to a small cave concealed there. Hastily, he wriggled behind the leafy trees and bushes, then leaned against the rocky edge and winced in pain. As he swore revenge upon the woman, he realized she had spoken to him in his language! Could it be, he wondered, that she was their lost queen? That she was indeed protected and guided by Odin? Surely no mere woman could have defeated two warriors, especially him, without divine help. Thorkel studied the dagger in his bloody hand, the one which Trosdan had given to Alysa. Upon its blade was etched a hanged man: the symbol of Odin.

Weylin charged the third man heading for Alysa and waved his sword ominously. The two clashed in fierce battle. As they fell to the ground and scuffled in dusty combat, the Viking seized a handful of dirt and flung it into Weylin's eyes, temporarily blinding him. Recovering his fallen sword, the raider rushed at the Damnonian lord to slay him while he was helpless.

Alysa had grabbed a crossbow from her horse and prepared to fire when and if the moment arose as in her strange dream. She released her arrow and it shot into the man's back with a thudding force, giving Weylin time to clear his vision and complete the kill.

Weylin joined her as their victorious band encircled her, shouting her praises. He smiled and thanked her for saving his life.

Alysa commanded, "We must gather any captives and return to the others lest they find us gone and worry."

"All are slain, Your Highness, except for the wounded man who escaped. Others are searching for him in the rocks. With his many wounds, he cannot go far. You have led us to victory as you promised. Long live Princess Alysa!" Sir Beag stated fervently and others quickly joined in to chant the words.

"You are kind and loyal, my valiant soldiers. You have shown much courage and prowess today and have given the bards brave and daring deeds for new poems. Lord Weylin, send men to burn the Viking ships as a warning to our invaders. Collect their weapons so we may arm more men to battle them. Seize their goods and take them home to the poor. Come, we must see if our wounded need help."

When they reached the Viking camp, it was a sorry sight. Many of Gavin's men were dead or injured. Others were tending them or loading bodies into a large cart. The ground was littered with slain foes, bloody weapons, scattered possessions, and battle-doused campfires.

Gavin came to meet them, looking fatigued and dirtied. Alysa hastily scanned his body for any sign of injury, and was happy to observe nothing more than a few minor cuts and scratches.

"I am glad you kept your promise and did not endanger yourself. It is also good we did not show our full strength, because several raiders escaped, no doubt to warn others of our attack. We will leave this evil place and camp miles away to rest before our journey home. We suffered many losses, but we are champions today."

"As are we," one of Alysa's men divulged excitedly, proudly.

Another rapidly related the news of their battle not far away. As he listened to the astonishing tale of the Vikings' entrapment, Gavin's eyes enlarged; then he squinted as he watched his wife.

"Not one man was lost. Princess Alysa planned our attack cunningly. Look there . . ." He motioned to the smoke which was rising skyward at the coast. "Their ships are burning and their supplies are being taken by our band. We captured no foe; we slew them all. Princess Alysa killed two raiders and fatally wounded another. She fought with sword, knife, and crossbow. She has more courage and prowess than any warrior in this land or in others."

Alysa did not try to quell her band's praises of her deeds and talents. It would be dishonest to feign modesty, and foolish to dampen their joyous spirits. Her followers were telling the truth, so she must not try to place the credit elsewhere. She had won their fealty and respect, and it was unwise to damage them to spare Gavin's feelings. She had proven her capabilities and leadership, vitally needed qualities for unity in the days to come. If she tried to downplay her role in today's events, it would destroy the enormous progress she had made, made at the risk of her life.

Gavin realized what the two battles meant in comparison. It appeared as if his wife had won the greater victory because none of her men had died while obtaining it. As leader and planner of his skirmish, he felt responsible for the lives which had been lost during it, a burden which any person in authority had to bear. Her plan revealed how cunning and daring she was. He had told her she was not strong enough to battle large men, yet, she had defeated three! He had said she was not a warrior or a soldier, yet, she had proven she was! He had claimed she was not trained or experienced in warfare, yet, no leader could have planned or fought better! He had practically challenged her to prove she was more than a bearer of future kings and princes, and she had done so!

Surely their subjects would prefer to follow her next time. Gavin was happy she had won her battle and relieved she was alive and unharmed. Yet he admitted he was slightly jealous of how easy and safe it seemed to have been for her band to triumph over their foes. He felt confused and distressed by fate, which had allowed this perilous matter to come between them. After this incident today, she would be even more convinced of the old Druid's insane words. It might be used as an example, or argument, or justification for placing Alysa in command of their troops. She had won today's battle, but could she lead their people to final victory? One battle did not make a war, and one defeat did not mean final victory.

Alysa noticed how quiet and watchful Gavin was. She wondered what was running through his keen mind. She said, "We saw the other ship landing and fear—decided your band was too weary to battle more foes. It was a simple ambush plan, but it worked because our men are brave and strong. We watched you from the hill and marveled at your prowess. There were so many Vikings present, but you conquered them. What can we do to help?" she asked sincerely.

Gavin focused on the matter at hand. "There are wounded to be tended. We must carry our people's bodies home to be buried by their families." He glanced around and continued. "There are too many foes to bury and we cannot leave them lying here to rot. We will make a great pile and burn them, as it is their burial rite. They are our enemies, but we are not barbarians who butcher or discard our foes. We took several captives. We will have them sent to Prisongate. When we are rested, we will decide what to do with them."

"They must be executed, my brave husband. We cannot free them, and we can spare no soldiers to guard them."

Gavin wriggled his shoulders to relieve their battle-tautness. "First, we must question them. Confined to prison, such men will get restless and will weaken. When they do so, their tongues will loosen."

"Your plan is right and cunning, my husband."

"You are kind, my wife, but the honor today belongs to you, because both plans were yours. Let us busy ourselves with our remaining tasks. The day grows late and we are weary."

Gavin and his band were exhausted; considering how long and hard they had fought, that was not unusual. Yet Alysa's band was filled with vitality after their quick and easy skirmish. They moved about agilely taking care of the chores at hand.

Alysa addressed the warriors in Gavin's group and praised their prowess, but, surrounded by pain and death, their moods were somber. She realized her glorious victory nearby had overshadowed this costly one and caused Gavin and his men to be depressed and disappointed. There was nothing more she could say to lighten their spirits and burdens, so she held silent.

Since Gavin was distracted, Alysa took the initiative and precaution of sending three of her men to track and slay the escapees. During future strategy, she wanted no foe to recognize any of them.

Two and a half days had passed since the battles. When their chores had been completed at the enemy camp, the Damnonians had ridden to Trill's Glenn to spend the night.

With the gravity of their losses weighing upon them, eating had been done in near silence. Gavin, Tragan, Lann, and Weylin had sat around a small fire and talked quietly about their slain friend and past days together. Not wishing to intrude on their grief and companionship, Alysa had remained with the others a short distance away. She was tormented by the fact her husband did not invite her to join him and appeared determined to avoid her. She could not help but resent his behavior, but she concealed her feelings from her subjects. She had slept little on the pallet beside that of Sir Beag, her self-appointed guardian.

The journey home yesterday had seemed longer than usual, no doubt because of the slow-moving carts and heavily loaded horses. Once more, Gavin had remained with his friends and practically ignored her. She hoped the others were too distracted to observe her husband's conduct, as it would reflect badly on him. She could not be faulted by fate's decisions, and she disliked being treated this way. She would give Gavin time to come to terms with his feelings, then she would speak with him.

Alysa had noticed how the alert captives had watched her closely and intently. They were rough-looking men who led violent lives. She had them guarded carefully because she knew they were sly and desperate foes. To prevent any escape plans from being discussed, she had ordered them held in different places. If Gavin were himself, he would have ordered those precautions. Alysa hated seeing him so withdrawn and inattentive.

Upon reaching Malvern Castle, they had been greeted by the servants and guards. Many locals had sighted them, sent word to the nearby villages, and followed them inside the gates to hear the news. Tales of the two battles had filled the air, and her people had marveled at her mastery. No victory feast had been held because of the dead and injured soldiers, but a nourishing meal had been quickly prepared and served to all present. Bodies had been placed near the base of the front battlement and covered, to be retrieved by families or buried tomorrow. The wounded had been housed in a separate wing of the castle and weary soldiers had been given places to sleep.

Dirtied and exhausted, Princess Alysa Malvern Crisdean had bathed, eaten, and gone to her bed as soon as she could slip away from the adoring crowd. She had been asleep when Gavin finally joined her, and when he had left her side at dawn.

Today had been devoured greedily by remaining tasks. Her men had returned from a successful pursuit of the flee-ing foes, which left no witnesses to their recent battle and identities. Lord Weylin had ridden to Land's End to reveal Sir Bevan's death to Lord Keegan. The captives had been taken to Prisongate—twenty miles away—by Sheriff Dal, Sir Tragan, and Sir Lann. The slain Damnonians had been mourned, lauded, and buried. Piaras and Leitis had busied themselves and the servants with tending the wounded and with sending word to families. Teague and Thisbe were see-ing to supplies for the wounded and for meals. And, shortly before dusk, Prince Gavin Crisdean had ridden off by him-self, to be alone.

It was late when her husband returned, but Alysa had waited up for him. "Gavin, we must talk." Her expression and tone were grave. She could not allow this distance be-tween them to continue or to increase. She had to make him relent, to understand.

The prince sighed loudly and replied, "It must wait until morning. I need rest, and my thoughts are elsewhere to-night."

"You are rarely here during the day," she reminded point-edly.

"There has been much to do. Would you have me laze around while enemies invade your land? Have you learned so much about warfare after only one battle to handle all matters henceforth?"

Alysa noticed his glazed eyes and knew he was plagued by some inner demon. "You are being unkind and stubborn, Hawk of Cumbria. I am not to blame for seizing a victory which was thrust upon me. If we had not ambushed the other Viking party, your band would have been too tired to defend themselves. Was it wrong to save lives?"

Gavin did not seem to hear her words. He poured two goblets of wine from the skin he was holding. "Let us drink to your victory."

Alysa shook her head. "I want no wine. I want to talk. I wish to tear down this wall which you have built between us. What continues to trouble you so deeply, my love?"

Gavin ignored her plea and insisted, "Then, drink to my victory, though a smaller one than yours."

"Your words are untrue and your feelings sour. Why must you spoil our happiness? Do you regret our marriage and settling here?"

Gavin pressed the goblet into her hand and ordered, "If you wish to please me and make me happy, drink to me."

Alysa realized he was behaving oddly and would not drop the matter until she obeyed. She lifted the goblet and said, "To you, my husband, my lover, my prince." She downed the liquid and set the goblet aside. "Now, will you talk with me?"

For a time, Gavin remained still and silent, and stared at her as if seeing through her. He did not empty his goblet, but placed it and the wineskin on a table. In a strange tone, he said, "Destiny calls to us, my warrior queen, and we must respond."

Suddenly, Alysa felt her head spin wildly and her vision blurred. A curious ringing filled her ears. Her body seemed light and tingly. The room began to waver like pond water rippled by a mischievous hand. Tiny lights danced before her eyes and the room dimmed. She could not speak or think clearly. Weak and shaky, she sank to the bed behind her. Still, Gavin only watched her as if waiting for something.

When Alysa fell unconscious, backward, Gavin lifted her body and placed her beneath the cover, then left a note beside her sleeping head. He gathered his possessions and the wineskin. As if a cunning thief, he left the castle without being seen.

Slowly, Alysa's drugged mind released her from its potent hold. It was midmorning. As her wits cleared, she recalled what had happened last night. She could not understand her husband's behavior, and she did not have to look around to know he was gone. She rubbed her grainy eyes as she sat up in bed. Noticing the note Gavin had left for her, she lifted the folded message.

Alysa shook her head to clear her wits and vision. Surely she could not be grasping the message clearly. She hurried to where Gavin kept his weapons and garments. All were gone! She headed for the door to search for him, but halted herself. She could not question the servants without revealing the problem. She had to think, to decide how to handle this stunning matter.

Alysa took a seat on a comfortable wooden bench to read the dismaying note again:

"Alysa,

A kingdom cannot have two rulers during a time of trouble. You have proven the people wish to follow you. I cannot relent to your destiny and I cannot watch it come to pass. Tell your people I am needed at home and have been summoned there by my father and king. Tell my friends I must be alone for a time. They will understand and accept my wishes. Do not seek me or worry over me. Let us test our love and bond by walking separate paths. We wed in haste and that changed my life completely. I need to recapture my joy of living and reclaim my prowess. For a time, forget me. Think only of defense and victory. If it is to be, we shall meet again.

Gavin"

Five

Alysa sat there a long time. She did not know where to search for Gavin. From his message, he had not even enlightened his friends to his strange departure. What would everyone think about his disappearance, even if she told the lie he had suggested in his note?

Alysa stood, went to a narrow window, and gazed outside. There was activity in every area of the inner and outer wards. So many people were present, and her responsibilities were great. Could she lead her people to victory? Could she survive without Gavin? Why had he done this horrible thing to them? Why had he changed so suddenly, so completely?

Deserted . . . Betrayed . . . The shocking and painful words echoed in her mind. She had been warned of this tormenting moment by Trosdan and in a subtle way by Gavin himself, but she had not believed it possible. Did he love her? Did he regret their marriage? Would he return?

There was a knock at her chamber door. Alysa hated to answer it and face anyone yet, but she knew she must. She opened the door to find Trosdan standing there.

The Druid High Priest remarked softly, "I sensed you needed me. The time has come, has it not?"

Alysa nodded. "Come inside, Wise One. We must talk."

71

Alysa led the white-haired man to the sitting area and motioned for him to take a seat near her. Her blue eyes were bright with unshed tears and her face was pale with distress. Her voice was tinged with anger and anguish as she said, "You did not tell me I would travel alone because of my husband's selfish betrayal. He is gone, Trosdan. I do not know where or why," she remarked sadly.

The man did not interrupt as Alysa related Gavin's behavior of late. She revealed his actions of last night and showed Trosdan the note he had left for her. She trusted this holy man and confided all to him. The old man read it silently, then returned his sympathetic gaze to her.

Tense, Alysa stood and moved about as she talked. "Why has fate changed him and taken him from my side? How can I win him back? I love him, Wise One, and I need him. How can I battle fierce enemies alone? What do I know of warfare and strategy?"

Trosdan smiled affectionately. "You have already proven yourself in battle, my valiant princess, as the Runes said you would. They do not lie. Did your dream not tell you what to do, and did you not follow its commands?"

Alysa looked surprised when the Druid mentioned her strange dream before the battle. Did the man see and know all things?

"Your powers are great. Believe in them, accept them, and use them. I saw his departure in my sacred chalice, but I could only prepare you for the truth. You must put aside your anger and pain, for they distract you. It is your destiny to walk this path alone; his departure could not have been halted, even had I warned you of it."

Alysa refuted, "If I had not gone into battle as Gavin desired, he would not have left me."

"Nay, he and the others would be dead, slain by those you slew. Our destinies are planned before our births. If we are stubborn and selfish and do not follow their leads, disaster results for us and for those we love. Do as you must, and all will be good again. You have conquered your first challenge and won your first victory. You are the sole ruler and leader of Damnonia, but the survival of all Briton kingdoms depends on you."

"How can I believe such words?" she asked gravely.

Trosdan went to where she had halted near a window and grasped her hands. "Remember my words in the cave: You must be strong, Alysa. You must put your destiny and victory above your own desires and dreams. Your narrow path is set before you. Do not let anguish halt your journey, or all is lost. You have seen many die and suffer. If you turn away from your duty now, destruction and death will fill your land and others. Your people believe in you and will obey you without question. Their hearts have been prepared to accept difficult words and times, as has yours. You must do as Gavin said in his note, as he is being controlled and guided by his own destiny. Soon you will begin your journey. It is as it should be. You shall meet and love again, of this I am certain."

Alysa wished she had the old man's confidence and foresight. What if Gavin were injured or slain during their separation? What if he decided never to return to her? "I must know where he is, if he is safe and what he is doing. Mayhap there is a good reason for his behavior, one he could not reveal."

"The Runes have not told me such things." As he fetched his bag, the Druid suggested, "I will use the sacred chalice to see if it will respond." Trosdan removed and placed several objects on a table. He poured a green liquid into a goblet, then chanted softly as he swirled it. Adding a sprinkle of yellow powder, the mixture sent forth wisps of blue smoke. Trosdan waved his hand back and forth over the chalice, causing the smoke to dance in the air currents and to fill his nostrils. When it ceased, he stared into the gently bubbling fluid.

Alysa waited eagerly for him to read the signs which only he could see. Her hopes were dashed when he lifted his head and shook it.

"They will not reveal such things to us. We must trust them."

Alysa was disappointed and vexed. She said, "I must search for him, Wise One. He must listen to me."

"Nay, if they wished us to find Prince Gavin, they would reveal his location. It is meant to be this way. That is why the gods and spirits hide him from our eyes, for he would halt you from the mission you must undertake. You have been prepared for this special moment. Your mother Catriona and your grandmother Giselde taught you the language of your Viking people. We have practiced it for weeks, though most of the Norsemen speak the Celtic tongue. They learn from their captives so they can give orders during their raids. It is a powerful weapon which will aid your cause."

Trosdan withdrew a small cloth bag, shook it, and tossed the sacred stones upon a table. He studied their etchings and arrangements. "Beware of a giant foe with hair that blazes as the sun. He seeks your heart and hand. He will help you fulfill your destiny, though he does not know this and does not wish it so."

Alysa replied knowingly, "His name is Rolf. He led the attack at Daron Castle." She repeated what Sir Teague and Thisbe had told her about the Viking leader, and of the stranger in a flowing robe.

"Yea, the man with Rolf is the Viking *attiba*. He is controlled by Darkness; he guides and protects Rolf. He is powerful and dangerous, Alysa. But there is another more deadly and treacherous than Rolf, and his wizard; a rival named Ulf. Beware of all three."

74

"Will we battle them face-to-face?" she inquired.

Trosdan's response was baffling. "If you follow your destiny, you will win this war with one great battle. Some of Isobail's hirelings escaped into Logris. They know your land and can lead attacks here if we do not prevent it. The warrior you wounded has survived and escaped. He will prepare the others for your brave task." Trosdan revealed his daring and perilous scheme.

Alysa listened carefully. If the plan worked, all would be saved without heavy bloodshed. She wondered if she was clever enough and brave enough to carry out her role in it. She went over his words from all angles. Knowing so much about the Vikings, she concluded it must be attempted, and soon. "I will do it, Wise One."

"First, you must reveal Prince Gavin's departure to his friends. They will be of great help while we are gone."

"Lord Weylin is at Land's End. He went to carry the news of Sir Bevan's death to their friend Lord Keegan. Sheriff Dal, Sir Lann, and Sir Tragan have taken the Norse captives to Prisongate. They should return by tomorrow at midday. I will speak with them together. Until then, I will tell no one of my husband's absence."

"After they return and you speak, you must go to Prisongate to question and execute the Viking captives. As long as they live, they are a danger to you, your land, and our mission. They could escape or lure others here to rescue them. If but one speaks of you and the prince, our foes could guess our strength and purpose."

"It will be as you say, Wise One," she agreed. "Will you remain here and join my meeting with Gavin's friends? They will be confused over his actions. They might insist on searching for him, or refuse to remain here under my command."

"They will heed and obey your words," Trosdan refuted. "I must return to my cave to prepare for our task, but I

75

will return for your meeting. Worry not, my princess, for we will succeed."

Alysa watched Trosdan pack his belongings and leave. She did not want to remain in the haunting chamber, so she dressed and went to visit the wounded men. They were glad to see her and their spirits were brightened. She chatted with each a moment or two, then left to speak with Leitis.

Alysa ordered the woman to make certain all present were fed and tended. She told the woman to serve her evening meal in her chamber, and said that Gavin would dine there with her after "his ride."

Fortunately she did not run into Teague or Thisbe in the large castle, which consisted of four two-story wings, two lofty towers, the Great Hall and their private chambers, and a gatehouse of interlocked towers. The inner ward of lovely Malvern Castle was private, but the outer one was filled with workmen and activities, and was surrounded by a tall and thick battlement. Situated beside a river, many of the rooms boasted of picturesque views. Several villages and hamlets were within walking or riding distance, and many of their inhabitants were castle servants. The castle was strong and constructed well for defense. With its wells, orchards, vegetable gardens, and private stores, they could hold out against an enemy attack for months.

Not wanting to find herself in a situation where she would be questioned about Prince Gavin's absence, Alysa returned to her chamber and locked the door. Soon, her meal was served. With little appetite, she barely picked over the mutton and vegetable pie and absently played with the warm bread.

She was restless and dejected. She put the food aside and strolled around the large room, stopping here and there to gaze out a window. From one, she watched the river flow, but its serenity depressed her even more. From another, she eyed the cool forest and longed to ride there, ride swiftly

76

on Calliope's back until the wind blew all worries from her head. How she missed Giselda, her grandmother, and needed her for comfort and advice, but the woman was far away and unknowing of her misery.

From another window, she saw smoke from chimneys which indicated villagers were preparing their meals, meals to be shared with loved ones. She leaned against the wall and gazed around the room. Prince Alric, her father, had occupied these chambers. He had lived and died here. Since her chambers in the south tower were too small for the married couple, she had had these royal chambers cleaned and refurbished for her and Gavin. Now, after only six weeks of bliss in them, she was alone, alone as Alric had been when Isobail had moved to other chambers while she plotted her treachery and evil.

"What shall I do, Father? I have been betrayed by love as you were. Must a ruler suffer so deeply for her people? Must their lives and needs always come before my own? I do not know if I am strong enough to bear this added burden. What if Trosdan is wrong this time?"

Alysa felt utterly alone. Gavin had vanished. Her parents were dead. Her grandparents were far away. Enormous responsibilities rested on her slender shoulders. She felt as if her vitality was draining away. She needed someone to help her, to hold her, to comfort her in this dire time.

"Why, my love, did you leave me?" she pondered aloud. "Was it so hard for you to accept me in your life? To let me rule my land and people? To allow me my destiny? To be myself? We had so little time together. Why did you not allow us more? We could have solved this matter together. From our first meeting, we were drawn tightly together."

Alysa recalled what Giselde had told her about trying to cast a lovespell over her and Gavin. Had it worked, only to fade with her grandmother's departure? Had Gavin loved her, or only been enchanted for a short time? If he had truly loved her, loved her of his own free will, he would be here with her this minute. If he did not love her, he would never return. That fear tormented her. She could not imagine life without his fiery caresses. She possessed wealth, beauty, and royalty, and was desired by countless men. Why not by her own husband? she wondered, and allowed the imprisoned tears to flow freely.

Darkness descended upon Damnonia, and with it came silence. It was as if all living creatures were asleep, all except Princess Alysa. She lay on her bed, staring into the blackness above her. Evil was black and wicked. She longed for light and peace. She rose and lit a candle, and watched its flame glow in the large room.

"Am I truly like this candle, Trosdan? Can I chase away the evil darkness which threatens us?"

Alysa heard fluttering at one of her windows. She glanced that way and saw a bird resting on the wide sill. It dropped something and sang merrily before flying away. Alysa went to the window and lifted the discarded object. Mixed emotions consumed her. She was happy, but she was baffled. Was it a sign or a happenstance?

She inhaled the fragrance of the tiny bloom, a flower like those she had once left for Gavin in the hollow of a dying tree in the royal forest beyond the castle, an unspoken message between her and her mysterious lover. She looked in the direction where they had met, but only a dark covering could be seen. So many times she and Gavin had met secretly in that forest to talk or to make love upon a grassy bed. How wonderful and passionate those meetings had been. She longed for his safe and swift return. Could he be camping there while trying to clear his head? Nay, she decided, for she did not sense his presence nearby. Somehow she knew he was far away, and traveling farther away from her with each hour.

Alysa rested her damp cheek against the cool stone wall

and gazed out the window, slipping into deep thought. She watched many destinies unfold before her mind's eye, trying to understand her loved one's motives and to forgive their past weaknesses. Her life had been filled with joys and sadnesses, with pains and pleasures, with victories and defeats. Love had provided the good moments, and evil the bad ones. If she was to have love and good restored to her life and land, she had to defeat evil. Was she, she mused anxiously, brave enough, clever enough, to do so?

Destiny had taken control of her life long before she was born, back in a time when her great-grandparents met and fell in love. Connal, a tribal chieftain in Albany, had been taken captive by raiding Norsemen. Having proven his prowess and earned the right to survival under their barbaric laws and customs, Connal had been compelled to deceitfully join the Vikings to live to defeat them and return home.

While existing with his foes, Connal had fallen in love with Astrid, one of the two heirs to the Viking throne with ancient royal blood, and Astrid had returned that love. A hopeless union there, Connal and Astrid had fled her homeland, calling down the wrath of the Norsemen upon them and birthing a fated path for many to follow. With the other heir too young to rule, the Norsemen had sought their lost ruler with a crazed vengeance. Attacks on Albany had been numerous and bloody, but the lovers had remained safely hidden. Her grandmother Giselde had been born of that powerful but ill-fated love.

Years passed, but the crime of Connal was not forgotten, nor was the hunger for Astrid's return. The time came when another warband sailed to Albany and brought with it a wild, sweet love for Giselde: Rurik, the other royal heir and very distant relative of Astrid. Rurik found Giselde irresistible and joined her side. With his help, the Norsemen were again defeated and repelled. The Viking *attiba*, wizard, declared this second betrayal by a royal heir a bad omen, a curse which only the recovery of a blood heir could dispel.

A daughter was born to her grandparents, Catriona, Alysa's mother. As a beautiful young woman, Catriona found a love of her own, Alric, the Prince of Cambria, one of the five kingdoms of Britain. Despite her parents' misgivings and the Cambrians' ill feelings, the lovers were wed. King Bardwyn, Alric's father and the ruler of Cambria and Damnonia, made them regents of this principality which was separated from Cambria by water. Bardwyn had hoped the rulership would mature his son and help their people learn to accept the "mixed-blooded, barbarian" princess whom Alric had insisted on marrying, a woman whom the people feared would bring down the Vikings on them. Yet times and people were hard on her parents, and Catriona returned home to Albany for a visit.

The angered Vikings persisted with their raids and hungers. They struck again. Connal and Astrid were slain, as was Rurik, leaving only two women with royal blood. Catriona and Giselde were rescued by Prince Briac of Cumbria, a man who had loved but could not wed Catriona for the same reasons Alric was advised against it.

After a lengthy rest and recovery at Briac's castle, where Giselde first met Gavin at age five, Catriona returned to Damnonia and Alric, with Giselde as her servant to prevent the people's fears and hatred and dissension. But Catriona had been away too long . . .

In a moment of weakness and despair, and doubting his wife's love and return, Alric, bored and restless, guilefully had seduced Isobail, wife of a feudal lord with whom Alric was quarreling. Although Isobail never learned of Alric's wickedness—a seduction which took place with the aid of potent drugs supplied to Alric by a sorcerer—she desired the prince as a means to obtain wealth, power, and high rank.

Lord Caedmon was slain mysteriously, by Isobail's hand or order, Alysa accurately suspected. As she was with child and Alric believed it was his, Lady Isobail was brought to live at Malvern Castle as Catriona's waiting woman, a rank the insidious beauty despised.

How sad that evil had entrapped her father before his wife's return. For when Catriona arrived, the lovers reforged their bond and made it stronger than ever. Peaceful months passed for her parents while Isobail plotted her wickedness and awaited the birth of her son, whose sire she did not know. Moran was born, and Alric secretly delighted in having a son. Shortly afterward, Catriona gave birth to Alysa, their only child, and Alric loved her more than anyone.

By then, evil had taken root in Malvern Castle. Isobail secretly poisoned Catriona when Alysa was nine years old, a fact Alysa did not learn until her father's death a few weeks past, a fact which Isobail had boasted of to torment the dying prince.

Following her mother's death, Isobail had pursued her grieving father until he weakened and wed her, only to sate his lust and to obtain his son, another fact which Alysa had only recently discovered. Isobail herself had never learned it before her violent death.

For years, Alysa had been tormented by her hateful stepmother and stepsister Kyra, and pursued for her rank by Moran, whom she had not known was her half brother until shortly before his death. It was a tangled web of deceits.

Alysa's troubled mind focused on the center of the evil which had torn asunder her own existence. Isobail—a blood heir of warrior queen Boadicea of the ancient kingdom of Iceni, now a part of Logris, and the scourge of the invading Romans—desired to rule not only this land but also all of Britain. First the greedy woman had obtained control of Prince Alric by poisoning him to the point of death and keeping him there until she was powerful enough to take over Damnonia before ridding herself of her second husband; then she had tried to steal this land before conquering all of Britain.

Alysa suspected her stepmother's evil and greed, and secretly battled them while trying to save her father's life and defend it. At her mother's death, Giselde—who had taken care of her since birth—vanished. Later, Alysa discovered the old woman living as a witch and healer in the forbidden royal forest. Alysa had visited "Granmannie" frequently, unaware the woman was her true grandmother.

It was Giselde who sent for aid from Kings Bardwyn and Briac, pleading with them to save Alysa and Damnonia, to send someone to check out Isobail's evil mischief. That rescue came in the form of "Gavin Hawk," a hired warrior who with his band of friends claimed to be there seeking adventure and riches. Alysa had met him in the forest while pretending to be Thisbe, her handmaiden and best friend at the castle. She asked the handsome mercenary for help in defeating the fierce brigands whom Isobail had hired to enforce her position.

Gavin Hawk made his presence known to Isobail and the raiders with daring deeds, then pretended to join the brigands led by a Norseman named Skane to defeat them from within, or so he had told her. His curious actions and secretiveness, despite their intimate relationship, had caused her to doubt him and to fear betrayal.

As the days passed, Isobail had Lords Daron and Kelton murdered and placed her men in control of those large feudal estates. If she had not been halted, she would have slain Lords Orin and Fergus and done the same! Isobail had been clever and daring, consumed by evil and greed. She had ensnared Sheriff Trahern and included her son in her evil scheme. Many were killed during Isobail's reign of terror. The people had feared her, been duped by her, and controlled by her.

One of her seeds had been more evil than the other, had been just like her: Kyra, her daughter by Lord Caedmon. Isobail had despised the child who had dared to reflect her lovely and innocent-appearing visage and who had dared to plot behind her back to steal all that Isobail craved. Princess Kyra and Earnon, her lover, and Isobail's sorcerer and adviser, had died mysteriously after their personal plot was uncovered and they were banished. Alysa had never learned who had slain them in the royal forest.

Things worsened as the days went by. Alysa had been unable to reach her father's drugged mind with the truth of what was happening in his land. She had been unable to rescue him in his sorry condition; if she had tried, Isobail would have overtaken them and slain them.

Once, mistrustful of Gavin Hawk even though she loved him and could not resist him, she had tried to flee to her grandfather's kingdom to enlighten King Bardwyn and to seek his aid in challenging Isobail's hold over Alric and Damnonia. But she had been captured by Isobail's brigands, only to be rescued by Gavin, with whom she spent several days in a hidden cave. She had confessed the truth of her identity, but, to protect her, he had held silent about his true name and his mission. He had claimed he was helping her by pretending to be one of the brigands. Returned home under the guise of a kidnapping by Skane's men, Isobail had turned against her brigand leader for such treachery. She had ordered Gavin to slay Skane and to take his place! Gavin, to further his ruse and to entrap Isobail, had done so.

Yet not all went well for Alysa's side. More perils and problems plagued them. Isobail and her son tried to force Alysa to wed Moran, unaware, as was she, he was her half brother. To stall for time, Alysa agreed to the offensive betrothal. But Moran was not satisfied with her partial submission and delay. He tried to ravish her to force her into a quick marriage. That horrid night, she clubbed him unconscious and, with Teague's help, fled the castle.

Teague was punished by imprisonment in the castle dungeon and tortured to obtain information. Thisbe, his love, was threatened with torture, too, rape, and death. Weakened from his beatings and fearing for his love's life, Teague revealed Giselde's location and prayed the two women were not at the cottage. Isobail guessed the woman's identity and interference, and ordered Giselde's death.

While her stepmother's soldiers were seeking them, Isobail had declared Gavin a wolfshead and Alysa a traitor. The evil and desperate woman had put out the news that Alysa, with Gavin and Giselde's help, had tried to poison Alric to take over this principality.

Things looked dark for Alysa's side. But a message had been taken to King Bardwyn by one of Gavin's men. While they awaited help, Giselde, Alysa, Gavin, his men, Teague, and Thisbe—who had been rescued by Gavin, Alysa, and *his* men via the secret passageway which nearly encircled the castle—were concealed in Trosdan's cave.

When her grandfather arrived with his large army to meet her for the first time and to defeat their mutual foe, many secrets were revealed in the Druid's hidden cave. Alysa learned who Giselde really was, and the truth about Moran, and the identity of Prince Gavin Crisdean. She discovered that her mother had been murdered by Isobail, and that Giselde had fled in fear of a similar fate.

Giselde had remained nearby to protect Alysa and to seek revenge on Isobail and Alric for Catriona's betrayal and death, as Giselde had discovered the truth about Alric and Isobail's liaison and their offspring! At one time, Giselde had tried to poison Alric herself, but had since realized that Alric was being used by Isobail and was innocent of Catriona's death. Although she could not forgive Alric for his wickedness, Giselde had decided the man had suffered enough for his past deeds.

Before the attack on Malvern Castle, Bardwyn had suggested Alysa and Gavin wed, as he had guessed their love and passion and they were more than suitably matched. Trosdan had performed the ceremony. That same night, Alysa, Gavin, and his men had entered the secret passageway to rescue Alric and other prisoners before opening the gates for Bardwyn's forces.

But tragedy had struck again. Her father had died in her arms before Isobail's downfall, died after confessing his sins to Alysa. The attack had been successful, and the villains had been conquered and slain, except for a few raiders who escaped after hearing of their defeat. Her grandfather, their king, had remained in Damnonia for two weeks to make certain all was smooth again before his return to Cambria.

During those two weeks, Bardwyn and Giselde grew close, and decided to wed. All seemed wonderful. Peace had been restored. She was wed to her love. Her friends had found their own happinesses.

Then, during the last few weeks, news had come of a new threat. More Norsemen were preparing to invade them and to take possession of the Last Viking Queen: herself, as they believed Giselde was dead—and Astrid, Rurik, and Catriona truly were. This time, the Vikings were more determined than ever to conquer this isle and to reclaim the "only blood heir" to their throne. By now, the stories of Connal/Astrid and Rurik/Giselde were legends, legends which said only Alysa's recovery could end the curse on them.

Yet few people knew the real reason for the Vikings' persistence and motives: to capture Alysa and to make her queen, by force if necessary. Even so, Gavin refused to believe he could not defeat them and protect her with his

85

prowess and wits. He did not understand or accept the power of destiny, or the power of magic.

Alysa gazed at the ancient wedding ring upon her finger and dreamily reflected on its history. The large stone captured the candle's glow and sent forth purple glimmers as if it possessed a life of its own. This wedding ring had been passed from Viking queen to Viking queen down through the ages. She removed it and gazed at the ancient Viking symbols inside the band, symbols which translated to the words: "I command Thor to protect my love forever." Legend claimed the ring had been created by Odin, the originator of the royal bloodline and had been given to the First Viking Queen, the only mortal woman to bear a child by him, a daughter who was protected and guided by Odin, as were all his heirs.

From daughter to daughter, queen to queen, the golden circle with its purple stone had been passed along until Astrid escaped to Albany with it and Connal. The ring, given to Giselde when she wed Rurik and to Catriona when she wed Alric, was old and priceless. After Catriona's death, Giselde had taken it with her to her hidden cottage in the forbidden forest, to pass on to Alysa on her wedding day, which she had done when Alysa married Gavin Crisdean.

Alysa studied the ring and murmured, "If you possess real magic and power, why did my love betray me and desert me? Nay, you are only an old ring. But a lovely and special one. I will never take you from my hand until Gavin is lost to me forever." A chill passed over Alysa at those intimidating words. If only her husband would return . . .

Astrid was never recovered. Nor was Giselde or Catriona. Now, she, Alysa, was last of the legendary bloodline. It was claimed the Norsemen could not be defeated as long as an heir of Odin's sat upon the Viking throne. With Giselde as a royal heir who had wed a royal prince, Alysa's bloodline was even stronger than Astrid's had been, and the Viking hunger for her was ever greater. Since Giselde was nearing seventy—too old to bear future heirs—and Catriona was dead, Alysa knew she was highly coveted by the Vikings.

Alysa pressed the flower and ring to her lips and whispered, "You will come back to me, Hawk of Cumbria, or I shall hunt you down and bewitch you when my task is done. Sleep well and stay safe, for you are mine." Alysa knew what had to be done and finally accepted her role in it. A curious feeling of resignation and contentment washed over her. She returned to her bed and fell asleep quickly.

Alysa had managed to keep anyone from realizing her husband had been missing for days. Dal, Tragan, and Lann had returned to the castle an hour ago. Lord Keegan arrived with Weylin to spend a day with his friends, mourning Bevan's loss. When word had been sent to her chambers of their presence in the Great Hall and their request to see Prince Gavin, Alysa had ordered Leitis to refresh them with food and drink until she joined them.

The young ruler donned a becoming lavender gown, her golden circlet, and matching cloth slippers. Her long brown hair was neatly braided into a large plait which hung down her back. A jeweled belt was secured around her slender waist and an exquisite medallion was about her neck and resting at the swell of her breasts. Upon her left hand was the legendary wedding ring. Its purple stone glittered each time light touched it, reminding her of its significance.

When Astrid escaped with her Celtic lover, she had innocently spawned a curse, a curse which alleged their defeat would be at the hands of their stolen heir if not reclaimed, a curse which would cease the moment their rightful heir was made ruler, by choice or by coercion.

The Viking who took her as his own would become undisputed leader, their High King. For years, the Vikings had lost track of the royal bloodline through Giselde and Rurik. But her wicked stepmother had learned the truth about Alysa and provided her Norse brigands with that priceless information. Isobail had wanted her slain or removed from this principality so the people would turn to her as ruler after she had secretly and cleverly murdered Prince Alric. Now, Alysa's foes knew of her existence and location, as a few of Isobail's brigands had escaped into Logris and had no doubt joined forces with the other Vikings there. If she did not do something desperate and daring to prevent their attacks to capture her, her land would suffer terribly. Only by using the superstitious curse and her heritage could she save her people.

Alysa went to the Great Hall to find only Leitis there. "Where are the others?" the young ruler inquired.

The head servant replied, "Trosdan took them to his chamber to speak privately. He asked for you to join them there. I placed him in the south tower in Kyra's old chambers."

Alysa smiled and thanked the tall, stout woman who had been at the castle since her childhood. "I hope all goes well with your new marriage to Sir Piaras," she remarked, happy that two people so special to her had fallen in love and wed.

Leitis's eyes sparkled with joy. She tucked a straying red-dish-gray curl back into her neat bun and grinned. "But we shouldna have waited so long, Princess."

The two shared laughter, then Alysa headed for the south tower. She had not been in this section since moving from the second floor after her marriage. Isobail's evil seeds— Moran and Kyra—had lived on the first floor, but both were dead now because of their mother's darkness which had engulfed them.

Trosdan answered her knock and she went inside. Weylin, Keegan, Dal, Lann, and Tragan were all present. The men were drinking ale while they awaited her arrival, all except Trosdan. Alysa took a seat and glanced at each man's expectant face.

Trosdan said, "You must listen closely to Princess Alysa's words and heed them. Before she speaks to you, there is something I must reveal," he began mysteriously, then related Alysa's Viking heritage and the Norsemen's superstitions about her.

The Cumbrian knights looked baffled by the man's words and by Gavin's absence. Their friend had previously informed them of his wife's ancestry and the Viking threat to her.

Alysa said, "Trosdan and I have a plan to defeat the Norsemen with little bloodshed, which I will explain to you in a moment. First, there is other news I must share with you, news which saddens me." She told them about Gavin's departure and read his note to them. "I do not know why he left or where he has gone."

Sheriff Dal exclaimed, "He would not leave without telling us!"

Alysa refuted, "It appears he has done so, Dal."

"But why would he vanish?" asked Lann skeptically.

Alysa held her chin high and kept her voice controlled as she replied, "He was angry with me for joining the battle and for claiming a victory which he viewed greater than his own. I have known Prince Gavin only a few months, but you have known him since childhood and have ridden with him for years. Perhaps you can understand better than I why he would do this to me, to us."

The men gave serious consideration to the perplexing matter. Weylin spoke up. "He was plagued by Bevan's death, and he has acted strangely of late. Perhaps he only needs time alone."

"If that were so, Weylin," she reasoned, "he could camp

in the forest or confine himself to private chambers. He is gone."

"Are you certain no message or summons came from his father, our king?" Tragan inquired worriedly. "Perhaps he only wished us to remain here to protect you and your land."

Again she reasoned, "If that were so, why not tell one of us? Of late, he has behaved and talked as a man imprisoned. Perhaps he only wished his freedom and will send for his friends soon."

"Nay," they all seemed to say in unison.

Keegan suggested, "What if Gavin has a plan to thwart the Vikings and did not want to worry us or have us resist it?"

"I do not believe that is so, Keegan. You have not seen him of late. He has been miserable here without his friends. He was restless. He longed for his old life and was excited by our impending war. When I took command, he changed. That is all I know."

Dal persisted, "But why did he not tell us of his pains and plans?"

"You know more of men's pride than I do. To say such things might be viewed in his eyes as a failure, a weakness, a mistake. Gavin is not a man to . . . accept any kind of defeat easily. He was a carefree warrior and was not happy being the bored ruler stuck in one place."

"I think there is more to this matter," Keegan decided aloud.

"As do I," Alysa concurred. "But until, and if, Gavin chooses to return and enlighten us, we must accept his wishes. By drugging me, he made certain he had plenty of time to get away. Enough of this depressing matter for a while. I will tell you of our plan to defeat our invaders. Trosdan and I will ride to their camp and I will declare myself their queen. I—"

"You cannot endanger yourself!" shouted Weylin.

Alysa smiled at the dark-haired man. "Hear me first, dear friends, then you can speak. I promise you the Vikings will not harm me; I am priceless to them. It will require time for me to prove my claim to them, then time for them to carry out a quest for their leader, my husband." When the men started to object again, Alysa lifted her hand and said sternly, "Be silent until I finish! The plan is complicated and cunning. It will work."

Trosdan refilled their ale cups from a clay pitcher. "Princess Alysa is right. Listen closely to her."

"We need time to train and prepare our forces. All men of age and strength must be summoned and taught to fight. Supplies and horses must be gathered. Weapons must be made and repaired. To obtain this time, I will distract them with my arrival and their quest. I will say I have returned to my people by choice and wish to lead them to victory over this isle. Once I prove I am their queen by right, they must obey me; it is their law. I can speak their tongue, and most of them can speak mine. I will give them Odin's instructions for choosing my mate, their High King. Trosdan will use his magic to frighten them into accepting me and my words. He will tell them of Odin's commands."

"What quest do you speak of?" Dal asked when she halted to take a breath and a sip of the water which Trosdan had given to her.

She explained, "They are superstitious people who will do anything their gods command. Trosdan will tell them Odin has prepared for this moment by concealing five objects in Logris: a sword, a helmet, a shield, an amulet, and a ship's figurehead. The Vikings must battle one another to decide which three warriors will win the honor of seeking the objects and my hand in marriage. Trosdan will give them clues for their search, carrying out one quest at a time. The man who finds the object must guard it while he seeks the next one. Do you not see? They will spend their time and energies on this treasure hunt and battling amongst themselves for the objects, and it will keep them in Logris. That will allow you time to prepare and train our forces, and to have Cambria and Cumbria do the same. When the quest is complete, I am to empower the objects with my magical ring at Stonehenge during a full moon, and to wed the champion."

"You cannot wed a Viking! You are Gavin's wife," Lann argued.

Alysa laughed softly. "I will not wed him. It is only a trick. Once I am accepted as their ruler and the quest is on, Trosdan will send a message to you to let you know all is fine. When the quest is complete and we are to gather at Stonehenge for the ritual, Trosdan will send you another message. You will gather all forces from our land and the others and attack while they are drunk during the feast. It is the only way we can become stronger than they and thus defeat them. I will place all of you in charge, under Weylin, to carry out the tasks here. The Norsemen will be too busy with me and the quest to attack here. Trosdan can keep them under control with his magic and I will do the same with skills he will teach me before we depart."

"What of your people? They will worry over your absence."

"Nay, Keegan, they will be too busy with preparations to realize I am gone. Each group will think I am with another. They are not to be enlightened until the day of the battle."

"What if Gavin returns?" queried Dal.

"Tell him of our plan and actions, but do not let him interfere. If he comes after me, all will be ruined and imperiled. This plan will save many lives and will ensure our victory. Do you not agree?"

The five men deliberated her words. They concurred with

Alysa's plan, even without the aid of Trosdan's bewitching elixir in their ale.

"What happens when they find no objects from Odin?"

Trosdan answered Weylin's question. "The sacred Runes told me of this moment and I prepared for it long ago. There are fake objects hidden in Logris and the sly clues are ready within my mind. I will arrange a special ritual to prove Alysa is their queen. With my help, she will use many tricks and skills to convince them of her powers as a seer and sorceress. They will fear us and believe us."

"You do not have to believe in magic to aid us, my friends, but you must believe in the powers of Good for us to be victorious. My husband was a doubter, but there are things we can do which others cannot do or explain. We will prey upon their fears and beliefs."

"It is a cunning but dangerous scheme. What if something goes wrong with the quest? What if you are injured or slain during the attack?" Weylin asked Alysa.

"All our tricks will persuade them to follow me. When the attack comes, I will conceal myself until all is safe."

"What if we do not win?" Lann ventured apprehensively.

"If we do not try this plan, all is lost anyway. We cannot sit by and await a certain defeat. This plan is our only hope, and it will succeed," she vowed confidently.

The men exchanged voting glances, and all nodded agreement. A bright smile from Alysa thanked them. "I will depend upon you to protect my people and to train them for the upcoming battle. We will slay our foes or push them back into the sea from which they came. When our task is done, we will search for Gavin, if he does not hear of our stimulating plans and rejoin us before our victory."

That idea pleased the men. "Surely he will hear of our training and hurry back to us," asserted Keegan.

"There is one last matter. We must ride to Prisongate to question the captives, then execute them. I doubt they will reveal anything of value to us, but it must be done. We need total privacy for our plans. We cannot allow them an opportunity to escape or to be rescued. These captives are a threat to our success. Do you agree?"

Sheriff Dal replied for the men. "Yea. If but one escaped and revealed your battle with them, they would suspect you of deceit."

Alysa knew from Trosdan that one man *had* escaped, but that was good because of what she had said to him and how she had defeated him. She wisely did not mention the wounded Viking to the men. "We will leave at dawn tomorrow for the prison. We must handle this matter ourselves for secrecy. We will test our plan on them. We will see how they react to my Viking words and claims. When we return to the castle, we will ready ourselves for our tasks."

After the men departed, Alysa looked at Trosdan. "All is coming true as you predicted, Wise One. Perhaps my love will return while I am gone. From this day forward, I will not dwell on his betrayal and reality until my task is done or he is at my side again."

"You understand what you must do in the enemy camp?" he hinted. "You must secretly beguile the three leaders to distract them and to cause dissension amongst them. Each must believe you desire him to win your hand. Can you carry out this difficult role?"

Alysa imagined another man's kisses and caresses, and winced. "I will do what I must to win this war, Trosdan. Anything."

Six

Alysa and Gavin's five friends rode to Prisongate, a small keep twenty miles from Malvern Castle. They arrived just in time to see the seven captives fleeing on foot.

Alysa's group rode after their foes. No man suggested she stay behind, which pleased Alysa. Only two Norsemen were armed with the guards' stolen swords, as other weapons were not allowed in the keep in case something like this occurred.

The Vikings were surrounded and Alysa ordered them to surrender. Their foes chuckled and prepared for hand-to-hand combat, unaware their captors wanted no prisoners taken alive. Gavin's friends dismounted and drew their swords, each seeming to choose his opponent, ready and eager to end this matter quickly. The remaining two Norsemen eyed the situation, five-to-five, and, ignoring Alysa, turned to flee.

Alysa knew they needed to escape to warn their friends. She also knew they did not make a grab for her, since they had no weapons and needed to use the time their friends were allowing them during their fights. Alysa drew her crossbow and fired into the back of one running man. He dropped to the ground, dead. The other one halted a moment and whirled to gape at the beautiful female. She was galloping toward him with a sword in her hand and a challenge on her face. He knew she would use it and readied himself for defense.

Alysa reined Calliope a few feet away and guided the well-trained horse toward the alert man. Sensing danger to his beloved mistress, Calliope obeyed her unspoken command to prance wildly before the foul-smelling warrior, bumping and shoving their foe until he stumbled. With that aid, Alysa gently pulled the dun's head aside and slashed across the Viking's chest, ripping through his shirt and flesh. With speed and agility, she and Calliope moved from the foe's reach before he could lunge at her with bloody hands.

The tag-and-strike game continued until the man was flustered and weakened. Cursing Alysa, he jumped at her to yank her from her saddle. Calliope batted the man with his forehead and threw him off balance. As the Norseman was falling backward, Alysa sliced her sharp sword across his throat, nearly decapitating him. This one she did not need to check for life. She returned to where the others were battling to see if any of her men needed help. None did.

Within a short time, the Viking captives were dead. Alysa gave her orders in a steady tone. "There is a crevice nearby. Tragan and Lann, you two place their bodies there and cover them with rocks. Keegan and Dal, see that our men are buried and replacements are posted. Weylin and I will return to the castle in case news arrives from other areas. Join us there when you finish your tasks. If it is late, camp here for the night and rest."

Alysa and Weylin headed for Malvern Castle at a leisurely pace. When they halted halfway to rest their horses, Weylin said, "After witnessing you in action twice, I have no doubts you can defend yourself on your journey. You are an amazing woman, Alysa Malvern."

Alysa smiled at him. "I only wish . . ."

"You wish what, Alysa?" he asked when she hesitated.

"I only wish Gavin felt and thought as you do. You are a good friend, Weylin, and I trust you completely."

Weylin took her hands in his and smiled encouragingly into her somber gaze. "There are times when men act strangely, Alysa. It is our curse to act the fool on occasion. Soon, his head will clear. He shoulders a heavy duty to you and your land. He must make certain he does what is best for all. One day he will be king and that is a great responsibility for any man. Surely he feels he must constantly prove himself worthy of both. He is full of energy and unaccustomed to lazy living. Give him time to adjust."

"You are as much like him as any man could be, Weylin. Yet you have adjusted. You have settled down and are happy. Gavin is strong in mind and in body. Why is it so difficult for him to be my husband and Damnonia's joint ruler? Would you be miserable in his place?" she asked unthinkingly.

Weylin almost flushed with surprise and guilt. He released her hands and ran his fingers through his sable hair, mussing it. His brown eyes did not look at her when he finally responded, "I am not as much like Gavin as you think, Alysa, so I cannot answer."

Alysa was astonished by Weylin's reaction. She had not realized he was attracted to her. She knew he would never intentionally expose such feelings or do anything about them as long as Gavin was in her life. To let the slip pass as if unnoticed, she laughed softly before she spoke. "It is good to have such a loyal friend as you, Weylin. I would be reluctant to go on my impending journey if you were not here to stand in for me. If Gavin returns, please make him see things our way."

"He *will* return. He could not live without you."

"If that were true, he would not be missing today. As long as I have you to stand by me and help me, I will be fine. My people like you best of all, Weylin, and they will obey you. We would not be displeased if you made Damnonia your permanent home." She glanced at the sky and added, "It grows late. We must ride."

As they traveled, Lord Weylin studied Princess Alysa from the corner of his eye. She was the most beautiful and desirable woman he had ever known, a stunning mixture of strength and gentleness, of daring and restraint. She was intelligent, brave, and genuine. He would give almost anything to find a wife like her. Whatever could Gavin be thinking to desert her, to hurt her even a tiny bit? Weylin swiftly chased forbidden desires from his mind.

Alysa ate a light meal in her room and took a long bath. She had vowed to herself and to Trosdan that she would keep Gavin out of her mind. But how could she? She loved him and missed him. She was worried about him and his curious state of mind. If he had not been acting so strangely for weeks, she would be tempted to think someone had placed an evil spell over him and driven him from her side!

Alysa recalled what Gavin had said to her only four weeks ago: "I cannot wait until we are alone for days on end. You are mine forever; Giselde told me so, and *this* tells me so." She touched her wedding ring to her lips and tears clouded her blue eyes.

Yet the ancient ring was what had come between them, for it represented her Viking ties and her duty and her destiny. Her responsibilities were heavy, but she was not running away from them as her husband had done. She did not have to test their love and commitment. For her, they were strong and real and forever. "Do not force me to resent you and this inexplicable decision, my love. Return before I leave, and explain it. In the dark days ahead, I need the strength and comfort of your love and acceptance. Fly back to me, Hawk of Cumbria; please come back to me before it is too late."

His lips ardently crushed against hers and she feverishly responded to him. His tongue danced around her lips and within her mouth, and she thrilled to the minglings of their flavors. He kissed her eyes and nose and tantalizingly roamed her face and throat. His wild, sweet caresses drove her mad with desire, and she craved him beyond reason or will. With deft hands, he quickly removed her garments and roamed her quivering flesh. Her breasts ached with longing when he kneaded them with gentle fingers and raced his tongue around their straining peaks. Her body was aflame and aquiver. She wanted him within her to feed this bitter-sweet hunger. Her mouth hungrily assailed his neck and shoulders as if she were trying to devour him. Sensuously her fingers teased over his supple flesh and aroused him to moaning desire. They entwined their flaming limbs and rolled upon the furry pallet, their mouths sealed and their passions blazing.

Just as he was about to blissfully enter her, his white-blond hair filled her vision. "Nay!" she shouted in her dream and pushed the Viking leader aside. "Not until we are wed, Rolf," she told him.

"I shall win your heart and hand, my warrior queen. There is no need to deny our passions until then. Forget your fears and doubts. Yield to me, my sweet destiny, the captor of my heart."

Suddenly, the unclear image of Rolf vanished and another man was beside her. In a husky, merry voice he said, "I will be the champion, my beautiful enchantress, if I can possess you this very night."

Alysa stared at the green-eyed warrior. His hair was dark-blond, the short beard on his handsome face light brown. A white scar was midway between his left eye and beard, and stood out most noticeably against his bronzed skin. His gaze was hot and playful as he removed his leather-and-fur garment, and his chest bore no royal Cumbrian tattoo. It was Gavin yet, it was not.

Alysa tried to escape, but he trapped her beneath his powerful body. His seductive smell was unknown, as was his aura. His mouth claimed hers with a savage tenderness which she found strange and irresistible. He tormented her with caresses and kisses until she pleaded with him to make love to her. Still, he stimulated and tantalized her until she was weak and shaky. This was no game as it had been with Rolf, a game she had nearly lost because she had been pretending it was Gavin with her. She wanted this man, this undeniable dream warrior.

As he spoke to her, he teased his tickly beard over her lips and nose. "Once I take you, my priceless queen, you are mine forever. You must make certain I win the quest so we can become lovers and rulers. Give me your help and your surrender," he entreated.

Unable to pull her gaze from his or to refuse his requests, she murmured, "Both are yours if you take me this moment."

His mouth fused with hers, as did his body. They made love urgently, wildly, recklessly, until the ultimate moment of rapture claimed them. As their damp bodies embraced afterward, he whispered, "You are my lover and my queen. Soon, you will become my wife. Tell me the answers to the riddles so this quest can end quickly and I can claim my beautiful prize."

Alysa traced the scar on his cheekbone as she replied, "Only the wizard knows the answers. I shall get them for you."

He kissed her passionately before speaking. "When you have them, my beautiful enchantress, I will return to your bed and arms forever."

As he walked away, Alysa cried out, "Nay, do not leave me."

As she jerked upward to pursue him, she was awakened. Her body and kirtle were saturated with perspiration. She was trembling and tears were rolling down her flushed cheeks. As her erratic breathing slowed, she cursed the dream and the tension within her. Her body ached for Gavin's, and her heart pained over his loss.

Alysa arose and went into the bathing chamber. She removed her wet garment and stepped into the wooden tub. Taking a pitcher of water, she rinsed off her sweaty body. After drying and pulling on a fresh kirtle, she braided her damp hair to get it off her neck. She retrieved some crushed leaves from a small pouch in her chest and mixed them with the wine nearby. She drank the bitter liquid hastily and returned to bed. Soon, the sleeping potion worked.

The next morning one of the spies returned from Logris to reveal where the main Viking camp was located, near the sacred circle of towering stones. The spy told her that the Vikings were building a large settlement which appeared to be a permanent one, proving their intent to remain on the isle, at least for a long time. He said they seemed in no hurry to go araiding, and did so only to obtain food and supplies. He reported that their foes were enjoying themselves and obviously feeling no threat from the Britons. "It was as if they were waiting for something to happen before starting their attacks."

Alysa summoned Trosdan and Gavin's friends to pass along this curious report and to finalize their plans. It was decided Alysa and the men would leave in the morning to travel the land from end to end, as one last appearance would make her imminent absence less noticeable and would show her subjects that Weylin and his group would be following her orders. Gavin had been gone since Saturday night, and she did not know if he would return before her departure. She announced that she would tell everyone that Prince Gavin was on a spy mission to assess their foes' strengths, and weaknesses. If he returned, he could take charge of the tasks being done here while she was away. Thinking of her husband hurt, so Alysa pushed her personal feelings aside and concentrated on the work before her.

Papers were drawn up with her royal seal to place Weylin and his group in charge during her absence. Servants were given orders to be followed during her "travels through the land to prepare our people for battle," the story to be used to cover for her absence. All questions and problems were to be directed to Lord Weylin or Sir Teague, who was entrusted with the truth.

The following morning, Weylin sent messengers to King Bardwyn in Cambria and to King Briac in Cumbria, asking them to secretly prepare their men and supplies for the joint battle. Sir Beag and Sir Tragan—who had insisted on carrying this vital news to his king—left knowing the importance of their missions. Tragan hoped he would find Gavin at home so he could enlighten the prince to certain matters.

The wounded at the castle were visited briefly before Alysa's party left the castle. For the next two and a half weeks, they visited villages and hamlets and farms and feudal estates to throw off suspicion during her impending lengthy absence. In all places, she spoke vigorously to arouse the people's support and to give them hope, determination, and confidence. She related how special camps would be set up all across Damnonia and all men must train to defend their land against invasion and enslavement. She asked her subjects to gather as many supplies as possible, to construct new weapons and to repair old ones, and to loan their horses and carts to their grateful leader. The people were awed by their valiant ruler, and persuaded to aid her in all ways.

Upon their return home, Alysa asked to speak with Weylin alone. The man observed how tired and hoarse she was from her many labors and speeches. He had witnessed the princess's effect on her people. Her words had been stirring and sincere. The noblemen and commoners loved her and trusted her, and would obey her. Almost like her children, they wanted to please her and make her proud of them. They truly believed their warrior princess could lead them to victory.

Alysa sank into a chair and sighed deeply. "All I can do here has been done, Weylin. I will rest today and tomorrow, then leave under the cover of darkness. Use any means you must to keep my location a secret. See that food is given to the poor in my name. Make certain all problems are solved quickly and fairly to prevent anyone from wanting my judgment. If trouble does occur, write out my command, use this royal seal, then deliver it to those concerned. Say I am busy with war strategy and cannot come in person to settle the matter." She handed him the supplies he would need for any emergency edicts. "When you go from place to place, issue orders as if I have just given them to you. Train them well, my friend. Keep them busy and high-spirited." Her voice altered as she added, "If my husband returns, he can visit places in my stead to keep the people's courage and hopes alive. It would be good for the people to see one of us on occasion. Another thing, Weylin: be sure no talks are held within the hearing of servants. If gossip spreads that I was in the hands of the Vikings . . . You know the results."

Weylin nodded understanding. Gavin had been gone for three weeks without a single word. If his friend was trying to punish or to frighten his wife, or to prove she could not rule alone, whatever his motive, his ploy had failed. Alysa was a strong woman, and a ruler who was unafraid to carry out her duties. Weylin was impressed by her cunning and daring, and he wished he could make this perilous and exciting journey with her. Gavin was missing so much by staying away from this unique creature. *You will regret this wicked action, my friend,* he decided, *and you will surely lose her if you do not return soon with a good explanation.*

Before settling into her chambers to rest, Alysa went to see her friend, Sir Teague's wife. Thisbe was not to be told of Alysa's true destination when she left tonight. Alysa trusted her friend, but people were prone to make slips when they were frightened for those they loved. Only Gavin's friends and Sir Teague would know where she was and what she was doing until time for the attack. And until Weylin's secret messages to King Bardwyn and King Briac arrived in those kingdoms.

Following her short visit with an ailing Thisbe, whom Leitis suspected was with child, Alysa returned to her chambers to prepare for her journey tomorrow night. Trosdan had delivered a sack of special items for her to use during their mission. After looking through them, Alysa reclined on her bed for some much needed slumber.

But sleep would not come. She was overly fatigued and stimulated by her weeks on the trail. To encourage her subjects and vassals, she had been compelled to remain full of energy and self-assurance. It had been a draining few weeks. And she was lonely.

How she wished she was lying in Gavin's strong embrace and he was kissing her and sharing his caresses. How she wished they were making passionate love, or even lying quietly together, or talking softly. Not knowing where he was or what he was doing, thinking, feeling, was maddening and frustrating. She had given her people courage and comfort and hope, but Gavin was not here to do the same for her. They should be together.

"If I truly possessed the powers which Trosdan claims I have, I would cast a spell upon you to make you miserable until you returned to me!" she threatened, though Gavin could not hear her words. "By the gods, I would punish your selfishness and stubbornness!"

Alysa fetched another sleeping potion to give her peace of mind and rest. "Your cruel ploy has worked, for I am the miserable one!"

Alysa worked with Trosdan in his guest chambers all morning. She quickly learned many magical tricks and skills which would baffle and deceive most people. Trosdan warned her that their main threat would come from the Viking *attiba,* who also knew such skills and possessed such talents.

"But do not worry, my princess, for I know many things he does not. It will come to a battle of wits between us, but I shall win."

The Druid wizard revealed how they would carry off the ritual to prove her identity and to obtain the Vikings' fealty. Her wedding ring was hidden in the secret passageway which nearly encircled the castle, and she was given a special fake one to wear. That ominous chill assailed her again as she removed her wedding ring, after vowing she would not do so until she was sure Gavin was lost to her forever.

Alysa returned to her chambers at midafternoon. Soon it would be time to leave her land and to challenge her destiny. It would require about a week to reach Stonehenge where the Norsemen were camped. If Gavin did not return within the next few hours . . . Alysa angrily pushed that hope aside and consumed more of the sleeping potion.

As arranged, Trosdan awakened Alysa at eleven that night to allow her time to dress for their midnight departure, as traveling in darkness through their land would thwart discovery. She donned voluminous pants, a linen shirt, and leather boots for easy riding. She braided her hair and stuffed it beneath a floppy hat to conceal her identity. Just before midnight, Weylin appeared to help her load her possessions and supplies, and to let them out the back gate.

The handsome knight whispered, "Be careful, Alysa, we do not want to lose you. Take no risks. Flee quickly if the plan does not work. If you get into trouble and cannot escape, send Trosdan's messenger bird and I will come to your side with haste."

Alysa eased to her tiptoes and kissed her friend lightly on the mouth. "Farewell, dear Weylin. I will see you at Stonehenge very soon. Take care of all I love while you rule it for me." Her pride forced her not to mention her husband again.

They embraced and Alysa mounted Calliope. The princess and the Druid wizard passed through the gate, across a narrow bridge over a deep moat, and halted. Alysa twisted in her saddle, waved to Lord Weylin, as she eyed her home a final time, and rode away with the old man.

Weylin watched them until they vanished in the darkness. "May the gods protect you, my cherished princess," he murmured, then sealed the gate. It was done; the perilous mission was under way.

Seven

Alysa and Trosdan had traveled four nights before camping at dawn in a secluded area on the Logris border. So far they had managed to avoid contact with anyone. Today, their schedule was to change. They planned to sleep a few hours, then ride again until dark. For the rest of the way to Stonehenge, they would travel in daylight.

As they set out two hours past midday, they rode with alert minds to prevent falling into the hands of peril. As they journeyed, Alysa mused on her Viking people. Trosdan and Giselde had told her that many raids were nothing more than compulsory exile for young men in order to control the Viking population and to prevent poverty. A proud and strong race, the Norsemen looked unfavorably on weaklings of any kind. Every warrior wanted to die in battle before he became a burden to himself and others. Raids were also viewed as the best way for a young man to prove his manhood and to obtain wealth with which to settle in his homeland. As a young man was no longer welcome at home after he came of age, it was his duty to go out and earn his own living, and the quickest and easiest way was through raiding. Many older warriors used their riches and fame to force out rivals in their areas or to reclaim property taken over by one, or as an excuse to get away from home for a while. Sometimes, famine inspired raids. Other times, they were based on colonization, or political expeditions, or searches for new trade routes.

Whatever their motives, they were fierce warriors and most lands cowered before them. From out of the mist on the North Sea, they swooped down on helpless villages with their hit-and-run attacks. They burned and plundered with great zest, to vanish again in another mist. But these ships of Norsemen had come not only to raid but also to conquer. They were shrewd strategists who often conquered lands by slaying king after king and terrorizing their inhabitants. These bold and tenacious pirates loved to strike at rich monasteries and wealthy castles. They craved anything which breathed or could be moved.

Most Vikings came from the Scandinavian countries of Denmark, Norway, and Sweden; and not all Norsemen were malevolent. Many were builders of cities and founders of states, writers of poetry and givers of law, adventurous explorers and supreme traders. Alysa liked to imagine that her ancestors fell into one of these groups.

All Vikings seemed to believe in the supernatural, in a variety of gods and goddesses, in shocking rituals, and in magic itself. Trosdan had enlightened and instructed her on their ways, and she prayed they could carry off their deception, especially when it came time for the human *hlaut*, a blood sacrifice, during one special ritual which took place every nine years and lasted for nine days.

She had learned that the Vikings prided themselves on the number of children they sired, even though it led to the overly dense population which was a problem for them. Any man who could afford to have a large family often had a favorite wife, concubines, mistresses, and under-wives. A slave was unimportant unless the man acknowledged her as

108

worthy of the attention and affection of his people and family. But no woman was more important and valuable than their queen by bloodright.

At that point in her reverie, Alysa wondered what had happened to Lady Gweneth and her two daughters, the family of her slain friend and feudal lord Daron. Even if the Damnonian women were captives in the camp where they were heading, there was no way she could rescue them. She hoped there were no Damnonian slaves in this camp, as she hated to appear traitorous before her people. But there was a ploy she was going to try in order to get all female captives released . . .

Alysa's eyes scanned their surroundings. Logris was a beautiful land, green and fertile, a land any conqueror would crave. She had to admit she was excited about meeting the Vikings and playing out the role fate had assigned to her. It was hard to believe that these barbaric people would bow down to her because of ancient laws and legends and superstitions. The only Vikings she had encountered had been Isobail's ruthless brigands, and she wanted to see if all Vikings were like those horrid men. She hoped they were not. After all, Viking blood ran within her body, so their history was partly hers.

Alysa wondered if the Norsemen would be on this isle if King Vortigern of Logris had not hired them as warriors to defend his land against another Roman invasion and against rivals in his kingdom. The largest and strongest footholds had been obtained as payments—not taken by force—by the Jute brothers, Hengist and Horsa. Now that they owned and controlled their own territories, there was no way Vortigern could push them out of his kingdom. Too, the brothers had grown more powerful by sending for more of their people, especially their warriors. Yet if reports could be trusted, Hengist and Horsa were not involved in any of the Viking invasions. The truth remained to be uncovered when she reached Rolf's new settlement.

Trosdan broke into her thoughts. "It is time to halt, my queen."

Alysa glanced at him, realizing how true that title was, as Trosdan was a Norseman by birth. "We will reach their settlement in three days, Wise One. I am both nervous and excited," she confessed.

"That is to be expected, Alysa. A great adventure awaits you."

The horses were tended and the three messenger birds were fed. Supplies were unpacked, fur mats were unrolled, and a small fire was built. They cooked a sparse meal and devoured it while they talked. Trosdan told her how they would make their grand entrance to the Viking camp, and Alysa smiled.

She held up her left hand and eyed the false ring. "Will it truly do magic tricks, Wise One?"

"Do as I told you, and all will be awed by it and you."

"And must I really wear the garments you gave to me?" she asked.

Trosdan noted her pink cheeks and smiled knowingly. "They will serve us well, my shy queen. They are like the garb of Valkyries. And," he added with a twinkle in his sky blue eyes, "they will enchant all men in the camp. You are to distract them from raids, remember?"

Alysa envisioned the skimpy, seductive garments of leather and fur. She laughed merrily. "Without a doubt they will do their job, Wise One. I am thankful this is not winter or I would freeze."

Trosdan, usually serious and quiet, chuckled. At seventy his loins still warmed over a pretty face and shapely body. He thought of Giselde and how much he loved that mixed-blooded woman. Alysa's grandmother did not know how many times he had been tempted to give up his powers to marry her. It was too late to think of such feelings and dreams; Giselde was wed to King Bardwyn. Perhaps it was for the best. Without his powers, he would be of no use to his queen, granddaughter of his true love. It was a wizard's fate to be alone, the price of his power and rank.

"You did not answer, Wise One," Alysa hinted.

"My mind roamed for a time. Repeat your question, my queen."

"Do you believe we can fool the Viking *attiba?*"

"The Runes say yes and the sacred chalice says yes. I have never doubted their messages to me. Another message came to me today while you slept. The Runes burned and tickled at my side," he remarked as he caressed the pouch hanging from his golden waist cord. "I tossed them upon the earth and they spoke strangely."

"What did they say?" Alysa asked eagerly.

"You will find a friend and helper in the Viking camp, but you must tell him nothing of our ruse. Though he bears the face of your lost love, you must remember at all times he is not Prince Gavin. He will flame your passions and you will wish to help him become champion, but you must not forget who and what he is. His name is Eirik."

Alysa stared at the old man and recalled her dream.

Trosdan watched her closely, then smiled. "You have already met him in the spirit world of dreams. Your powers are growing stronger, my queen. They will become stronger still if you do not resist them. Open yourself to them. Hone them. Obey them. Use them."

"What if I forget he is not my love?" she asked worriedly.

"What you must remember is that he is not your husband. Evil will place many temptations and pitfalls in your path. You must be strong and brave; you must be true to your calling."

"I did not expect this task to be so difficult," she remarked sadly as she called the dream to mind and studied

111

this irresistible warrior named Eirik. She wondered fearfully how much of the dream was a warning and how much was a foresight.

Four days later, Alysa and Trosdan cautiously approached Stonehenge near midday. They left their horses and all their possessions except for those items needed during this first encounter concealed.

In the distance, the Viking camp was in view. As their spy had reported, it was a large settlement of longhouses, *shielings*—small houses or huts—and many *kviviks*—byres and barns combined. She noticed several large corrals which held countless horses, cattle, sheep, and goats, and gazed at the large fires in the open areas where cooking could be done and meetings held. It was obvious from their labors that the Vikings intended to remain here a long time.

Alysa could not even begin to count the number of Vikings present, for they were everywhere in the camp. No doubt the structures were also filled with more foes. Apprehension flooded her. How could she fool so many men? How could she compel them to accept and obey her? She was only nineteen, a small, slender female. She had only an elderly man to help her. What if—

"Do not worry, my queen. All will go as we planned and practiced," Trosdan vowed soothingly.

Alysa smiled at the Druid wizard. She glanced before them at the towering circle of megalithic posts and lintels, and was awed by their size and Druid history. The site was surrounded by a circular ditch five feet deep. Within it were many pits whose use she did not know. From Trosdan's previous words, she knew the open end of the ditch ran for miles to the Avon River.

She recalled what the man had told her about this place. There were four ranges of stones. The outermost circle of one hundred feet was of sarsen stones, large and linteled. The second circle consisted of smaller blue stones. That circle enclosed a horseshoe-shaped arrangement of five linteled pairs of large sarsen stones. Within it was a smaller horseshoe-shaped collection of blue stones which enclosed the Altar Stone which they would use during their ruses. Near the entrance from the ditch was positioned the Slaughter Stone. In certain areas around the main structure were tumuli: burial mounds.

Today, many stones were toppled over from desecration by their Roman invaders. Looking at the site, a sense of well-being and power filled Alysa. She followed Trosdan's lead across the ditch and through the graywether stones. She was glad no Viking was present. In fact, there seemed to be no guards posted around the camp.

At the Altar Stone, she and Trosdan prepared for the moment they had awaited for weeks. Trosdan was attired in a flowing black robe with symbols of a Viking *attiba*. He carried a wand of yew in a cresent shape with tiny bells attached. His nearly gray hair was uncovered and hung halfway down his back in soft waves. His snowy beard teased below his heart and was thick and silky. A medallion with Odin's image was around his neck. He placed his small drum on the altar until he was ready to use it to summon the Norsemen.

Alysa was clad much differently. The leather cups which held her breasts were edged with soft fur and remained in place by straps over her shoulders and around her back. Upon each one was an image of Freyja, goddess of love and protector of the heart. Strips of leather were sewn to the band beneath her breasts and dangled past her waist, doing little to conceal her slender middle and swaying provocatively when she moved. She was wearing a female warrior's apron over a snug leather garment which just covered her hips and private regions. More strips of leather dangled

113

from it to her knees, and were attached to the lower garment with studs which displayed etched images of Odin, whose startling eyes served to remind everyone he was the Seer of all things. The waist and thigh openings of this lower garment were also edged with soft fur to prevent binding and discomfort.

Gold armbands encircled her wrists, upon which there were carvings of Njord—god of wealth and seafaring. She put on the bronze helmet which depicted Frey, goddess of the mind, ruler of the body. Her long brown hair cascaded from beneath it and flowed down her back to her waist. Atop the helmet was the symbol of royalty. The sword buckled around her slim waist revealed another etching of Odin, protector of warriors, creator of man, ruler of heaven and earth. The medallion around her neck matched the one which Trosdan was wearing. On her shield was the image of Thor—god of power and victory, guardian of justice and law. A mighty thunderbolt was poised in one hand and a powerful hammer in the other.

Alysa's feet were encased in leather boots which rose to her knees. Upon her finger was the false purple ring Trosdan had given to her. Twisting this way and that, she eyed herself as the strips wiggled sensuously. Her leather and fur garments made her look the perfect image of a Viking queen or a mythical Valkyrie.

"Position yourself, my queen. It is time to begin."

Alysa stood upon the altar, facing the direction from which the Vikings would approach. She stood straight and tall, proud and lean, her expression one of confidence and courage. Her feet were planted slightly apart, the stance of a warrior about to speak. The large shield was standing on edge to her left, her fingers holding it face forward and motionless. Her sword was drawn, its point touching the stone below her at her right. The midday sun beamed down on her, sending reflections off the metal on her helmet, garb, and weapons.

Even if Trosdan had not begun to beat the small drum to seize the camp's attention, it would have been captured soon by the strange glitterings from the sacred site. Alysa watched the settlement come to energetic life. She saw warriors grab weapons and hurry their way. She took several deep breaths to steady her nerves and to clear her head. Soon, they would be surrounded by numerous foes.

Most of the Norsemen were clad in brown cloth shirts and pants, not in the leather and fur she had expected. Of course, she decided as they raced through the monoliths, this could be their attire for camplife. She watched her foes halt abruptly at the inner range of blue stones which enclosed the Altar Stone to absorb the strange sight before them: a black-clad wizard and a beautiful female warrior. She noticed how many eyes gaped at her in undisguised lust, while others revealed astonishment and confusion and intrigue.

Two leaders pushed their ways forward through the crowd of rough men. They stepped to a few feet of the altar and stared at her.

Alysa was relieved that her cheeks did not pinken as she posed provocatively, haughtily, before so many wide-eyed strangers. In a clear tone, she announced, "I am Alysa Malvern, heir of Connal, Astrid, Rurik, Giselde, and Catriona. I carry the last of the royal Viking blood from Odin. I have come to take my rightful place as your queen and to lead you to victory over this isle. I command you to kneel and to swear your allegiance to me and Odin."

The crowd continued to gape at her in surprise and disbelief. But the two leaders eyed her much differently, desire for her and her rank shining in their eyes. Upon his return to camp, Thorkel had told them of the Damnonian princess's words and deeds, and here she was as promised. The waiting was over. As wild and wonderful thoughts raced through their minds, neither spoke nor moved.

Trosdan called out, "Do you wish Heimdal to sound his war horn for *Ragnorak?*" Trosdan knew every Viking feared the end of the world and the god who was to signal it. "Urd, the goddess of destiny, sent me to Queen Alysa's side to convince her to take her place of honor and duty. She has done so. She is here to reclaim what was stolen from her by foolish ancestors. It is our law; we must obey her."

"How do we know she is our queen?" one of the leaders asked, although he did not doubt her identity.

Trosdan and Alysa glared at the man who had to be Ulf. His body was large, but with muscle, not fat. He was wearing a helmet with a hole in the top through which his hair was drawn. His beard was as red as his hair, and his cheeks were flushed with excitement.

Trosdan lifted a limp white bird and showed it to the man. "Is it not dead?" he asked coldly.

Ulf casually examined it. "It is dead."

Trosdan handed the well-trained creature to Alysa, who had lain aside her shield and sheathed her sword. "Show them your powers, my queen."

Alysa looked skyward as she called out, "Hear me, great Odin, creator and ruler of all things. Send your life-giving power through me to rebirth this dead creature. Show your people I am who I say I am."

Alysa positioned her hands as Trosdan had taught her. She eyed the fuzzy coverings on the bird's legs and knew their message to Weylin was hidden beneath them. She prayed she was not sending this message of success prematurely. She eyed the sun and lifted her left hand, catching its brilliance and creating a beam of light with the clever cut of the stone. The purple ray touched the white bird. It wiggled, then sat up in her hand before flying away. Alysa smiled as she watched its flight a moment; the ruse was in motion, the missive on its way.

The crowd was stunned into silence, then a raucous cheer arose. Alysa's gaze went from Ulf's stunned expression to the playful grin on the face of the very tall and muscular man at his side. His hair was white-blond and grazed his massive shoulders. His features were strong and handsome. His hazel eyes engulfed her. At last, the image of Rolf had a face. She recalled her past attackers' words: "Rolf wants her." Judging by his mood and gaze, those words were true.

The blond man informed her, "Thorkel told us you would come to us when it was safe. We were going to seek you when our camp was complete. But you have kept your word. Now the curse upon us can be dispelled. This is a joyous day."

Another man worked his way through the chattering crowd, a man in a dark flowing robe with golden symbols. With black eyes, he studied Alysa and Trosdan. "There is another female of royal birth in this land, Giselde. How do we not know she is to be our queen?"

The towering man grinned. "But Einar, Giselde is an old woman, too old to bear heirs and to rule our people."

Einar, their *attiba*, was merely a talented trickster who knew a little alchemy. He wanted to test the powers and skills of this competition to see if Trosdan was truly a wizard. If so, the old man could be dangerous. "I say this female does simple magic. I say she must prove her claim as our queen on the sacred altar. Legend says our queen cannot be harmed by a sacred flame."

Trosdan spoke up. "There is a full moon tonight; that is the time for such a test. After she has proven herself, she will give you the message from Odin for conquest."

Einar was shocked and dismayed by the wizard's quick and easy acceptance of his challenge. He knew of no way a person could survive such a test. He looked at Alysa and

117

warned, "If you are not who you claim to be, the test will slay you. Do you understand and agree?"

Alysa's blue eyes focused on the deadly villain below her. "Be glad I will not seek you as a blood *hlaut* to be sacrificed after my victory, Einar. I do not like to be questioned or doubted. But I am a *volva,* so I know we have need of you later. Only for that reason will I spare your life after your insulting behavior."

"Prove you are a female Seer," Einar boldly challenged.

"I will do so tonight, after the ceremony," she replied smugly.

Trosdan warned, "Beware of such dark feelings, Einar. Do not let Loki steal your wits and fealty. Loki loves evil and he has a sharp eye for a foe's weaknesses. Loki is clever and deceitful. He is cruel and vicious and filled with self-interest. He attacks all gods, even though he is Odin's half brother. Odin is with us, so Loki must try to attack us. An *attiba* wields great power and must not be disobeyed. Do not allow Loki to use you against us and Odin."

To Rolf, Alysa said, "I am weary after my long journey. I must rest before the ritual tonight. Can you find me lodgings here?"

Rolf lifted his hand and helped Alysa from the altar. "You will stay in my dwelling. I will have food and—"

"Nay!" Ulf shouted and seized Alysa's other hand, as Rolf had not released his gentle grip on her. "She will lodge with me until this matter is settled."

Alysa suggested, "We will have a game to see where I will stay until tonight, then I must have my own dwelling." She presented them with her back to prepare for it. She turned to the two men. "The man who finds the stone is the loser," she announced, holding out her balled hands to Ulf.

Ulf looked at both hands, then touched the right one.

Alysa opened it to reveal a stone. "I go with Rolf this time. Come, Wise One."

Ulf could not behave the irate fool before the others, so he nodded and stepped aside for them to pass. Trosdan collected his possessions and trailed the couple. At the doorway into Rolf's longhouse, Alysa opened her left hand and gave him the second stone. "I do not like warriors who behave as small children with ill tempers. Keep it for good luck during your upcoming challenge."

Rolf closed his hand over the warm stone and smiled. "You are very brave and clever, Alysa. Ulf is not a man easily or wisely duped."

"It takes little to fool any man when his wits are not where they should be," she replied mirthfully. "Do not misunderstand, Rolf. I tricked Ulf to punish him, not to charm or impress you," she added to wipe the cocky grin from his sensual lips.

They entered Rolf's longhouse. The *skali*—living area— was first. The *eldhus*—kitchen—was next, followed by the scullery and privy. Sections of the living area could be curtained off for privacy when a man needed or desired it. The dwelling was clean and well lighted. It was sparsely furnished with wooden items covered by soft furs. She took a seat.

A pretty female slave brought food and drink within minutes: cheese, fruit, and bread, with wine for Alysa and ale for the two men. Knowing she had interrupted the eating hour, she assumed Rolf would join them for the meal, which he did.

As they ate, Alysa related what she knew of her history, the story colored to impress and beguile the attentive Rolf. This was her chance to study one of the leaders before things changed with the quest. She was genial and ever so slightly seductive. "When Trosdan came to me and counciled me, I knew I must come here and join my people.

119

Odin had prepared me for his words and my destiny through many dreams. The calling was strong, too strong to be resisted or ignored. After our conquest of this isle, I will rule from Damnonia. There, I can serve both my peoples wisely and fairly."

Rolf's eyes slipped over her. "Can you lead us to victory, Alysa? You are a very young and gentle woman."

She locked her blue gaze to his hazel one. "When my evil stepmother Isobail tried to take what was mine, I defeated her and destroyed her. I chased her brigands from my land, those I did not slay in battle. I can use all weapons, Rolf, use them with skill and victory. I do not boast or lie. I planned many of the battles with our past foes, so I know how to use cunning and daring."

Rolf chuckled. "Such words must be true, for Thorkel bears the wounds of your battle with him."

Alysa sneered contemptuously. "If he had not fled as a coward that day, I would have slain him as I did my other attackers. If he had listened to my words, his friends would have survived and escaped. He sought glory so hard that he lost his wits. I could not reveal myself to the Damnonians by siding with them when they were outnumbered. Thorkel should be punished for his stupidity and recklessness."

"Were three wounds not enough punishment?" Rolf teased. "If he had not survived and brought us news of you, your land would have been conquered by now, which would have endangered you. We restrained ourselves, as we planned your capture if you did not keep your word."

"So it was Odin's hand which stayed mine so Thorkel could prepare the way for my return. Then I will forgive him for his weakness."

"We were told you had wed a Cumbrian prince. Where is he?"

Alysa had anticipated this question and was ready to re-

120

spond cleverly. "He is a weakling and a fool, so I dismissed him from my sight and land. I can have no mate at my side who doubts me and resists me. He is jealous and selfish. He tried to halt me from this journey to prevent my destiny. I could not allow it."

"How could you so calmly dismiss a man you loved and wed?"

Alysa exhaled and rolled her eyes scornfully. "I wed him because my grandfather, King Bardwyn of Cambria, arranged the marriage. It was a reward for his help with Isobail's defeat, though I did not truly need his assistance. He was too cautious and ignorant. The victory could have been won earlier if he had not hesitated or made wrong moves so frequently. I was not myself at that time, or I would not have allowed Grandfather's wishes. I had fought a long and difficult battle, and my father had been murdered. Once I was rested and my grief passed, I realized my mistake. I am the queen of a powerful race. Never again will a mortal man rule me or deny me my dreams."

"Where is this unfortunate husband now?" Rolf persisted.

"Like an injured dog, he raced home to his father with his tail between his legs. I care not for what King Briac thinks or says, I will not take the bumbling olf back! I do not need his son as my husband to become the future queen of Cumbria. I shall rule all of Britain."

"Why are you so angry, Alysa, if it does not matter to you?"

Alysa looked Rolf in the eye. "Would you not be angry if you had allowed others to use you and sway you in a moment of weakness? Would you not be angry with yourself for even having one? Would you not be angry if your wife tried to halt your destiny?"

"I have no wife," Rolf replied, his expression enticing.

"Surely you jest," she responded seductively. "A man

121

such as you should have been wed by now. What age are you?"

"I am twenty-nine."

"Why have you not taken a wife—many wives? Is that not the Viking way, except for royalty?"

"I have not found a woman to please me. I want no female who whines and crawls. I want a woman whose strength and dreams match mine. Too, I have been araiding for years."

Alysa glanced toward the *eldhus* area and teased softly. "What of your lovely slave? Does she not please you and serve you well?"

"If she did not, she would not be in my dwelling. But she, like others, is not of my liking and bloodline, as you are," he added.

"I am honored by your words and feelings, Rolf, but it is not my place to respond to them. Odin will select my true mate."

"I do not understand." The handsome warrior frowned.

"After the ceremony tonight, you will," she promised.

"What if you do not survive the test of the sacred flame?"

Alysa teased her fingertips over the back of his hand and murmured, "Odin did not bring me here to be slain or rejected. I must rest," she hinted. "Do you mind my using your bed?"

Rolf's eyes glowed with desire as he imagined her in his bed. "I will leave you to refresh yourself, Alysa. And I will pray you are our queen," he added.

He called the slave and they left Alysa and Trosdan alone. Alysa sank back in her seat. "Did I do well, Wise One? You never spoke once."

Trosdan smiled at her. "Perfect, my queen. Go to sleep. You will need your strength and wits tonight."

"What of this Eirik?" Alysa inquired, eager to meet him.

"I did not see him. Perhaps he is gone araiding."

To envision the image of her love slaying and plundering distressed Alysa. She asked, "Can you help me sleep, Wise One?"

Trosdan fetched his bag of potions and aided her.

Leaving the slave outside, Rolf entered Einar's abode. "Tell me what you think of this woman and her claim, wizard."

"She is the queen we have awaited and searched for, Lord Rolf. The only way to end the curse on our people which Connal and Astrid began is by conquering her. The warrior who lays claim to her will become all-powerful here and in our homeland. If she is willing, good. If she is not, she must be forced to obey her destiny. Astrid and Rurik sided with our foes, why should their heir not side with us? She carries the last royal blood and must be compelled to honor her rank."

"If you believe her, why did you battle her?" Rolf queried.

Of necessity, he lied. "To prove her identity to the others before you win her. With her as your mate, you can become High King."

"What if she fails the test tonight?"

"She will not. The wizard with her is powerful."

"More powerful than you, Einar?"

"He is the right hand of Odin. None can defeat him."

"Then she will be safe tonight. How do I win her?"

"By passing the test she will reveal tonight. She is a brave and smart woman. She will accept only the best man among us."

"We must make certain that is me," Rolf commanded.

"I will do all in my power to aid you, Lord Rolf. Be

cunning with her. She is not a woman to respond to an easy conquest."

"It is hard to resist her, Einar. Already my loins burn for her."

"Douse your flames with your slave so they will not burn out of control," the man suggested.

Rolf watched Einar depart, then called his Logris captive inside. "Lie with me. I have need of you," he told the lovely woman.

Obediently she removed her garments and reclined on the bed. She knew it was futile to refuse her captor anything, and she was enthralled by him.

Rolf undressed and joined her. He closed his eyes and pretended she was Alysa and he was making tender and passionate love to her.

Just before midnight in Rolf's dwelling, Trosdan and Alysa prepared for the ritual. He explained what would happen to her and gave her instructions. He rubbed her back with a special powder, then gave her the leather pouch to conceal in her lower garment.

"Are you sure this will work?" she inquired anxiously.

"Have no fear, my queen, it will fool them—even Einar."

Trosdan put the fur cloak around her shoulders to hide their ruse and guided her to the door. He kissed her cheek and smiled into her worried face. Grasping her quivering hand, the Druid led her outside where they were joined by Rolf, Ulf, Einar, and the Vikings.

They walked to Stonehenge where Alysa reclined upon the Altar Stone. With Einar's assistance, Trosdan placed a forked oak limb at her head and feet with the "Y" shape downward. He tossed a covering over her which was supported by the two points. Oak branches were piled around the altar and set ablaze.

As Trosdan chanted, Alysa worked swiftly beneath the tent to rub the wizard's special powder over the remainder of her body. She felt the heat rising and she began to perspire, causing the powder to work its spell.

Time passed and the heat increased. Alysa wondered why the covering did not catch fire, but Trosdan had told her it would not, and she praised his alchemy skills. She felt moisture gather on her face and dampen her body. She could hardly breathe in the nearly suffocating tent, but she told herself she must endure this test.

When the flames died down, Alysa heard the clue in Trosdan's words. She tossed the covering aside and stood upon the altar. With the aid of the "magical" powder, her body glowed as if she were ablaze from within. Alysa was thrilled to see the ruse working perfectly. Despite her faith in Trosdan, she had feared something terrible would go wrong. Her confidence was restored as she took in the crowd's expressions of awe and intimidation. The full moon and firelight caused her wet flesh to glisten like sun upon snow. She felt a heady sense of power and pride rush through her body, as if she could accomplish anything. She felt magical, stimulated, enchanted. She turned slowly, allowing everyone in the ever-expanding circle to view her from all sides. She heard their reactions of amazement and pleasure, and was delighted by her victory. She watched them kneel before her.

The night breeze cooled her flesh and dried her perspiration, and gradually the powder lost its strength and brilliant glow. Trosdan retrieved the covering, concealing a pouch of combustible liquid within it, and tossed it into a nearby fire. A burst of flame ignited it and it burned slowly, proving there was nothing protective in the cloth.

Alysa stated in an authoritative tone, "I have proven myself to you, my people. You must accept me and our laws. It is time for your oaths of fealty upon the ring altar. After

125

our ritual toasts, I will tell you of the great quest which has been revealed to me by Odin."

The ceremonial stand was brought forward and placed before the altar. Upon it was an arm ring and a sacrificial bowl for a blood offering. In the bowl was the blood of a sheep which Trosdan had ordered slain. With an oak twig—as oak was the sacred tree to Druid and Viking alike—Alysa sprinkled each man's chest as he stepped forward to swear his fealty to her and to Odin upon the arm-ring altar. When the lengthy *hlaut* was completed, the toasts were given.

The ceremonial horns were passed back and forth over a flame by Trosdan, who was in charge of this ritual, then passed around to each man several times. The toasts were given in order of importance: first to Odin for victory, to Njord and Frey for good harvest and peace, to Alysa as their queen, and to the dead who had entered Valhalla before this special moment.

At last, the two rituals were completed. "This is the ninth year," Alysa began meaningfully. "It is time for our great feast. But first, we must pass Odin's test, as I have passed yours tonight."

A Viking warrior who had been observing these curious events from a distance joined the ecstatic group and asked, "What is this quest, my queen?"

Alysa turned toward the familiar voice and stared at the man coming forward. It was, but it was not, her lost love.

Eight

Alysa's gaze slowly swept over the warrior who stood below her at the altar. He was so much like Gavin, yet he was different, noticeably different. His shoulder-length hair was trimmed shorter and a deeper blond. It displayed no flaxen streaks. His green eyes seemed darker and their gaze unfamiliar. A short beard and mustache covered his rugged jawline and above his upper lip, whereas, Prince Gavin Crisdean was always clean-shaven. No blue royal crest of Cumbria was tattooed over his heart. Only a bronzed chest was exposed beneath the snug leather jerkin. There was an old scar on his cheekbone; Gavin had none. His manner and aura were unknown to her, as were his changing expressions.

Yet his size and physique were the same as those of her missing husband. His voice nearly matched Gavin's but for a slight intonation difference. There was no way she could explain these physical and mental variances. If this man was her husband, he did not know it. The look on his face revealed that she was a stranger to him. But if by chance this *was* her love, something—or someone—had altered him. There was nothing she could do except observe him, test him, and keep her head clear.

Alysa's study of the Viking had been done swiftly. Having

been prepared for this moment and having heard the voice, she seized control of her emotions and reactions before turning to face him. "Who are you? And why do you interrupt my words? You did not join the oath and toast. Do you challenge me as queen?" she inquired in a stern tone with a nearly scornful gaze.

He answered smoothly, "I am Eirik. I have only just returned from raiding. I saw everyone here and came to see what was afoot. My friends told me of your arrival and deeds. I will swear fealty to you and drink the sacred toast, my queen."

"Trosdan," she called to her friend, "see that . . . Eirik does as he vows. I want no trouble, for we have much to do."

She waited patiently while Eirik and his band were sprinkled with the sheep's blood, swore allegiance on the arm ring, and drank their ceremonial toasts. She watched the virile warrior closely as she pretended to merely be observing the new men as if to test their loyalty.

Trosdan and her dream had told her she would find a friend and helper in this camp, a Viking warrior who would reflect her lost love's visage. But Trosdan had warned her this man was not Gavin, that he would be a dangerous temptation, perhaps a pitfall if she were not careful and alert. The powerful wizard had also warned her that Eirik would inflame her passions and she would desire him to become champion of the false quest; already those words were true. Yet she must "not forget who and what he is." She tried to ignore Eirik and her tumultuous feelings to carry out her ruse.

Alysa remained on the altar where she could be seen and heard better in the large gathering. "Every nine years my people hold a special nine-day feast. Soon it will be the day for it to begin. Before our human sacrifices are chosen and slain for the *hlaut,* we have a task before us. I have

128

ome to you, my people, to claim my destined mate so we
an lead you to conquest over this isle. Odin has spoken to
ne in dreams, and to Trosdan through the sacred Runes
nd in the sacred chalice."

It was alleged by the Vikings that Odin had created the
unes, so the men held great faith in them and in a reader
f the magical stones. "We must cease all raids on villages
nd castles, in this and in other lands, until our quest is
omplete." She noticed the reaction that command received
nd hurried on to explain her meaning. "There is no need
or any of my warriors to die in simple raids or retaliatory
attles when victory can be grasped under the leadership
f an all-powerful and invincible champion, your High
Ling, my husband."

Ulf injected, "How will we live if we do not raid?"

Alysa looked at the man and replied calmly, "We will
ake only the goods we need for nourishment, and waste
o precious time plundering any area. Next, we must release
ll slaves. They will slow us down and only give us more
nouths to feed. We can take plenty of captives after our
uest and feast, or before we sail for our homeland after
ve have conquered this isle. If we decide to remain here
orever, it is foolish to slay our future subjects and to de-
troy property which will belong to us soon. We must spend
ur time and energy on our sacred quest. With slaves in the
amp, men must be left here to guard them. Odin com-
nands that all men participate in his quest. It is known that
ome brave men and women allow themselves to be cap-
ured to act as spies. If any slave escaped, he could warn
is people of our plans and delay us with battles."

Rolf asked, "What is this quest you have mentioned many
imes?"

Placing her hands on her hips, Alysa glanced over the
lert faces. Fearing a loss of her self-control and concen-
ration, she was careful not to look at Eirik. Trosdan had

told her to relate the quest, as her beauty and newly estab
lished rank and manner of dress would inspire trust an
admiration and would weaken any opposition. The wis
man knew the warriors would be less likely to disagree wit
their queen.

As she spoke, she turned this way and that to addres
everyone, causing the dangling leather strips to sway an
to reveal glimpses of her slim waist and shapely legs. Th
leather cups over her breasts exposed their generous siz
and firmness, her lower garment did the same for her hips
She was a stunning vision, and the men had trouble keepin
their minds on her words. "We must have a contest in th
battle ring to select three champions. Those warriors wil
choose three bands to aid them with their quest for fiv
objects which Odin's helpers concealed on this isle lon
ago when our great Seer knew such a moment would come
Odin has given clues of their locations to Trosdan. One a
a time, he will pass the clues to the three leaders who mus
solve the riddles and find the objects. The man who hold
the five prizes when the quest is complete will become m
husband and your High King."

Alysa held up her left hand. "This ancient ring from Odi
will be used to empower the objects upon this altar. Yo
have witnessed its power this very day. This quest is a tes
of strength, cunning, and bravery. Not only must the object
be found, they must be guarded during any followin
searches. A man must prove he is the best champion—th
one warrior worthy to become my husband and your Hig
King—by holding on to what he has obtained, as it is fai
for the other two questors to try to take them from him b
any means but death. It is his band's duty to help him an
to protect his prizes. I will travel with a champion durin
each of the quests, to be chosen from the winning stone i
a basket. That way, each of you will know I offer no hel

130

to your rivals. Odin controls our destinies and will aid the man he desires to rule us and to wed me."

Alysa motioned for silence and attention a moment longer before questions were asked or remarks were made. "When this task is done, we will gather here for the empowering ritual, my wedding ceremony, and the great feast. Afterward, under our invincible champion, we will leave here to conquer this entire isle. What say you?"

Rolf asked, "What are these five prizes, my queen?"

"An amulet of Odin to protect the warrior and to receive our god's magical aid in battles. A sword from Thor to give the champion power and victory in battle, and justice amongst his people. A helmet from Frey to protect his head, ruler of his body and actions, and symbol of future peace. From Njord, a figurehead for our champion's ship to bring him wealth and to guard him at sea; upon it is an eye for divine guidance. From Freyja, a shield to protect his heart. The prizes are ancient and valuable. One man must possess them all to make him indestructible. Once Odin sends his power from the heavens, through this ring, these weapons and possessions will make him and our people unconquerable. If no man possesses all objects after the quest, the man who holds the greater number must battle the other two in the ring for theirs." Her voice lowered to a grave tone and the crowd strained to hear her. "I warn you now of Loki's mischief. This quest must be done before more raids. Do not let him blind you to Odin's commands. This ring holds no power to enchant the prizes unless it remains upon the hand of the Last Viking Queen. Odin has given me this honor to remove the stain upon my bloodline which Astrid and Rurik placed there. What of Hengist and Horsa? Are they with us?"

Ulf scoffed, "They refuse to join us. They have become lazy and content in their new lands. If they do not aid Vortigern against us, we will let them be."

Eirik spoke up. "I came to join Hengist's forces, but Ulf is right. They are sated for a time and seek no adventure and prizes. I left his castle and joined this band. I seek plunder, conquest, and excitement. A warrior cannot test his prowess sitting down at home. Nor does a worthy leader hire out to fight another's battles."

Einar questioned Alysa, "What did Odin say of Hengist's help?"

"He was not in my dreams and visions. Let the people vote if they are to be approached about joining us. What say you? Will this quest and victory be ours alone, or do we invite the Jute brothers to join us?" Alysa was relieved when the vote was no.

Eirik did not know how Trosdan and Alysa had passed the test put to her, but he suspected it was a clever ruse. He knew that wizards could perform inexplicable magic and cunning delusions. He was impressed and intrigued, but he was also wary and doubtful of the Celtic princess's sudden appearance. Yet he was consumed by desire for her and for the prizes she offered. The people believed her and accepted her as their queen. If he could win her and the quest, he would have all a man could desire. To seize her attention and interest, he ventured boldly, "You are the ruler of a land nearby. How do we know this quest is not a cunning trick to distract us from raids while your warriors prepare to attack us?"

Anger filled her blue eyes and they sparkled ominously. "My warriors would not invade King Vortigern's land. Damnonians are a peaceful people who only practice defense, not conquest. They would not even attempt such a task if I am not there to lead them."

"What if they come to rescue you from us?" Eirik added.

"They believe I am in Cambria visiting my grandfather, King Bardwyn. When the time comes, they will allow a peaceful takeover by us. They would never battle me or disobey me. Besides, my land is small and my knights are not skilled or experienced enough to challenge this force. Your questions speak of suspicion and reek of insult. Even if I deceived you, they could never risk an attack with me in your camp. Any warrior who wishes to continuing raiding can do so. As your queen, I will not command against it. But while he and his band are raiding, the others will be carrying out the quest. Unless he plans to win all prizes in the battle ring, he would be wise to join the quest."

Alysa waved her right hand over the crowd. "I am a stranger to you. If you need time to trust me, then have me guarded each day and night to allay your doubts. Though I have proven myself tonight, I would not be insulted by your caution. I have nothing to fear; Odin guides me and protects me. Is that not so, Thorkel?"

The man she had wounded in her trap nodded. "She speaks the truth." He withdrew her dagger and held it out to her.

"When I opened your body with that blade, Odin opened your heart to the truth, for it bears his sign of the hanged man. It is a gift to you, Thorkel. One day soon it will save your life."

Einar spoke up again, "What of your test as a Seer?"

"I told you at midday I would prove that claim tonight. While I slept this afternoon, Odin revealed a message to me. I will tell you what I envisioned, but you will not know I speak the truth until the contest is over. I shall tell you the names of the three champions."

Everyone became still and silent as she looked around the crowd of over seven hundred fierce warriors. She closed her eyes and announced, "Ulf . . . Rolf . . . Eirik." When she opened them, she glanced briefly at each man. "Prepare the rings tomorrow. We must begin our task at dusk. When only three champions remain, your bands will be selected and the clues given. If there is no more, I am weary. Dawn is nearly upon us, and this day has been long and hard."

"My house is yours to use, my queen. I can stay with my friends. There is plenty of room for you and your companion. I have no servants or slaves. Do you wish me to find some for you?"

Alysa stared at Eirik. This action was unexpected. "I am not sure I can accept the kindness of a man who doubts me as you do."

Eirik chuckled. In a devilish tone, he countered, "I do not doubt you, my queen. I only asked the questions which others feared to ask but wished answered. My fealty and life are yours. You and your companion have more need of a dwelling than I do. It is yours."

Rolf was annoyed by the other warrior's intrusion on his plans. "Our queen can use my dwelling. Then she will not have to move when I win her hand in marriage," he stated confidently.

"She used your house today, Rolf. It is my turn to have her," Ulf protested selfishly.

Trosdan said, "We will let Odin and the Runes settle this matter. The man who withdraws the one blue stone from the bag will give his dwelling to the queen until she weds one of you. Is it agreed?"

All three men nodded. Trosdan shook the thick leather bag and opened it, holding it out to Eirik first. Eirik wiggled his fingers inside and pulled out a blue stone between them. He grinned.

Recalling Alysa's trick with the other stone, Rolf hinted warily, "How do we know they are not all blue stones, wizard?"

Trosdan untied the string again and dumped six stones into his palm: five of sand color and one blue. Rolf smiled, relieved he had not been tricked. Ulf snorted in vexation and departed.

Eirik cocked his arm in invitation. "Come, my weary queen, I will show you your new home."

Eirik grasped Alysa's waist to help her across the ditch, their gazes fused for a moment before he released her. The contact had an affect on both of them. Heady desire raced through their bodies.

They walked to camp, and Eirik waited at his longhouse with Alysa while his friends—Aidan and Saeric—and Trosdan retrieved their possessions from Rolf's dwelling. Calliope and Trosdan's horse had been brought to camp earlier and placed in a corral for safety and tending. Later Alysa would check on her cherished dun and see what kind of mount Eirik rode. If it was Trojan . . .

"How old are you?" Alysa inquired suddenly. Her probing gaze walked over him from head to foot, without her awareness. Where a blue royal tattoo should be, if he was Gavin, was instead a splotch of dried blood from the ceremony. She wanted to seize a cloth and water to wash all dark spots of the barbaric custom from his virile chest.

"Thirty, my queen. And you?" He smiled mirthfully at her obvious interest in him and her futile attempt to conceal it.

"Nineteen," she responded, knowing her love was twenty-seven.

Eirik stepped closer to her. "Why did you choose me as one of the battle-ring winners?"

"I did not," she retorted as his engulfing gaze unsettled her. She realized she was being too friendly with this . . . stranger. Next, she fretted, he would be seducing her for her aid as he had done in her strange dream! "I revealed the names which Odin gave to me. I have no favorite among you."

Eirik was amused and delighted by her defensive reaction. "What if your guesses are wrong?"

The man's smile warmed Alysa. She had the wild urge

135

to invite him inside for a long talk just to be near him longer. Recalling her dream about him, she quivered in panic. If he was indeed a stranger, and a seductive foe, she could not yield to him! "They are not my guesses, and Odin does not make mistakes. You will be a winner in the battle ring, but it remains to be seen if you will become my husband and High King. Are you the best man here?"

The roguish warrior ignored her challenging words. "What if Ulf is the winner? He has many wives at home. Will you force him to put them aside and take only you?"

Alysa was well acquainted with the Viking customs and laws. "A High King can have only one wife. If Ulf wins and he so desires, he can have many concubines and mistresses. As queen, I rule only my people, not their king."

His voice was husky and haunting when he murmured, "Why would a man require others in his life with you at his side?"

Alysa's fingers reached up and traced the scar on his cheekbone. "I will make certain he does not. What of you, Eirik? Why have you not taken a wife?"

He trembled at her gentle and arousing touch. His eyes flamed with the passionate fire she had kindled within him. He hungered to take her inside his abode and possess her. He lifted the medallion around her neck and looked at it closely. As he replaced it, his fingers grazed her bare flesh at the swell of her breasts. He heard her breath quicken and saw her flush from an inner heat. "I have found no woman special enough to conquer me."

To protect herself from this intimidating peril, she moved away as she nonchalantly remarked, "That is what Rolf said. Perhaps you and he are too choosy."

"Perhaps," he concurred mischievously.

Trosdan and the men arrived with their possessions, and Eirik introduced her to his friends. Alysa greeted Aidan and Saeric genially, then bade them all good night.

Eirik chuckled. "It is dawn, my queen."

Alysa glanced at the rising sun on the horizon. "Yea, the dawn of a wondrous new day for us. Sleep well, Eirik, as you will have need of your strength and wits." She went inside, and was pleased to find the dwelling clean and comfortable. As she placed her belongings in a corner, she became aware of Eirik's manly smell, and her passions were enflamed anew.

When Trosdan joined her, she asked abruptly, "Do you know if Queen Brenna had twins or two sons? Could one have been stolen as a baby by the Vikings?"

Trosdan eyed her strangely. "I have never heard such a tale. Why do you ask?"

Alysa admitted, "There is something about Eirik which troubles me, Wise One. He is like my husband, but he is not. I am confused. If he is Gavin's brother, that would explain their similarities."

"What you really ask, Your Highness, is if he can be Gavin." Alysa turned and her somber gaze locked with his sympathic one. He smiled worriedly. "It is possible, but I think not. Even so, he is still one of them and must not be trusted. I will watch him closely to see if he is enspelled. Perhaps this is only a trick by the Evil One to thwart us. Gavin is your one weakness; do not allow Evil to use it against us. You must control your desire for this Eirik until we know more of him and his purpose. Take heart, all will be good again one day."

Alysa knew "this Eirik" was attracted to her. That delighted her, and alarmed her. If it were her lost love under some terrible bewitchment, could she save him? During their separation of many weeks, had he been unfaithful to her? She knew what many raiders did in the villages with helpless women. Had this man behaved in such an unforgivable manner? Even with such a sin against him, she caught herself hoping it *was* Gavin and he *was* enchanted, because that would excuse his betrayal and would put him within her reach for rescue.

The old man warned, "There are more perils in this strange matter, my queen. If others see you too frequently and intimately with Eirik, it could arouse their suspicions and endanger both of you. If Prince Gavin's face has been seen by any of them, such as a spy on you in Damnonia, it would appear as if you two are in a daring ruse together. The captives were slain, so they cannot escape and imperil either of you, and Thorkel did not see Prince Gavin before he was wounded. I am also certain there is no threat from Isobail's old raiders. I have seen none here, so they must have joined forces with Hengist or Horsa. You must not inspire Ulf and Rolf to become overly jealous by your attention to their rival. If you become reckless, your feelings will be exposed in your face and actions. If Eirik wins, or seems to be winning, they might suspect you favor him and aid him. That would cause us grave trouble. It is best to avoid Eirik."

Alysa reasoned, "But what if he *is* Gavin? What if he needs our help, your help, to break the spell over him?"

"Even if such is true, I could not disenchant him before our task is done." When Alysa started to argue, Trosdan said, "Let me explain. Do you not recall Gavin's feelings and behavior before his strange departure? If he became himself again, what would he do? We both know, Your Highness, and we cannot permit his intrusion. He would seize you and carry you home to safety, by force if need be."

"Nay, Wise One, he would help us carry out our task."

Trosdan's expression revealed his doubt. He reasoned cunningly, "Could he do so knowing the peril you are in? Could he conceal his fears and worries? His feelings for you and this task, good and bad? Could he continue to live as Eirik? To fool the Vikings?"

138

Before thinking, the fatigued Alysa scoffed, "I do not wish him to think and live as a Viking!"

Trosdan clasped her pale face between his hands and locked their gazes. "Even if by saving him for yourself, you lose all?"

Tears dampened her eyes and lashes. Her voice was ragged as she said, "It is unfair to make me pay such a high price for victory."

Trosdan observed her and realized how much she loved and missed her husband. He feared she would weaken in her task if she saw Eirik with another woman. "If you wish, I can make him desire only you."

Joy brightened her face. "Do so, Wise One, and I will obey you."

When a desperate idea struck her, she questioned eagerly, "Can you reveal the riddles' answers to Eirik in his dreams?"

"I do not understand."

Alysa explained, "If anything goes wrong, I wish Eirik to be the winner of this false quest. If I have to go beyond the marriage, it must be with him. I could not yield to Rolf or Ulf for any reason."

When Trosdan lowered his head to ponder her request, she added, "It is not as if I ask you to use your powers for Evil, Wise One. There is no real quest, no destined Viking husband. What does it matter if *we* choose the winner of this false quest?"

"What if there is an Odin, Alysa? I am a Viking by birth. I am working to destroy them. What if Odin has led me here to punish and destroy me?" he questioned to mislead her.

"The powers of Good will protect you, Trosdan. Have no fear," she told him with childlike faith. "Defeat is not our destiny."

"If only you understood the powerful forces which are at work here, you would tremble in fear as I do."

Alysa tugged at his arm playfully and teased to lighten his shaded mood, *"You* are the power here, Wise One. Do not doubt your skills and knowledge." Her tone and expression waxed serious as she continued. "I trust you with all things; that is why I am here today."

"What if I have misread the sacred Runes? What if my mind and skills have weakened with age and doubts? What if . . ."

Alysa embraced him affectionately. "You will be convinced when Eirik, Rolf, and Ulf win the contests in the next few days."

"They will win," Trosdan replied absently.

"See, you have not lost your confidence."

"It has nothing to do with confidence, my beloved queen, only a matter of perception. They are the strongest here."

"Nay, Wise One, *we* are the strongest. We control their lives. Will you seek Gavin once more in the sacred chalice? Now that we have met Eirik, surely it will give us clues about him."

"There is no need to do so again, Alysa. I cannot tell you where your husband is, or if Eirik has stolen his body and mind." He urged, "Be content in knowing the Runes vow Gavin will be returned to you after our task is done." Trosdan knew this was his last chance to save Alysa, the girl who would have been his granddaughter had he married his love Giselde long ago. He had to save her from the Viking threat which constantly loomed over her head; he had promised Giselde. The ruse was clever and simple. The only peril lay in Alysa's irresistible attraction to Eirik. What, he mused worriedly, could he do to prevent temptation from overwhelming her when Eirik would be thrust before her every day? Whatever the situation required, he decided.

Nine

In Damnonia at Malvern Castle, Lord Weylin was talking with Sir Teague in private chambers. The knight had been told to check the cage at Trosdan's cave every morning for the messenger bird's return, and he had done so earlier. After retrieving the small missives which had been concealed beneath the furry coverings on the creature's legs, Teague had summoned Weylin from the training field.

A broad smile traveled Weylin's face and softened his brown gaze. "Wonderful news, Teague; all goes well with Alysa and Trosdan. The Norsemen have accepted her as their queen. I will send word to King Bardwyn and King Briac of her success to cease their worries."

Sir Beag had journeyed across land to Lord Fergus's estate where he took a boat to row across the Sabrina (later to be named the Bristol Channel) to the coast of Cambria. There he traveled overland to the castle of Alysa's grandparents, Bardwyn and Giselde. After enlightening them to their granddaughter's desperate plans, Beag had been given their assurances of help with a joint attack and a promise of no interference with her ruse. Both considered Alysa very brave and cunning, and never doubted her ability to succeed in this daring matter. Giselde had told the men Alysa would be perfectly safe with the Druid High Priest who was a

141

powerful wizard. Bardwyn and Giselde were told that a second messenger bird was to arrive after the contest ended, and a third after the quest ended: their signal to attack in four days. Afterward, Sir Beag had returned home, one day after Alysa's departure.

Lord Keegan had done much the same, also heading out by boat from Lord Fergus's. Keegan had traveled along the coast of Cambria in the Oceanus Hibernicus (later to be named the Irish Sea) to the shore of Cumbria, then across his homeland to the castle of his rulers, King Briac and Queen Brenna.

Gavin's parents had listened to the startling tale with interest and dismay. They were concerned deeply about their son, who had not returned home during the time he had been missing from his wife. They had told Keegan that whatever their son was doing, there was a good reason for it, and Keegan had concurred. They had agreed to aid Alysa's clever plans, and promised to send Gavin back to Damnonia the moment he arrived, if he did so.

Keegan had told Gavin's parents all he knew about Alysa and about the recent events in Damnonia. He had explained her ruse in detail and revealed why it should work. They, too, were proud of Alysa and looked forward to meeting her soon. After swiftly visiting family there, he had returned to Weylin's camp three days following Alysa's departure, to find Gavin still gone.

On advice from Trosdan before his departure, the three lands were to train their men for five weeks and prepare their supplies for a joint battle. A messenger line was set up between the two rulers and Weylin so that word could be passed along quickly and efficiently. On the sixth week, all forces were to gather at their Logris borders and await Alysa's signal that the quest was over and they were to join her at Stonehenge in four days. The joint forces were to cautiously encircle the special area and be ready to swoop down on the Vikings when the final signal was given.

Teague was in charge of collecting the messages from the first two birds and relaying them to Weylin, who in turn was to send their news to Briac and Bardwyn. The third bird was trained to fly to the old Roman baths at Aqua Sulis where Weylin would be camped, ready to send word to the other forces to unite and swoop down on the Vikings.

Weylin could not help but warn Teague, "Alysa said the contest would take weeks, as would the quest, but we must check for her messages every day. If anything goes wrong, we must know of it swiftly. No matter where I am working, you will know of my location. Waste no time in alerting me to a change in plans, or to her peril."

After the men parted, Weylin sighed longingly. When he had returned to his estate to place Lady Kordel in charge during his absence, he had been surprised by the lovely woman's behavior toward him. The look in her glowing eyes and the warmth of her manner had enticed him strangely and potently. He craved to spend time with her, to test these new and unexpected feelings between them.

Alysa was aroused from her deep slumber an hour past midday by Rolf's slave. The young woman nudged her almost roughly. "The day grows late, Your Highness. It is time to rise and eat." The female captive had been told to serve Queen Alysa when she awakened, but the slave could not resist annoying her ravishing rival for Rolf in any way. "I have brought you food. Is there more you desire?"

"Who are you?" the Damnonian princess inquired sleepily as she sat up, stretching her taut body and rubbing her grainy eyes. The past four weeks had been hard on her, and she needed more rest. Yet she could not lie abed in an enemy camp with things to do.

The haughty response was, "My name in Enid. I am Lord Rolf's slave. He commanded me to serve you. What are your needs?"

Alysa gazed at the honey-haired female with dark-brown eyes. She noticed the tension and antagonism in the woman, and guessed the reason for them: Rolf. "I will eat, then I wish to bathe. I saw a brook nearby. I will go there."

"Are you permitted to leave camp?" Enid inquired crisply.

Not fully awake, Alysa replied to her sullenness with an uncharacteristic chill. "I am not a lowly slave. I am Queen Alysa, and I can come and go as I wish. You may leave the food and return to your chores. It is wise for a slave to control her tongue and manner."

Seeing that this beautiful woman was fearless and quick-witted, Enid did not retort. She nodded and bowed in false respect and left.

Peeved with what could be an unforeseen problem, Alysa eyed the food and wondered if it was safe to devour it. What if Einar had put something in it to loosen her lips, or the ruffled slave had done so to trick her? What if the Vikings did not believe her or trust her? What if they were only leading her along until she exposed herself? She could not imagine what those vicious men would do to her and her friend.

Trosdan entered and observed her frown. "What troubles you?"

Alysa explained the conflict with Enid and her worries. Trosdan tasted the food and drink, and told her it was untainted. As she slowly consumed it, they chatted.

"The Vikings speak of nothing but your return to them and the impending quest. Their blood runs hot with the excitement of competition and victory. Have no fear, Alysa, for they are duped."

"Soon, we will see," she replied, as if unconvinced.

144

When Alysa finished her meal, she gathered her possessions to head for the brook. Rolf was waiting for her outside, and she wondered how long he had been standing
there. She was glad she and Trosdan had spoken in whispers
to prevent being overheard. She cunningly said, "I wish to
bathe in the brook over there," and motioned to it. "Will
you select several loyal men to escort me and guard me?"

"It is too dangerous, Alysa. You are a beautiful and desirable woman. Foes could be lurking nearby, eager to capture you as a hostage," he quickly stated. "I, too, enjoy
leisure baths. I have a large tub in my home. You may use
it as often as you wish. My friend Sweyn will guard the
door for your privacy."

She inquired in a polite tone, "Is that wise, Rolf? Others
might think I favor you for your kindnesses, and cause
trouble."

Rolf smiled. "You are queen. It would be wise to show
others you make your own decisions. Come," he urged her.

Alysa relented and followed him into his dwelling. She
waited patiently while Enid filled the tub and finally left
her alone. She knew the captive was annoyed by Rolf's
attraction to his new ruler, and realized she must handle
that matter promptly.

Before leaving his dwelling, Rolf told Alysa to ask for
anything she needed. He ordered Sweyn, a large and strong
warrior and best friend, to stand guard outside.

Alysa barred the door and closed the openings for air.
She stripped and stepped into the tub. Because of the strenu-
ous ritual last night, it felt wonderful to refresh herself in
the tepid water. She scrubbed the gritty residue of Trosdan's
powder from her body.

She wondered what was taking place back home. How
had her grandparents and Gavin's parents taken the news
of her ruse? She wished Sir Beag and Lord Keegan had
returned from those two kingdoms before her departure to

145

enlighten her. Somehow she felt that Bardwyn and Giselde would go along with her deceit, but what were the reactions of Briac and Brenna? Did they blame her for their son's curious behavior? Would they aid her cause?

The only way to receive news from home, was to arrange a spot which she would visit during part of the quest. Until then, she had to believe and hope both lands would honor her requests.

And there was Gavin. Was Eirik her missing husband? If so, what had happened to him? If not, was he back home yet?

Where are love? What troubles you so deeply? I need you, Gavin. I love you. I must know if you are well and safe.

Alysa dried herself and put on her garments. She donned a flowing white kirtle in a soft material which was visually impenetrable. She encircled her middle with a gold chain allowing the extra lengths to dangle down her left thigh and slid her feet into slippers which matched the kirtle. She brushed and braided her long hair, and the heavy plait hung down her back to halt near her waist. She positioned a gold crown atop her dark hair and touched the image of Odin which was displayed on the raised section above her ocean-blue eyes.

Bending her head forward, she slipped another gold chain over it, settling its jewel-encrusted medallion at her heart. She had decided against wearing any weapons, even the exquisitely bejeweled dagger that had replaced the one which she had used on Thorkel. She slipped wide gold bracelets with more glittering stones over her wrists. She wanted to appear a regal queen with an intoxicating blend of strength and softness. Her image and aura were vital to her ruse and success. Not once could she allow the Vikings to forget her rank and power, or what she meant to them.

Alysa checked her appearance. She must keep her foes

enthralled and intimidated. For the contest to be lethal to many Norsemen, she needed for them to desire her and all that went with winning her. The more foes that were slain or injured, the fewer to battle later. To hold their fealty and to remain safe, she needed to prey on their fear of their head god Odin. Not for even one hour could she allow them to forget their superstitions, their ancient laws, their *curse*.

This was a barbaric camp of savage men who lived and thrived on greed, and lust, and power. These were rugged men who constantly needed to prove their prowess to themselves and to others, men who loved fighting and killing and conquering, warring men of fierce pride and determination—all things which she could use against them.

Alysa straightened up and gathered her possessions, leaving the tub for Enid to empty and clean. She opened the door and, after thanking him, dismissed Sweyn. As she walked toward Eirik's house with her bundle, she thought of all the reasons she must avoid him. Besides making the other two rivals vengefully jealous and risking his dangerous temptation—she could arouse suspicion about Eirik, her motives for coming here, and about the two of them as a guileful pair of foes.

"Where is Rolf?" Eirik asked from behind her. He had seen her leave Rolf's dwelling, fresh from a bath and no telling what else, and was plagued by jealousy and worry.

Alysa halted and turned to face him. A sensation of weakness attacked her as she gazed into his dark-green eyes. She eyed the neatly trimmed beard and mustache, and wondered if Gavin had worn facial hair before his arrival in Damnonia. Considering the amount of time since his departure and the rapid growth of his whiskers, it was easy to explain this one change in him. But the others . . . Why were his eyes darker, and exposing expressions she had never seen before? Why was his hair a deeper blond, nearly light brown, and where were its sunny streaks she had loved to finger? Granmannie, her special name for Giselde, had once removed his royal tattoo with powerful magic. What had happened to it this second time? Who else possessed such awesome skills and knowledge? How had his voice changed slightly? How did he know the Viking language although most everyone here spoke hers each day?

Alysa's anxious gaze continued to scrutinize him. Where had the scar come from which now traveled his cheekbone? It did not look fresh! Most importantly, what was the motive behind this ruse, if it was one? It was such a mystery, if this man was Prince Gavin Crisdean. In all honesty, she could not decide, a dilemma which alarmed her.

"Why do you always stare at me so strangely, my enchanting queen? Do you seek to bewitch me?" he teased.

Alysa watched the grin which lifted one corner of his mouth and seemingly tickled his eyes to bring them to smiling life. It was Gavin's expression, one which enflamed her senses and haunted her. Yet her voice was curt when she demanded, "Who are you, Eirik?"

The man stared oddly at her terse question. At times, his irresistible ruler seemed drawn to him; at others, she seemed repelled. He was utterly baffled. Perhaps she was only worried about his not winning the quest and her! "You wish to know more about me?" he hinted with pleasure and smugness.

To still his curiosity and destroy his conceit, she replied, "There is something about you which . . . which worries me. I do not feel as if I can trust you. I must ask Trosdan to study you in the sacred chalice. Tell me, Eirik the Bold, are you friend or foe?"

Her words visibly stunned him. His eyes widened briefly, then narrowed. He informed her in a level tone, "You are my queen. All I have is yours to command. How can I prove myself to you?"

"By telling me what it is you want most from life," she answered.

He looked confused, but replied, "To survive with honor. To win all battles and challenges. The best of all things."

His words and manner did not remind her of her husband. True, Gavin wanted honor, victory, and good things, but his reply would not have been the same. The fact this man responded so quickly and easily and differently pained her. She probed almost desperately. "You are a man who loves raiding and killing. Is that not so?"

The handsome warrior looked even more puzzled than before. Was that not what Viking life was all about? he mused. Yet her expression and tone were contemptuous of his way of life! Surely that was not her intention. She was seeking something which he could not guess. Even though he did not trust her fully, he craved her with a fierce desire. He wanted to win both the quest and this woman. She was beautiful, she was powerful—his queen, his path to victory, the answer to all his needs. Surely she was his destiny, even if he must seize her by force or deceit! He answered tentatively, "I raid because there are things I desire and I am strong enough to take them. But I do not kill unless I am forced to do so. I give my conquests the chance to yield or flee. If they do not, I slay them. Is that not our way, Queen Alysa?"

Closely observing Eirik, she asked, "Why do you enjoy such a life? Explain your feelings and desires to me."

Without delay he said, "It is like a cliff. To live on its edge is stimulating and empowering. Nothing sharpens a man's skills and wits more than facing perils every day he breathes. There is a nourishing thrill to winning. It makes life worth all perils and sacrifices. What way is there to better myself than with challenges?" He did not expect an answer, so he went on. "A warrior should never be satisfied with himself or his possessions. He must always be hungry

149

for more. He must be daring and eager to face any danger to gather his dreams. If he is not, he becomes lazy, slack, careless, and weak. He becomes vincible. Would you desire such a man?"

Alysa did not answer his troubling query. "What of those loved ones left behind if you should fail and die? Or while you are gone if foes should strike your land with raiding and killing and conquering in mind? Are such pleasures worth those sacrifices?"

"They should be glad I died bravely with a sword in my hand. But there are no loved ones left behind, my queen. My family is dead. I have nothing left but my skills and hungers."

Alysa knew it was reckless to ask what those "hungers" were, so she did not. She did not know this man, whoever he was. Yet she was potently attracted to him, as if she could not help herself. If he was an enspelled Gavin, that did not matter. But if he was not . . .

"You have that strange look again, my queen. Why do you doubt me? I would not harm you. I shall win you in the quest and cherish you forever," he vowed, then clenched his jaw in vexation. He had not meant to reveal such things to her so soon! To rush past his annoying confession, he asked, "What are your needs? Do you wish slaves to tend you? I will supply your every wish."

"My needs have been filled, Eirik; I have food and shelter, and my people have accepted me. I wish no slave in your house. I love my privacy. Rolf commanded his captive to see that I am fed and tended. He placed Sweyn on guard before his door while I bathed within. It was dangerous to use the brook, and your dwelling has no tub."

Eirik grinned happily at her revelation. "I have none, for I bathe in the stream, my queen."

Noting his look of relief, she hinted, "There *is* something

150

ou can do for me, Eirik. After I put away my possessions,
wish to visit Calliope. Will you escort me there?"

"Who is Calliope?" he asked.

Alysa smiled. "My horse, a beautiful grayish-brown crea-
ure. He is used to daily rides and visits. He is in a strange
lace and will worry if he does not see me today. Do you
now where he was taken?"

Looking relieved again, Eirik nodded and grinned.

At the makeshift corral, Alysa spent time with her be-
oved horse while she probed Eirik for more information.
Which one is yours?"

"There," he said, pointing to an energetic dun.

Alysa eyed the beast which was not Trojan, Gavin's tawny
ide mount with blond tail and mane. Disappointment
hewed at her and was exposed in her expression, until she
ealized how closely Eirik was watching her. "When do you
ight? Have the lots been drawn?"

The contest was to begin at dusk and continue until mid-
ight. There were seven hundred and sixty-eight Vikings in
amp. Using six rings, one hundred and twenty-eight men
vould pair off in each. After each round, lots would be
rawn for their next opponent in battle. It would require
even battles to leave one victor per ring. Those six men
vould compete in an eighth fight to leave three champions
vho would become the band leaders for the quest. Consid-
ring how long each battle took, she would probably witness
round ten to fifteen today.

Starting tomorrow, the contests would be held from
welve to six, then eight to midnight—allowing for about
wenty fights per day. At that rate, the contest should con-
ume nine to eleven days.

Although the Norsemen would be distracted during the
ontest, it was not the time to attack them, as only one fight
vould be in progress in each of the six rings. That meant

151

not all foes would be fatigued at the same time, fatigue enough to lose a battle to her forces.

"I drew a high number, so I fight in a day or two, if the men battle hard and long as I believe they will. There is much at stake in this contest and quest. Will you stand at my ring during each fight to inspire me to victory?"

She bravely met his enticing gaze. "You need no encour agement from me, Eirik. You will be one of the three cham pions, as will Ulf and Rolf. It is the will of Odin as was revealed to Trosdan in the sacred Runes and chalice. My presence will not affect any fight."

"Did they reveal who the winner of the quest will be?"

"Nay, my curious warrior. Even so, I could not tell you."

Eirik's gaze devoured her hungrily. "What if your choice does not match Odin's?"

Alysa stroked Calliope's forehead and looked at the ani mal as she responded, "Odin will select the best husband for me and High King for our people. I must trust him and accept his decision."

"Even if that choice is Ulf? He is not a good mate for you."

Without glancing at Eirik, she divulged playfully, "I must confess you and Rolf are more pleasing to a woman's eyes but that is not the most important thing in choosing a hus band."

"What does a woman like you desire in a mate?" he asked seriously as he patted Calliope's head so their hands would make contact.

Alysa moved her hand, almost jerking it away too swiftly and revealingly. Eirik's allure was potent, and frightening She craved to fling herself into his arms and cover his mouth with urgent kisses. She yearned to make wild, pas sionate love to him, wanted to shake him and awaken him from his dark enthrallment. She missed him and needed him. Frantic over her increasing weakness for this compel

152

ling stranger, she had to put distance between them. "I must return to your house and rest. This night will be a long one."

"You are afraid of me, Alysa. I wish that was not so. Do you fear to open your heart to me before I win you in battle? Or do you fear to desire a man who might not be Odin's chosen one?"

Alysa looked up into his tender gaze. "It is reckless to pursue and desire a woman you may not win. It is also rash to make others think we favor each other—especially my future husband, if that is not you. I do not want any of you to doubt my honor and behavior. Do not expose feelings for me before the others, Eirik, for you may find yourself craving another man's wife and inspiring trouble."

Alysa turned abruptly and walked away, leaving him standing there and observing her hasty retreat. *Craving another man's wife?* Never, he vowed, determined to have Alysa Malvern.

As the sun set, Enid arrived with the evening meal for Alysa and Trosdan. Alysa was feeding the two birds in a small wooden cage. The beautiful creatures were cooing to her as she spoke to them. Enid watched the tender scene and smiled wickedly.

An hour later, Trosdan guided Alysa to a raised dais where she could speak, witness the fights, and relax during the lengthy evening.

The men fell silent at her beauty. They listened to her words with keen interest.

Alysa looked over the large open space before them and said, "We have gathered in this *ve* to obey Odin's commands. Only three of you can become champions and lead

153

your followers in the quest. Once my husband, your High King, is chosen by his victory—we will have need of our warriors to conquer this isle. If you realize you cannot beat an opponent in the ring, yield to him before he is forced to slay you to continue his destined path. There is no shame in bowing to a friend's superiority. Vikings are the best warriors in the known world. When the moment of life or death is before you, yield if you must and live to battle our foes with us. May Odin guide your hands and minds for justice and mercy. Prepare the rings, Wise One."

Trosdan left her side and went to each large ring in turn, each of which was outlined on the ground by a circle of rocks, a boundary which the contestants must honor. He brushed their surfaces with sacred oak branches and cast sacred powder on them. As he did so, he chanted melodiously, "Great Odin, purify this space of earth where your commands will be followed. Protect the warriors you have chosen to ride at the head of your sacred quest. Hear me, Urd, goddess of destiny, guide these men as they seek their fates. I beseech you, Thor, give Odin's chosen ones power to defeat their opponents. Use your great power to keep Loki away from this special site. Gentle Frey, instill wisdom in all men who battle here so they will know when to yield. Beautiful Freyja, goddess of love, instill mercy in the hearts of our warriors. Let no man give or take a life without just cause."

Trosdan returned to the dais and lifted his hands skyward. "It is time, my people, to heed the calls of destiny. Go to your rings and let the contest begin. Fight with honor and wisdom and mercy."

Each man obeyed by going to his assigned ring and crowding around it to await his turn within it. Einar joined Alysa and Trosdan. The Viking *attiba* asked, "Since you say you are a *volva* and know the winners, will you witness the battles, my queen?"

She glanced at the man who was not attired in the same manner as Trosdan. Today, Trosdan was clad in the ceremonial garb of a Druid High Priest: a long and flowing white surplice with a gold brooch at one shoulder, a gold torque about his neck, and a garland of sacred oak leaves around his head. Trosdan's feet were bare and he held a yew staff. The Viking wizard was clad in a black robe.

"Yes, Einar, I will visit each ring during the contests. I wish to observe the strengths and skills of all my warriors, even those who must lose. I will warn you of one thing, do not use your skills to aid your master Rolf. He has been chosen by our god to be one of the three questors, and your magic could interfere with his victory."

Einar looked surprised by her warning. "I would not interfere in Odin's plans, my queen. I am confident Rolf will win you and the quest. Is that not also your desire?"

"My desire is to serve and obey Odin," she responded.

"As it should be, my queen."

Alysa strolled from ring to ring as she observed the contests. Some fights were quick and easy victories, some were long and difficult ones. Some men fought to the death, while others wisely yielded when lethal defeat was within sight. Others were injured, but spared by their opponents. The clashings of weapons and muscled bodies were loud in the clearing, as was the noise of cheers for encouragement and victories. Soon, the odors of dust, sweat, and blood could be detected.

The wounded were taken away to be tended, while the dead were piled aside to be burned on funeral pyres by Odin's command and their custom. It was Odin's law that fallen warriors be cremated with their belongings. The ashes were either cast into the sea or buried in the earth. The possessions of the dead warrior were destroyed with his earthly shell so that enormous smoke would be made. The higher the smoke ascended into the heaven, the higher his spirit could travel skyward toward Valhalla, Odin's great Hall of the Dead, their heaven. Alysa hated to imagine the stench of burning bodies, yet dead men could not battle and slay her people and other innocent victims.

When she needed to rest, Alysa returned to the dais. She had seen Eirik at one of the rings and Ulf at another, but neither man had approached her to speak. Rolf had followed her from his ring.

His hazel gaze roamed her appreciatively. "You are even more beautiful today than yesterday, my queen, if such is possible. It will be my turn to battle for you tomorrow. Will you stand at my ring?"

Alysa considered his request and any consequences of it. Perhaps it would lessen Eirik's boldness if he saw her watching Rolf closely. Too, she needed to beguile the stalwart blond giant and to prevent his discovery of her intrigue with his rival. She smiled and said, "Yea, Rolf, I will witness your battle for me. If . . ." she hesitated seductively, "you promise not to allow me to distract you from victory. I would not wish Loki to use me as a weapon to defeat Odin."

Rolf displayed satisfaction with her response. "Do you wish something to eat or drink, my enchanting queen?"

Alysa sent him a warm smile of gratitude. "I am fine, Rolf, and you are most kind. Soon, the fights will end for tonight and I must sleep. It was a long and tiring journey back to my people. I have not fully recovered from its demands."

"I eagerly await the night when you will sleep at my side, Alysa," he murmured in a husky voice which exposed his desire for her.

Alysa glanced around to make certain no one was within hearing distance. She lowered her voice to a near whisper as she teased, "You should not speak so openly of such feelings, Rolf. We do not wish others to think we become too close before the outcome of the quest. Your rivals might then suspect I give you the answers to the riddles so you can win my hand as you seek to win my heart."

"Would that your heart is as easy to win as a battle, my queen. Only victory in the quest would please me as much as winning you as my wife. As my love," he added.

Alysa sensed a threatening stare on her and, without revealing her perception, sought it from beneath lowered lashes. She located Enid spying on them from the corner of a nearby house. The coldness emanating from Rolf's slave crossed the span between them and alarmed her, as it could endanger her success here. Few things were more perilous than a love-blinded female who saw another as her rival.

Alysa tried to end the meeting quickly. "I will think on your feelings for me, Rolf, but the choice of mates is not mine. It is Odin's, and we must obey his command. We must beware of the eyes of others upon us. We cannot allow ourselves to create doubts and dissension. All must know you won fairly, if you do so."

"I did not think of causing trouble with my actions and words. You are wise and right, queen of my life and heart. I will try to avoid you until we are alone on the quest, then I must reveal my heart. You captured it the first moment I saw you standing upon the altar. I will prove to you and Odin I am best for the last champion."

"I will be honored to become your wife and to follow you as king, if that is Odin's will for us. Leave me now, so others will not cause us trouble in the days to come," she urged softly.

"Yea, I must go. Else I will forget all and seize you this night. There is no sweetness greater than your lips or any thrill greater than being in your arms. I will await such pleasures impatiently."

157

"Go quickly before our eyes expose us, Rolf," she entreated.

The Viking warrior engulfed her with his ravenous gaze, then walked away. Alysa glanced toward the house where Enid had been lurking, but the woman was gone. She glanced toward the rings, to find Eirik's piercing stare on her. As if guilty of some wrong, she nervously licked her lips and broke their locked gazes.

She was relieved when Eirik did not join her. She did not know what to say to him. Each time her eyes touched on him, she wanted him more urgently than the last time. Fierce cravings had been born within her and they were growing rapidly by the hour. She had to master her personal feelings as they were dulling her wits.

Fortunately, the signal was given to end the contest for tonight. Trosdan escorted her back to Eirik's house and she collapsed on his bed.

"I saw you with Eirik today and with Rolf tonight. Tell me of your visits with them," the old man entreated.

Alysa complied, then added, "It seems as if we have been here a long time, Wise One. It is strange, but sometimes I forget we are in the midst of foes and have a vital task here, or that we have another life elsewhere. Yet other times, I am aware of nothing else but those things. There are matters of Eirik and Enid to cause us problems. I must find clever ways to deal with them."

Trosdan then offered advice and some suggestions which delighted Alysa.

Ten

Just before noon, Enid arrived to bring food and drink to Alysa and Trosdan. The captive did not speak to either person today; she went about her task sullenly, then departed.

The contests began at midday and continued until shortly before dusk when everyone halted for two hours to rest and eat. Alysa was conscious of the fact that Eirik and Rolf intentionally kept their distances from her today, no doubt because of her clever warnings to them. But Ulf had asserted before her that soon she would belong to him. He had made the words sound more like a threat than a vow of desire. Alysa could not help but despise and fear the malevolent man.

It was during the evening period when both Ulf and Rolf fought their first contests. The flaming-haired Ulf wore his battle helmet and worked himself into a war-rage before attacking his opponent. Alysa watched the man and was glad Eirik would not have to fight him, if Trosdan's foresights were accurate, and she prayed they were.

In less than twenty minutes, Ulf had slain the other warrior; he had wounded the man so savagely, he could not ask for mercy, and Ulf offered none. Perhaps, Alysa thought, that was to reveal his power and determination to his future opponents as means of frightening them into making mistakes or into a hasty surrender.

Rolf's battle was different. Alysa stood at the front of the crowd at his ring and watched the action intently. As with Ulf, Rolf won his contest quickly and easily, for he was strong and cunning. But he did not slay the injured man. He glanced at Alysa and bowed. "Our queen has asked us to spare the lives of her warriors so they can battle our foes after the quest. This is a contest amongst friends, not a war with enemies. For her warrior and our friend, I show mercy. Go tend yourself, Sigurd, and thank our queen for your life."

The wounded man was taken from the ring for the next event to begin. When Rolf looked at Alysa, she smiled and falsely nodded her gratitude. He returned the smile before leaving the area to refresh and clean himself. Alysa slowly made her way to each ring until she reached the one where Eirik was standing across from her.

Without making herself obvious, she looked through the tangle of opposing bodies. The image of her husband kept his attention on the fight between them, or so Alysa thought.

Eirik pretended to focus on the two men hacking at each other's swords with nothing but victory and survival on their minds. He had been furtively watching their ruler since this contest began yesterday. As it would determine her future mate, he wondered why she was not more excited or intrigued by what was taking place. Even though she observed the battles, it was as if her mind was far away, as if she did not care who won, or if anyone did . . . Or maybe the old man had told her who would win, and the name displeased her.

Eirik recalled how she had behaved with Rolf last night. His fury still burned brightly within him. Although he had not overheard their words, their moods had been apparent to his keen eyes. The Briton princess had flirted subtly with his rival, and that did not sit well. Did she, he mused angrily, have a preference for Rolf? Would she dare help his rival win her hand? Perhaps she did not care who won her as long as she was a powerful queen! Nay, he told himself. He had noticed the scornful look in her eyes as she had watched Ulf fight, one which had come and gone quickly and cunningly.

As Alysa turned her head to speak with the man beside her, Eirik studied her. Her brown hair was hanging free today. How he longed to run his fingers through its silky strands and to inhale its sweet fragrance. The dark-blue tunic over her white kirtle matched her deep-blue eyes, eyes which seemed to sear his soul each time they met his gaze. Her skin was incredibly soft like newborn fur and he ached to touch it, to caress her from head to foot. Beneath that enticing flesh, her body was lean and hard, its tone that of a well-honed warrior's. She moved like water flowing peacefully in a rock-free gill, the gentle sway of her hips capturing every man's eye. Her laughter was more pleasing to his ears than the song of any bird. And her voice, her voice caused his body to tingle and enflame whenever he heard her speak. The tightening in his groin warned him to change his thoughts and to shift his gaze from the bewitching creature.

Bewitching, yea, that was Alysa Malvern. All men here desired her. But only one man could possess her. Whatever it took, it had to be him or . . . Or what? he wondered. He could never forget this woman. She had become like a fierce hunger which had to be fed. He could not let her go to another!

Alysa quivered as she felt Eirik's potent stare on her, and she feared locking gazes with him. She feared that everyone would see the uncontrollable desire for him written there. It had been weeks since Gavin had left her arms, and her body traitorously craved this man who was so like her lost

161

love. She loved and desired every inch of Prince Gavin Crisdean, and she missed his nearness terribly.

The fight ended most timely, as Alysa could not gaze across at Eirik another moment without bursting into tears from her anguish and tension. Hurriedly she left that ring and returned to her dwelling.

She tossed and turned for two hours. She could not get Eirik and Gavin off her mind. Each time she dozed, their images overlapped to tantalize her with one irresistible man, then separated to battle each other as vicious foes, tormenting her into wakefulness. She tried to think of other things, but it did not help her restless spirit. She fretted over something going wrong with her ruse. Even if the contest and treasure hunt went according to plan, what if the attack failed? What if the Cumbrians and Cambrians did not join her people? Could the Damnonians crush this mighty force alone? She did not think so.

As for seeking help from the king of Logris, that was impossible. Vortigern was the reason Vikings and Jutes were here. He hired them, used them, and tolerated them for his own evil and selfish purposes.

As for the peasants and noblemen of Logris, Alysa did not know where to locate villages and castles in this foreign land, and she could hardly ask for directions. Time, distance, and risks made approaching either group unwise, at least for now. She would not know whom to trust, and why should *they* trust a female ruler of another kingdom?

Stonehenge was situated on flat, open land which prevented a stealthy departure even under cover of darkness. And, given that she *could* get out of camp unseen, she would have to search for villages, awaken peasants, convince them to take sides with her against their king and terrorists, and return before dawn and discovery! She was brave and smart, and determined to have victory, but she would not act impulsively or rashly. Yet she needed some backup strategy.

There were so many areas where unanticipated problems could arise. What if one of the messenger birds was captured and devoured by a hawk? What if Enid started to bother her? She could not allow the woman's intrusion, nor did she want to order the captive's punishment or death. What if Rolf became too romantically inclined and aggressive? What if he and Eirik exposed an open rivalry for her? What if Eirik really *was* Gavin and he was unmasked? What if Ulf tried to challenge her rank or motives? The redhead was a mean, unpredictable man and must be watched at all times.

"You cannot sleep?" Trosdan asked from the corner pallet where he slept each night.

"My mind and body are too restless tonight, Wise One. I am sorry I have disturbed you. Do you have a sleeping potion with you?"

Trosdan prepared the liquid and handed it to her. Hastily and gratefully Alysa downed it, frowning at its bitter taste. "What did Gavin give me that night?" she inquired. "I tasted nothing in the wine, and I did not suspect such a foul deed from him."

The old man replied, "There are plants without noticeable taste which bring on deep sleep, but they grow far away. While we are on the quest to the North, I will gather some in case we have need of them at the end."

"Please do not use that word, Wise One. It has a frightening tone of finality and defeat."

The Druid explained gently, "We do not believe as the Norsemen do, my princess. Death does not end our lives on earth. Our spirits will transmigrate into another form, that of another human or an animal. The soul is immortal, indestructible. Only fire and water can prevail over it, if the right conditions are met."

"But I wish to live as Alysa with Gavin at my side. Do you think perhaps one of the Vikings we slew took control of my love's body?"

"Nay. When I was with him, I did not feel warning tremors of such a dark deed. I cannot tell if Eirik is Good or Evil. Beware of him and yourself, my princess," he cautioned out of necessity. He had to keep her strong, and true to her destiny. Soon, the threat to her would be destroyed, and all could be made right again.

Trosdan looked into his ruler's serene face and smiled lovingly. He tucked her in as a small child, as his cherished child. Returning to his pallet, he surrendered to dreamless slumber.

The morning and afternoon schedules were the same as yesterday's. When Alysa returned to her borrowed dwelling to eat and rest before the evening's games began, she found a large wooden tub in the kitchen area. Immediately she realized it was not the one she had used at Rolf's. She knelt to retrieve the wildflowers inside it.

Enid entered with Alysa's food and drink. She saw the queen standing in the *eldhus* and staring dreamily at the flowers in her grasp. "They are from Lord Eirik," she quickly clarified.

Alysa turned and smiled genially, masking her surprise and pleasure. "It is good that I will not have to trouble you each day with this added chore. You have been kind and helpful, Enid. I know I have been an extra burden for you each day, but I am grateful for all you have done. Rolf asked if I needed a captive to serve me, but I thought you would rather remain in his dwelling and serve me from there. I hope you do not mind, but there is little room here

164

for another person. If you wish to make yourself a place in the *eldhus,* I will ask Rolf."

The female realized the queen was giving her that choice and was astonished. "Do you wish me to leave Lord Rolf's?" she asked, skepticism creeping into her eyes and voice.

"Nay if you are satisfied there. I am sure it is difficult being a captive, but you are strong and you manage your fate well. Surely it is easier for you to serve Lord Rolf and to tend me from his dwelling." Alysa took a small brooch from her bundle and handed it to the woman. "Take this as payment for your kind services, Enid."

Enid clutched the jeweled brooch and gaped at it, then slowly lifted her curious brown gaze to Alysa's entreating blue one. "Lord Rolf commanded me to serve you. There is no need to pay me."

Alysa saw how much the woman wanted to keep the jewel. She smiled and pushed away Enid's outstretched hand. "It would please me if you kept it. Think of it as a reward for your many kindnesses. If Lord Rolf questions it, I will explain. I have told him how good you are to me and to him. You are a valuable treasure, Enid."

Enid did not know what to say. She slipped the gift into her pocket, bowed, and left. She was thrilled to remain with her lover, but she could not ascertain the queen's motive for allowing it. If the ruler was jealous of their closeness and desired Rolf for her own, Alysa would have ordered her to move from Rolf's dwelling. Perhaps the queen desired Eirik more than Rolf. Happiness surged through the captive and she was tempted to let Rolf know Alysa did not favor him. But Enid knew that was foolish, as it would no doubt challenge Rolf to pursue Alysa feverishly.

Within minutes of Enid's departure, Eirik arrived, and knocked at the doorway. "There is something I need from inside, my queen. Do you mind if I fetch it?" he inquired politely.

Alysa stepped aside and motioned for him to enter. She watched him go to a large chest and retrieve a cuirass, a tough leather garment which covered the chest and back to prevent any minor cuts from slashing blades. "You fight later, do you not?" she asked to start a conversation.

He halted his departure to reply, "Yea, my queen."

Alysa realized he was distant today, as he turned again to leave. She touched his arm and stayed him once more. "I wish to thank you for the tub, Eirik, and for the flowers. I had need of both."

"Of both?" he queried, eyeing her strangely.

She met his gaze as she explained. "I am far from home and living with strangers. My responsibilities here are great, and often they frighten me. I do not know why the gods chose this perilous destiny for me, and its importance intimidates me." She strolled a few feet away and presented him with her profile. "There are times when I know all will go well for us. Then there are times when I doubt myself and the task before us. There are moments when I feel weak and scared like a child. But there are moments when I feel strong and proud like a queen. The differences are so great between ruling a peaceful land and leading the conquest of many lands. Sometimes it is so confusing for me. Duty to one's fate can be difficult and demanding. The flowers and your kindness brightened my spirit and calmed my fears."

Eirik closed the distance between them. Her revelations touched him deeply. It seemed as if he had misjudged her. She was so young and gentle to become a warrior queen. Destiny had played unfairly and harshly with her life. "Do not worry, my enchanting queen, all will be fine. You shall have me at your side to protect you and to—"

When he ceased his words, Alysa looked up into his trou-

166

bled gaze. Their eyes locked and their emotions ran rampantly. For a time, they simply stared at each other. Eirik's hand lifted to caress her cheek, and Alysa closed her eyes and dreamily nuzzled it. Helplessly his hands cupped her face and he lowered his lips to hers. Their mouths fused in a heady kiss which caused both to tremble with powerful desire. For what seemed a long time, they kissed feverishly, and further enflamed their bodies. He held her soft body tightly against his hard frame, and she yielded to his embrace.

Hungrily and urgently they each savored the mouth of the other. Soft moans escaped between kisses, and eager hands began to roam wildly and freely. It was Eirik who parted them, with enormous difficulty.

"I shall carry these kisses as your favor into battle, as your knights carry such signs into jousts. I must go, for soon I fight for you."

"You will win each battle, Eirik, for Odin has willed it."

"What of you, Alysa? Who is your chosen one?" he probed.

Alysa lowered her gaze. "I must not speak such words aloud. It is wrong for us to behave this way. It must not happen again. Go and prepare yourself. Be careful, Eirik. I would not want you slain by Evil or by Good to punish me for this weakness."

"It is not a weakness to yield to your future husband," he teased. "It is good that you desire me as deeply as I desire you. When I watched you at the ring, I saw and felt your desire for me, even though your eyes tried to avoid me as mine tried to avoid you. It is impossible, for the bond between us is too strong."

Fear enlarged her blue eyes and she trembled. "I revealed it before others!" she gasped in panic. "It will cause trouble. You must go and not return to my side until the quest is over. Then, do so only if you are the winner."

"Do not worry, m'love, others did not see or feel what I did. You hide your feelings with great skill. I feared I had repelled you."

Alysa stared at Eirik when he used Gavin's favorite endearment for her: "m'love." Was it a sign? A coincidence? A trick by Evil? "We cannot do this again, Eirik. It is too dangerous for all concerned. If others suspected I desired you, they would believe I aid you with the quest. That would lead to peril for us and for the task before us. I cannot stain my honor, for I am to wed the champion."

Eirik caressed her cheek and murmured, "I will go, m'love, and make this no harder for us. It is enough to know you feel as I do. I would never dishonor or imperil you."

Unable to halt herself, she told him, "I will be at your ring tonight. Let no blade touch you or my reaction will expose us."

They kissed briefly, and Eirik left with the cuirass over his arm. Alysa sank to his bed and tried to master her breathing and tremors. She suddenly realized that to avoid Eirik or to treat him coldly would arouse as much suspicion as being overly friendly with him. The answer to her dilemma, she decided, was to treat all the men equally in public.

Alysa went to Eirik's storage chest and opened it. Nothing of Gavin's was there—no weapon, garment, or possession. Nor had she seen anything familiar with Eirik, and the horse he rode was not Gavin's Trojan. If only she could find clues—one tiny piece of evidence, more than an endearing word—to prove he was Gavin!

Moments ago he had seemed so like her husband in speech, manner, and behavior. How could he not be her lost love? This could not be a clever or mischievous pretense on his part, else he would have told her by now or she would have discovered it herself. Nay, this man truly believed he was Eirik.

She recalled her words to Gavin before the battle: "Clear your head of all things except survival and victory. Forget I exist . . ." Had her "powers" worked on Gavin? Was she somehow his enspeller? Was he by her words and her destiny enchanted? Would victory be the key to unlock his imprisoned mind?

Gavin's last words had been, "Destiny calls to *us,* my warrior queen, and *we* must respond." His note had said, "If it is to be, we shall meet again." But meet as strangers? Foes? Had Gavin been sent here as Eirik to protect and love her?

When it was his turn, Eirik stepped into the ring and assumed his position. He was wearing the leather garment which he had taken from his house. His hips and upper thighs were covered by a battle apron, and his feet were encased in furry boots with overlapping straps. Gold armbands reached from his wrists to within inches of his elbows. His dark-blond hair was secured with a leather strip at his nape to prevent it from falling into his face and obstructing his vision. He looked so handsome and virile, so strong and proud, so invincible.

His opponent joined him, a huge man with massive shoulders and arms. Alysa tried not to appear frightened or overly interested in this particular match. Rolf stood beside her, so she had to be extra careful how she behaved. The signal was given and the two men came to alert, each poised to attack his opponent and to defend himself. Slowly they circled each other as they awaited an opening to charge. Their eyes were locked as they searched for weaknesses and strengths. It was obvious both men were ignoring the loud noises from other rings where contests were going on simultaneously. Swords clanged and the match began.

Both warriors were skilled fighters. The match continued for a time, and sweat beaded on their faces and shone on their arms. But Eirik was quicker on his feet and stronger with his sword arm. With flashing speed and agility, Eirik sidestepped the man and sliced through the back of his leg near the knee, sending the man toppling forward to the ground. With such an injury, the man could not stand on it or move about to continue the match. He clasped the wounded area with one hand and tried to defend himself with the other. It was unnecessary, as Eirik did not attack him again.

The victor said, "It is over for you today, Leikn. Do you yield to spare your life as our queen desires?"

The man knew he was helpless, so he nodded. He was removed by friends and carried away to be tended. Several areas had been set up for the wounded, a place where Trosdan spent much of his time as he pretended to use his healing skills to evoke the Vikings' gratitude and loyalty toward him and Alysa.

Alysa walked to another ring with Rolf and watched the action there. The men were serious about this contest and fought desperately to win each match. She thought about the pile of bodies near camp and knew there would be a great funeral pyre tomorrow when the first set of matches were completed. She dreaded having to observe that barbaric ritual, but knew she must.

"What troubles you, my queen?" Rolf asked.

"I was thinking of how many noble warriors have been slain. I wish more would yield and survive to travel with us on our great journey."

"All men here wish to be champions, to become your husband and our ruler, my queen, so they fight to the death.

It is hard for a man to admit defeat, even in a friendly contest."

"But they are friends and we have need of them later. I wish the contest were not so deadly. Let us speak of other things," she entreated, her lies having a bitter taste on her lips.

"Enid told me you do not come to bathe at my house anymore. She said Eirik stole a tub from a village for you," he remarked in an provocative tone.

To allay Rolf's obvious jealousy and vexation she replied nonchalantly, "He did so because I asked why he did not have one. Bathing daily is a task which many do not find a great pleasure as I do. He felt it his duty to bring me one."

"Do you desire a slave of your own? Or a gift of Enid?"

"Nay, Rolf. I do not care to have servants underfoot in a small dwelling. I am accustomed to large and private chambers at my castle. To have someone chattering and hovering about me at all times would annoy me and dampen my spirits." She glanced at him and smiled sweetly. "You are kind to share Enid with me. She works hard, and is respectful. You could have no better servant to tend you and to care for your home."

"That is all she does for me," he whispered meaningfully.

Alysa smiled faintly as if that news embarrassed her. She did not believe his statement to be true. "I do wish to ask about other captives you have taken. Many weeks ago you attacked a castle near the Logris border in my land. You captured a raven-haired woman and her two daughters who lived there. They are the family of a past friend and feudal lord. What has happened to them? I have not seen them here." In fact, she had recognized no slave here as Damnonian, which relieved her.

Rolf was intrigued. "I gave them to Horsa, Hengist's

brother, as a truce offering. Do you wish me to buy them back for you?"

"Nay, I only wished to know their fates. Lord Daron once saved my life when a poacher mistook me for a peasant girl who had witnessed his crime. If they were here, I would want no harm to come to them when it is time to release the slaves to begin our quest."

"How did you know I attacked there?" he asked.

Alysa laughed softly. "Those who escaped came to my castle to report to their ruler. They described the leader as a handsome blond giant who was accompanied by a wizard wearing a black robe with strange symbols upon it. When I saw you and Einar, I realized the victory was yours."

"Had I known the queen of my heart and destiny was so near, I would have stormed your castle and lay claim to you."

Again Alysa laughed. In a playful tone, she scolded, "You did much damage and terrorized my subjects. In the future, we must be careful not to destroy property which will soon belong to us."

"To *us?*" he echoed with a broad grin.

"I meant to us as Vikings, Rolf. Do not play with my words," she teased him as he chuckled.

"Come, I must take you to your house to rest and sleep. Perhaps we can ride tomorrow. Your horse must need exercise by now," he added so she could not refuse his offer.

"If there is time, I will do so," she replied noncommittally.

When Alysa was snuggled in bed, she decided that things must be going as planned back home. If not, she would have known by now. When this matter was settled, she would find a way—either by force or ransom—to get Lady Gweneth and her daughters back safely.

Come lie with me, my love . . . She mentally summoned Gavin before drifting off to sleep to dream of him.

* * *

Rolf did not take her riding the next morning because he and a band of Vikings raided a villlage an hour away for supplies. Now she knew the location of at least one village if an opportunity to sneak there safely presented itself. Alysa strolled about the settlement and watched the men honing their skills for upcoming bouts in the rings. Needing to release energy, Alysa collected her sword and shield and headed for the practice ground where Thorkel was working. She approached him and asked him to exercise with her, since Eirik was not around to use this ruse to be together.

Thorkel flashed her a toothy grin. "Only if you tell me how you beat me last time. You are a woman, a small one."

"Your pride is your weakness, Thorkel. You assumed you could best me because of what you viewed—a woman, a small one!—so you did not think me competition for your size and skills and did not fight your best until I had the advantage over you. Then you allowed anger to dull your wits and desperation to create mistakes. You also allowed me to distract you with my looks and words. You must keep your head clear and your mind alert to your opponent's trickery."

Alysa and Thorkel tapped swords as if to say, "Ready." Flashing sword crossed flashing sword time and time again. They moved quickly and nimbly, but were careful not to wound the other. Alysa wielded her weapon with an expertise and ease which amazed the viewers crowding around them. Once, she ducked and slammed her head into Thorkel's belly, jarring him backward. He hastily recovered his balance and laughed mirthfully to conceal his embarrassment.

"Wait one moment. My boot is coming off," she told him.

When he lowered his sword to obey, she whirled and placed the tip of her blade at his throat. She reminded, "Re-

173

member your opponent's trickery. Never slack off and never give him the advantage. A warrior who seems lest harmful often offers the greatest peril."

The men around them cheered loudly for their victorious queen and teased Thorkel, who seemed to take his defeat good-naturedly. To make certain, Alysa said, "You are a superior fighter, Thorkel. I am glad you restrained yourself to let me work out with you. Had our fighting been genuine I doubt I could have won this time."

The shaggy-haired warrior was delighted by her words and manner. He grinned and thanked her. "I have seen you use a sword and dagger, my queen. Do you have skills with the bow and lance?"

"I have practiced with them many times. Shall we try them?"

Targets were swiftly set up by eager men, and Alysa was handed a lance. She gauged the distance, wind, and weight of the large weapon. She lifted her right arm and positioned it before taking several rapid steps and releasing the lance. It hurled through the air and struck its target in the center. Twice more she was encouraged to repeat her action, and twice more she was successful. The crowd, which had grown larger, cheered and praised her.

"Which do you wish, my queen, the longbow or cross bow?" one of the warriors inquired.

"You choose," she told him, and he selected the longbow. Alysa laughed softly, knowing most believed that weapon required more skill.

After emptying a quiver of arrows which all found their assigned targets, the men gaped in awe at the beautiful woman before them.

"Truly she is a warrior queen as legend claims," one man said.

Alysa remarked, "It is nearing time for the contest to continue. We must go and prepare ourselves. May Odin

174

watch over you and guide you." She turned to leave and saw Eirik's eyes gazing upon her from the corral. The look on his face was one of amazement and obvious pride in her skills.

She joined him. "Would you take care of my weapons while I give Calliope a good run? I will not go out of sight."

"You are . . . magnificent," he said, choosing a word which only halfway described this unique woman. "Shall I ride with you?"

"Nay, it is unwise. Wait for me here with my weapons. We can steal a moment longer when I return for them."

Alysa mounted Calliope bareback and guided him out of the rickety corral. She smiled at Eirik, then gave her horse his lead. Off they galloped across the clearing, the wind seizing her hair and spreading it out like a flowing brown cape behind her.

Eirik observed her intently as she raced back and forth, remaining in view as promised. He could tell how much she loved the dun and riding. She looked so alive, so radiant. Few men or women could ride bareback, and especially so gracefully and expertly. What a stunning creature she was! He wished he could join her and they could escape into the forest for a private meeting. But as she had warned, it was too dangerous for them.

Alysa returned to the corral, nearly breathless and with pink cheeks. Her eyes seemed to sparkle as blue jewels beneath a blazing sun. Her loose hair was tangled and cascaded around her shoulders. For the first time, Eirik realized she was wearing loose pants and a linen shirt. Yet the manly garments looked fetching on her. He secured the corral and went to help her gather her belongings.

As they walked toward his dwelling to put them away, he teased, "You did not tell me you were a skilled warrior. I heard Thorkel's tale, but thought it a wild story which could not be true."

Alysa replied in words which were honest, but not with the meaning Eirik would grasp, "It seems as if I have been training for this destiny all my life. I have ridden since childhood, and used weapons longer than I can remember. I was taught to track and how to use my wits. Until recently, I did not know I was preparing for such a great moment in my life and in our history."

"How did you know it was time to return to your people?"

"Trosdan came to me and told me. At first, I battled his words, for they were strange and frightening. I have lived a rather peaceful existence; now, I go to war as a foreign queen."

"Do you always trust and obey this wizard?"

A look of love and respect brightened her features. "Yea, Eirik, for he is wise and powerful. Many times I have been shown he speaks the truth. I possess a gift which I cannot explain or control. I see things in dreams, then they come true. When peril surrounds me, some force protects and guides me. When I have need of proof, it is provided. Do you believe in such things?"

"Yea, m'love, I believe in the powers which surround us and guide us. I cannot explain them, but I know they exist. Have you seen *me* in your dreams?" he asked unexpectedly.

Alysa flushed with guilt and turned her face from his keen eyes. Eirik entreated, "Tell me what you saw, m'love."

"I cannot."

"Will you say if it is good or bad?" he persisted.

Eleven

Before Alysa could reply, Trosdan joined them. As if Eirik were not present, the old man focused on Alysa. "Enid has prepared your bath, my queen. You must hurry to get ready for the contest."

The Damnonian princess nodded respectfully and left them. Eirik remarked, "You have much control over her, wizard. I pray you only use your powers wisely on her and on my people."

The Druid's sky-blue gaze met Eirik's concerned one as the warrior scrutinized him closely. There was an air of mystery, reverence, and potent authority about the white-haired Viking—an aura which implied he possessed great skills and knowledge about the secrets of life. His clear eyes were gentle, but impenetrable. His manner was kind and easygoing. Yet Eirik sensed he was a man who could not be swayed from his beliefs.

In a voice which was almost musical, the old man responded, "Alysa is like my own child. I would never endanger her or misguide her. She is the Last Viking Queen. She will obey her destiny, no matter her fears or desires; have no doubt of this, Eirik. It is cruel and wicked of you to tempt her to disobey the gods. To turn her aside from her destiny would bring down havoc on all."

"Do you see and know all things, Wizard?" Eirik asked, ignoring Trosdan's subtle warning.

Trosdan's pervasive gaze remained locked with Eirik's. "The sacred Runes and chalice reveal much to me, but not all things. Beware of your craving for her and the trouble it could cause. She is young and knows little of men's powerful desires. Her heart is good and she does not know what terrible things fierce men will do to sate their hungers. She does not recognize the fires she ignites in them or the destructions which they can do when burning out of control. You cannot hide your lust for her and all that goes with the quest, but you must control it, before others and if you are alone. To inspire others to doubt her will endanger her, and will endanger you, Eirik. If you do not wish her harmed or mistrusted, be strong and remain distant."

Eirik questioned a matter which haunted him. "What of her husband? Will he not come searching for her? Will he not try to rescue her and carry her home?"

Slyly the old man answered, "Nay, Prince Gavin will remain where he is. He does not possess the power or wits to seek her."

"How could he not love and desire a beautiful and unique woman such as our queen?"

"Do all women love and desire you? Or any one man? Nay, as not all men can love and desire her. It is sad, but Prince Gavin cannot and will not come for her."

"Did she not love him when she wed him?"

"Her grandfather, King Bardwyn, commanded the marriage, and she obeyed. I was present and carried out the royal order. It was before the Sacred Runes revealed her true destiny to me, else I would have prevented the wedding and brought her here."

The warrior reasoned, "If she is loyal to her king and people, why did she leave her land and husband to obey your strange words?"

178

"Because she knew I spoke the truth, and she knew what had to be done. The gods speak to her in dreams, but she does not realize how strong her powers are. Often they frighten and confuse her, but she obeys them, as it should be. There is no need to worry; her Celtic marriage is not real or binding in the Viking world, and she views herself a Viking. I caution you, Eirik, do not intrude. If it is the gods' will for you to win her and the quest, you will do so. If not, you must not trouble her with your perilous pursuit."

Eirik ventured, "You fear me, do you not, old Wizard?"

"Nay, I only fear what your desires can do. If you but realized the perils you can create with them, you would shudder in terror and not go near her again until after the quest."

"Tell me who will win the quest, and perhaps I will obey you."

"Whatever my answer, you would not. You are a passionate and restless man, Eirik, one who recklessly pursues his dreams no matter the price. It is her safety and destiny which concern me, and I will do all to protect them. If your heart is good and wise, you will heed my words. If not, I will be forced to prevent your doing evil to her."

"You threaten me, old wizard?" Eirik asked with a grin.

Without fear or hesitation, Trosdan informed him, "Nay, my foolish warrior, I make you a promise. If she has stolen your heart as well as your eye, you will desire her safety more than her body."

"I will think on your words. But if I obey them, it is for her safety, not because of your threat." Eirik walked away.

The matches continued from midday until dusk, completing the first round and leaving sixty-four men—thirty-two pairs—in each ring. Before the group separated for the eve-

179

ning to rest, lots were drawn for the next set of fights which would begin tomorrow. With low numbers, both Eirik and Ulf would face competitors early.

Alysa was astonished when Ulf approached her and handed her a gift: a jeweled belt which had undoubtedly been stolen from a wealthy, highborn lady during a vicious raid. She wanted to refuse it, but could not humiliate him before others. She smiled and thanked him.

"Wear it the day we wed," he stated almost like a command.

She could not stop her retort. "If such does not happen, Ulf, I will return it so you can give it to the head wife you already possess."

A mocking grin captured Ulf's face and contorted it into an ugly mask. As he chuckled, the long red lock of hair atop his head shook wildly and his beady eyes ravished her. His flaming beard needed a trim, and his breath was foul. He was a bullish man in appearance and manner, and Alysa could not imagine lying with this repulsive male.

Rolf came to where they were standing and argued in a merry tone, "Nay, Ulf, she will become my wife. Forget her."

"We will see, Rolf," Ulf replied, cocky and undaunted.

The blond Viking asked, "Will you join me to eat, my queen? Enid has prepared a special meal. I gathered supplies this morning while you were defeating Thorkel a second time. Many told me of your skills when I returned. You will make a fine queen, and a cherished wife."

Ulf began to laugh so hard that he choked. He coughed and cleared his throat before speaking. "Do not woo my future wife, Rolf, or I will be tempted to think you will do so again after we are wed."

Alysa tried to control her quavering voice as she chided, "Wooing is not the same as winning, Ulf. Nor will it cause me to be unfaithful to my husband, or myself, or our gods.

180

Do not insult me with unfair suspicions. I vow, only my husband will touch me and claim me."

Alysa looked at the grinning Rolf. "I am weary tonight, but I will join you another day. Until morning," she said, and left.

When Alysa was inside her dwelling, she tossed Ulf's present on the bed. She would never wear a gift taken from a helpless victim, a female who was no doubt ravished and enslaved or killed! She was angry. She was restless. She was tense. She paced the longhouse of stones with its turf roof. The narrow slits for ventilation could be sealed inside and outside to shut out cold and rain or for privacy. In the winter, the space between the inner and outer shutters was filled with turf for added warmth. Tonight, only the inner shutters were closed. She envisioned herself there with Er— Gavin.

Alysa walked to the opening in the dark kitchen. She unsealed it and stared at the unobstructed scene beyond the settlement: Stonehenge, which was outlined against a sky that went from black, to violet, to blue, to sweeps of more violet, to mingled hues of pink and gold and deep purple near the earth. The dark site looked eerie against the colorful backdrop of the last remains of the day. She wondered what had taken place there in ancient days, and what would take place there after the quest.

Eirik entered her line of vision as he headed toward the Druid temple of towering stones. As if sensing her stare, he halted and turned. Locating her at the window of the house which he had won in a bet only weeks ago, he met her gaze.

Alysa tried to move from the window, but could not. She found herself suspended there by the power of his allure, as he did hers not far away. Her body seemed weightless and serene. Her mind drifted dreamily. She did not look away, could not look away.

181

Eirik watched her, noting her response to him. His mind was in a quandary. He wanted to go to her, but knew he should not. She was bewitching, and he lacked the strength to resist her pull. He wanted to hold her, to kiss her, to caress her. It seemed forever before the quest would be finished and he could do so. Trosdan's warnings thundered across his mind, and he dared not endanger her. If only she would help him obey the wizard . . .

She was seductive. Compelling. How could he battle the invincible force which was drawing them together? It appeared the same for her, and that conclusion thrilled him. Yet it worried him, as it meant he would receive no help from her with his emotional struggle. If she but once summoned him . . .

Eirik's friends Aidan and Saeric shouted to him and broke the spell between him and Alysa. He turned and answered their call. He glanced toward the window, but she was gone and a feeling of emptiness plagued him. His head ached strangely and he was tense. He felt bewildered and flustered. He felt as if he were smothering in a trap. To relax the tautness in his chest, he inhaled deeply and slowly exhaled. He headed to join his friends in a game of toss-the-stones.

The Viking Queen was aroused the next morning by the noises which filled her ears and the stench which attacked her nose. She sneaked a look outside and saw billowing smoke heading skyward: the funeral pyre had been lit. The offensive odor of burning flesh stung her nostrils. She was glad it was being carried out beyond the settlement, but the mild breeze was wafting in this direction. She did not know how many foes had been slain or had died from wounds, but the pile was large. As was their custom, the men's possessions were burned with them to create more smoke to carry their spirits heavenward and to supply them with riches when they arrived in Valhalla.

Enid came with Alysa's food, and was cold to her rival again. Irritated, Enid remarked, "Lord Rolf was unhappy last night because you would not join him for his late meal. He desires you greatly."

"Only because I am queen, Enid. What warrior would not wish to become High King? To do so, he must win the quest and wed me. It is not my command; it is Odin's. No matter who the winner is, you will remain his slave; I promise."

Enid glared at Alysa before leaving without another word.

When Trosdan arrived to escort Alysa to the rings, she revealed Enid's visit and decided to contend with the problem today. Trosdan agreed.

Alysa stretched out on the bed to await Trosdan, who was finishing his guileful chores with the wounded. She had been tempted to pretend to assist the wizard while secretly slaying her helpless foes by poisoning or smothering them. Yet it seemed too cold-blooded and barbaric to kill an injured man. Also, she had been tempted to lessen her enemies' number by stealthily slaying as many as possible. But how could she safely dispose of their bodies? If men were found dead or missing, suspicions would arise and intrusive guards would be posted around camp, lookouts who could interfere with future ploys. She had to use caution, patience, and wisdom.

Suddenly she was exhausted and fell immediately asleep.

The matches began, and soon Eirik was battling another rival. Alysa was overjoyed when it ended within minutes with Eirik unscathed. His overly confident opponent had been no threat to him.

When the triumphant warrior left the ring, he also left

183

camp for a tension-releasing ride and to avoid Alysa while he cleared his head. Never had he faced such a dilemma in his life, to want a prize so desperately but to be unable to go after it and seize it! He had no one special in his life as all his family was dead. How good it would be to make a home and to have children with this enchanting goddess. If he did not win her, his emptiness would be even greater than it was now. What a strange and powerful emotion love was!

Ulf fought again, and slew another man. Rolf remained at his assigned ring to study his future combatants. And Einar's eyes seemed to trail Alysa's every move.

Alysa returned to her dwelling before the contest break for the men to eat and rest. She was thinking about Eirik as she strolled homeward. Sometimes he was so like Gavin, other times he was nothing like her husband. If only she could solve this mystery!

Alysa's early entry surprised Enid in her daring mischief. The woman was about to release the birds which the queen seemed to love so dearly. Alysa commanded sternly, "Nay, Enid!"

The captive whirled and paled. "I—I was a-about to feed them."

Calming herself, Alysa stated simply, "You lie. But I know the reason for your wicked deed. Be assured, I do not seek to steal Rolf from you. I know you love and desire him and wish to remain at his side."

"He has not wanted me since you arrived," the woman scoffed.

"I have found a way to prove to you I am not your enemy. If I help you with your love, will you keep our deed a secret?"

Enid locked the cage door and came forward. Her look

was one of mingled mistrust and intrigue. "Explain your meaning."

"First, you must promise to tell no one of our magic."

"Magic?" she echoed, her interest snared.

"Yea, a love potion for Rolf," Alysa clarified, and Enid smiled. "I will give you a vial of liquid which you can place in his food each time you desire to lie with him. It is powerful and must not be used too frequently. Once he has eaten the enchanted food, he will be unable to resist you for hours. You must be careful not to arouse his suspicions by using too much or too often. If I give you the love potion, will you forget your hatred of me and keep my gift a secret? If we were caught at such daring mischief, we would be tortured and slain."

"Will it truly work?" Enid asked eagerly.

"Yea, but use it with care. Even if he wins the quest and must wed me, at least you will have him to yourself until that day. Even after we are wed, I will allow you to use it when you wish and sneak into his bed to sate your desires. I have been wed before and I cared not for bouts in bed beneath a man. I will be glad for you to do that chore for me. The potion is dazing, so he will not guess you take my place." Alysa placed the vial from Trosdan in the slave's open hand.

Enid hid the vial in her pocket, then smiled at Alysa. She was convinced of the queen's words and was ecstatic over her good luck. "I will obey you, Queen Alysa. Ask anything of me."

"You serve me well, Enid. There is nothing more I need. I am glad you wish to do this chore for me. Rolf is handsome and kind, but I do not desire him as a man, only as a friend. Later I will have refreshments with him at his dwelling to prevent his suspicions when you use the potion on him tonight."

* * *

The evening round of battles ended with Rolf at her side. She smiled genially and asked, "Do you have wine you can share with me?"

Pleasure danced in his greenish-brown eyes as he nodded. He led her to his dwelling and invited her inside. Enid served them wine and small meat pies. They talked for a short time as Rolf related many of his past adventures and conquests, with Enid hovering nearby to seize any scrap of emotional food which was dropped by Rolf.

Alysa stretched languidly. "I must go. You need your rest. You are to fight again tomorrow."

Rolf escorted her to Eirik's dwelling, then returned to finish the cup of wine he had left on his table.

Within minutes, his loins ached for release. He stripped and lay on his bed. Visions of Alysa stormed his mind, and fiery passions consumed his body. He called to Enid, and the naked girl joined him.

For hours, Rolf made love to the slave girl, who was filled with gratitude to Alysa and with love for her Viking master.

Rolf battled during the afternoon, after sleeping late. Still amongst the winners, he went to his dwelling to ward off his unusual fatigue. Enid served him tea to enliven him, tea mingled with a special herb which Alysa had given to her today to invigorate Rolf.

By dusk, the second set of matches was concluded, leaving thirty-two men to pair off for the next one. Lots were drawn once more before the evening meal and rest period.

Afterward, Eirik fought and won his third match. Again he vanished from sight, convincing Alysa that he was indeed avoiding her. Yet his absence only increased her longing for him.

Rolf fought again, and won narrowly. Alysa summoned

Enid and cautioned the girl to hold off using the magical liquid until the contest was over, else a malevolent rival like Ulf could slay him. The slave girl agreed, smiling dreamily after her passionate night.

Within four hours the next day, contest three was finished, leaving sixteen men to pair off in each ring. As was expected by Trosdan and Alysa, Ulf won another match, leaving another enemy dead.

During the rest period, which had come early because of the end of round three, the remaining rivals practiced anxiously and refreshed themselves with stimulating food and ale.

One of the male slaves brought an armful of wood to Alysa's dwelling for heating water and to ward off the chill of an occasionally cool night. Alysa had been observing all the captives closely and felt she could trust this one. Hatred gleamed in his eyes for his foes, and she knew he had been whipped many times for defiance and scorn. After glancing outside to find no eyes on her abode, she closed the door and barred it. She told the baffled slave, "You must hide here until darkness, then I will help you escape our pagan enemies."

"What trick is this? I will be found and killed!" he argued with the queen of the men she was insulting and betraying.

"No one will search the queen's privy for a runaway slave. Conceal yourself there until I summon you. I am here to defeat these barbarians who rape and plunder our lands, but I may need the help of your people." Hurriedly, she revealed her ruse to the astonished blacksmith who had been captured to care for the Norsemen's horses and arms. "Tell your people to make weapons and to practice with them.

Carefully pass the word along to trusted men in other villages. If my forces fail to arrive or to defeat these vicious foes, the people of Logris must help me rid our isle of them. Soon, we will all be free and happy again. Expose me to no one, my trusted friend."

The prisoner was amazed by her shocking words, brave deeds, and cunning plan. He was inspired by them and by her enormous courage. "It is an insane plan, Your Highnesss, insane enough to work. I will do my part to aid you, but convincing others to defy our king and his wicked hirelings is another matter."

Alysa sent him a grateful smile for his honesty and courage. "Do your best, my friend; that is all I or our gods can ask of any man or woman. The moon will be high overhead before you can sneak away. The search for you will be over before that time. I must go now. Hide yourself and pray for victory."

Alysa went for a ride on Calliope. The animal was happy to be with his mistress, racing across the open land. Ever so often, she would rein him to catch his breath. While he did so, she stroked his neck and talked to him.

"Soon you will get plenty of exercise, Calliope." She spoke gently to her dun. "We will gallop far and wide on their foolish quest. I wish we could ride for hours today but they would wonder where we are. We must do nothing to arouse their suspicions, especially today. May the gods aid his safe escape and convince these peasants to help me end this tyranny."

She dismounted to walk a while. The dun trailed her with obedience and affection. When she stopped, she hugged his neck and her thoughts shifted to Eirik. "Did you see him, Calliope? Is he my lost love? You did not recognize his scent and touch. Should that warn me of peril? Have I placed a curse on our love by removing my wedding ring? said I would not do so until Gavin was lost to me forever. Can such a grim fate be mine? Trosdan said I had powers, but what are they? How can I bring them forth and use them? Why can I do nothing more than see things in dreams, things I do not understand and cannot control? If am so special and powerful, why can I not free my love of this evil spell? I have done no real magic, Calliope, only tricks which Trosdan taught me."

Alysa hugged her horse again as she murmured, "I am such a weak and foolish creature, for he stirs my blood as much as Gavin did. What am I to do if Eirik is not my lost love? What if this Viking warrior is my true destiny as Rurik was Giselde's? What if Gavin was driven from my side so would be driven to Eirik's? What of Gavin then?"

Alysa's gaze traveled past her beloved animal to settle on Eirik, who was poised in the distance upon an unknown horse. She made it apparent that she saw him, but he did not join her. Sighing heavily, she mounted and rode back to the settlement.

The first funeral pyre had completed its task and cooled enough for the ashes to be buried. Alysa gazed at the enormous black spot upon the ground. She wondered if those violent men thought nothing of killing and dying. How could they be duped so easily by clever lies and golden promises? By silly superstitions and curses and legends?

Before she left the corral, Eirik rode up and put away his horse. She glanced at him as he worked, then turned to leave without speaking. After all, he was the one being cold and distant.

"You should not ride alone, my queen," he softly scolded her.

"You were guarding me. Or were you spying on me?" she asked.

Eirik caught her frosty tone and understood it. "I was

189

protecting you, nothing more. I thought it rash to join you. Why look so sad?"

By that time, several men were within hearing distance. As if speaking casually, she remarked, "The deaths of so many of my warriors depresses me. The funeral pyre was too large and burned much too long for a friendly contest. You have spared your opponents; for that, I am glad. I do not understand how men die so easily and freely."

"Dying is not hard, my queen, if done with honor and a sword in your hand. From the time a man is born, he is trained to be a warrior, to die without fear or regret. He is taught to forget wounds during battles, to forget the weather and events around him. He must think of nothing except victory. If he must die, then he is happy to join Odin in Valhalla. To survive, he must train with all weapons and try to be the best with each one, including his bare hands. I have prepared myself for battle, and for death if necessary. That is our way."

"It is the Viking way, and I am Viking now. Soon I will learn all things about my people. To understand, I must ask questions."

"Ask what you will, my queen, of any man here."

"I have no more questions today. I must go prepare for tonight. You were kind to guard me and to enlighten me. Farewell, Eirik."

Before Alysa reached her dwelling, she witnessed the discovery of the blacksmith's daring "escape." Orders were given to search for the slave so he could be recaptured and punished. She was asked to check her abode to make certain the foolish thrall was not hiding there, and she pretended to do so.

When Enid brought her meal, she gave most of the food to the concealed man. She did not ask his name; that way she could not let it slip from her tongue and incriminate herself. "Soon the contest will continue and the search for you will be called off. They are convinced you are not in the settlement and are searching the surrounding areas. During the battles tonight, sneak to the stone temple on your belly. Wait there until all are asleep, then flee swiftly. May our gods protect you, my friend. Wear this to hide your light hair and shirt," she advised and handed him a dark-green cape.

The smithy smiled and thanked her. "If my body is not returned by midday on the morrow, you will know I have succeeded."

All of round four was fought that night, leaving eight men to pair off for round five in the morning. If the matches continued at this speed, rounds five, six, and seven would be carried out tomorrow, and one winner per ring would remain to compete the following day to leave three champions. That meant the contest would be over in two more days. Then the quest and attack loomed before her.

In the fourth match that evening, Rolf, Ulf, and Eirik all remained victors in their rings. Before parting for the night, lots were drawn for match five tomorrow.

As the combat period was short this evening, Trosdan left camp with several men who had been eliminated in battle. He went to gather healing herbs in the closest forest and glen, as certain ones had to be harvested at night for potency. To keep the Norsemen fooled, he still spent much of the time with his healing arts and tending the wounded.

Another funeral pyre was set ablaze, and the stench nearly sickened Alysa. Many gathered around it, and she stayed a while as if praying for the souls of her slain subjects. When she thought it all right, she slipped away from the smoky circle. She locked herself inside Eirik's dwelling

191

on the pretext of bathing and resting. The slave was gone. She prayed for his survival and success, and decided not to worry Trosdan by revealing her deed.

Shortly, she heard a soft tapping on the *eldhus* window from which she had watched Stonehenge and Eirik the other night. Surely none of her men would risk coming here! What if it was the escaped slave? She crept to it and asked nervously who was there.

When the manly voice said, "Eirik," her heart skipped a beat, then began to race madly. She wondered what she should do. This was insane. Exciting! Dangerous!

"I have something to give you," he said, keeping his voice low.

Alysa opened the shutters and asked, "What is it?"

The opening was not large enough for a person to slip through, but he could touch her. He captured her right hand and carried it to his lips. After kissing each fingertip and her palm, he pressed it against his bearded cheek. He felt her trembling, and himself.

Alysa watched his actions with a baffled gaze. His whiskers were soft against her hand, and she longed to caress every feature on his handsome face. His hair was mussed and fell across her hand, tickling it. Every part of him that touched her enticed her, enflamed her. Her voice was shaky as she inquired, "Why did you come here? It is mad to tempt fate. Go before you are seen."

His hand released hers so he could reach inside the small opening to caress her cheek, causing hers to slip to his bare chest. It remained there, as if she also needed their flesh to be together. Her contact was gentle, intimate. His was stimulating and possessive. "I had to touch you and see you closely, if only for a moment. I dream of nothing but the day when you are mine. If I lose this quest, I will not let another have you. I will steal you and carry you far away," he revealed to test her reaction to such a daring deed.

Alysa protested weakly, "You cannot. You must not. Fate is not battled like a foe. To challenge it is perilous. We must yield to it."

"I can yield to no power except the one you have over me. It is the force which drives me, the only force I cannot conquer."

"I have no power over you, Eirik. Fate controls me and my life."

"Nay, you have enchanted me," he accused in a husky voice. "Upon my honor, I have not used magic to ensnare you."

"You are magic, my beloved enchantress. I cannot resist you."

"Do not say or think such things. If it is not to be—"

He silenced her with a finger to her lips. "It must be, Alysa. We both know that. Yet we resist it as if it is wicked. How can love be evil? It is not something we can birth or slay at will. Surely you feel this bond between us, as if it has always existed and can never be broken. Something within me cries out that we are destined for each other. I have not known such feelings before; they have baffled and intimidated me. I have tried to control them, but they are too powerful, invincible. I do not want to imperil you or frighten you, but I cannot keep my distance any longer. I must win you or—" He sighed in frustration. "Or surely I will be incomplete without you."

His impassioned words and mood touched her deeply. But her dream at the castle . . . She murmured, "If you are here to entice my help with the quest, I cannot betray myself and my destiny. I cannot give you the riddles' answers."

"Is that what you saw in your dreams? That I would trick them from you with words of love?" Her look told him he had guessed right. "That is why you do not trust me and why you pull away each time we are drawn together. I swear, I will not ask you for your aid."

193

"There are other ways to ask for help than with words."

"You fear I will weaken you and steal them between kisses?"

"If I allowed myself to fall under your spell, I could not help but aid you. If you win, it must be done fairly."

Voices were heard, and the both of them knew Trosdan and his helpers were returning. Quickly, he kissed her and vanished into the shadows. Alysa closed the shutters and hurried to her bed. Without removing her kirtle, as she had already taken off her *bliaud,* she slipped under the cover.

When Trosdan entered, she sat up and smiled. "I am glad to see you home safely, Wise One. It is late."

Trosdan was distracted so he failed to notice the guilty look on her face. By the time he had put aside his cloth bags of herbs and turned to her, she had composed herself.

"I found many plants we can use, plants they do not know or understand. I will gather others when we ride northward, herbs to dull their minds during the feast. They will be unable to defend themselves when our forces attack. All foes will be slain and the threat to you and your land will be over."

That news did not overjoy her. It sounded as if they were planning a merciless slaughter of helpless victims. She had been here long enough to get to know many of these men, and she hated to think of murdering them while they could not defend themselves. Nothing was worse for a Viking than to die without a sword in his grasp. Yet these foes had to be slain or else they would continue their bloody and lethal raids. She had known of this requirement, yet she had not really thought about it. Too, the Norsemen had been strangers and foes when this ruse was planned; now, many were not . . .

Her mind raced in many directions at once. Trepidation filled her. What would happen to Rolf? To Enid? To Saeric

194

and Aidan? To her people during the attack? To Eirik, if he was not Gavin . . .

Trosdan read her concerns and cautioned, "Do not weaken now, my beloved princess. They are our foes and must be destroyed. If we do not complete this ruse, they will destroy us and other lands."

Alysa sighed heavily. "I know, Wise One, but it makes slaying them no easier. Are you certain you can slip the weakening herbs into their ale casks without endangering yourself? I do not want you harmed."

Trosdan smiled and entreated, "Do not worry. It will be simple."

"The quest should be completed in three weeks. Are you sure our people will be prepared to battle the Vikings by then?"

"Yea, my princess, and we shall triumph over them."

"Do you think my grandfather and King Briac have joined forces with our people?"

"I am certain of it. They know our plan is cunning. If they did not aid our cause, their lands would soon be imperiled. They are wise kings; they will join our struggle for survival."

She related her talks with Enid, and Trosdan was pleased.

"Sleep now, my princess, for tomorrow will be a long day."

The four matches in each ring took place within two hours after midday, ending the fifth round and leaving two matches in each to go. Saeric, Eirik's close friend, was eliminated without any severe wound. Lots were drawn again before the men rested for a while, as the remaining competitors would engage in three battles today.

Round six required a longer period, as these men were the best warriors in camp. The closer the men came to final victory, the fiercer the fights became. Aidan and Eirik were paired off in the same ring, alarming Alysa. She observed the match intently, fearfully. But Aidan soon realized that Eirik was the superior fighter between them and yielded before either of them was injured. By the time that round ended, Alysa's body was taut with anxiety. She could not help but wonder how Gavin would feel and behave if fate paired him with Weylin with her and a kingship at stake.

The remaining twelve combatants were weary and bloody, and desperate to continue their struggle for one of the three championships. Before the evening meal and break of several hours, lots were drawn for the seventh bout which would leave one victor per ring for tomorrow's final matches.

Alysa could not eat. She was too nervous. Eirik had one more fight today, then one tomorrow. If he could become a champion—

Enid encouraged, "Eat, Your Highness. I prepared this just for you." The slave girl set a small vegetable-and-meat pie on the table. "Why do you worry so? You know who the winners will be."

To conceal her motives and real fears, Alysa replied, "I know who Odin has selected and shown to me. But Loki has many evil powers. He always seeks ways to defeat his half brother Odin. Loki is cruel and deceitful, and he is clever. If he prevents Ulf, Eirik, and Rolf from winning, my people will think I am not a Seer. They will think I have misled them. If I am doubted and cast out, all is lost."

"With the other gods behind Odin, Loki cannot beat him."

Alysa glanced at the happy slave and asked, "Have you come to believe as the Vikings do? Have you cast aside your Celtic ways?"

"I love Rolf. I must believe as he does if he is to desire

me and keep me. Can I use the potion tomorrow night after the last fight?"

Alysa realized that the woman was utterly enslaved—physically and emotionally—by Rolf. "Yea, it will be safe to do so. After the three champions are chosen, we will rest for several days before we leave on the quest. If Rolf does not take you with him to serve him, you can have him each time a journey is over and he returns for the next riddle. Will that please you, Enid?"

The female smiled dreamily and nodded.

Alysa dressed carefully that night to look every inch the ruler of these people. Clad in a shimmering gown with flowing sleeves and skirt, she donned her Viking crown and many jewels. The greenish-blue shade of her garment enhanced her coloring and the cut of the gown with its low neckline and snug bodice was stunning and sensuous. Her cascading brown mane was unbound, and held in place with her golden circlet. With the dusty-blue powder from Trosdan, she lightly covered the area between her eyes and brows, making her eyes appear startlingly blue. She rubbed a pale-pink liquid over her lips, giving them more color and glow.

The matches began in the six torchlit rings. Sweyn, Rolf's friend, was defeated by a wound to his sword arm. Thorkel defeated his opponent by using the dagger which had belonged to Alysa, wounding Kirvan, another close friend of Rolf. As Alysa had told him when she gifted him with the dagger, it had saved his life.

Ulf viciously opposed his rival and ran his sword through the man's body. Afterward, he lifted it skyward and howled like a mad wolf. He growled and laughed and shook his broad shoulders, causing his long red lock to flop about upon his head. He seized a wineskin from a nearby man, threw back his head, and poured it down his throat. The red liquid overflowed his mouth and ran down his beard and chest.

Rolf fought long and hard, but won his match. He walked to where Alysa was standing at the edge of his ring and bowed to her, sending her an engulfing smile which exposed his burning desire for her. Even so, she realized how different he was from the offensive Ulf.

Two other warriors won in their circles: Horik and Olaf.

Alysa quickly moved to another ring where Eirik was furiously battling his rival. The men slashed at each other with glittering swords which sent off sparks like tiny bolts of lightning. The noise of their struggle was loud, often hurting her ears. As they labored inside the ring, firelight danced eerily on their bodies. Dust filled the cool night air as their boots moved swiftly upon the dry ground. Despite the gentle breeze, the men's exertions caused them to sweat heavily. Beads of moisture ran down their faces, their chests, their arms. Garments were soon damp and clingy. Determination filled their eyes and minds.

Both men received minor cuts and scrapes. The battle seemed to go on forever. Alysa tried to mask her fear and desire for Eirik, but it was difficult to maintain her self-control. She prayed that her presence was not distracting for Eirik, but she had to be there.

At last, the match ended. But this time, Eirik was forced to slay his opponent because the man refused to yield. Alysa noticed how swiftly and mercifully her warrior took his rival's life. Eirik walked to where she was standing and knelt before her.

"Forgive his death, my queen," he asked with a bowed head.

Alysa reached forward and touched his shoulder. "Arise, Eirik, his fate was of his own doing. You fought well, and I am pleased."

Before the man stood, Alysa turned to leave, not daring for their gazes to meet while others were staring at them. The crowd parted for her to walk to the dais. Standing in the midst of a large crowd of rough men, she said, "There are six opponents left: Olaf, Horik, Rolf, Eirik, Thorkel, and Ulf. Tomorrow they will battle until only three champions remain. We will have one large ring where the battles can be viewed by all. As with our great nine-year feast, this competition will require nine days. Surely that is a good omen. When the matches are over, we will celebrate with good food and drink. Then we must rest and heal for two days before we divide into three bands to begin our journey. May Odin's will be done."

In Rolf's dwelling, Einar, the Viking *attiba,* handed him a small mandrake root and instructed, "Wear it tomorrow and on the quest, but keep it hidden at all times. It has the power of invincibility, and the power to find treasure. It will assure your victories."

The handsome blond warrior gazed at the plant root which was in the shape of a human form. All believed that the mandrake possessed great power and magic, but few knew how to use it and most feared to even touch it. If not gathered correctly, it could strike a man dead. If used recklessly, it could destroy its owner. Rolf trusted his friend and adviser, and had faith in the man's alleged skills. He grinned.

It was near midnight when Ulf met secretly with his friends Thorkel and Horik. "Tomorrow we must slay Rolf, Eirik, and Olaf. We must become the leaders in this quest. We cannot let them live to give us trouble along the way. Eirik and Rolf both desire our queen. They will do anything to possess her, even challenge the champions or the quest. They must die tomorrow. Fight any way you must to win."

"With them dead, one of us will become High King and lay claim to the queen. She is a prize to die for."

"Yea, Horik, one of us will be king," Ulf vowed, knowing he would do anything—anything—to win this challenge.

Twelve

The next morning, lots were drawn by the six remaining warriors to determine their opponents and match numbers. One large ring was marked on the ground and the area was consecrated by Trosdan. The Vikings gathered and formed a human fence around the large circle where six fates would soon be decided. Queen Alysa was standing in the front of the crowd with Trosdan at her side. Einar, clad in his *attiba* garb, was nearby, as were the six rivals for her and the kingship.

Alysa was attired in a tunica of bold blue and yellow, her waist encircled by a jeweled belt with blue and red and green gems. The gownlike garment was sleeveless, revealing her supple arms. About her shoulders was a thin *sagum,* a cloak which was fastened by a decorative jeweled fibula at her right shoulder. All her garb was soft and flowing, giving the impression of grace and serenity. She was wearing leather sandals which overlapped her ankles and calves. Her hair was braided with tiny golden chains, the heavy plait left unsecured to hang down her back. Naturally her Viking crown from Trosdan was in place. She was glad the clever wizard had made suggestions for her wardrobe and had supplied many of the special items which created the desirable impressions on their foes.

Rolf looked handsome in his snug, earthy garments. His muscled body was clad in a short brown tunic with sand-colored borders at the hem and neckline and his tight brown pants were tucked into thin leather boots which climbed to his knees. There was a wide belt around his waist which displayed a large bronze buckle embossed with the image of Odin. It was easy to see that his body was hard and well toned. His arms and shoulders, exposed by the sleeveless tunic, seemed to shine as if greased lightly with a delicate oil. His white-blond hair was cut shaggy on the top and sides, as if to prevent it from falling into his eyes and blinding him at an untimely moment.

Alysa's gaze drifted to Eirik as the men readied themselves for competition. Eirik was wearing knee boots and a brown leather warrior's apron with side slits for easy movement. As with Rolf, his narrow waist was spanned by a wide leather belt with a carved buckle which depicted the god Thor in battle. It was his upper garment which seized most of her attention, as it was just the kind of accessory her husband would select. Very large bronze shields were strapped over the tops of his shoulders to protect them from sword blades. Its leather straps, which were buckled at his lower back, crossed in the form of an X over his chest, where another but smaller bronze shield guarded his heart, a place where no blue royal tattoo could be found. All three shields were skillfully decorated with symbols of the Viking deities. Her body trembled with raging desire for him.

As with Rolf, Eirik's hair had been cut this morning to keep it out of his face. His darker locks fell smoothly over his forehead and to his nape. It looked soft and shiny. She wanted to stroke its waves, to bury her fingers in its thickness.

It was clear Eirik's body had been honed for years with hours of daily attention. Hard and nimble muscles could be found beneath that sleek, tanned frame. His well-defined features gave him a breathstealing visage. His mustache was gone, but his short beard was not, making him look only as if he had not shaved in a long time, and causing him to appear more like Prince Gavin. His face and body were a golden brown, and she yearned to let her fingers travel both, slowly, sensuously. Alysa's gaze roamed down his arms to where his wrists were covered by leather armlets. She eyed his hands and envisioned them caressing—

Her gaze defensively shifted to Ulf, who was dressed in a short dark tunic with a white border at the hem. A fur mantle was thrown about his robust shoulders and held in place with a bronze brooch. A leather belt with large bronze buckle was secured about his thick waist. His feet were encased in heavy leather boots and his wrists in bronze armbands. Today, his red hair was knotted and twisted atop his head to make it stand erect to give him the illusion of more height. His facial hair had been removed except for two long sections of mustache which fell around his mouth and halted at his chest. He looked ominous, and struck fear in her thudding heart.

The signal was given for the first match: Rolf and Thorkel. The two men circled each other and crossed swords tentatively. Then the conflict began, fiercely, coldly, confidently on each's part. The heavyset warrior fought the blond one in a manner which indicated a life-and-death struggle, not unexpected considering the prizes which awaited the winner of the final battle. The conflict raged for over an hour with the loud, often ear-splitting, clanging of weapons filling the manmade arena. The combatants were evenly matched in skills and strength. It was obvious that the victor would be the warrior who made no mistakes in judgment and movement.

Anxiety chewed at Alysa, as she did not want Rolf slain, or her vision doubted. Thorkel fought as if he had forgotten the *volva*'s words which had included Rolf amongst the

203

three champions, along with Eirik and Ulf. Clearly he did not intend to lose this match, or to yield. The end came quickly when Rolf tripped his rival and sent his blade homeward to Thorkel's heart. Rolf glanced at Alysa and smiled broadly. After nodding in respect, he left the ring.

Time came for the second match. Ulf unfastened his brooch and removed his furry mantle. He chuckled as he tossed it to a friend to hold for him. With a cocky walk and smug grin, he stepped into the ring. He and his friend Horik had been paired, and his friend Thorkel was dead. Yet nothing, Ulf decided, would prevent him from becoming a victor in his match! The flaming-haired Viking grinned satanically. He did not care if Horik yielded and he hoped the man would not, as he must slay his carelessly acquired confidant to prevent future trouble with a disgruntled loser.

The battle got under way. For a time the friends fought casually, as if this were merely casual exercise. Horik seemed playful and at ease, and failed to use his superb skills and wits. Not once did he imagine the dark, evil thoughts which were consuming his companion and close friend of so many years.

Noting this careless and gullible flaw, Ulf pressed his advantage, as he knew Horik would not expect to be severely wounded, much less slain by him. In a tight clinche, Ulf whispered, "Fight, Horik. Make it look as if we care nothing except for victory or we look the fools."

The unsuspecting friend complied. The two men warred violently, and Horik was wounded in his sword arm. Still, the man continued with vigor and ignorance. When the moment presented itself, Ulf drove his sword through Horik's body with enmorous force. He cruelly twisted it as if trying to open up the man's belly and spill his innards to the bloodspattered earth. The wounded man gaped at the lethal wound, then at his grinning "friend." There was no time to speak a warning to others about Ulf's dark guile before Horik fell dead in the circle.

As he had done after each victorious match, Ulf lifted his sword heavenward and sent forth eerie wolf howls. He wiped the traitorous blade on his dead friend's tunic and walked to the man holding his mantle. Even though the day was warm, he tossed it around his shoulders and fastened it. With a triumphant grin, he swaggered to Alysa and said, "Soon, my queen, you will be mine."

In a calm voice, Alysa replied, "If it is the will of Odin, Ulf, so be it. You have shown yourself to be a superior champion, but I am distressed over your lack of mercy to your friend. He was wounded beyond more fighting. Why did you not let him live to heal, to ride with us another day?"

Ulf was enraged and embarrassed by her scolding before the others, but he masked his feelings. He lied easily. "When we battled closely, Horik said he wished to die or win. Since he could not win, his fate was sealed by his own words."

Alysa sensed the darkness and danger in Ulf and knew he was lying. Yet she said in a deceptively gentle tone, "I accept your words, Ulf, but his death still saddens my heart. For a warrior to reach this point in the contest proves he is a man of expert skills, skills we have need of in our imminent conflict for this land."

Ulf shrugged, as if throwing off any blame or guilt. "He died with a sword in his hand, my queen. He has joined Odin in Valhalla. What more can a slain man desire?"

"Nothing," Alysa responded, and smiled falsely at the cruel man.

It was after midday. The crowd dispersed to eat before the final match between Eirik and Olaf. After witnessing the bloody and fatal battles this morning, Alysa was frightened for the image of her lost love. She asked Trosdan, "Is

205

there nothing we can give Eirik or do for him which wil ensure his victory?"

"He will win," the old man replied confidently befor leaving to make certain Olaf was not strong enough to de feat Eirik.

Eirik and Olaf stepped into the human enclosure which had formed again to observe this final battle for a third champion. This match would test their prowess, in body and mind, and would determine their fates.

Alysa glanced at each man and gave the signal to begin She was tense, unnerved by the thought of her love's imag losing his life. She tried to conceal any telltale reactions to Eirik and his peril.

Olaf's gaze was mocking, defiant. He eyed his rival who was standing with shoulders squared proudly and with boot firmly planted apart and watching him with that same in tense and probing gaze. He studied Eirik's movements in an attempt to outguess his opponent, to catch him unaware for just an instant.

Eirik was doing the same. He knew what was at stake in this battle, and it was much more than his human exist ence. He noted how Olaf held his sword, the sun glistening off the sharp blade. He observed the man's movements and tactics; and he always watched Olaf's eyes, for it was there where attacks and errors could be first sighted.

Sword was assaulted by sword, slashing, charging, par rying. Each evaded the other's sharp blade with deft handi work and nimble feet. Rapid and masterful blows were deflected to their rights and lefts, before their faces and legs. Each knew that a simple split-second delay in retali ation or defense could cost him his life, or severe injury Each knew this probably would be a life-and-death struggle as had been the two previous contests. Each hungered to win, but each was prepared to die while seeking victory.

Remaining on full alert, the two warriors circled each other while battling fiercely and confidently. The sun glistened off their sweaty bodies. Damp hair clung to determined faces, strong necks, and powerful shoulders. The men fought with enthusiasm, dedication, and greed. Olaf slashed at Eirik, who averted the charge by quickly stepping aside. Eirik's avid blade followed his movement and sliced across Olaf's right forearm.

Olaf briefly glanced at the minor injury, and chuckled. His mind and body felt light, invincible . . . He pretended to begin an upward swing with his weapon, only to halt it and jab at Eirik's stomach. Eirik was swift and alert to the cunning tactic; he defeated the movement with a skilled parry.

Eirik knew that a wounded man was dangerous and desperate, so he paid close attention to his temporary foe. The keenly alert Eirik noticed the glint in Olaf's eyes, a strange gleam which implied his foe was possessed by some unknown spirit or force, or perhaps the evil god Loki. The men used most of the large circle as they fought to and fro. Each time they came near the human fence, the observers were careful to avoid injury.

Suddenly, Olaf's sword was knocked from his wet grasp. As he leaped to the ground to recover it, he entangled Eirik's legs and sent his rival sprawling and his sword flying away. The two men fought upon the ground, thrashing wildly and urgently for the upper hand. Although both men possessed great stamina and brute strength, fatigue and the strain of a crucial battle were exposed in their taut faces and bodies. Their labored breathing and grunts of exertion could be heard in the stillness which surrounded them.

As the men came to their feet, Eirik threw his shoulder into Olaf's unprotected gut, causing a rush of air to leave the man's lungs and knocking him back to the ground. Eirik jumped on him, and the two rolled again upon the ground in a desperate scuffle. Eirik flung Olaf aside and scrambled for his sword. With waning energy, the handsome warrior knew he should end this conflict as soon as possible. When a man became fatigued, he made mistakes, costly mistakes.

Olaf lunged for Eirik's legs and, grabbing one ankle, tripped him before he reached his shiny weapon. With hard kicks from agile feet and staggering blows from powerful shoulders and hands, the fight continued. Both men seized knives from their sheaths. Olaf slashed upward in an attempt to carve open Eirik's chest and abdomen, but Eirik diverted the blow with his leather armlet, resulting in a minor cut. While doing so, Eirik nicked Olaf's sword arm, a deep cut which sent blood flowing down the man's arm. Rapidly, Eirik slammed his back into Olaf's and knocked the man off balance. With speed and skill, Eirik slashed Olaf's calf muscle.

Eirik surprised everyone when he backed away to allow Olaf time to consider surrender. The rival cut a strip from his tunic and bound his wound. Struggling to his feet, Olaf playfully motioned Eirik forward to resume the fight. Eirik wondered why no one else seemed to notice Olaf's curious behavior and expression; to him, the man looked as if he were drunk, though not on spirits.

It was clear to everyone that Eirik had the advantage, but was being patient and cautious with the injured man. Olaf recovered his sword and charged Eirik, shouting loudly and stumbling awkwardly as he did so. He slashed wildly and frantically, but Eirik avoided the blows. Soon it was apparent that Olaf would not yield, and it was foolish to continue a battle where reckless errors could be made by underestimating a wounded opponent. Either Eirik could slay Olaf or cruelly play with the man until he was exhausted.

Eirik called out, "Yield, Olaf. Do not force me to slay you. Live to battle another day," he urged.

Olaf sneered at his rival. "Nay! It is to the death of one of us. I have tasted victory and cannot live with defeat. Fight or die!"

"So be it," Eirik replied reluctantly. Eirik whirled with lightning speed and sliced his sword across Olaf's throat, ending the man's misery.

Olaf collapsed to the ground, dead. A roar of cheers went up for Eirik, for showing mercy and for winning his match.

Unaware she had been holding her breath in the last few minutes, Alysa exhaled with relief. Eirik did not look her way, and she wondered why, as Rolf and Ulf had acknowledged her after their victories. Perhaps Eirik was angry because he had been forced to slay a friend.

Einar walked into the ring. As he turned, he shouted, "It is true; our queen is a *volva*. From over seven hundred warriors whom she had never seen battle before, she revealed the three champions. Truly Odin speaks to her and through her. Long live Queen Alysa!"

The crowd immediately picked up the words and chanted them over and over. Alysa smiled and nodded to every man whose eye she captured. In spite of her faith in Trosdan, she was amazed by the accuracy of his predictions, and relieved to have her status as a Seer proven. Finally the chanting ceased, but the people were still stimulated.

Einar asked, "Is there more you see in our future, my queen?" He hoped that his deceptive status would not be exposed. Whatever it took, he must not make enemies of Alysa and Trosdan. He was amazed by their powers and insights, and he believed in them, envied them.

Prepared for this moment, Alysa commanded, "We must rest for two days, tend our wounded, and get ready for our journey. All who can must ride with us on this great quest. We shall divide into three groups, with a champion to lead each one. Friends may go with their chosen leader; others will draw lots for their band number. On the third morning from this joyous day, we will gather here for Trosdan to give us the clues from Odin for our first quest. Each band will seek the hidden treasure, then return to camp for the next quest. Do not forget," she cautioned the three victors who had been gently shoved into the ring, "you are responsible for safeguarding each treasure you find. You may use any means, save death, to steal it from another."

With greedy eagerness shining in his eyes, Ulf asked, "Why can we not leave tomorrow for the first quest? We are warriors and have no need for rest. The wounded can join us on later journeys."

Alysa noticed that Ulf and Rolf's gaze was focused on her face, but Eirik was eyeing the ground as if paying little or no attention to her and her words. She explained cleverly and convincingly, "Trosdan, who is a wise and skilled wizard, says the stars and planets will be in fated alignment Friday; we need that good omen when beginning our glorious task. We must wait for Odin's signal. Do you not agree, my people?"

Firm believers in the power of astrology, the crowd concurred with her. Einar shouted, "We must heed their words for Odin sent them here to lead us. Do as our queen and *attiba* say and a glorious victory awaits us."

Alysa smiled at Einar and went on. "Before we depart we must release the slaves, as they cannot be trusted to be left here with our defenseless wounded and we cannot take time or men to feed and guard them. Different warriors will be selected to remain here as guards during each quest to tend and protect those who cannot travel. Tonight, we must celebrate the victories of our three champions. Have the slaves prepare food and drink. At dusk, we will feast."

Another round of cheers filled the air. The Vikings were eager and ready for a celebratory feast and the upcoming quest. Following the seven hundred and seventy-one contests, one hundred and eighty foes were either dead or wounded. That left close to two hundred men for each band, unless more were slain or injured during the quest. Almost six hundred healthy Norsemen still presented enormous odds and prowess for her countrymen to battle soon.

Alysa turned and left the area with Trosdan at her side. She entered Eirik's dwelling and sank wearily to his bed. She closed her blue eyes and inhaled deeply several times to release her tension. She realized she had not given her husband much thought lately and knew why: she believed Eirik was Gavin Crisdean and her love was within close proximity of her. But, she fretted, what if Eirik was not Gavin? Nay, she told herself, it had to be true! Her love was here with her!

She sat up and looked at Trosdan, who was gathering items from his bundles. "You picked the winners, Wise One. I fear there were times when I doubted your skills and insights, but they have come true. Forgive my weaknesses."

The elderly man smiled and responded, "Good fear is not a weakness, my sweet princess. It makes one careful and alert. The Runes never lie or deceive; they revealed such things to me."

"If only they would reveal the truth about Gavin to us," she murmured, then reclined once more.

"There is a reason why such news is kept from us; perhaps it would harm us during this perilous time. Perhaps it is his destiny. Trust me and our gods, Alysa, and all will be right again."

"You are good and kind, Trosdan, and I do trust you and the gods. But it is hard not knowing of Gavin's fate and whereabouts. Worse is not knowing if Eirik is my lost husband and what has happened to him. If only I could make certain—"

"Nay, my princess. If you learned that Eirik is your enpelled mate, it could imperil all we have worked for not to mention our lives. Your love for him would be exposed by accident or intention. If this warrior is Gavin, he does not know it. If you rashly enlightened him, he would think us mad, liars, beguilers, dangerous foes. Until the truth is revealed, you must accept him as Eirik and treat him as Norseman."

"I will obey," she replied in a dejected tone.

Trosdan warned sternly, "Be on guard at all times, my princess. Ask him no suspicious questions and make no reckless hints. Living as a Viking, Eirik would betray us even if he is your enchanted Gavin."

"It will be as you say, Wise One," she vowed.

"I must release the second bird to take a message to Lord Weylin. It will tell him the contests are over and the quest is to begin in a few days. He will send word to the other kings, and all will prepare for the joint attack. Our cunning task will be over in three weeks. Once victory is ours, I will help you find your lost love."

Alysa smiled with misty eyes and thanked him.

The Druid said, "Rest a while, then bathe for the feast. I must go and slip potions into the wine casks to test their strength. It is to our favor if you bewitch them with your beauty tonight. Plagued by a thirst for you, the men will drink heavily and sleep like death all night, if the potion is strong enough and I use the right amount. Do not drink from the casks, only from the wineskin which I will give to you. While they are lost to this world, I must go to the sacred temple of standing stones and offer a sacrifice to our gods. There, I must fast and pray all night for divine guidance and protection during the quest. Bar the door before you sleep, as I will not return until dawn."

The feast was noisy with laughter, singing, and talking. Large quantities of food and drink were consumed, by Vi king and captive alike. Alysa remained at the wooden table which had been prepared for her, eating and drinking only what Trosdan placed before her. As high-spirited men came by, she chatted genially and pretended to be having a time of great enjoyment.

Rolf and Ulf both stayed at her side, as if smugly exposing their claims on her. When Eirik made no appearance and she grew weary of entertaining the two bantering champions, she politely excused herself to stroll around to visit the wounded. As she moved about the large settlement, she wondered where Eirik was. His absence was obvious and distressing. Surely others would notice it and be curious.

She recalled the last time they had touched, and it warmed her body. The burdens on her were enormous, and she was lonely and intimidated. She longed to be held in his soothing arms and to make love to him. Her body ached for his and her spirits were low. He had bruised her heart deeply with his mysterious departure, and his selfish actions before it. Did Gavin truly love her? Did he miss her? His disappearance was a bitter desertion to her when she needed him most. At times, her tightly leashed anger toward him surfaced anew, but mostly she missed him and yearned for his return. If only they could have a few moments alone to talk, to steal a few kisses and caresses . . .

Alysa noticed how the crowd was thinning rapidly and the noise was lessening. Obviously Trosdan's herbal potion was working by now. The drunken and drugged men were retiring for the night in their dwellings or falling asleep anywhere the potion took effect. She headed for the table to bid her people good night.

The moon was high overhead, so the hour was late. With all the strong spirits the men had consumed and the time of night, no one should suspect Trosdan's deceit. Rolf and Ulf had gone their separate ways during her absence, but the Druid was waiting for her.

As he walked her to her dwelling, he reminded, "Do n¢ forget to bar the door. I will be at the stone temple unt the sun rises, praying and seeking the aid of our gods. have taken a lamb to sacrifice, and I must consult the star The gods are on our side, Queen Alysa, so fear nothing an no one. The quest will be victorious."

The wizard's choice of words was fortunate, as neithe noticed the figure standing in the darkness near the corne of the longhouse.

Trosdan fetched his belongings for his rituals and de parted. She watched him walk toward the awesome sigl of towering stones. She glanced around her. It was qui¢ and peaceful. Nearly all were asleep.

Rolf had not consumed enough of the treated ale to b disabled for the night. Yet Enid had laced his last drin liberally with the love potion from Alysa. Intoxicated wit lust and his loins enflamed, he hurriedly stripped Enid wit insistent hands. The blond Viking tossed his willing captiv upon his bed and fell atop her, driving his fiery manhoo into her. He labored urgently to appease his savage nee¢ He could not seem to have enough of her, taking her ove and over until he was exhausted. Still unsated and arouse¢ she worked upon his body with skilled hands and lips, giv ing him blissful pleasure and relief.

After pacing the floor and downing the remainder of th wine in the leather skin to relieve her anxiety, Alys stretched out on her bed garbed in a soft kirtle. Her hea was spinning dreamily from fatigue and the heady win¢ As visions of Gavin filled her mind, her body flamed wit desire and ached for his touch.

A soft knock came at the door. Drowsy, she glanced th.

way but did not move. It came again. She thought Trosdan must have overlooked something, as all others should be slumbering deeply. She left the bed and unbarred the door. Opening it, she smiled and asked, "What did you forget, Wise One? I was nearly asleep."

It was Eirik, fully alert and looking troubled. He stood there, staring at her, silent, moody, mysterious. Alysa tried to clear her wits and keep her poise. "What is it, Eirik?" she inquired, her voice quavering and her body trembling. "Where have you been?"

Still he did not move or speak. His intense stare made her unsure of herself, enflamed. "Is something wrong?" she asked.

Eirik grasped the edge of the door and pushed it aside so he could enter. Alysa stepped backward without protest, intrigued and enchanted. Eirik closed and barred the door. He turned to face her. He seemed to be waiting for something, some word, some sign.

The candle burning near her bed cast a romantic glow in the room and on his handsome face, on her beloved husband's image. His searching gaze roamed her features, and consternation was exposed there. He looked as if he had just awakened from a dream. "I had to come," he murmured softly, his voice sounding like water moving tranquilly through a brook.

"Why?" she inquired just above a whisper.

As if dazed, he confessed. "You have bewitched me, my beautiful enchantress. I cannot get you off my mind. I know it is perilous to tempt fate, but I cannot help myself. My heart aches and my body burns for you. I feel as if I cannot breathe or survive if I do not make you mine. I rode swiftly for many miles trying to cool my fiery passions and to clear my muddled head. It did not work. The farther I traveled from you, the more panic I felt. I could not stop myself from rushing back to your side. Forgive my boldness in

215

deed and word, but I am ensnared in a trap which I cann
escape. Nor do I wish to flee. I need you, Alysa, more tha
air or food or victory."

Alysa engulfed him with her loving gaze. She was weak
ened and enthralled by his physical changes. With shorte
hair and a cleanly shaven jawline, he was Gavin Crisdea
to her. . . . It had been many weeks since she had lain wit
Gavin, and it seemed to be her husband—her lost love—
whom she was seeing tonight, hearing this very momen
reaching out to her. A fierce and irresistible hunger gnawe
at her. Her loneliness and misery faded, and her wits de
serted her. She lifted her hands and cupped his face, bring
ing it downward to fuse their lips in answer to his unspoke
question.

Eirik's arms banded her body and held her possessivel
as his mouth ravenously assailed hers. His lips eagerly trav
eled her face and neck, then returned to hers. One enticin
kiss dissolved into another until they were both breathles
and quivering. He lifted her and carried her to the be
lowering her at its side and fusing their gazes. Their eye
exposed their urgent desires, their willingness to challeng
fate, their search for love.

Without hesitation or inhibition, Alysa removed her gow
and stood before him naked, her golden body revealed i
the candlelight. Boldly she removed his tunic as she ha
done to Gavin in the past, the missing tattoo never enterin
her mind to warn her to halt her rash deed; nor did the sca
upon his shadowed cheekbone stay her hands. Her hand
and lips roved his chest and neck, leaving a trail of ho
kisses and stirring caresses behind.

Eirik moaned in rising desire. Never had he imagine
she would respond so eagerly, so freely, so ardently, as
she, too, were uncontrollably drawn to him. He remove
his clothing and pressed their naked bodies together. Th

ontact staggered their senses. They sank to his bed, locked
n a lover's embrace.

He smiled into her softened gaze and drove any remain-
ng hesitation from her mind. He pulled her tightly and pro-
ectively against his hard body, and she heard the thundering
f his heart. "You have captured my heart and thoughts,
my beautiful enchantress. Even if the gods slay me for this
ffense, I must have you this night."

Alysa looked into his smoldering green eyes and read
he truth of his words written there. "As I must have *you*
onight," she replied.

His lips fused with hers as they explored her sweet sur-
ender. At that moment, he desired her more than any treas-
re, more than any honor, more than his life. He felt her
very soul cry out for his possession. She wanted him to
onquer her, to make their bodies one.

Alysa's arms encircled his torso and her fingers drifted
p and down his back, a back which was so familiar to her.
t was wondrous to have him in her arms again. It was
timulating to make love to him, to have him make love to
er. Her mind whirled with pleasure as he stormed her
enses. His touch, his nearness, were all consuming.

Her body tingled with blissful sensations, as did his. She
was alive again. She was happy again. She was where she
belonged again. His hot breath teased over her face and
body, causing her to tremble with anticipation. Her starving
body was sensitive to his caresses, susceptible, aroused. As
f discovering his virile body in her dreamy mind, her fingers roved it leisurely, enticingly, skillfully. She knew what
pleased her husband, and she touched him in those ways.
There seemed no inch of him which she did not caress or
kiss. His bronzed body was enchanting to her. She could
not get him close enough, taste him enough, touch him
nough.

His mouth feasted at her breasts and made her writhe

upon his bed. Rapturous feelings assailed her and daze
her. His wild, sweet caresses drove her mad with pleasur
creating a greater hunger by the minute.

His deft fingers trailed over her fiery flesh, halting her
and there to labor lovingly in special areas. Yet her flame
were not extinguished, only brightened. Moans escaped he
parted lips. Her fingers buried themselves in his dark-blon
hair. Her mouth placed kisses everywhere they could reacl
She shuddered when his experienced and gentle finger
stimulated her woman's domain. She sensed his arousa
Closing her hand around his manhood, she brought forth
deep groan from his lips. She wanted to prolong this tar
talizing stage of lovemaking, but her body would soon b
consumed by the fires which were blazing out of contro
within her. She urged him to take her, to reclaim his los
treasure.

For Alysa, this union was too long awaited, too long de
nied, too long anticipated since finding her love again. Sh
murmured, "Take me now, Eirik, or I shall die of need fo
you. For this night, I am yours."

For Eirik, this was their first union of bodies. He ha
craved this woman since first sighting her. She had be
witched him, enticed him, tormented him. Hunger for he
had been driving him wild. She was his queen. She was hi
enchantress. She was his life, his fate, his dreams. Surel
he would cease to exist if he could not have her. He wante
to give her great pleasure this first time, and he was amaze
by how enflamed she was by him.

Eirik entered her, and never had he experienced anythin
so wonderful, so special. His hands imprisoned her beautifu
face. He stared into her enslaving eyes as he set the rhythr
which would bring both of them blissful release. He ha
not bedded a woman in a long time and his loins ached fo
sweet relief. But his heart ached for something more tha
mere physical pleasure. The need to win this woman as hi

own was overwhelming. She was a rare creature who could fill all his needs. He had enjoyed and sought no woman's company more than he longed for hers. No other woman had captured his eye and heart, not since meeting this one. Only Alysa could arouse and sate him.

His body moved with skill. He brushed his lips over her face, then fused their gazes once more. This was the only woman he needed and wanted, now and forever. Even if it was because she had cast a magical spell over him which caused him to respond only to her, he did not care. He watched passion's glow brighten her cheeks and daze her blue eyes. Happiness filled him in knowing she enjoyed his actions, ached for more of them.

Alysa relented to his powerful spell. She was mesmerized by his enticing gaze and intoxicated by his lovemaking. Her body moved in unison with his, and he smiled disarmingly. She clasped his face and lowered it so their mouths could labor with their bodies. Ravenously, she kissed him as her stunning release came forth.

Eirik's mouth muffled the cry of bliss which would have escaped her lips and possibly been overheard. The intensity of her release overjoyed him. He cast aside his weakened self-control and plundered her lips and body as he had plundered many countrysides. He guided them over crest after crest until passion's flood subsided, then held her in his embrace, unwilling to release her even for a moment. His fingers tenderly roamed her damp flesh and his lips pressed to her hair. She was perfection; she was his. Nothing and no one would ever change that fact, he vowed.

Alysa snuggled against him and smiled tranquilly. Soon, he was slumbering quietly in his arms.

Eirik gazed into her radiant face, still flushed from their union. His green eyes traced the curves of her naked body. She was cuddled against him where she belonged! Was it possible, he wondered, that she had truly bewitched him?

219

If not, why had he been unable to sate his needs with other women? If he was not to be the quest victor and she knew that fact as a *volva,* why had she yielded to him tonight? He had overheard her words to Ulf and Rolf: "I vow, only my husband will touch me and claim me." Was it a sign, or a weakness for him? If he was not to be the winner, would she give up her rank and destiny to escape with an adventurous warrior? Was that too much to ask of a High Queen? Too great a sacrifice to expect? What if she only desired him as a man, but did not love him? Or love him enough to choose him over her crown? She seemed totally committed to her destiny, to obeying Odin. If he abducted her, could he flee with her without getting caught and slain by his people? The days ahead would supply his answers.

There was soft knocking at the door. Alysa and Eirik came to instant wakefulness, their gazes locked on each other. With a look of panic and disbelief on her face, she stared at him. She did not know what to do. Had she actually slept, made love, with Eirik? What if he was not Gavin Crisdean? At this moment, he was nothing like her husband. He was only a tempting stranger, a beguiling Norseman. Where and why had her wits deserted her? This was both foolish and perilous!

Eirik knew he could not stain her honor by being found naked like this with her. He had not meant to fall asleep beside her, but it had seemed so natural and easy to do so. If discovered, Odin's wrath would not even compare to that of any outraged Vikings! He rapidly reasoned on their problem, then pulled her close and whispered, "I will hide in the woodbox in the *eldhus* until I can slip out later. Come help me."

He rose quickly, donned his garments, and rushed into the kitchen area. He climbed inside a large woodbox which fortunately was empty, as Alysa had dropped the logs into the privy pit to conceal the runaway slave's visit. He told her to throw a fur covering over him.

Alysa hurriedly pulled on her kirtle and checked the room for any sign which would expose her wild and crazy mischief. She went to the door and unbarred it, rubbing her sleepy eyes and yawning.

Trosdan entered, and was fooled by her behavior. "I should have slept at the temple and not disturbed your sleep, my beloved princess. The Runes have spoken to me. I will share their news with you."

Horror flooded Alysa as she realized her Viking lover was hiding nearby and would overhear anything they said.

Thirteen

Alysa was relieved when Trosdan said, "I will visit the wounded to see if any man needs tending, then nap a few hours. Return to bed and sleep, my princess, for you look very tired. After we are refreshed, we will talk." Trosdan gathered some items and left again.

Alysa leaned against the door and sighed heavily. Her heart was pounding in fear, and from guilt. She hated deceiving the old man, but she knew what he would think of her wickedness. She angrily scolded herself for being so weak last night, as her actions could complicate this dangerous situation. Foolishly she had allowed herself to forget Eirik was not Gavin Crisdean, at least in mind. She did not even want to imagine the consequences of her wanton behavior.

Eirik threw aside the covering and rushed to her side. He gathered her trembling body in his arms and embraced her. He knew how frightened she must be and he wanted to comfort her. If anyone learned of their passionate adventure, they would both be imperiled. Loving her fiercely, he could not allow any harm to befall her, or to tarnish her golden image. He had achieved much with his impulsive visit; he had unleashed her love for him and had revealed his love for her. Now that they were one in body and spirit, nothin could part them or come between them. With tormenting tenderness, he whispered into her ear, "Do not fear, my beautiful enchantress. I will sneak out while he is gone. I will let no one see me and I will tell no one of last night. We will talk when it is safe." He captured her pale face between his hands and kissed her very gently, urgently. Eirik peeked outside and, sighting no one about yet, slipped out the door and closed it.

Alysa collapsed upon the bed. She felt weak with fear and indecision. Eirik's manly odor assailed her warring senses. She turned over the pillow to prevent it from arousing her already heightened desires. She wanted Eirik to remain here with her, but that could not be. She yearned to talk seriously with him, to open his mind to the truth, to seek comfort and passion and assistance from him. She was fascinated by Eirik, and she wondered how much of Gavin's personality and character were in him, things about her husband which she had not been given time to discover. She liked this unknown side of her love, and she hoped he remained this way when the spell over him was broken.

Gavin loved this kind of life, which offered him excitement and danger and challenges. Would he become bored, restless, and moody again when it was over and his spell was broken, a spell which made him compliant to her? Was that why fate had bewitched him? Gavin would have battled these foes head on, and probably lost all. He had refused to believe victory must be won with wits, daring, and guile. She doubted she could have found a way or words to convince him of that truth. Had the fates made certain he would cooperate?

When it was all over, would Gavin leave her again to seek more adventure and daring deeds? She had to admit that she liked him better this way, as Eirik, or as the mysterious warrior she had first met months ago. She liked being accepted for herself and being included in on all matters, not being the woman Gavin wanted her to be after their marriage. Why could he not stay like this?

If he was Gavin . . . She trembled in alarm and confusion. She had made love to no man except her husband. After her passionate night with Eirik could that claim still be true? She closed her misty eyes and prayed that he *was* Gavin. If not, how could he ever forgive her for lying with another man, a fierce enemy? How could she ever forgive herself for such a weakness? Or forget Eirik?

She wondered, too, what Eirik would do now that he had possessed her? How would he behave before others and to her? Did he view her surrender as love? As her choice of him as victor and mate? As a means of help with the quest, which he did not know was false? If she refused to aid his cause or if he did not win, would he threaten her? Betray her? What if her forces did not arrive or did not win their battle? What if Ulf or Rolf won the quest and no one appeared to save her? What if Eirik won, but he was not Gavin and no help arrived in time? Could she wed him and continue this farce until . . . Until what?

Trosdan had warned her to stay away from that perilous entanglement. She had promised to obey. In a moment of weakness and need, she had fallen prey to Eirik's irresistible charms, to his likeness to her lost love. Alysa bolted upright in bed and frowned worriedly. Except for adding the missing royal tattoo and removing his facial scar, it was almost as if Eirik had made himself appear more like Gavin before trying to ensnare her! If such was true, how much did he know about her and her husband? Had the cunning warrior practiced disarming guile on her? Was he a weapon which the dark forces sent here to defeat her?

Alysa frantically deliberated this predicament. There was no way she could discover if Eirik was an enspelled Gavin. What if her love had been snatched by the dark forces and was being held captive somewhere while this replica enchanted and defeated her? Shape-changing was known to happen, but it was dangerous, as a man or force could be entrapped forever in that chosen body. Who was this man, this demon or spirit, who had stolen her love's image to dupe her?

Yet perhaps he was Gavin, but a Gavin deeply entranced. How could she free him? Free him before he destroyed her without knowing the truth about them? She could not risk enlightening him, as he would not believe her. How clever of Evil to use Gavin against her! Evil knew she would surrender to him! Evil knew she would never harm him even to save her own life!

There was only one way to protect them and to prevent a disaster with this task. She must avoid Eirik. Yet that would not be easy. She had to be careful not to arouse the curiosity of others or to vex Eirik with her behavior. If he was sent here to entrap her, he would be hard to dissuade. But if he was a bewitched Gavin, she had to protect him until she could break the spell over him. If he was not, should she ask Trosdan to end his threat and magical pull? Nay, she could not avoid him, but she must resist him. If only the gods would reveal his true identity and motives . . .

Alysa heard Trosdan at the door. Quickly she snuggled beneath the cover and pretended to be asleep. He entered quietly and went to his pallet. Soon, his breathing told her he was slumbering. A sudden fatigue claimed her, and she cleared her mind to enter the beckoning blackness.

Another series of knocks at the door awakened Alysa and Trosdan near midday. Trosdan left his comfortable pallet and answered it to find Enid standing there with their meal. Hungered by the delectable aromas, he invited her inside, and she placed the food on the table. Trosdan followed her.

He remained in the *eldhus* area and drew a curtain for Alysa's privacy.

The smiling captive approached the rising Alysa and whispered, "It was wonderful last night, my generous queen. This time, he called my name, not yours," she happily divulged as she straightened the bed.

Putting aside her memories of last night, Alysa smiled. "This is good, Enid. I am happy for you. Perhaps the love potion works on more than his physical passion. Perhaps he loves you and does not realize it. You are a strong and special woman, but a captor does not expect to fall in love with his slave. He sees me as a path to the kingship, so he pursues me. Give him more time to understand and accept such feelings. No matter what happens, Rolf will be yours."

"Do you think he will marry me if he does not win you?"

Alysa whispered conspiratorially, "We will make certain of it."

The Logris captive left with glowing eyes and cheeks. Alysa joined Trosdan and took her seat. "All goes well with Enid. She is happy and duped. She will hate me when this task is over, for her love will be dead, lost to her forever in this world. I wish Rolf were not a Viking foe, as he is a good and kind man and Enid loves him."

Trosdan stopped eating to remind her, "He must be slain with the others, for he is a strong man who could not accept our friendship and truce. He would seek revenge upon us, and he knows the truth about you. This task is to free you of all threats from your Viking ties. If but one lives, so will your peril."

"Yea, Wise One, I know that truth only too well."

"Do not look so sad. Remember, they are enemies."

She admitted, "We have spent too much time amongst them. Many have endeared themselves to me. Their deaths will come hard."

"It is only because we have lived amongst them as

friends, as queen and *attiba*. If such were not true, we would despise them. You have not forgotten how they attacked your land and others, wantonly destroying all in sight, pillaging and burning and raping. They are cruel and brutal men. Their greed is evil and powerful. They prey on others who are weaker than themselves. Think of what your fate would be if you were not their queen, only their captive or helpless victim. Think of the danger to your children when they are born. You do not want your son or daughter stolen by them and raised as a Viking, to rule barbarians far away instead of ruling your subjects here in Britain."

"Such words are true, Wise One, but they trouble me. By blood and heritage, these are our people, yours and mine. If things had not been changed for us by fate years ago, we would not feel this way. We would think and feel and behave as they do."

The old man reasoned gently, "But fate *did* intervene, my princess. We were born to defeat the forces of Evil. We must be strong, for we represent the forces of Good."

"Good?" she echoed. "How do we know what is good or bad? What is good for one is bad for another. We kill them, or they kill us. Murder is murder, Wise One. Where does the difference lie?"

"You know the truth and the difference, my beloved princess, without me explaining," he said, and she did.

Alysa and Trosdan finished their meal, but remained at the table. When Trosdan spoke again, his words stunned Alysa.

In a grave tone, he revealed, "As I fasted and prayed last night, the Sacred Runes spoke to me. The gods knew you were weakening and sent this message to you. They said, be strong, Alysa, for your love awaits your reunion. He will be with Lord Weylin when they attack our foes at Stonehenge and will share in our great victory. Nay, Gavin will lead it. You shall be reunited at the stone altar in the sacred temple and never parted again."

Alysa gaped at the wizard. This could not be true! Must not be true! If so, she had . . . The gods had sent their message too late! Was that why Evil had tempted her last night? Gavin was coming with Weylin and their joint forces? He was at home preparing for this momentous event while she was surrendering passionately to Evil? Nay, her warring mind argued, it could not be true! Her love was here, was he not? Yet the Sacred Runes had never been wrong . . .

"Gavin will lead the attack on that fated day?" she inquired.

"Yea, my princess, and he will be pleased with all you have done. His will know you have only yielded to fate. No longer will he doubt you and your skills. He will again be the man you loved and wed. All will praise your courage and cunning. All foes will be slain."

Only yielded to fate? her mind screamed in anguish. If Gavin discovered her . . . If all would be good between them again, that meant he would never learn of her betrayal with Eirik. Did that mean Eirik would be slain before he could expose her sin? Why did that thought torment her? If Eirik was evil, why did she object to his death? If he was evil, how could he be so gentle, so wonderful? Nay, she could not so misjudge him or be so blind and gullible! If Eirik was not Gavin, they must be closely related, perhaps twins or brothers! Otherwise, they could not be so alike.

After knowing Eirik so intimately, how could it ever be the same between her and Gavin? How could she forget or excuse Gavin's wicked deeds against her? He had deserted her. He had doubted her. He had denied her what she needed. If he had returned home, where had he been? Why had he left her side? Was he happy only because he could lead the charge which would save her, which would defeat

228

heir Viking foes? Terrible, unwanted feelings consumed
her.

Trosdan inquired, "What troubles you, my princess?"

"Men," Alysa stated simply.

"I do not understand."

"Even if fate took Gavin from me and will return him
to my side, I am angry with him. When Isobail threatened
my kingdom, he wanted to save it without my help. When
the Vikings threatened me and our land, he wanted to defeat
them and leave me home. When I told him my destiny was
to save my people, he laughed. Now he will lead the attack
against our foes and expect all the credit. If he does not
receive it, will he behave as he did when my victory was
greater than his before his selfish disappearance? I need a
husband who believes in me, who knows I can perform my
duties, all of them. I am not a child or a weakling. I am a
queen, a warrior, the ruler and defender of my people.
Gavin deserted me when I needed his love and understanding, when I needed his aid. He betrayed our love and
commitment. I do not know if I can forgive such offenses."

Alysa did not realize she was speaking from feelings of
anguish, guilt, and frustration. Eirik had accepted her as
she was, when Gavin had not. Eirik was here, when Gavin
was not. Eirik believed in her, when Gavin had not. Eirik
was sharing her fate, when Gavin was not. Yet how would
Eirik behave if he knew the truth of her ruse? How had
Rurik behaved when he had fallen in love with Giselde?
He had sided with her Celtic people against the Vikings!
Maybe Gavin was not her destiny; maybe he had only prepared her to fall in love with Eirik.

"It is only natural to feel such things, my princess," Trosdan replied knowingly. "But Prince Gavin Crisdean is your
fate. As you must know by now, when fate calls, a person
cannot refuse to answer. That is how it was with your husband. He did not understand such things. He feared for your

229

survival. He battled them in mind and body. When you see him again at the Altar Stone, he will know and accept such things. Do not blame him for his deeds," the wizard urged.

"What of Eirik? What is *his* fate?" she asked unexpectedly.

"When the battle is over, Eirik will be no more. Forget him. Avoid him as you would death and evil. Eirik can bring on our defeat."

Alysa envisioned the handsome warrior lying dead on the battlefield, then his virile body burning upon a funeral pyre. Never see him again . . . Betray him and destroy him . . . "Have the Runes never been wrong, Wise One?"

"Never," the Druid High Priest replied, eyeing her closely.

Forget him, she agonized. How could she when she had given him all her love last night? How could Evil be so splendid, so kind, so unselfish, so tender? Nay, something was wrong . . .

"I will think on your words and the message from our gods."

"Do not think on them, Alysa, obey them," he commanded.

Later that afternoon, Alysa went to Rolf's dwelling. Only Enid was there, singing happily as she worked. She told the captive, "I will ask Rolf to go riding with me. We are friends, so he will expect me to spend time with him. We must do nothing to arouse his suspicions against us. Here is another vial of potion for you to use. Take care, dear Enid, for it is more powerful than the last."

Alysa left to find Rolf, locating him with several friends. She asked, "Will you escort me while I ride today? Calliope needs exercise."

Rolf beamed with pleasure. "Yea, my queen, I will be honored. Come, we will leave immediately."

Alysa mounted her dun, a grayish-brown horse with black tail and mane. Sweyn, Rolf's closest friend, joined them to prevent gossip. The three rode for many miles along the lovely bank of the River Avon, chatting and laughing genially as if they had been friends for years. Alysa urgently needed to relax, as her nerves were taut and her mind in turmoil. After a time, they halted to rest their horses. Rolf asked his friend to wait there while he and Alysa walked a ways to talk privately. Sweyn nodded and sat on the grass.

Alysa knew she had to let Rolf romance her to fool him and to dissuade Eirik's pursuit. She realized such actions would anger Eirik, but he was a proud man, hopefully too proud to cause her trouble in public. The only way to protect herself, Trosdan, and their ruse was by keeping Eirik at a safe distance. What better way to make him think she was interested in another man, his rival? That she had yielded to him in lust or guile.

They entered a wooded area which was cool and lovely, leaving their horses to graze nearby. When they were out of Sweyn's sight, Rolf captured her hand and halted their progress. When she looked up at him, he was smiling, devouring her with his hazel gaze.

"I have craved to get you alone for even a moment, my beautiful queen. Each day my hunger for you grows larger and stronger." He carried her hand to his lips and covered it with kisses.

Alysa was about to slow Rolf's chase when beneath his raised arm she sighted Eirik's face peek from behind a large tree not far away. Quickly, she fused her eyes to Rolf's, pretending she had seen nothing. What was Eirik doing here? she wondered. She had not seen him trailing them across the open downlands. They had traveled over rolling upland country with grassy slopes, a landscape which offered few, if any, hiding places. It was as if he were lying in wait for them to arrive so he could spy on them!

231

Alysa resolved herself to carry out her desperate ploy. Rolf's fingers wandered through her thick brown mane, and she smiled with pleasure and enticement. His hand gently stroked her cheek and teased over her uplifted chin. Slowly, as if fearing she would stop him, Rolf bent forward and sealed his lips to hers. When she did not refuse him, his mouth ardently crushed against hers, and she responded as she had in her dream of him at the castle weeks ago. His tongue danced around her soft lips and within her mouth, and he thrilled to the minglings of their flavors. He kissed her eyes and nose and tantalizingly roamed her face and throat. As if he could not get enough of her lips, he kissed her until they were breathless.

Alysa did not repel him as his hands drifted down her back, caressing its supple line before he pulled her tightly against his hard body. He was enormously strong and his embrace was snug. His mouth urgently ravished hers and she bravely allowed him to continue his ardent behavior. She knew he was becoming highly aroused and she cautioned herself to control him. As his mouth journeyed down her neck and over a shoulder bared by pushing aside her upper garment, her arms encircled his muscled frame and her lips nibbled at his neck and chest.

Rolf groaned as flames of desire licked fiercely at him. His mouth covered her ear with kisses, between which he confessed, "I must have you, my queen, before I go mad with hunger. I have wanted you day and night since we met. Lie with me as lovers."

"Nay, Rolf," she murmured, sounding reluctant to cease their intoxicating actions. She pushed gently against his brawny chest and met his burning gaze. "I cannot, not until we are wed. Soon you will have me, all you desire of me, for surely you will win."

Confidently the handsome Viking murmured, "Yea, I shall win your heart and hand, my warrior queen. But there is no need to deny our passions until then. More than I wish to become king, I wish to become your husband. Forget your doubts and fears. No one will find us here. Yield to me now, my sweet destiny, the captor of my heart."

Alysa's hand went to his cheek and caressed it. He nuzzled it and lavished kisses in its palm. She entreated with a soft and innocent voice, "I beg you, dear Rolf, do not ask me to roll upon the grass like a common strumpet. I am your queen. My honor must remain intact. Do you not realize the peril we would face if caught in such a manner? Our first time together must not be rushed. It must not be when we are frightened of being caught naked in each other's arms. I would be shamed forever if others witnessed such a special moment. Be patient and kind. The quest will be done in but a few weeks."

Rolf coaxed, "Even waiting one day sounds like forever when I am starving for you. I trust Sweyn with all things and secrets. He will stand guard for us."

Alysa reasoned, "How could I ever look into Sweyn's face again knowing that he stood guard while we stripped and made love so close to him? How could I win his respect and fealty when he would know I had disobeyed Odin to yield to lust for you before you became the last champion? What if he suspected us of cheating during the quest so we could have each other? The price of one hour's pleasure is too great, dear Rolf. We must be strong and brave."

Alysa smiled sweetly into his eyes and hinted seductively, "If we crave each other today, think of how much more our bodies will be pleading when we are forced to control them for two weeks. The eagerness and anticipation of coming together will be stimulating. We will increase our appetites until we are so starved that our first night together will be wild and rapturous. The fires we have kindled today will be fueled each hour until our marriage. The moment we touch in your bed, our bodies will burst into fiery flames.

Think of how wonderful it will be when we can finally have each other. Whet your appetite by yearning for me. Then soon you will feast wildly upon me until your hunger is sated. I will deny my husband nothing. Nothing, Rolf."

"A hunger such as I have for you, my warrior queen, can never be sated. When you are mine, I will pleasure you as no other man could." A dark scowl lined his tawny face. "But what if I do not win you?"

Alysa embraced him and rested her cheek near his heart. "Do not lose faith or confidence, dear Rolf. You are a superior warrior. I cannot help you with the quests' riddles because I do not know the answers. Only Odin and Trosdan know such things, and I cannot ask the wizard to help us cheat on a sacred quest. We must do nothing to arouse anyone's suspicions about us. Do not worry about winning. Even if you do not, we will find a way to be together. If I am compelled to wed either Ulf or Eirik, we will get rid of my husband when it is safe, then wed. There are many ways for warriors to die accidentally."

She leaned back her head and fused their gazes. She read his willingness to do anything to have her—even defy his gods. Clearly he was potently obsessed with her. *Poor Enid,* she thought, as the captive would never win this man. "Do your best to win the quest, Rolf. But even if you do not succeed, I will be yours soon. If you do not become my husband, we will find ways to meet secretly until our rival is slain cleverly. I will not be happy until you are my husband and High King at my side. Is this promise not sufficient to make you strong enough to resist me for two weeks?"

Rolf chuckled at her playfully provocative expression and tone. "Yea, my sweet destiny, it is more than enough." His mouth closed over hers and they kissed feverishly.

When they parted, she smiled. "My ankle hurts. Could you carry me back to my horse? We must go before Sweyn

234

thinks we have sated our hungers instead of tormenting them."

Rolf swept her into his powerful arms and headed agilely for their mounts. Alysa knew Eirik had been too far away to hear their words, but close enough to witness their actions and moods. With luck and caution, both men should be right where she needed them.

As they rode back toward the settlement, Alysa asked casually, "Who is this Eirik? Did I not hear someone say he has not been with you long? Why was he allowed to join your group? There are many things I do not know about my people. Do you often accept strangers?"

"He came from the camp of Hengist six or seven weeks past. He was seeking adventure, but Hengist is content to win land and wealth with patience and cunning, not by his sword and skills. A warrior cannot prove himself while warming a castle with his backside, so Eirik came to join us when he heard of our presence."

The two men laughed before Rolf continued. "He was forced to prove himself in the ring before he was accepted amongst us, as is our way. He was challenged by Gritar the Bold. When Eirik beat him, he was given Gritar's dwelling and rank. He is from Juteland, near Denmark. He is a skilled warrior and we can use such men of prowess and hunger. He possesses no family, so he has no reason to return home."

"Has he proven he is loyal as well as skilled?" she asked.

"Yea, my queen, he has led many raids and won great fame among us," Sweyn replied begrudgingly. "Once, he saved my life."

"Where did he get the scar on his face?" she inquired.

"It was there when he joined us. I have not asked."

Alysa's gaze slipped over Rolf at her right. She smiled and remarked, "You have no scars, Rolf. No man has been strong enough to mar you. That speaks highly of your skills."

Rolf grinned with pleasure and admiration. Sweyn noticed the interchange between his queen and best friend. It pleased him. If Rolf became High King, that meant his rank would heighten.

"Let's race," she suggested, needing to diffuse her excessive energy and tension. The men agreed and off they galloped.

Alysa's mind traveled as swiftly as her beloved Calliope's sleek legs. She thought about Eirik. The timing of his arrival here perfectly matched that of Gavin's disappearance! He looked, sounded, and most times behaved like the Gavin she had first met, not the strange Gavin he had become shortly before deserting her. What if the Runes only meant he was not Gavin *at this time?* What if the dark powers had Trosdan and the forces of Good fooled? What if Gavin had been sent here as Eirik to aid them?

The scar, her keen mind hinted. It was far more than weeks old! Even if he was not Prince Gavin Crisdean, the two men could be related and not know it. What if Eirik was not a weapon or trick of the dark forces? What if he was only a close image of Gavin, a coincidence? Or, what if he was her real fate? What if she had been led here to do more than defeat their invaders? What if she was also meant to find Eirik, to choose him over Gavin?

After what he had witnessed with Rolf, he would be jealous, mistrustful, possibly hurt by her betrayal. She had not meant to arouse those feelings in him. If he were innocent of her mental charges against him and he truly loved her, her actions could turn him away. Did she want that to happen? Did she want to return to Gavin if things were the same as when he vanished? Could she bear to see Eirik slain during the attack by her people? She had acted rashly and cruelly, which was unlike her. If Eirik was not Gavin, she was ensnared in a trap of her own making. She could not remain the Last Viking Queen and marry him! And after her ruse was exposed, could she ever hold his trust and love?

Those were all matters which Alysa did not want to ponder or decide at this time. She cleared her mind of her worries and doubts to enjoy a carefree ride. Soon, others sighted and joined them.

The small group rode joyously over the downlands, circling Stonehenge several times before they returned to the settlement corral with Alysa in the lead. After dismounting, she chatted with some of the men who were pleased to spend time with their queen.

Rolf said to the others, "She rides like the wind. No queen could serve us better. All men and kingdoms will envy us."

Alysa laughed gaily. "Only because I have ridden since childhood and I possess the best horse in all the world. I would die if anything happened to my beloved Calliope." She hugged the animal and stroked his neck. Calliope responded by nuzzling her cheek. "All kingdoms will envy us because we will rule this land one day. To our great victory!" she shouted above the noise, and the men cheered louder.

Ulf walked up to them. "Will you join me to eat tonight, my queen? I have asked my captive to prepare a matchless meal for you."

"I would be honored, Ulf. But first, I must refresh myself. I will join you soon," she replied, knowing she could do nothing less if all three champions were to be treated the same in public.

On the way to her dwelling, Alysa met Eirik. Again, he was moody and mysterious. His green eyes were narrowed and a frown creased his forehead. His body was taut with warring emotions, evidenced by his walk and stance. She wished she could explain her behavior earlier today, but she could not. She nodded a greeting to him and kept walking.

Eirik trailed her. "Where have you been, Alysa?"

She halted and replied, "Riding with Rolf and Sweyn, and others. Why did you not join us?"

"I was not invited," he said, his tone exposing his anger.

"Nor were the others, but they joined us nonetheless," she retorted.

"We must talk privately," he stressed.

"We cannot. Others are watching us this very moment. I must reveal no favoritism in public. I explained this to you."

"Yet in private you do," he said in an accusatory tone. He was jealous, furious, and baffled. He wondered how she could play the wanton with his rival after spending such a passionate night with him.

"What is your meaning?" she inquired, stalling for time to think.

"Are you afraid of what happened between us last night? So afraid that you seek comfort and protection in another man's arms?"

Alysa glanced around to make certain no one was within hearing distance of them. She scoffed, "Nothing happened between us last night, Eirik. It was only a dream. Are you trying to charm me, to beguile me, to entrap me? Do you not realize you are only confusing me and endangering me? If your feelings are real and strong, you will leave me alone to do my duty to my people and my destiny."

Before she could walk off defensively, he challenged, "Is it your *duty* to romance all three champions? To play me for a fool? To tempt me and torment me? To enchant me, then spurn me to steal my wits so another can win you in the battle ring?"

She tried to glare at him, but failed. "I can treat none of you three differently before the others. I am new here and

238

must be careful what I do and say. I am queen, and all watch me."

"Nay, you are mine, Alysa, mine," he argued.

"Nay, I belong to no man. I am not a piece of property. I am not a prize of war or conquest! I belong to Odin and to my destiny! If such was not true, I would be home in Damnonia with a weakling of a mate who does not understand me or accept me as I am. I need a strong man who trusts me and who does not interfere in my duty and destiny. I need a man who does not question my every word and action when I only do what I must to prevent trouble and suspicion. I need a man who believes in me and who will stand at my side no matter what happens. I need a man who loves me more than his own life and dreams. A man who loves me and wants me, not who wants to use me. If you are such a man, prove it by ceasing your temptation and pressure!" With those enlightening statements, Alysa walked away.

Eirik watched her depart and considered her heated words. Her desire for him had not been concealed by her anger. He realized something vital: she was frightened and desperate! Was that why she had turned to Rolf in the woods? Was she testing her feelings for him? Was she trying to dupe Rolf into believing there was nothing between her and himself? Was she only worried over their safety?

Eirik recalled how she had yielded so passionately to him last night. Their wild, sweet caresses had driven them both mad with desire and pleasure. But it had been more than a physical experience. Alysa was not a woman to yield to lust, or to yield to *anything* lightly. Her feelings could be nothing less than love! As were his. Yet she appeared almost terrified. Did she want him, but knew he was not to be the winner of the quest? Or was there more to her fears and doubts? There was only one way to find out . . .

Fourteen

When Alysa arrived at Ulf's longhouse, she was amazed to see the amount of food being placed on a large wooden table in the *eldhus*. "You have planned a feast, Ulf. Will your friends be here soon?"

"No one will join us, my queen. I did not know what you liked to eat, so I had my captive prepare a choice of many things."

Her blue gaze swept up and down the overloaded table. She mentally scoffed at the amount of waste at innocent victims' expense. "There is so much food, Ulf. If we feasted for weeks, we could not consume so many dishes. But you are kind to go to such trouble for me."

"It was no trouble," he replied accurately, as the slave had done all the work, using food stolen on vicious raids. "If there is food and drink left, she will serve it to my friends or to the wounded. None will go to waste," he remarked as if reading her mind.

Alysa took a seat at the end of the long table. She closed her eyes and inhaled deeply. Delectable aromas filled her nose. She smiled at the captive, and complimented her labors.

Ulf took a seat to Alysa's left. The slave continued her task in silence. Ulf reached for a joint of meat and slapped it on his wooden platter, jarring both the platter and the table. As if ravenous, he piled food around it and filled another side platter. "Where are the bowls, stupid woman?" he shouted at the captive.

With haste and fear, the woman fetched them. Ulf ordered, "Are you still a dumb and lazy cow? Fill them for us!"

"Which soup?" she inquired in panic, her voice quavering and her hands shaking.

"My queen?" Ulf inquired of Alysa in a mellowed tone.

As she mastered her anger at the woman's treatment and concealed her pity for enthrallment to such a vile creature, Alysa eyed the potage and the mutton stew. "That one," she replied softly, then thanked the woman after being served. The slender female glanced hurriedly at the beautiful queen, her eyes filled with a hunger for kindness and freedom. Alysa smiled again and the woman's eyes misted.

Ulf frowned in annoyance. When the woman went to bring the hot bread, Ulf chided in a whisper, "If you show them such kindness, they get lazy and disrespectful. She is here to serve her master, not enjoy herself. She will cause me trouble if you soften her."

Alysa wanted to lift the large carving blade from the table and drive it into the vicious man's heart. Soon, she vowed, such cruelties would halt and men like Ulf would pay dearly for their evil. Yet she forced a genial smile to surface as she teased, "Does not sweet cinnamon taste better than bitter verjuice, Ulf, and bring forth more gentle flavor, even in people?"

He laughed as if she had told a joke. "Yet verjuice makes food more tender and causes it to last longer. So which is more valuable and agreeable?"

Alysa grinned and nodded as if she stood corrected and agreed. She tasted the mutton stew, which was laced with tiny chunks of bacon, veal, and venison. It was seasoned

241

and cooked perfectly. She nibbled on the white wheaten bread which was smeared lightly with butter. She decided on a breast of spit-roasted duckling over the rabbit or lamb or tripe sausages. She passed over the onions with peas to slowly devour fragrant and tender cabbage with slivers of pork. Between bites she sipped wine and listened to Ulf rave about his past conquests.

The man related raids in other lands and in other areas of this isle. From his descriptive words, it was obvious he loved to hurt people and destroy property. Clearly he believed it was a show of manhood and prowess to cower others and to take anything he desired from them. He spoke of how many warriors he had slain and beheaded, revealing how he enjoyed piling their heads high and counting them before leaving them to feed the vultures and wild animals. Age and sex meant nothing to him, for he slew and maimed both with great zest. He talked of the weapons he used, and which ones he preferred. As could be imagined, he favored those which inflicted the most horrid of deaths.

She tried not to watch the man stuff himself crudely and talk with his mouth overflowing, but she could not stare at her platter until this meal ended. Neither could she leave so quickly after her arrival nor admonish his sloppy behavior. To fool Ulf and others, she had to endure this sickening chore. Hopefully it would be the last time she would be compelled to show she favored none of the three champions by spending time with all three. Yet she detested this Norseman who was so unlike Rolf and Eirik. Ulf was a barbaric savage!

Ulf lifted his bowl several times and gulped down his soup, trying the potage first and the mutton stew second. He seized the gigot of lamb from his platter and tore off large hunks with yellowed teeth, eating like a wild and starving animal. As if a wild beast trying to beat another to a fresh kill, he grabbed half of a duckling and ripped ieces off the bone, appearing to swallow them whole. When it was devoured, he reached for half a rabbit and did he same.

Alysa prayed she would not get nauseous witnessing this offensive sight. Ulf chopped and slurped and belched. Whenever meat got stuck between his teeth, he clawed at it with his dirty fingers or picked at it with a small knife. Ever so often he wiped his greasy mouth on his sleeve, leaving behind stains and pieces of food on the thin material. He quaffed down a pitcher of ale and shouted for another one, which was brought quickly.

Alysa daintily used the cloth which she had brought with her to clean her fingers and lips between bites. Even if Ulf had provided one, she had feared it would not be clean. To avoid such an offering and to be prepared, she had tucked a clean cloth into a pocket. She wondered how long and how much the large man could ingest.

Ulf lifted several tripe sausages, smacking and sucking on them until their juices were removed before gnawing heartily on them. Bits of food lined his mouth and stuck in his mustache. His face and hands were shiny from grease. His platter looked like a pig's trough. She was repulsed by him.

For a time, they had eaten in silence. Then Ulf began to ask her many questions, about herself, her heritage, and her homeland. Between unwanted bites and sips, she planned her next words. She lightly went over her bloodline and history, and talked about Damnonia, telling the man little, but making it seem as if she was revealing a lot.

Finally, Ulf pushed back from the table to give his distended belly more room. "What plans do you have for us, my queen?"

"After the quest and my marriage, we will begin our conquest of this isle. I have many ideas in mind, but I will explain them later when all can discuss them."

243

He remarked, "It will be hard living without captives to serve us."

"We are a strong and clever race, Ulf. We can tend ourselves. During your many travels, surely there were times when no woman was around to wait upon you. It is simple to roast a deer or fowl or pig upon a spit. And it is no trouble to throw meats and vegetables into a cauldron to make stew. We will manage fine on the trail. Slaves would get in our way and slow us down, and we cannot leave them here alone." To change the subject, she coaxed, "Tell me what of your family back home? How many wives and children do you have? What of your property and rank?" She turned the conversation on him to pass the time and to protect herself.

"I have four wives and three other women who . . . tend my needs. I have a large appetite to fill," he remarked, his lewd grin exposing his real meaning. "They have given me thirteen children, but only four little ones are still in my house. I own much land, and I am a lord in my area, a chieftain as you Celts call it."

"Why did you leave such wealth and pleasure to come here?"

Excitement filled Ulf's beady eyes and widened them. "There is no greater pleasure and honor than to go araiding. A lord always needs more riches to support himself and to ward off rivals. We live as many do on your isle, in tribes or clans. I am head of my clan. We only unite for battle or raiding. Such will be true of Rolf when his father dies. But Eirik has no land or tribe or wealth or family. He is a wanderer, nothing more."

Alysa caught the undertones of his remarks. So, she concluded, Ulf had a fierce rival back home who wanted his lands and rank, and the heartless beast did not like Rolf and Eirik. "Who protects your lands and families while you are away?"

"My four sons. They have houses near mine. We go araiding one at a time while the others see to chores and defense. When I return home, I will take them plunder and pretty wenches as gifts."

"You do not plan to remain here after our conquest?"

He looked at her as if she were mad. "Nay, this is a land of weaklings. Good for nothing more than plundering and catching slaves. You will rule in our land, from my home," he added smugly.

Alysa refuted as politely as she could manage. "I must remain here; that is Odin's wish, for me to conquer this land and to control it. If you become my husband, you must remain here, too. If you desire, you can move your families here. I will see that my husband gets the best area and castle. Of course, your present wives must be reduced to concubines, as a High King can have but one. You may keep them in another castle and visit them when the mood strikes you."

Ulf chuckled and shook his head, causing his unbound red hair to flutter wildly about his shoulders. "As king, I will be the master of our home, the giver of orders. We will live and rule where I choose. It is the man's right and duty."

"A common man's, yea; but the Last Viking Queen's husband, nay, Ulf. You can become my helper and mate, but not my ruler or master. Surely you know our laws better than I. Even without them, Odin has spoken, and his command is to remain here."

"We will decide such matters after we are wed," he told her, already plotting how to bend and break this strong and vexing woman. She was beautiful and desirable, and he imagined himself greedily and forcefully ravishing her body. He would keep her with child every month so she would be forced to stay home, out of his hair and business. He would rule his people, not this spirited wench with

245

mixed blood! Once she produced him a royal heir, if she disobeyed him, she would be dealt with swiftly.

Sweat beaded on Ulf's face from the strong drink and lecherous musings. He called to the captive, "More ale, sluggard beast!"

The nervous woman rushed forward, stumbling and sloshing ale on Ulf's shirt. The man jumped to his feet and bellowed at the frightened slave, "Stupid fool of a nag! Beg for punishment, will you?" He backhanded her cheek with great force, sending the woman to her knees. She covered her lowered head to ward off his blows, whimpering and pleading for mercy.

Alysa also jumped to her feet. She commanded, "Nay, Ulf! It was not her fault. My foot was spread too far and she tripped upon it. I am to blame for the spill, not her. It is foolish to whip a good slave, to injure her beyond serving you further. I know there are plenty of slaves to be had here, but we have no time for them. Few women can prepare such meals or tend you as well as she does. Leave the poor creature be," she urged firmly.

Ulf's face was suffused with rage at both women. Never had any female corrected him, and especially before another one! This bold and haughty queen would pay for her rash deed when she belonged to him! Yet for now he must use wisdom and caution. He lowered the hand which had been about to beat the woman and shrugged. "I did not see the accident. She is clumsy all the time. Only punishment can help her."

Alysa helped the woman to her feet and checked her injury. "I will have Trosdan come and tend it for you in the morning. Go, wash your face and calm yourself." As the grateful woman obeyed, Alysa explained to Ulf in a gentle tone, "She is clumsy, Ulf, because you terrify her. If you cannot be kind in manner and gentle of voice, at least do not be loud and cruel. You need not show your power over her with such brutal actions; she knows you are master and she must obey. My castle is large and I have many servants. They do not disobey and become lazy because I treat them as people. Nay, they serve me better. If you do not believe such words, try them and see I am right."

"As you wish, my queen," he said, lying in outrage.

"It is late and I am weary from my long ride. Thank you for a wonderful meal and good company tonight. I will see you tomorrow."

Ulf walked to the door with her, then closed it after she left. He turned to the petrified woman. "Come to me, old hag."

The captive knew he was enraged, but she was helpless. She ordered her legs to obey, going to stand before him. Yet she felt hope tonight, as the new ruler was kind and gentle . . .

Ulf stripped her, bound her to his bed, and gagged her. "I will teach you to make the fool of me before the queen. She is stubborn and stupid as you are." To release his fury and to punish the woman in Alysa's place, he beat the defenseless victim like a madman. When she was nearly unconscious, but still thinking how to reach the queen tomorrow with a warning about this evil man, he drove his manhood into her and ravished her brutally.

Afterward, he arose and stood looking down at her bruised and battered body. A malicious grin spread over his ruddy face, then he laughed with satanic pleasure. He wiped the sweat from his face, then spat upon her. "I know how to deal with you, old hag. I will follow the queen's orders tomorrow, and I will persuade the others to agree. She likes slaves, does she? I will punish her by showing her what a pagan slave like you is good for—to feed the wolves and vultures. Soon, she will be the one in your place!"

Ulf retrieved his knife and plunged it into her body many times, chuckling as he did so. When he ceased, he wrapped her in a blanket and carried her body far from camp. He shoved it into a gulley and sent forth a wolf howl, as if calling them to supper. Feeling aroused again by his wicked deed, he rode to the nearest farm to find another innocent female victim to ravish and slay.

When Alysa reached her dwelling, she closed and barred the door and leaned against it. Trosdan watched her, then asked, "What happened, Alysa? Did he harm you?"

"Nay, Wise One," she replied, then related the events at Ulf's. "I despise him. I am glad not all of my ancestors' people are like him. When the attack comes, I wish to slay him myself!"

"If the time comes, I will do so before that day," Trosdan vowed.

"Nay, Wise One, take no such risks," she protested. "If he died not at the hand of a foe, you would fall under suspicion, as would I."

To put her mind on other matters, Trosdan ventured, "Would you like to hear the first clue and where the treasure can be found?"

Alysa joined him and responded eagerly, "Yea, Wise One."

When he finished his tale, Alysa smiled happily. "You are very clever, Wise One. Soon our task will end in victory."

"By now, the second bird has reached Lord Weylin. It will not be much longer before we can return home as victors and live in peace. We must guard our last bird carefully, Princess, as he is the signal for attack. Our timing must be perfect."

In Damnonia, Weylin read the first part of the message again with a broad smile and sigh of relief:

248

"All goes well. Contest over. Quest begins Friday. Be prepared. Leave message at healing waters as planned."

In the morning he would send this good news to King Bardwyn and King Briac. Within two weeks, the three forces would take their positions near their borders with Logris. A messenger line would be set up from camp to camp for swift passing of information. Then he would camp at the old Roman baths to await Alysa's summons. All was prepared. Men were trained and practicing and supplies had been gathered. So far, no one had realized that Princess Alysa was away.

Weylin thought about Lady Kordel back at his estate and how much he missed her. He had managed two visits while gathering supplies and collecting men to train. His heart warmed, as did his body. Dreams of Alysa no longer plagued him; perhaps fate had only used her to prepare his heart and mind to open to a special woman like her. He was in love with Kordel, truly in love for the first time, and he found this reality pleasing and timely. He wanted to marry the woman, to share all things with her, to live here in peace and prosperity. He had confessed his feelings to the lovely woman, and she had agreed. When Alysa returned, he would ask the ruler to betroth them.

Weylin's attention returned to the message which was written in tiny letters on the back of a furry skin. He had taken it from around the skillfully trained bird's leg. He focused on the last part. Later he would discuss the curious request with Gavin, but he knew what had to be done at this time. He wrote out his reply and sent for Piaras, the castle trainer of knights and squires. It would be less noticeable for the aged man, dressed as a peasant, to carry the message to the old

Roman baths and conceal it. Hopefully, news of Gavin would ease Alysa's anguish and worries . . .

The next afternoon, Alysa left her dwelling dressed in a thigh-length tunic over comfortable pants. As she headed for the corral, she saw Aidan and Saeric, and cunningly invited them to be her escorts. While riding, perhaps she could learn more about Eirik.

It was harder than she had imagined, as the two men were not very talkative. They seemed awed and intimidated by their beautiful queen, and responses had to be pulled from them. She asked them many questions about themselves, but was not truly interested in their answers. She did not want to get too friendly with men she was going to have slain! Their deaths troubled her, yet could not be prevented, as they were foes, something she had to remind herself of many times these days.

"What of your friend Eirik? Where is he today?" she asked.

"He left camp early this morning. He is restless to begin the quest, as I would be in his place. He will win," Aidan boasted proudly. "He can fight as ten men, with any weapon, even his bare hands."

"Yea, Aidan," Saeric concurred, "he will become our king. He is a brave and handsome man, my queen. He will make a good husband and ruler. We will follow him proudly as we follow you."

"If he wins the quest," Alysa teased merrily to relax them.

"Few compare to Eirik. He will win."

"You like him very much, do you not, Saeric?" she inquired.

"He is a born ruler, a matchless leader of men, a warrior without weaknesses. Yea, my queen, he is our friend."

"It is good to have such friends as you two. Only a special man could influence others so deeply. That pleases me." Alysa thought of Gavin's six friends, then reminded herself that Bevan was dead. Yea, it was good to have friends one could depend on and trust fully. In this manner, Eirik was so like her husband. She called Eirik's image to mind. Where had the scar come from and how could it have healed so quickly if he was Gavin? Only powerful sorcery could have placed it there, removed his royal tattoo, and changed his memories. Einar did not possess such awesome powers. Then, who did? And why?

Alysa repeated them the same question she had asked Rolf. "You have not known him long to be so close. Is he not new here?"

Aidan and Saeric glanced at each other and passed an unseen message between them. They did not want the queen to think their friend unworthy of her and the rank of High King because of his length of time with them. With Saeric's mute agreement, Aidan lied. "He has been in this camp only a short time, but we have known him many years. We have shared countless adventures in other lands and visited him in Hengist's camp after our arrival here. He has no family at home, so he continued his adventures while we returned to our families for a time. He was restless in Hengist's camp and unhappy, so we persuaded him to join us again. Many times over the years he has saved our lives and helped us obtain much treasure."

"What of the scar on his face? How did he get it?" she asked.

A friend would know the answer, so Aidan replied cleverly, "On one of our raids long ago, we were attacked by savage barbarians. There were three to five foes to each of us. Eirik slew many, but was wounded while saving my life. If it is needed, mine belongs to him."

Saeric added, "He will make you a perfect husband, my

251

queen. You will be good for him. He is lonely. Already we see how his eyes follow you and adore you. Pray to Odin for Eirik to win, as he is far above Ulf and Rolf."

"I will not be displeased if Eirik wins, but the choice is not mine and I can show no favor to him. Nor is Rolf a bad choice, but I do not care for Ulf," she confessed cleverly to pretend as if confiding in them, hoping they would do the same with her.

"You are right, my queen. Ulf is not liked among us."

"Why does he have such power and high rank?" she asked.

"He won them, and no warrior has been able to take them from him. He kills without mercy, even his friends. The man he fought in the last match was his friend. He is evil. Perhaps Loki rules his heart."

"I feasted with him last night, and your words could be true." To test the men's feelings, she revealed what Ulf had done.

Both men scowled, and Alysa was pleased but tormented. "We must head back. Soon the evening meal will be served."

As they neared camp, billowing smoke caught their attention. From the smell and color of the smoke, all knew it was a funeral pyre, a large one. The sickly sweet odor of burning flesh and bone filled her nostrils and caused Calliope to prance nervously.

Of necessity, Alysa gasped, "Can so many of my subjects have died from wounds? Why must it be so amongs friends?" At the corral, Alysa made a startling and horrifying discovery.

Ulf joined them with several others. He grinned and said, "It is done, my queen, as you wished. We have ridded ourselves of the troublesome slaves. They will be no threat to us. Come morning, we will be ready to ride and all will be safe here for those left behind."

"What do you mean?" she asked, unable to conceal her dismay. Somehow she knew what had taken place during her absence, and dread filled her. Yet she rapidly mastered her feelings.

Rolf walked over to them. Alysa met his solemn gaze and inquired, "Have you slain all prisoners?"

Without returning her smile, Rolf replied, "All but five trusted captives. Ulf said you wished to be rid of them to-day. Why did you not tell me before leaving camp with Eirik's friends?"

Alysa's wide gaze flew to Ulf's devilish expression. This man could not be trusted. He was bold and daring, cruel and deceitful. She took Ulf's deed as a challenge. She had no choice but to call his bluff, even if it meant calling him a liar! "I gave no such command to Ulf or to another. Why did you not wait to question me, Rolf? I said the slaves were to be released before our departure. They were help-less women, not strong manly foes to be slaughtered proudly and bravely by my warriors."

Ulf responded quickly with feigned innocence. "I mis-understood your wishes and orders, my queen. Forgive me. It is too late. While you were gone, we slew them. Now they burn."

Alysa glared at the flame-haired man and used the best insult she could imagine, "This is a bad omen, Ulf. Odin said to free the captives, not slay and burn them. This very moment their foul stench burns his nose and displeases him! What threat were silly females to us? None. They were to return to their homes and villages and tell all of our power so their people would tremble in fear of us. This dark deed will turn the peasants against us and cause trouble while we are trying to carry out our sacred quest. To enslave some frightens them, but to slay their women gives them the ha-red and courage to harass us!"

The men began to mumble amongst themselves, agreeing

with Alysa and speaking against Ulf, who had misled them. She took advantage of the grim situation. "Now we must leave men here to guard our camp against their families' revenge. They will be unable to join our glorious quest. I did not realize I had not made myself clear on this matter," she scoffed sarcastically.

Rolf was pleased with her reaction and words, as was Eirik, who was concealed nearby and listening intently to this heated discourse.

"Tell me who was spared." She directed her query to Rolf. She was relieved when Enid's name was among the survivors, spared to serve her. Yet she was angered by the death of Ulf's pitiful slave. She felt responsible for this brutal slaughter, for surely her behavior last night had spurred Ulf to commit such an evil deed.

By now, many Vikings had gathered around the angry scene. Alysa shouted to be heard by all, "Hear me well, my people. No more slaves are to be taken until after the quest. There must be no more raids on villages and hamlets until we are ready to conquer this land. If we rashly stir up the peasants and lords, they will be compelled to retaliate even at the cost of their lives. We have no time for such one-sided battles until our invasion is under way. Take only the supplies you need for survival, but attack no place or person. You are warriors with much experience and wits. You know how men, even peasants and serfs, react when their wives and children are slaughtered. You can cower men who are frightened, but you cannot control men who are challenged, even if they are weaker. There is another peril in such deeds. If the people seek their king's protection from us, Vortigern will ride against us, or pay Hengist and Horsa to do so. We need no such trouble at this time. They ignore small raids, but will not ignore us if we rashly terrorize their land. Be patient and use restraint, my people, until we are ready to challenge and conquer all in this land."

Rolf shouted above the agreeable murmurings, "Our queen is right. We must think of nothing but our sacred quest."

"When dawn comes, I will meet with you at Stonehenge. Trosdan will give us the first clue. Tomorrow our quest begins, my people. May Odin guide us and protect us as he chooses his king and my husband."

In her dwelling, Alysa paced the floor. She was angry, angry at herself for letting Ulf best her, angry at Ulf for daring to do so, and angry at the others for letting Ulf dupe them. How she had longed to call him a liar and to pierce his heart with her sword. She had thought that unwise at this time. There was no way she could prove he had betrayed her and used them. Too, he was a warrior who few, if any, wished to challenge. That ominous reality distressed her.

"You are mine, foul beast of Evil," she resolved softly.

What of Eirik? her mind shouted. She had noticed his presence as she was leaving the group, but he had not approached her. There had been a strange look in his green eyes, one which baffled her heart and mind. The words of his friends returned to haunt and confuse her, as did Trosdan's new warning. For some reason, she did not believe them. Eirik had appeared just when Gavin vanished! She believed in their love, their entwined destiny. The forces of Good would not treat her so cruelly while she was working for them. Gavin was here by design, here for a good purpose just as she was. No matter what anyone or the Runes said or how things seemed, Eirik had to be Gavin.

Alysa went into the dark kitchen area to fetch some wine to soothe her taut nerves. Night had enwrapped the land in its embracing shadows, but Trosdan was still tending the wounded, pretending to ready them to join the quest. She poured the wine and, feeling as if she were smothering,

255

went to the window for fresh air. The moon highlighted many areas, including the one which Eirik was crossing as he made his way toward where she stood. Quickly, she fetched a candle, hurried to the table, and sat down. Trosdan's possessions still filled the table. An idea came to mind.

Before Eirik reached the window to summon her, Alysa decided to help him win this quest, no matter who or what he was. She pretended to be praying to Odin and seeking the Viking god's divine guidance. She was relieved when Eirik did not interrupt her, as she saw him from beneath the hair falling over the side of her face.

She whispered softly and urgently, "Hear me, Great Odin, for I have failed you today. Do not punish us for disobeying your commands, as your people were misled. Surely Ulf is controlled by Loki and seeks to defeat your orders. I must be wary of him, for he cannot be trusted. I have felt the evil flowing from him, an evil which seeks to conquer and destroy me. At times, I have been weak and afraid here and have followed my desires over yours. I will not do so again. If I have not offended you, prove it by showing me where the first treasure is concealed. I vow to tell no one."

She lit the candle beneath the crucible which Trosdan had been using earlier. Taking the knife which was lying beside it, she cut off a short lock of her hair and tossed it into the bowl, then lifted a container of green liquid and poured some into the heating bowl. From a pouch, she took a pinch of yellow powder and added it to the mixture, as she had seen Trosdan do. Wisps of lacy blue smoke began to rise.

"Hear me, Great Odin, show me the path to your treasure."

The mixture boiled quickly and she removed the crucible from the flame. Placing it before her, she added a pinch of red powder to it, creating colorful smoke. She tried to en vision the best and quickest way to the place where Trosdan had told her the amulet was hidden. She had never visited this kingdom, but had studied maps of it. The conquering Romans, who had withdrawn from their isle years ago, had constructed imperial roads which ran in every direction and to every tribal area. There were large roads, secondary roads, trails, trackways, and canals. She mentally placed a map of Logris before her mind's eye.

She gazed into the smoking liquid and murmured, "Yea, I see the trail growing clearer. We must travel the North Downs trackway toward Maidstone, but not enter it. When we reach the River Medway, we must follow its banks northward. I see where the conqueror Caesar battled with Cassivelaunos for a third time, a place where Androgos revealed his treachery. It is a place of death and victory, many times over. Family slaying family . . . Three trees standing forever like the three sisters who fiercely battled each other there. At the river's edge, I see a large rock, a rock which looks like the lost head of one of the sisters. But I do not see your amulet of protection, Great Odin."

She dropped in more yellow and red powder and created more colorful smoke. "There, yea, I see it now, beneath the rock. It is a good symbol, Great Odin, a dagger with circles like the two heads of the traitorous sisters. It will warn your people against such evil."

Alysa hesitated a moment before she entreated, "Will you show me the face of the winner, Great Odin? The one who will become my husband?"

The liquid was cold by now and the vapors had ceased rising. She waited, pretending to search the clear surface for a mirrored image. "You do not answer, Great Odin, and perhaps that is best. It will be between Rolf and Eirik, but which will win, I wonder . . ."

She sipped the wine and sighed deeply as if exhausted. "Both are good and handsome men. Both are superior warriors. Both seek to win my heart and hand. Each would make a great king and a worthy husband. Have I the right to desire one to win over the other?"

Alysa stood and cleared away the disarray her potion-making had caused. She knew Eirik was still listening nearby, as she sensed his presence. He had his first clue to victory, and the gods help her if she had chosen to aid the wrong man.

Eirik smiled and left. He could not let her learn she had aided him without meaning to do so. His heart soared, for surely the gods had led him to her window tonight to receive such help with his victory. He knew where those battles had taken place. It would only be a short search to locate the trees and rock near the river. Yet he could not make it look too easy or find the amulet too quickly, else others might think he had cheated. Or worse, that she had cheated.

Eirik gazed eastward. He wondered what Hengist would do when they swept through his area in search of a prize worth dying for.

Seized by an emotional maelstrom, Rolf paced his long-house, as he had lost the mandrake during his ride with Alysa and Einar did not possess another magical root to give him. When Enid queried his behavior and mood, he angrily divulged, "I have lost my sacred amulet, and I needed its help on the quest and its protection during the last contest in the battle ring else I will fail and be slain."

Much as the enthralled slave did not want her love to wed another woman, Enid could not let death take him out of her reach. "Do not fret, my lord; I am from Logris and I can aid your victory. You saved my life when Ulf tried to slay me with the other captives. Command anything of me, and I will obey. Anything, my Lord Rolf."

Fifteen

Enid came early the next morning to bring their meal. Trosdan sat down to eat while Alysa walked to the door with the frightened slave. The lovely princess said, "I am sorry about the slaughter yesterday, Enid. I did not order it, and I have commanded no more deaths. Ulf is a dangerous and guileful man. Be wary of him."

"Lord Rolf refused to let him slay me. He said I was needed to serve you. It was terrible," she remarked with teary eyes. "Only a few Celts who have joined sides with them were spared."

Alysa's blue eyes flashed with anger as she told Enid of Ulf's evil mischief to the defenseless slave. "I despise him. But he is powerful, so we must be careful. Watch him and report his deeds to me. But take no risks, Enid, or he will slay you and make it appear an accident."

"What if he wins the quest, my queen?" she asked worriedly.

"Nay, Odin will not permit it. Ulf is the weapon of Loki, and Odin will soon destroy him. Will you take care of my bird while I am gone? One has died, and the last is very precious to me."

Enid glanced at the cage and remaining bird. "He will be safe with me. I will feed him and guard him for you."

259

* * *

Shortly before noon, the people gathered at Stonehenge. Alysa stood upon the Altar Stone to be seen and heard by all. "It is time to begin our quest for our king and my husband. Einar, come forward."

The Viking *attiba* obeyed, eyeing her with intrigue. Alysa handed him a leather pouch, then summoned the three champions. She forced herself not to look overly long at either man. "Hold the bag over your head," she instructed Einar. She positioned her hand and looked skyward as she prayed, "Hear us, Great Odin. We have gathered in this sacred place to begin our task. Send down your power to aid us."

The purple ring, a cunning duplicate of the ancient one, captured the sunlight and cast a purple glow on the bag in Einar's grasp. Believing the power of Odin was touching him, the false wizard's hand trembled and he nearly dropped the pouch. The crowd of warriors was awed by this sight and stared at the scene with great reverence and interest.

Alysa informed the small group before her, "Each of you must pull a stone from the pouch which Odin has blessed. There are numbers on them which give the order of our next drawing. I ride with the winner who selects the blue stone. It will be done this way each time."

Rolf, Eirik, and Ulf reached into the pouch and withdrew their numbered stones. When the second pouch was blessed, Einar held it before Ulf first, who withdrew a white stone. Rolf was second, and withdrew the coveted blue stone. Einar dumped the other white stone into Eirik's palm; his fingers closed tightly around it. Ulf scowled, deepening the lines on his face. Eirik's expression, when he lifted his green gaze, remained impenetrable. Rolf grinned at his first victory and held up the blue stone for all to see.

Alysa said, "I ride with Rolf this time. Your bands have

260

been selected and are prepared to leave when we finish here. Wise One, come forth and give my champions their first clue." Alysa was helped by Rolf from the altar and she remained at his side.

Trosdan climbed upon the Altar Stone and gazed around him. "After the matches were over, I fasted and prayed here all night. Odin has provided the first riddle. You must solve it, locate the prize, and return to camp with it. Once all have seen the first treasure, you must protect it from cunning theft by the other two champions."

The three men nodded understanding and obedience.

Trosdan's voice was deep and clear as he related the enigma. "In the days of the Roman conquerors, this land was divided into many tribes and areas. The one you seek was known as Cantii. In it, you search to locate a place where many battles have been fought, where death respected no bond or tie or sex. Long ago, two foes—the Mighty Caesar and a hero from this land—battled fiercely for a third time at this spot. Many warriors were hanged from trees and left to rot. Others were beheaded, their heads left upon their own spears to feed wild birds."

Trosdan watched the three men beneath him as they listened intently. "Another tragic battle knew this same ground. Leir, son of Bladud, a legendary Celtic king, had three daughters: Goronil, Riganna, and Cordaella. Leir loved only Cordaella and wanted her to have the Crown of London after him. To dupe his other girls and people, he created a test of love, a vain test Cordaella failed before all eyes, and after which she was banished. Leir grew old and his two remaining daughters were his curse. They weakened him and tried to destroy him. Leir sought out his lost child and begged her forgiveness and help. Cordaella, a queen of another land by marriage, returned to this mighty isle and challenged her two wicked sisters. A great battle was fought. Goronil and Riganna were slain and beheaded.

261

Upon the piles of their soldiers' heads were placed their own. To mark this spot forever, three trees grow; one is tall and lovely, and two are as bent and ugly as the sisters. Find the lost head of Riganna, and you will find the prize. Odin, the Seer, the master of runic magic, observed these battles long ago. There, he placed an amulet of protection for one of you to find this great day. Go, solve the riddle and seek your first prize."

"How can we find a woman's head which rotted long ago? Her skull would look no different from all others. How would we know it? It makes no sense. Where were these ancient battles fought?" Ulf asked.

"That is for you to uncover with your wits. This quest seeks the one man whose wits, skills, and courage stand above the others'. The amulet is to protect the winner against the treacheries such as this place has witnessed, and to give him guidance from the Great Seer when we go to battle. Your quest lies within two days of here."

"But in which direction? We do not know this land or its history. Your words are silly," Ulf ranted foolishly. Then he accused, "Rolf has the advantage. Our queen knows this isle and can reveal clues to him along their journey. She will help him win today."

Rolf argued, "Perhaps that is the reason for her presence. I won the right to have her join me and council me. Just as she would have been with you had you pulled out the blue stone. The choosing was fair, Ulf, blessed by Odin. All witnessed it. Is this not true?"

The people were compelled to concur. As Ulf stormed off with his friends, he whispered, "We will find peasants to answer our questions and provide us with facts to solve the riddle. Surely the people of this area know their kingdom better than a Damnonian princess."

Sigurd, who had been mercifully spared in the contest by Rolf, teased, "See, my friend, it does not matter that she travels with Rolf today. No doubt she will distract your rival by slowing his wits with her beauty and his pace with her fragile body."

"Yea, Sigurd, perhaps I am the one with the advantage. Come, let us ride quickly. We will cut out any Celtic tongue which refuses to solve this mystery for us."

Trosdan joined them with his possessions. After his talk with Alysa, he had to make certain this malevolent warrior did not cheat and that he did not win, even though the quest was a ruse. He knew that Alysa would be safe with Rolf, but Ulf had to be watched closely. There was no guessing what lengths that vile human would go to for victory, and he must be controlled. "I ride as the numbered stones revealed. You chose the stone marked One, so I go with you, Ulf."

Eirik left the area without speaking to Alysa, as he feared his gaze might expose his feelings and perhaps hers. Soon, he, Aidan, Saeric, and his band had departed. Between the wizard's clues and the queen's unknown slip, he knew exactly where to look for the amulet.

Alysa headed for the corral to meet with Rolf, who had been to see Enid. She feigned a regretful smile and told him, "I fear I can be of little help on this adventure, Rolf. My father never allowed me to travel into King Vortigern's land, so I know little about it. If I am being sent along to aid you, it makes no sense to me."

He caressed her cheek, uncaring of the many eyes on them. "Do not worry, my queen. Your company is all I desire from you today."

The large group mounted and galloped eastward. There

was a sly grin on the blond giant's face, for his captive was of this land.

Alysa's group rode hard all day, halting only to rest their horses when necessary. It was dark when they made camp that first night.

Rolf told her apologetically, "I am sorry if I push you too hard and fast, my queen, but I am eager to beat the others to the sacred site. If you become weary or sore, tell me and I will slow our pace."

Alysa smiled gratefully. "You are a kind and generous man, Rolf, but do not worry about me. I am strong, and I am accustomed to riding every day—at least before I came here and found myself so busy. Go at the pace you desire, as I can keep up with any man. For the quest to be fair, I must not become a hindrance, and I will not."

They were sitting near a campfire which was separated from the others. Yet they lacked the privacy to speak freely. Even so, Rolf's eyes adored and caressed her, and his body ached for hers. Over and over her words and responses in the forest returned to increase his craving for her. She was right; having to wait to feed his ever-mounting hunger served to whet his appetite to a greater height. "Truly you are a warrior queen. I feel great pride and love for you. I must obtain the amulet and all other prizes to win you. The day you are mine will be a happy and glorious one."

Alysa glanced around to see who was observing them. No one seemed to be eavesdropping, but his behavior made her nervous. Her expression warned Rolf of his rash slip. He shrugged and smiled ruefully. She asked, "Have you solved the riddle? Do you know where to look? You seem to be heading to a certain spot at a swift speed."

A sly grin made him appear even more handsome than the reality. His hazel eyes sparkled with devilment. He whispered, "This is Enid's land, and she told me where to search. It is good she was not slain with the other captives, for she will aid me each time. Fate is on our side, Alysa, and soon we will be together as husband and wife."

Alysa tried to conceal her astonishment and dismay. She had forgotten that Enid was a Logris captive. If Eirik stalled his search to keep from arousing suspicion, Rolf would beat him to the location!

She quelled her panic, as it did not matter who won the false quest. Strange, but at times she forgot it was all a ruse! She would find herself caught up in the excitement and anticipation of the events. Perhaps that was good, because it aided her guileful behavior.

The second day of travel got under way early. They rode along the North Downs trackway through picturesque landscape. Rolling hills were covered with green grass. The land would soon be changing colors to announce the end of summer. But for now, the trees and grasses were still verdant, and wildflowers were abundant. To avoid contact with this land's inhabitants, they skirted villages, hamlets, and farms.

There was a good reason not to raid in this area: the Jute Hengist who was in King Vortigern's employ to guard his land against invasions. If they appeared a threat to either man, trouble could occur, and Trosdan had warned the Norsemen about such a rash move during the choosing of bands two days ago, as she had done earlier. All had agreed to be cautious during the quest. Alysa had made no plans to deal with the Viking warlord Hengist who was firmly established in this kingdom, as he seemed to have no interest in her or in her land. Until now, Hengist and his brother Horsa were content to beguile land and wealth from Vortigern. If the Jute brothers became too greedy or dangerous, surely King Vortigern would deal with them. Yet Alysa could not afford for

Hengist to join the alleged quest and increase the Viking strength. If that happened, the Norsemen would number the same—or more—than her united forces! She had to depend on, prey on, the greed of her subjects to keep Hengist away! Too, Hengist would be a threat to her love if he arrived and exposed Eirik's false tale.

Darkness engulfed them before they reached the River Medway, so they were forced to camp again to await daylight. They had not seen the other two bands, but assumed they were heading in this same direction. Food was quickly prepared and consumed, and the tired band unrolled their pallets for the night.

At dawn, Rolf awakened everyone, as he was anxious to finish this journey in victory. They reached the river and rode northward along its banks, searching for the three trees which came into view.

Rolf scowled when he saw a band camped near them. He galloped forward, and Alysa hurriedly followed him. Eirik greeted them with a wide grin, holding the amulet in his hand.

"How did you solve the riddle and get here so quickly?" Rolf demanded, his eyes narrowed and his tone chilly.

Eirik chuckled. "Have you forgotten, Rolf? I lived in this area with Hengist and I heard the Celts' legends many times. It is an old and favorite tale which is related constantly. I have been to this spot before, so it was easy to find again. Come, let us return to camp so our second journey can begin."

"Where was the amulet? How did only you find its hiding spot?" Rolf asked, gazing at the envied prize in Eirik's tight grasp.

The handsome victor led them to the riverbank. He pointed downward and explained, "When I was here before, an old peasant showed me this rock which looks like the shriveled head of a woman and claimed it was a symbol of one cut from the body of Queen Cordaella's evil sister. The peasants say it is cursed and refuse to touch it. When the wizard gave his riddle, I remembered his words and looked beneath it. The amulet was there. It is from Odin, for it bears the image of a hanged man upon its blade. Look, the grip forms two heads, those of the unlucky and traitorous sisters."

Ulf arrived at that moment, furious. The tale was repeated and the prize was displayed before Eirik tucked it safely into his sheath.

Eyeing his two clever rivals, Ulf scoffed, "We would have been here first if this feeble old wizard had not slowed us down. Stone or no stone, he shall not ride with me again."

Trosdan refuted, "It was not I who slowed us down, Ulf. You halted your band many times to beat clues from peasants. You even took precious time to torture and kill the slave who escaped your camp not long ago."

Ulf sneered, "He was rousing the peasants against us. I had no choice but to make an example of him."

Queen Alysa was distressed by that news. She scolded, "You were warned against such deeds, Ulf. You will cause trouble for all with your selfish mischief. There must be no violence here to call attention to our comings and goings. Use your wits to buy information, not your strength to obtain it at a terrible price. There are four more prizes to be won. Obey Odin's commands, or he will rain havoc on us."

"I have obeyed," Ulf argued boldly and rudely.

Just as boldly, Alysa retorted, "Nay, twice you have created bad omens for us. Now you seek to refuse Odin's command for Trosdan to ride with the man who picks the number-one stone. We do not know the reason for this requirement, but Odin has given it and we must obey. If you cannot follow Odin's rules for this quest, you cannot be a part of it," she threatened, her unwavering gaze drilling into Ulf's cold one.

Ulf glared at her, but relented. "As you command, my queen."

Alysa could not let him have the final word, especially in that condescending tone. "Nay, Ulf, not as your queen commands, but as our god commands. Yet as I am a part of this quest, one of the prizes, I will make certain it is done fairly and honestly."

This time, Ulf did not respond, and his body shuddered as he forcefully withheld what he wanted to say and do to the bold female.

Alysa did not look at Eirik as she walked away with Rolf. They mounted and rode for their settlement. On the trip back, she remained with Trosdan to avoid all three men. She questioned him about the smithy's death and was relieved to learn the man had not betrayed her.

They reached camp late Monday night. Alysa told the group, "We will rest until midday, then meet at the stone temple for our next riddle." Fatigued, she hurried to her dwelling and collapsed on the bed. Within moments she was asleep.

Enid brought her meal an hour before noon, and Alysa eagerly consumed it. Afterward, she soaked in the hot bath which the captive prepared for her in the *eldhus*. The water was refreshing, and she remained in the tub—a gift from Eirik—a long while. Stepping from it, she dried her invigorated body and dressed. As with the first journey, she donned a short tunic over linen pants and placed around her waist her leather belt with its dagger sheath.

As she worked, Eirik filled her thoughts. Had her clues

268

aided him, or would he have been able to solve the riddle without them? Had he made up the story about the peasant to cover his secret knowledge? Or was there truly a legend about the trees and rock? If so, when had he heard it? She wondered how familiar Gavin was with this territory, and if such memories were still intact.

She left the dwelling and headed toward the towering stones. Weaving her way between tall monoliths and linteled trilithrons and gathering men, she made her way to the altar. Trosdan was there waiting for her. They exchanged smiles.

The wizard whispered into her ear, "Take care if Ulf wins your company this time. There is no way I can control the draw with Einar in charge. Ulf is dangerous and unpredictable. But he would be more dangerous if we aided either Eirik or Rolf and he discovered that fact. We must let this ruse take its own winding path."

Alysa nodded. "Do not overtire yourself, Wise One. These journeys are difficult and you are unaccustomed to such rides."

Trosdan did not reply because others joined them. Alysa stepped onto the altar and called Einar, Rolf, Ulf, and Eirik forward. Three men approached. Alysa asked, "Where is Eirik?"

"Here, my queen," he called out, moving through the crowd. He had waited for everyone to leave camp before sneaking into his old longhouse to hide the amulet in the least suspected place: Queen Alysa's dwelling! No one would dare search for it there. He knew Ulf and Rolf were having him watched, but he had eluded his spies during some cunning maneuvers around camp. He was certain no one had seen him enter or leave the queen's dwelling.

Alysa struggled to hold back a happy smile at his arrival, as even his brief absence had frightened her. "Einar, we are ready to draw stones again." She handed the pouch to the Viking wizard and repeated the ritual from yesterday.

Einar felt a sense of power overcome him. Odin had not struck him down for duping his people. Perhaps, Einar decided, Odin knew he was doing his best to serve him and them with his meager skills and talents. Einar proudly held the bag out to the men, one at a time.

Rolf drew stone number one, so Trosdan was to go with him this time. Eirik drew number three, and Ulf pulled out number two. The first man drew from the second bag, and Rolf came up with a white stone and a look of disappointment. Ulf shoved his fingers into the bag and wiggled the two remaining stones, withdrawing one, a white one. His frown was even more intense than at the last drawing.

Einar turned the pouch up and dropped the blue stone into Eirik's hand. Eirik gazed at it, then handed it back to Einar to return to the bag. He did not look up at Alysa, whose eyes he felt upon him. He did nothing to show he was excited or impressed by this luck—until, he finally lifted his head and engulfed her with a look of mischief.

Alysa stepped down and took her place at Eirik's side. She hoped her trembling was not visible. They would be together for days, but not alone, she thought irritably. She must watch herself closely, as her desire for him was growing stronger each day. She could not forget the passionate night they had spent together, and she longed to repeat it. No matter what anyone said, she *knew* he was Gavin, so there was no harm in lying with him as lovers, even if Eirik did not understand her willingness. Although she had made love only to Gavin Crisdean, she felt that no two men could make love in the same manner. But Eirik had. Her body flamed at his nearness and she craved to be held in his arms, to feel his lips against hers. Some day soon, he would discover the truth and he would belong to her again. Trosdan and the gods had promised her. With all her heart and soul she loved and desired only this man. She was no longer angry with him because she knew his behavior was uncon trollable. She fused her gaze on Trosdan and held it there by sheer willpower.

Trosdan was speaking. "We ride for a place where Queen Boadicea ruled in the ancient land called Iceni, two and a half days from here. There, she battled Roman conquerors, slaughtering foes as bravely and continuously as her invaders. Many claim she slew as many as seventy thousand before the Roman governor attacked her in great force. The warrior queen was beaten and tortured, and her family was brutalized and murdered. Seek the place where Boadicea took her life to end her madness and torment. Travel the Icknield Way into her once-ravished lands. Look across the North Sea to our homeland. Look where another great fleet landed their dragon-prowed ships and stepped upon this kingdom to begin a clever conquest of this isle. Look where Vortigern sought help against his rival Prince Ambrosius after slaying the prince's father and sending his rival into exile; yet he feared his return. What you seek is the figurehead of a ship, a spirit prow. Upon the dragon's head is an all-seeing eye for guidance upon the waters and protection from our god Njord. Find a curved gulley filled with rocks and sand and water. Claim this second prize and sail to many victories and riches."

Ulf asked loudly, "Why can we not receive the next clues at the next sight and so forth? Why must we return to camp after each victory? It takes much time and energy."

Trosdan cleverly explained, "There is no assurance all three bands will go to the same place, Ulf. We would waste more time and energy seeking them to join us at the right location. It is best to meet here. But there is a more important reason: Odin wishes the clues to be given here at his sacred temple."

"But it is a pagan temple to Celtic gods!" Ulf said scornfully.

To fool everyone, Trosdan lifted his shoulders and stiffened in indignation. He stared at Ulf as if the man were mad, contemptuous. "Nay, Ulf. Question any Celt. They know naught about it, as it has been here long before their memories; they only use it. It was built by our gods long ago and has awaited our arrival and conquest. Look around. It was placed in the *ve,* as is our way," he explained, referring to the open downland which surrounded Stonehenge. "The Druids and Celts worship in forests and groves or in manmade temples. Our gods dropped these stones from the heavens, marking this spot for our sacred quest. Surely you do not think any man or group of men could bring such enormous stones here and upright them, and place heavy lintels over some. This place is a Viking temple to Odin and our other gods: Thor, Frey, Njord, and Freyja. Each stone represents one of our gods. The smaller ones honor the land spirits, the following spirits, and the *disir*—our lady spirits. This is holy ground. Speak no further evil upon it. Be content to be among the champions."

Many stared at Ulf in displeasure, as he was becoming more and more quarrelsome and disrespectful of their queen, wizard, and gods alike. They did not care to see a man of his rank and prowess acting as a bad child or a foolish woman. Those who traveled with him were disgruntled and longed to be members of either of the other two bands.

Ulf noticed this perilous reaction to his behavior and he cautioned himself to control himself to get his way. There was something about their new queen which caused him to act rashly. He could think of nothing more pleasurable than taming her by force. When she was in his possession, he would do just that, he vowed sardonically.

He grinned and held silent. He did have a stroke of luck this time; he knew where Hengist's great fleet had landed. While his rivals were gathering clues, he would be riding there as swiftly as a thunderbolt traveled. One good thing he surmised, Alysa had not aided Rolf, and had better not aid Eirik! From appearances, she seemed to favor Rolf as a man. So, if she knew the riddles' answers, Rolf would have found the amulet. *The amulet . . .* If Eirik had not tricked his men, the sacred dagger would be his by now. Since it was not in Eirik's sheath, that meant he had hidden it somewhere between the site and the camp. But where? It had to be close by as Eirik would have to produce it that last day to show he still had it.

As the group was dismissed, Ulf quickly called his men together and left camp at a swift pace. Without the nosy wizard along, he could make some clever plans to slow down his rivals.

Rolf did not know where Hengist, the Jute chieftain and paid warrior for Vortigern, had landed on this isle. He suspected that Eirik knew and would rush there, so he had the man watched. He hurried to his dwelling to question Enid. All the enslaved woman knew was the general area, and that lack of aid angered Rolf against her. There was nothing he could do except ride to the shore, skirt it, and look for a clue to the hidden gulley. He gathered his band and Trosdan and departed, noticing that Eirik was still in camp.

Eirik escorted Alysa to the corral. She tied her small bundle to her saddle, mounted Calliope, and they joined his band. The men, following their victory, were in high spirits. Unaware that Ulf knew the location, Eirik did not rush Alysa. The handsome warrior knew where Hengist had landed with his fleet of hired men. In a little over two days, he decided confidently, he would have the second prize. Soon, he would win the best prize of all—the woman at his side. But for now, he was satisfied to spend time with her.

They rode for hours, with Alysa between Eirik and Aidan. As they traveled northeastward, they encountered yellowing grasses and trees. Alysa was reminded again that winter was only months away. She would be glad to get this ruse completed and return home with her husband. She envisioned them snuggled beneath furry covers, making love and exchanging thoughts about this exciting event in their lives. How wonderful it would be to have peace again, in her land and with her beloved.

She glanced at Eirik, and he looked at her. She smiled, and he returned it. Their pace was steady, but not swift. Even so, she did not try to converse with him, as the band was behind them. From the corner of her eye, she studied his virile body and handsome profile. He was lean and hard, and golden-skinned. His short-sleeved tunic exposed his muscled arms, and she imagined them holding her. His legs, clad in long trousers, were long and agile. She pictured herself lying between them, and quivered. Her gaze roamed to his hands, hands which could be strong or gentle. How she yearned for them to caress her. As he moistened his sensual lips, she did the same, thinking of how passionately he kissed and how his mouth could drive her wild with pleasure as it roved her body. She was glad he did not look her way, as she always became lost in those green eyes. It was a face and body she knew well. Yea, she concluded happily, this man was her lost love, had to be Gavin. Gods above, how she loved him and needed him!

Eirik was aware of her intense study of him and stirred him from head to foot. His heart yearned to win her. His loins burned to possess her. His soul thirsted to make her happy. Never had he dreamed of making a woman his, totally his. Yet this woman, this rare creature, gave him longings he had never experienced before. She had enchanted him, possessed him, enthralled him. She filled his mind during wakeful hours and consumed his dreams at night. His life seemed centered around winning

274

her and making her his. Yet he wanted more than passionate nights with her; he wanted the happy *days,* each minute of them, with her. He wanted to share her laughter, her tears, her victories, her defeats, her dreams, her destiny. For the first time in his life, marriage was agreeable, very agreeable.

Eirik tried not to think of losing this quest. Yet if he did, he could not lose her. No matter what she believed was her destiny and duty, if he lost, he would steal her away and convince her only their love mattered.

They reached a lovely area at dusk. A serene glen with a deserted hut was before them. Eirik lifted his hand to stay the men. "We halt here for the night where there is shelter for our queen!" he shouted.

The band was more than agreeable. Camp was made quickly, provisions were unpacked, and a hearty meal was prepared. The men supped on ale, bread, and roasted meat. They sat around fires an enticing distance from the hut in the trees.

Alysa settled herself in the hut, unmindful of its dust and mess. She fluffed the straw mattress and flung a blanket over it. When Eirik came to bring her food and drink, she smiled and thanked him.

Eirik had decided not to press her and frighten her further. He must woo her slowly and carefully, gently and tenderly. While slyly tempting and stimulating her, he must prove to Alysa that he was the only man for her. "You are a superior soldier and queen, my enchanting Alysa. Few men possess your skills, courage, and wits. Each time I hear you speak, I am awed. You ride like a weightless cloud moving across a tranquil sky, and you fight like a warrior with great prowess and experience," he complimented her. "Sometimes I fear you cannot be real and this is only a cruel dream. I am glad you are here with me. There has been so little time to get to know more about

275

you. Soon the quest will be over and I must win you or perish trying."

Alysa was moved by his tender words and stirring mood. In a softened voice, she cautiously replied, "I pray you will find a second victory on this journey, Eirik, and I wish I could aid your search. Do you know the place where Hengist landed?" she asked, ready to enlighten him with what little information she had gleaned from Trosdan.

Confident and happy now, he replied, "Yea, my enchantress. I know this land well. I was here a long time with Hengist, and I stay alert to all things around me. There is no need to worry about failure. Eat before your meal grows cold and unappealing."

As he reached the door, she ventured boldly, "The food is not what appeals to me or worries me, Eirik."

He halted and turned to face her. Their gazes fused and searched. Their passions blazed. "Name your worries, my queen, and I will appease them. Speak your desires, m'love, and I will fetch them for you."

She could not go another day without having him again. She needed his solace, his strength, his acceptance, his love. "You are both, Eirik," she responded bravely, helplessly.

Eirik was surprised by her confession. His heart pounded in joy and in panic, and his loins responded to her. But they were not alone. Over a hundred men were camped outside this hut, men who would slay him for doing what he was thinking. Should he be strong and wise? Could he be either tonight with her so entreating? "Our band camps nearby. There is little time and much danger," he reluctantly reasoned against what he desperately wanted—to make love to her tonight.

"Yea, I know," she murmured, going to stand before him. "I fear I am weak and wicked, Eirik, for you torment me day and night."

"What can I do to ease your pain, my queen?" he inquired.

ervously as his hand reached out to caress her flushed cheek. He trembled at the contact and her enticing gaze.

"That is for you to decide, Eirik, my love."

Sixteen

Eirik's heart sped up at her inviting words. "There is b
one thing to decide, m'love: if we will risk all to sper
only a short while together. I can do so easily, but I do n
wish to endanger you, nor do I wish to take you so swift
at such a special moment."

Alysa was trembling with need. "You said I possesse
courage. Now I shall prove it. Stay with me, Eirik, if on
for a brief time."

He did not have to ask if she was certain; her gaze to
him she was. For Eirik, the decision now seemed simpl
irresistible. "Tonight we must rush our union or the othe
will wonder why I stay with you so long. But soon we wi
have all the time we want together."

"Tonight my only desire is you, Eirik. Do not leave n
aching with hunger for you. Can you not see you are th
only man I want?"

"I love you, Alysa. I swear I have never said that to
woman before, nor have I desired or taken one since mee
ing you. You have shown me what my life is missing, ar
you have filled my heart with joy."

That brave declaration made her heart and spirit soa
Her arms encircled his waist and she snuggled against h
hard body, resting her cheek at his heart. She heard

ounding swiftly. "You do not know what it means to me) hear those words from your lips," she murmured, thrilled at this new Gavin would also fall in love with her.

"It does not frighten you to know how fiercely I love nd desire you? That I will do anything to have you, even bduct you after the quest if I do not win it?" he inquired, is voice heavy with emotion.

Alysa lifted her head to fuse their gazes. "No matter what appens in the quest, or after it, we shall be together for ll time. But do not act rashly before we make our plans," he cautioned him, as she realized he was serious about aving her one way or another. It was imperative that he ot panic and kidnap her before the attack, else her forces vould walk into unspeakable danger. It was also vital that, ˙ she could not break the spell over him before the two ides clashed, she make the bond between them so tight nd strong that he would side with her that awesome day.

"As long as I know you will be mine for all time, nothing lse matters," he vowed, spreading kisses over her face and air.

"I am yours, Eirik, now and forever. But there are other natters which must be handled wisely before anyone learns ur secret. First, I must do my duty here or great havoc vill follow us. Once they have a king, they will have less eed and hunger for their queen."

"After the quest, if I do not win, will you give up your rown to escape with me?" he asked, needing her answer onight.

"It warms my soul that you would sacrifice all to have ne. I can do no less. When my task here is done, we will e lovers and rulers or we will leave together. We will return) my castle in Damnonia and live there. You will love my nd and people as I do."

Eirik was too consumed with love and desire to hear the varning clues in her words or to read them in her eyes. He

cupped her face and looked deeply into her misty eyes. H
asked worriedly, "What of your husband, the Cumbria
prince?"

Alysa wanted to shake him to his senses and shout, Yc
are my husband! For now, she was speaking to "Eirik" an
she had to continue this pretense. Her hold over him wa
not powerful enough to compel him to defy his gods, 1
war against his friends and people, or to accept the tru
about himself and their relationship. Later, Gavin would u
derstand her actions. "He will not come between us. W
are destined to live as one."

Eirik embraced her tightly. "What of your people?"

Alysa's fingers trailed over his facial scar and wondere
if it would vanish with his spell. No matter, it was not di
figuring. "They will see how much I love you and nee
you. They will accept you at my side. We shall be happ
and prosperous there."

Eirik clarified, "I meant, your people here. You are quee
They have craved your return for many years. What if the
pursue us?"

Alysa wondered why he did not say, *our* people and *v
have craved. She put her arms around his neck and lifte
herself to brush her lips over his. As she did so, she e
treated, "Do not worry about such problems tonight. O
time together is short and precious. We will handle ar
trouble and decisions later."

In response, Eirik's mouth covered hers. They kisse
many times before he carried her to the musty straw ma
tress and placed her there. He pulled the linen shirt ov
her head and dropped it to the dirt floor. He unlaced tl
ties at her waist and wiggled off her loose pants over supp
hips and sleek legs, baring her golden flesh to his fie
gaze. He wished he had more time to enjoy her and the
stolen union, to give her immense pleasure. Quickly, he di

280

carded his own clothing and joined her on the rough, blanket-covered bunk.

Their lips meshed feverishly and their hands caressed ardently. Passions were ablaze within them both, so they did not have to ignite them. Yet each touch fueled those brilliant flames and increased their raging desires. Both knew time was short, so they united their bodies and sought sweet pleasure and relief. Their mouths never parted until rapture's peak was in sight.

Eirik gazed into her seductive eyes and increased their pace. Soon, they were falling over ecstasy's precipice. They clung together, lips, arms, bodies, while they savored each magical moment. Their heads spun dizzily at the swift climb and rapid descent of their passion. Yet they participated happily, knowing this was only one of many times they would share.

Eirik held her until his breathing had calmed so he could speak. "I tried to stay away from you, but I could not, Alysa. We must be careful until the quest has ended and we can be together. When I saw you in the forest with Rolf, my anger and pain were boundless. Why did you turn to him after our night together?"

Alysa told as much of the truth as she dared. "I knew you were there. That is why I behaved so boldly with him. It was an impulsive and cruel thing to do, and I am sorry. There were many reasons, Eirik. I needed for you to avoid me so we would not be endangered. I needed for you to be strong for both of us, to prevent us from offending our gods. I was frightened and confused by what we had done, by what we feel for each other. I feared what we were doing was wicked and perilous, but I cannot stop myself from wanting you and yielding to you. You have some power over me which I cannot resist. Too, I needed to fool Rolf. He was worried about us being too close. I feared he would suspect the truth about us. I knew he would not if he believed I desired only him. I saw you behind the tree and knew you could rescue me if I could not control his ardor. I am sorry I deceived you and hurt you. Can you understand and forgive me?"

His gaze and voice were filled with tenderness when he replied, "Yea, m'love, I understand, but there is nothing to forgive."

Surprise was exposed in her eyes. "You trust me and believe me? You will allow me to do what I must?"

"Yea, m'love, for all such things are part of you. If any danger approaches you, I will be nearby to aid you. You are skilled in all things, Alysa, so I have no doubts in you or your prowess."

Suddenly he sounded nothing like Gavin Crisdean. Tremors passed over her. She coaxed, "Tell me all about you, Eirik. It is strange and frightening to have a stranger in my heart and bed. I know so little about you."

He chuckled, looking and sounding like her lost love again. "I promise to tell you all in the next few days while we are together. There is nothing to fear, m'love. Soon you will know as much about me as I do. For now, much as I wish it were not true, I must leave you."

She had to agree. "Go, my love, before others worry and question us. We will speak tomorrow."

Eirik used her water bag to wash himself, removing all hints of lovemaking from his body. He smiled at her and kissed her before departing, with helpful words. "Call out if you need anything from me."

Alysa rose from the bed and bathed herself. She picked at the chilled food, but ate very little. She aimlessly paced the small hut to relax her body. Was there, she asked herself, any doubt in her mind that Eirik was Gavin? "Gods be merciful, for I am not certain."

* * *

The following day passed swiftly because they traveled just as rapidly as time did to reach the ancient land of Iceni. Somewhere on this coast, Hengist and Horsa had landed their great fleet and hired out to King Vortigern. The shoreline was too far to make today, so they halted again to camp, this time at a deserted Roman villa from days long past.

They were near the Broads where many lakes formed a vast estuary of blended brackish freshwater and brine, where many species of fowl made their homes: water hen, bittern, snipe, heron, and kingfisher. Here and there trees grew along the banks of snaking waterways which were seldom more than nine feet deep, but linked by several rivers and covering many miles. Grasses and wildflowers grew in abundance, and lightly wooded areas could be seen. It was a beautiful area, a peaceful and secluded one.

They had not sighted the other two bands during their journey, but surely they were within miles of them, if they had guessed the clues correctly. Tomorrow they would reach the coast which looked toward their homeland, to begin their search for the second treasure.

During their journey, Alysa had been given no time or privacy to speak with Eirik, to allow him to keep his promise of last night. She had to learn more about him. She needed to know his history.

She wandered through the crumbling villa as their meal was being prepared in the camp nearby. When dismounting earlier, Eirik had whispered in her ear that he would sneak inside to visit her again, again in a rush which tonight rankled her. She hated being dishonest with her husband, and hated this tormenting confusion on her part. Either she believed he was Gavin or she did not. If she did not, she should not be giving herself to Eirik! Perhaps, she concluded defensively, it was only fatigue and tension which assailed her.

When Eirik brought her evening meal, they ate in sight of the men, within the tumbledown wall of the villa, but not within their hearing. Though they sat close enough to speak privately, their bodies were not close enough to inspire gossip. Both were careful to appear calm and friendly, but not intimate or secretive.

Between bites of roasted fowl, she reminded, "You said you would tell me all about yourself. Please, do so now."

Eirik shrugged and complied. "There is little to tell, m'love. An adventurer's life is much the same day to day. I have seen many lands and met many challenges. If the pay and my mood were right, I accepted any job for money or stimulation. I left home many years ago to go araiding and to seek excitement. At that time, I did not realize it was to seek happiness, peace, and fulfillment more than wealth or recognition. I needed to find respect for myself and from others." Looking as if these memories pained him, Eirik continued after a few bites. "My father was a cruel and greedy man. When I was sixteen, nearly the size I am now, he slew my mother and replaced her with another wife. He claimed she had plotted with his rival against him and had lain with him during his absence. If such claims were true, I never witnessed them or suspected them. Yet he was my father and our chieftain, so I could not call him a liar and killer without proof."

He gazed off at the horizon, looking vulnerable and tormented. "My father kept many women around him. There were few days when all were not bearing his seed, for his appetite was large. Some say, and I do not doubt them, that he slew many of his newborn to keep his house under manageable number. We quarreled often, and I hated him. At first chance, I left home and seldom returned to visit."

Eirik met her sympathetic gaze. "The gods finally punished him. He was attacked by a rival and all in his dwelling were slain. I could not grieve over his death, for he was wicked and selfish. I saw no reason to challenge for his lands and rank, so I remained at sea or in foreign lands. Saeric and Aidan have been my friends for years. We have shared many adventures and perils. When they came here, I asked to join them once more. I had been with Hengist since winter departed, but he lacks spirit and hunger, and I needed a new challenge."

"Why did you not wish to challenge your family's killer? And why did you not want your father's lands and rank? Is your spirit so restless that you find home boring and must constantly be on the move?"

"Nay, I was restless because I was not wanted there and it was constant war with my father and his many families. I traveled only to find peace and distraction to consume my days and nights. Until now, I have found no one and nothing of value to settle me down. But I am weary of such an existence and am eager to share a simple life with you. I was the only child of my slain mother. The other wives were not of our tribe. The lands which my father held had been taken by force from the rival who reclaimed them, as was his right and duty. Would you have risked your life to aid the clan of Isobail?"

Alysa thought about those words. "Nay," she replied honestly.

When Alysa questioned his facial scar, Eirik told her the same tale which Aidan had. Even so, she detected a glimmer of deceit in him, as if his new friends had revealed that conversation and he had repeated it. Perhaps he was only doing so to keep her from doubting him and his friends. "Does your arm pain you?" she asked, changing the subject to avoid deliberation on the scar and his false tale.

Eirik glanced at the healing wound from Olaf during their contest. "Nay, it is fine. Did you watch him? He appeared strange."

Alysa wondered if Trosdan had drugged Eirik's opponent

285

as he had hinted, and wondered if the wizard had compelled Eirik to desire only her as she had insisted. She needed to ask Trosdan those disturbing questions. "Yea, he seemed possessed by Loki. I am glad you won."

"As am I," he concurred with a broad grin.

"What of Hengist? Does he offer us any peril? Had you heard of me?" she probed, eyeing him closely for any further sign of deceit.

"Yea, m'love, I had heard the legends about you, as had the Jute chieftain. Many times Hengist spoke of Isobail's evil in your land. Some of her brigands were renegades from his band. He did not crave you at such a high price, as he does not wish to lose his stronghold here or to become king of the Vikings far away. He is content to remain in the lands which he demanded as pay from Vortigern. But if his greed and guile become too large and obvious, Vortigern will come to fear and distrust him and will push him out of Britain."

"I am glad you did not remain with him, else we would not have met. But what of your wandering spirit after we are wed?"

"Since I have met you, it troubles me no more. I am ready and eager to settle down with you as my wife in our home, with our children. Do you wish to know more about me?" he inquired. "Ask any question and I will answer it."

Alysa considered his query and realized that, if he was Gavin, he had been prepared well. Therefore, his answers would provide no clues to his identity and enchantment. "When we are together for all time, we can speak more on our pasts."

"The day will come, m'love, when we know each other as well as we know ourselves. Think of the many talks we will have, the many nights and days we will share. I can imagine no better fate."

"You will not become bored and restless with such a dull

286

life? You would not desert me to seek excitement?" she teased.

"How could any man become such with you at his side? If we desire adventure, we will seek it together, as you are a better warrior than most men. Now that I have found you, Alysa, I would never risk losing you or making you unhappy."

She grinned and jested, "I will remind you of such words when you grow weary of me and our mundane homelife."

"That day will never dawn, m'love." He inhaled deeply. "I must leave you for now. I will sneak to you after dark."

Alysa watched him rejoin the men before entering the villa. She went to the sunken pool and filled it from a neighboring well. She scrubbed her body and prepared herself for her love's stealthy arrival.

Alysa was awakened to tantalizing caresses and kisses. Her heavy lids fluttered and opened. She smiled into Eirik's grinning face and whispered, "I fell asleep awaiting you. What kept you so long?"

"I waited until the men were imprisoned by sleep or ale. I almost left you slumbering, m'love. You looked so tired and comfortable. Am I forgiven for awakening you?" he asked in a husky tone.

"Forgiven if you join me quickly."

Hurriedly Eirik stripped and lay down beside her. Alysa rolled half atop him and covered his neck and chest with fiery kisses. Her fingertips grazed softly over his tawny flesh, savoring and admiring the rolling landscape of his muscular body. He closed his eyes and let her continue her seductive journey. Her lips trailed down his right arm, to nibble and kiss his fingers. Then they traveled upward again, across his chest which was rising and falling rapidly with heightened excitation, to journey down his left arm and tease his hand with her adoring mouth.

Alysa covered his lips with hers and tantalized him with her taste and skills. Her hand drifted down his sleek side. His torso rose and fell slightly where muscles were enlarged and honed with power and use. He was a magnificent creature, a splendid creation by the gods and his own labors.

She kissed his eyes and imagined gazing into their dark-green depths. Her lips passed over his finely chiseled cheekbones and jawline, brushed over his shapely nose. Again, they sealed with his full and sensual lips. Yea, her dreamy mind told her, it was the noble face of a handsome prince; it was a face which she knew well.

Through the broken roof, moonlight flowed over his frame and lovingly caressed it, just as her hands were doing. The provocative glow caused his flesh to appear a deeper shade of bronze, but that was only a trick of the lighting. Yet his darkened hair had no sunny streaks to capture the silvery light and reflect it. She pressed her lips to the scar on his face and helplessly wished it away, but it did not vanish. She kissed the area over his heart and ordered the royal crest of Cumbria to reappear there, but it did not.

Her hand boldly ventured lower, stimulating the skin along his hips and thighs. Her hand carefully wrapped around his straining manhood. Slowly and sensuously and appraisingly she massaged it. Again she told herself this familiar body was Gavin Crisdean's.

Alysa desperately wanted to recover Gavin's memory. They were locked into this mission now, so it was too late for him to halt it or to refuse to continue it. She straddled his hips and slipped his manhood within her body, hoping this action would refresh similar times from the past. She made love to him wildly and freely.

Eirik gripped her waist with his hands and matched her pace. His undulating hips gave them both immense pleasure. His hands left her waist to cover her breasts. Gently, he kneaded them, causing them to grow taut with arousal.

They moved together until blissful sensation claimed them. Alysa bent forward and fused their mouths. Eirik rolled them over and continued driving into her welcoming body until all spasms ceased. It was an experience of enormous rapture and satisfaction.

Later, she whispered, "There is a small pool nearby if you wish to bathe in it before leaving."

Eirik lifted her and carried her to the pool. Before washing himself, he bathed her.

Alysa teased, "If you do not halt this stirring play, we will need to join our bodies again."

"Yea, you cause my body to burn as no woman ever has." He kissed her and caressed her, his hands moving up and down her flesh.

She gently pushed him away and warned, "You must go, Eirik."

Reluctantly he left the pool, dried himself, and put on his garments. He knelt to kiss her again and to murmur, "I love you, Alysa."

"Hurry, before I refuse to let you go tonight," she jested.

He grinned, then sneaked from the villa.

Alysa left the pool to dry off and dress. She stretched out on the pallet and closed her eyes. "Soon, my beloved, you will remember."

At midmorning, two of Ulf's men raced toward them. When they halted, the men shouted, "We have been attacked! We need help! Come quickly or all will be slain!"

The group rode swiftly behind the two men for over an hour, northward. Finally, Eirik ordered them to stop and

289

questioned, "Where is this attack? What were you doing in this area?"

Leikn rubbed the healing leg which Eirik had injured, knowing he would limp forever because of that wound behind his knee. "Only a few more miles. We were pursued by a great force of brigands and had to flee this way. Before we were entrapped, Sigurd and I escaped to seek help. We are lucky you were in our path. We must go quickly."

Eirik suspected they were being cleverly waylaid. But if they were not, they had to go to the aid of the other band. He let the two men guide them for another few miles, then halted again. "Either you are lost, Leikn, or you trick us," he accused.

Leikn grinned, aware this band had lost too much time to thwart Ulf's victory. "The wizard and queen said the champions were to use their wits and daring to obtain victory, and Ulf has done so. His trick has worked. You will reach the coast too late to find the second prize. By the rules, no one was harmed and the victory is fair."

Eirik's narrowed eyes seemed to blaze with green fire. He had been made to look the fool before his love and the others. He should have suspected guile, had suspected guile, but had allowed his love-dulled wits to be swayed. "We ride to the coast!" he shouted angrily.

When they reached the shoreline, they galloped southward. They swept past a small coastal village where peasants stared at them in dread and surprise. The sky and sea were a dark blue; the land was brown and barren. As feared they sighted men camped beyond them: Ulf's triumphant band, and Rolf's sullen one.

As they dismounted, Ulf grinned broadly, tauntingly "You are too late, Eirik. The treasure is mine," he remarked smugly. He pointed to the figurehead which was being cleaned by several of his men.

The curved wooden prow was mostly brown and appeared very sturdy. Oddly, it looked old, yet new. The "neck" was carved to appear like hundreds of overlapping scales. The dragon's nostrils were large and flared, and Alysa could imagine smoke and flames coming from them as ancient legends spoke of fire-snorting dragons. Its eyes were wide and glaring, as if trying to mesmerize or terrify its intended prey. Its gaping mouth exposed long teeth and a snaking tongue. Atop its head were raised bumps from which short horns protruded. It was a fierce and intimidating sight, the kind which had struck horror into the hearts of numberless victims. But what held her attention was the large eye in the middle of the beast's forehead—a blue eye with a penetrating gaze, as if it could pierce flesh and soul, the all-seeing eye of Njord which Trosdan had spoken of in camp.

"Is it not beautiful, my queen?" Ulf hinted at her left side.

Alysa eyed it again and replied, "It has great power and rugged beauty, Ulf. I am awed by it."

Ulf boasted of how he had located it and revealed its hiding place. He motioned to a moody Eirik. "We both have prizes, but Rolf has none," he taunted the tall blond warrior.

Rolf bristled noticeably. "The quest is not over, Ulf. There are three more to be found."

"I will seize them all," the redhead bragged confidently. "This one will be guarded closely so it cannot be stolen or tricked from me."

"As you tricked us today?" Eirik sneered angrily.

Ulf laughed mockingly. "It was done fairly, and it worked."

"I hope you do not get into real trouble, for we will not answer your summons for help again," Eirik warned.

"We must ride for camp so the next quest can be undertaken."

"Nay," Alysa said. "It is late and all are weary. We camp here."

Ulf argued, "If we ride tonight and tomorrow, we can reach camp quickly. Stay here if you wish, my queen, but we head for home."

Alysa was vexed. "The quest cannot begin until all return to camp, Ulf, so you waste your time and energy with such reckless haste."

The redhead grumbled, but knew he could not change their minds.

Alysa was amazed by Trosdan's preparations and cunning. She looked around and inquired, "Where is Trosdan? Was he not with you?"

Rolf revealed, "He was tired and ill, my queen, so I encouraged him to return to camp so he would not slow us. He is very old and weak."

Distress was exposed in her gaze. She was tempted to follow Ulf's suggestion so she could check on the elderly Druid. After her words against such haste, it would look selfish. "Did someone go with him to tend him and protect him?"

"Nay," Rolf responded. "We were not far from camp and he said he could make it back alone."

Alysa sighed worriedly. "He has many burdens upon his back. The journey here was long and hard on him. Perhaps I will ask him to remain in camp instead of going along with a champion each time."

"That will be good, my queen," Ulf remarked, "as he slows us."

Alysa did not retort, though she wanted to do so. "Make camp and rest so we can ride at dawn."

Rolf and Eirik both asked if she needed anything.

"Only food and sleep," she replied honestly.

* * *

As she gazed across the blue water, she wondered what her ancestor's land was like. She asked Rolf if his land was far away.

"Yea, Alysa, many days by ship from here. I have missed you."

Without looking at him, she cautioned, "Be on guard, Rolf, for Eirik appears jealous when he sees us together. We must do nothing to arouse his suspicion against us. Do not worry about the prizes and quest; you know our plans. But tell no one, not even your best friends."

"I will obey, queen of my heart and life, but it is hard."

"Leave me before someone wonders why we speak too long."

Just as Rolf departed, Eirik approached her. "Point toward your land and pretend you are telling me about it," she instructed him. As Eirik complied, she related her conversation with Rolf. "We must be more careful than ever, my love," she cautioned.

Eirik warned, "It is unwise to tempt Rolf. He will be dangerous."

Alysa pushed windblown hair from her face as she whispered, "It is the only way to control him, my love. Trust me," she urged.

"I trust you because you have proven your love to me."

She hinted, "In the days to come, Eirik, I might be forced to act strangely. Be patient and do not doubt my love and my promise."

"Act strangely?" he echoed. "I do not understand."

"For our protection, I must dupe Ulf and Rolf with devious words and deeds. Before our people, I must act as if the only things which matter to me are the sacred quest and my impending marriage. If I appeared to weaken toward you and my destiny . . ."

Eirik inhaled the sea air. "I understand. Do not worry."

They left the shore to join the others to eat and slumber.

* * *

Far away, many unexpected and startling things were taking place in Damnonia, in the Viking settlement, and at the site of quest number three.

Two days later, the rapidly traveling bands reached camp after dusk. Trosdan was among those who left their dwellings to greet them.

Alysa embraced the old Druid. "How do you fare, Wise One? I have been so worried about you."

The wizard smiled and nodded. "It was nothing more than something foul I ate. I have rested, taken a healing draught, and recovered fully. Tell me of the quest."

Ulf did so before Alysa could answer.

During the redhead's boasting, Trosdan glanced at Rolf and Eirik, who were both silent and moody, and watching Alysa with desire. He accurately surmised that more than losing the second prize to Ulf had them sad and worried. He furtively eyed Alysa, and fretted. It had been foolish to instruct her to romance the three champions. It was unnecessary, as her beauty and rank would enchant them sufficiently. She should have remained aloof and regal, tempting, but out of reach and peril. Now, Eirik and Rolf were too bewitched by her actions to think clearly, and Ulf was provoked to winning her unfairly. It was a hazardous situation. But soon her head would clear of its confusion and she would think of nothing except victory and survival.

The schedule was made for the next day and they disbanded.

Inside Rolf's longhouse, Enid welcomed her lover home eagerly. She prepared him a cup of ale, laced with the love potion. As he drank it, she handed him the amulet Eirik had found on the first quest. She explained, "I saw him hide it where none would suspect—in the queen's dwelling. After everyone left camp, I stole it for you, Lord Rolf, to make you happy and to lessen your anger against me."

Rolf stared at the sacred dagger in his hand. Now he possessed one prize and Ulf possessed one, and Eirik had none. Ecstasy flooded his body. "How did you do this clever thing?" he asked, impressed.

Enid smiled seductively. "I saw Eirik sneaking toward the queen's house, so I concealed myself behind the curtain. He slipped inside while all were at the sacred temple and hid the amulet in his belongings. He knew she could say nothing if she discovered it there. How cunning of him to pull such a trick, to force her to aid his victory for her. You must tell no one you have this prize or Eirik will try to recover it. He will not know the dagger is missing until he goes to fetch it for the final ritual; then, it will be too late. He will believe the queen found it and gave it to you. I wish I could steal Ulf's prow for you, but it is too large and heavy. I love you and will do anything for you."

Rolf's astonished gaze met Enid's enticing one. "You love me? But you are my slave. How can this be so?"

"There is no man with more beauty and prowess than you, Lord Rolf. You have been kind and gentle. You have taken me with a passion which enflames my heart and body. I wish only to remain with you and to serve you in all ways."

Watching Rolf, the enthralled woman feared she was being too bold. She had to help her love win the quest or he could be slain in the final battle for all prizes. "I am certain you will win Alysa and become High King, for you are the best man here or anywhere. I will keep my eyes and ears open to help you win your desires. Surely that is why the gods spared my life when Ulf slew the others."

The potion was taking effect on Rolf. His loins burned for attention. His mind soared with joy and confidence. He felt that the gods were smiling upon him, and aiding him through this captive. Enid loved him and would obey his every command. He should reward her.

Rolf's wits were not so dulled that he did not realize how he could use this woman to his advantage. She had a weakness for him, one to exploit. He told her softly, "You have done well, my beautiful slave. I am lucky to own you. Do you wish me to reward your wits and courage by enflaming you again tonight?"

"Nothing would please me more, Lord Rolf. I love you."

As Rolf undressed Enid, he stirred her passions by his words. "I shall give you the greatest pleasures of all tonight. Lie upon my bed and I will send your mind and body to paradise."

Enid obeyed while Rolf yanked off his garments. She looked at his manhood and smiled. "Do you not wish me to pleasure you?"

"Later, after you are fully sated. Tonight, I will be the slave and you will be the master. Give me any command to please you."

Enid was trembling with desire and anticipation. "Do whatever you desire with me," she entreated hoarsely.

"As you command, Lady Enid," he murmured, his hands and lips feverishly assailing her fiery body.

When Trosdan finally returned to Alysa's dwelling, she asked, "Are you certain you are well?"

"I was never ill, Alysa. I only used that excuse to get away from the bands so I could gather the plants and herbs which we will need later. I did not tell you before you left camp because I wanted your reaction to be convincing. I am sorry I worried and frightened you."

"It is so good you are not ill, Wise One. I would no

know what to do if anything happened to you. All would be lost."

As a precaution, Trosdan gave her the remaining clues and locations for the quest. He told her which tricks to use to "prove" Odin was supplying them to her in his stead. "Ulf halted me after I visited the injured. One of his spies told him I did not return to camp until this morning. I said I was too ill to travel and made camp until I was well enough to return. He said he does not trust me. I warned him of my rank, but it did not matter to him that *attibas* are to be honored and obeyed. He is dangerous, Alysa. Be wary of him and alert for his spies. It would be wise not to be so friendly with Eirik and Rolf."

"It is too late to change my behavior or they will wonder about it. Each believes I love him and desire him to win me. I have not tried to fool Ulf, for I could not bear it or convince him of such a ruse."

"Find some clever way to lessen their hunger for you. It has reached a perilous height in both men. We have Ulf to worry about with tricks; we do not need two other men adding to our distraction."

"I will try, Wise One, but it will be difficult with Eirik."

"Be especially careful around him, Alysa."

"He is Gavin; I am certain of it," she disclosed.

"Nay, he is not your husband," Trosdan refuted sternly.

"How can you be so positive?"

"The Runes told me so, and it is true. Beware of him."

"Did you drug Olaf so Eirik could beat him?"

"Nay, I was given no chance to do so. Besides, the Runes said Eirik would be one of the champions, so it was unnecessary."

"Did you enchant Eirik so he would desire only me as promised?"

"Nay, my cherished princess, I felt it was too dangerous.

Eirik's pursuit of you alarms me. I wanted nothing to strengthen it."

"Then, he loves me. I can sense he is being honest and sincere."

"Even if that is true, it must not matter to you. Do not betray yourself and your husband by returning Eirik's love and passion."

Seventeen

The Norsemen were filled with anticipation for their third adventure. The bands gathered in three separate areas to eat and to prepare for the impending clue and their departure. The remaining slaves, along with several Viking helpers, cooked food in each area and served the bands hot stew and bread with tepid ale.

When the meal was finished, the people gathered once more at Stonehenge for the drawing of lots. Trosdan was chosen to go with Rolf again. Eirik was to ride alone. Alysa was to go with Ulf.

Trosdan stood upon the Altar Stone to give his third riddle. "There is a tale of a blemished prince who could not become king because of his terrible disease. He was forced to dwell alone with only a few servants to tend his sores and needs. One day a peasant came by and told the prince how his dying dog was healed after falling into a hot spring. Bladud sought the Waters of Sul and entered them. A prince was dying, but he was healed. A circle of mud with flames beneath. Two springs of water, one hot and one cold. Find his healing bath and be shielded from pain and death. What you seek can be reached today with plenty of time to return to camp before darkness covers this land. You will know your prize by Freyja's image and signs. The goddess of lov[e] will guard your heart from pain and death."

Ulf grinned mischievously, as he had visited the crum[bling] ruins of Aquae Sulis not far away. He knew it ha[d] been a favorite spa of Britain's past conquerors. But the[re] were three pools there, not two. The Great Bath had bee[n] spanned by an arched vault which was decorated with carv[ings] and sculptures. It was said to be guarded by the Celti[c] goddess of the spring, Sulis, whom the Romans called S[ul] Minerva. Long ago, the luxurious resort had been enclose[d] within a wall, all twenty-two acres. It had boasted of priva[te] apartments, clean streets, shaded colonnades, and exquisi[te] gardens with secluded walks.

It had been a marvelous place which had fallen into rui[n] long ago. The locals were said to avoid it because it re[-] flected their days of bondage to the decadent Romans. [It] was considered an evil place where wanton orgies had oc[-] curred. Ulf envisioned those days of drunken, licentious fes[-] tivity. How he would love to have been there during thos[e] times of unbridled indulgence of all passions. It was a goo[d] sign that Alysa would be accompanying him on this pa[r-] ticular quest.

Ulf rushed her to her horse and ordered his band to de[-] part quickly. The men obeyed and off they galloped. The[y] traversed the open downland which encircled the stone tem[-] ple. They encountered light vegetation, then dense wood[-] land. They passed a hilly area called *wolds* where th[e] woodlands were thinner and more scattered. It was a variet[y] of landscape which flashed by rapidly in Ulf's hurry.

Alysa wondered where the other two bands were, as sh[e] had not seen them since leaving camp. That was strang[e] because the way to Aquae Sulis was on a direct line fro[m] Stonehenge.

When they halted briefly to rest the horses, Alysa aske[d]

Ulf, "Have you cleverly tricked them again? They are no-where in sight."

Ulf did not know why, but he was glad. "Perhaps they are dumb, my queen, and have not guessed the riddle as I have."

"Perhaps you are right," she replied casually, then smiled. She could not resist playing with this malevolent man. "I have viewed your great prowess many times in the battle ring, Ulf, but it seems I underguessed your wits and daring. That pleases me, for you are a man of high rank. How did you trick them this time?"

Ulf grinned slyly and did not answer her question. "Come, we must ride before the sluggards catch up with us."

They reached Aquae Sulis, and Alysa was amazed by what she observed. Legend said these hot mineral springs possessed healing powers, and had cured Bladud of his leprosy. The Romans had built them and used them for that same reason: healing. It was said the baths had offered hot and cold pools and heated chambers. The largest pillared hall and pool were enormous. She was fascinated. Next to it had been constructed a temple to Minerva. She eyed the shaded walkways, the Roman statues, the carved columns, the impressive sculptures. From the past to the future, these hot springs would flow forever. Houses were situated here and there, evincing their luxury of the past. It was a wondrous place with an earthy atmosphere, an enchanted aura. Too bad the Celts refused to keep it in repair and use it.

"You have never been here before?" Ulf asked.

"Nay, my father never allowed me to leave Damnonia. I was compelled to live a very gentle and sheltered life. It must have been beautiful and tranquil here," she remarked with feigned naiveté.

"Stay and look around while I join my men to seek the prize," Ulf encouraged, wanting her to absorb the carnal aura there.

Amidst scurrying treasure seekers, Alysa strolled along the colonnades. The floors were still in good condition, as were many of the private chambers into which she peeked. The smaller, spring-fed pool was clear and inviting, but the water was surely chilled. The larger one, which had been filled by pipes and pumps, was filthy, displaying an abundance of green growth and bits of trash. She heard a joyful shout, and surmised its meaning. Annoyance nibbled at her.

Ulf hurried back to her side and held up a shield. "The third prize is mine, as *you* soon will be, my lovely queen. It was hanging in the temple. Eirik and Rolf will envy me."

Sigurd and Leikn were behind him. Alysa falsely smiled and congratulated his second success. She wanted to laugh in the man's face, as the shield he was holding up bore the image of Minerva from whose temple it had been taken. She was eager for Eirik to arrive so she could tell him of Ulf's error. "If you are in no rush to return to camp, Ulf, may I enjoy the magical healing pool for a short time?"

The foolish Norseman replied with smugness, "Yea, my queen, there is no hurry now. Seize your pleasures here while we rest and celebrate outside."

"Sigurd and Leikn, stand guard beyond the doors for me," she commanded, mistrustful of Ulf. She had not reached the pedestal yet which held the message from Weylin. She needed more time to look around and privacy to read it, to make sure all was going as planned.

The men left her, forcefully closing the warped door behind them. Ulf glanced at his friends and jested lewdly, "Soon, she will be yielding to more than silly pleasures in watery pools. Let no one disturb her. When she is finished, join me outside to await the others."

Alysa made her way around the unsightly pool to the far end. She had not wanted to approach that area or draw attention to it until she was alone. It was good that her group had reached this area first and that Ulf was distracted

302

by his victory. When the others arrived, they would not intrude on her privacy. She shoved on the heavy urn atop a moldy pedestal. With force and determination, it moved aside and exposed a hidden compartment, and Alysa wondered how Trosdan had known of it. She reached into the hole and withdrew a bound message. She untied the leather strip and unrolled the paper to read it:

"Alysa,
The birds arrived. We are ready. All forces will reach their borders soon. If all is going according to planned, in eight days hence I will be camped here awaiting your third message. When the bird arrives, I will send for the others to join me. This site is closer in case something goes wrong. At your next sign, we will encircle Stonehenge and await your signal to attack. There is another message hidden where this one was. Seek it and cease your worries.

Weylin"

Alysa sighed in relief, as their schedules were matching perfectly. By next Monday, her three forces would be poised at their Logris borders. By Tuesday, Weylin would be camped here, and the bird should reach him by nightfall that same day. By Friday or Saturday, twelve to thirteen days from now, this task would be over.

Alysa recalled Weylin's last words. She went to the urn and reached inside again, withdrawing another bound message which had been shoved to one side, nearly out of reach. She untied it and read:

"Alysa, m'love,
I am sorry I have been selfish and cruel and rash with my words and deeds. Many things troubled me and confused me. My life was changed before I was

303

changed. I needed solitude to clear my head of such wickedness. When I left your side that night, I rode home and my parents helped open my mind and heart to the truth. They told me of your daring ruse and fear struck my heart. I carefully pondered your plan and it is a good one. I will not intrude. I am at our castle now helping to ready our forces to join the others. I will meet you at the attack site and never leave your side again. All goes perfectly with us and our allies. Soon we will seize a great victory and all can be righted once more. I have accepted your destiny and will aid it. Let nothing happen to you, m'love, for I cannot survive without you. I have missed you and feared losing you because of my weaknesses. I love you, Alysa, and want nothing more than a life here with you. Forgive me for how I have wronged you and injured you.

Gavin"

Alysa paled and trembled, slowly sinking to the floor. She could not believe what she was reading. Gavin could not be at home with Weylin! He was here with her as the enspelled Eirik! She read the two messages again. There was no denying it was Gavin's handwriting and words. Her shocked mind screamed, *But how?*

Alysa did not know what to think. Gavin was her husband, her love, her destiny. He was coming soon to reclaim her. He had accepted their fates; he had accepted her as she was. He had admitted his mistakes and begged for forgiveness.

But what of Eirik? Who and what was he? If Eirik was Gavin, these enlightening messages could not have been sent to her. There was no way Gavin, as Eirik, could have gotten word to Weylin to send a false message, or to include his own personal one. She and Trosdan had sent news to

Damnonia far away. These answers had been brought from there by Weylin's messenger. If Gavin had not returned home, he could not know of their actions here or of their plans and of the birds. He could not know to leave his letter in this hiding place, unless Weylin had told him. And Weylin could not have done so unless Gavin was with him! Nay, the stranger with her could not know such things or be responsible for them. That meant . . .

Alysa shuddered again. She had been forewarned that Eirik was not Gavin Crisdean, but she had resisted the truth, ignored it, battled it. The physical and mental differences between the two men had plagued her. Trosdan had cautioned her. The sacred Runes and gods had advised her. The tales of Eirik's friends and Eirik's history had alerted her. Why had she not heeded those numerous warnings?

The truth could not be denied or ignored; Eirik could not be an enspelled Gavin. Even if they were brothers or twins, and even though this mission was vital to her land's survival, that did not excuse what she had done—not once, but three times—with Eirik, her foe, a Norseman, a stranger, and no telling what else.

Tears rolled down Alysa's flushed cheeks. She was weak and wicked. She had been lustful and traitorous. She did not deserve the forgiveness of her husband and their gods, and probably would not receive them. What if she bore a child? Would it be Gavin's or Eirik's? Far worse, how could she love and desire two men equally? Yet, in all honesty, she did. No matter who or what Eirik was, she *did* love and desire him. But she could have only one of them. To keep Gavin, Eirik had to die and carry her wanton secret to his grave. To have Eirik, she had to sacrifice everyone and everything to flee with him, if he still loved and wanted her after she was exposed.

She mentally pictured the two men. At times, they were so alike; at others, they were so different. If only they were the same man! Frustrated, Alysa yanked off her garment and dove into the smaller pool. An excellent swimmer, she traveled one end to the other until she was cold and exhausted, but still did not feel clean or relaxed. She climbed out of the Roman bath and retrieved the two messages. After tearing Gavin's into many pieces, she stuffed both back into their hiding place. She shoved the urn into position. Jerking on her clothes, she mentally shouted, *Curse you, Gavin Crisdean, for this is your fault! If you had not deserted and betrayed me, I would never have yielded to Eirik, be he your image or nay! The deeds are done, and I must live with them.*

Alysa moved aside the urn again to place her response for Weylin there. She had nothing with which to write Gavin a message, and would not have done so if she had! At that moment, her anger with him was as great as it had been after awakening to find him gone.

Tormented, she scoffed silently, *Let him worry and suffer in doubt as I have done!* Since Gavin had admittedly vanished of his own free will, she needed time to decide if she could understand his behavior and forgive him, or ever trust him again! Now she had crucial work to do. She had no time or energy for regrets and anguish. Perhaps she had failed herself, the gods, and her destiny, but such would never happen again!

She stalked from the pool to the doors. She pounded upon them and they were forced open. In spite of her consternation, she smiled and thanked her guards. She walked outside and glanced around. Her timing was perfect, if it could be called such: the other two bands galloped into the area and dismounted.

Rolf had to be restrained from attacking Ulf as the blond warrior shouted in fury, "You have tricked us again! I shall slay you!"

Ulf scowled. "I tricked no one. I rode straight here and found the prize. We have been awaiting you for hours."

"You drugged the food or ale! All have been sleeping for hours!"

Ulf appeared honestly shocked. "Nay, Rolf, I did not. It was the gods who did so. Do you not see I am their chosen champion?"

"You are ruled by Loki, and Odin will destroy you both!"

Ulf noticed the anger which was confronting him. "I know not of such potions. Where would I get enough herbs to drug so many men? How could I have slipped it into your food and drink? I was never near your camps or cauldrons. Ask the slaves who did this evil!"

"They were also drugged, for they ate from the same pots and drank from the same casks! You shall pay for this dark deed."

Ulf scoffed, "If that was my doing, I would accept the credit for such cleverness. No one was harmed and the rules were not broken. But I did not trick you this time."

"Then one of your men did so upon your command!"

"Nay, fool, it was not of our doing!" Ulf glanced at Trosdan and his beady eyes chilled. "Ask the wizard; he knows of such things. He is a stranger amongst us, and I do not trust him. He hates me and insults me each day. He must have done this mischief to cause me trouble. To have me banned from the quest as he threatened."

Trosdan stepped forward, looking indignant and vexed. "Why do you darken my name and show contempt for my sacred rank? This is twice you have called me a liar. Prove such claims or cease them."

Rolf added, "Yea, Wizard, he only seeks another to blame for his dark mischief. He has been disobedient and disrespectful from the start. I say the *attiba* is right; Ulf should be banned from the quest."

When others agreed, Ulf shouted, "Hear me, warriors and

friends! *Someone* has done this evil thing to push me out of the quest. Perhaps Rolf ordered his friend Einar to do so. Einar knows of such matters. Or perhaps Eirik did it; he, like Trosdan, is a near stranger amongst us and might know such tricks and skills."

Rolf and Eirik's men loudly protested Ulf's accusations, saying neither champion had been given the opportunity to carry out such guile, and would not do so if they had! They scolded Ulf for such words.

Rolf scoffed, "Why would we drug ourselves and our bands so you could seize the prize we hunger for? Nay, you lie."

Ulf vowed in outrage, "I am innocent. I will prove myself in the battle ring with any man who doubts me and challenges me."

No one wanted to fight Ulf, not even Rolf or Eirik. Gazes skipped from eye to eye, and no one stepped forward to challenge him.

Ulf shouted, "I will swear my honesty upon the sacred altar when we return to camp. Even if no man wishes to risk his life to clear me of this dark stain, I will clear myself. Let Odin judge me."

Trosdan nodded and agreed. "It shall be done, Ulf, and I will do the same. From that moment hence, you will not challenge me."

"Nor will you challenge or doubt me, Wizard," Ulf retorted.

The men headed for their horses to return to camp before nightfall. Rolf went to Alysa's side to escort her.

Alysa lowered her head and whispered, "The shield which Ulf carries homeward is not the shield of Freyja. Remain here and seek it. Look between the hot and cold pools in the mud bath."

Alysa went to Calliope and mounted. Not once had she looked at Eirik. Her hair was wet and braided; her garment were still damp and clingy. She watched Rolf announce his intention to remain behind for a time to rest his men and horses. Trosdan joined her, and they galloped for the Viking camp.

It was dark when they arrived. Eirik was close behind. He asked to speak with her at the corral. Alysa nodded to Trosdan to comply, and the old wizard reluctantly left them alone.

"You seem pale and different, m'love. What troubles you? Did Ulf harm you? If he did, I will slay him."

Alysa's gaze roamed him before she replied, "I have acted rashly, Eirik. I have allowed lust for you to sway me from my destiny. And you have allowed your hunger for me to distract you from the sacred quest. This . . . thing between us cannot continue until we have done our duties. Until I discover the truth for myself, you must not approach me again. If you dare to abduct me before I agree, I swear I will hate you forever and will try to escape you at every chance. I am confused and troubled, so do not add to my woes at this time. If you truly love me, keep your distance until I summon you."

Stunned, Eirik watched her almost race toward her borrowed dwelling. Much as he longed and was tempted to do so, he dared not pursue her, for she had appeared totally serious. Her words troubled him. Why had she said "lust" instead of "love"? How could she doubt her feelings for him, or his for her? What of the way she had seduced him in the hut and had taken him in the villa? What of her revelations and promises? "We shall be together for all time." "I am yours, now and forever." "We are destined to live as one." "I love you and need you." Why this sudden and agonizing change? She had accused him of being distracted from the sacred quest. Even though she had vowed he would win her regardless of the outcome, did she think he had given up trying to become king and husband at her

309

side? Nay, he had not! In fact, he wanted both coveted ranks.

Once she had told him to be strong for both of them, to prevent them from offending their gods and bringing down their wrath upon them. Was that what she feared, being "wicked and perilous," being exposed? He had promised to trust her even if or when she was "forced to act strangely." All he could do was give her time to sort out her thoughts and feelings, to believe in their love and bond.

Presently, he had another worry. Ulf had two prizes, and he could not allow the evil man to find the last two. It would make Ulf's position in the final battle too powerful. After much thought, he realized these people would never allow them to escape together, so he had to win her and remain here.

Alysa entered the dwelling and faced Trosdan. She confessed, "Ulf did not find the right shield, so I told Rolf where to search for it."

"Why did you choose Rolf over Eirik?" he inquired.

"Each champion needs at least one prize to keep him equal with the others and to keep him involved in this ruse." She then related the information in the two messages.

Trosdan observed her closely. "You do not appear happy with such news. Why is that?"

"I do not know if I can trust my husband to be honest and sincere. What of the next time he grows restless and doubtful? I would rather have left him furious at home than have him vanish to punish me."

Trosdan advised in a softened voice, "Long ago, I told you of your imminent reunion and of your love's change of heart. You must not blame Gavin for doing what the gods compelled him to do, for being led astray by a fate which he could not resist. If he had remained at home, you would not be here now and victory would not be within our grasp. You do this deed to free yourself and your heirs of peril."

Alysa frowned in dismay. She knew that Eirik's close reflection of Gavin was not his only appeal to her. Eirik was a special man. She respected him and enjoyed him. He was a heady blend of strength and gentleness. He was responsive to *all* her needs—physical, mental, and emotional. If she had met Eirik first, there was no doubt in her mind that she would have fallen in love with him. "The gods have been cruel to tempt me with Eirik. I truly believed he was Gavin, sent here to help me with this task. Eirik has been the man Gavin should have been. Eirik has Gavin's looks and good traits, but none of his flaws. I cannot order his death, for he has touched my heart. What am I to do, Wise One?" she implored, her eyes tearing.

Trosdan placed his arm around her sagging shoulders. "Trust in yourself and in your destiny. The gods will not make you suffer. There is a reason for this happening. Have faith, Alysa. Be strong and patient," he coaxed sympathetically.

"I want this task over with quickly. Is there no way we can rush it? I must return home and . . . I need peace, Wise One."

Trosdan eyed her intently. She looked so young, so fragile, so vulnerable. Perhaps he had been too hard on her. Yet he could not push her toward Eirik to ease her anguish.

Alysa saw Trosdan's concern for her. She forced a smile to surface. "I will be fine by morning. I only need time to accept this surprise. It was so unexpected."

"All things will work out as you desire, cherished one."

"Will they, Wise One? Will they?"

As Trosdan lay on his pallet in the darkness, his mind was plagued by Alysa's pain, for he was responsible for it.

311

Even knowing what he did now, he would take the same path again. Yet he realized that he had underestimated the power of their love, the strong forces of their entwined destiny, the irresistible bond between Princess Alysa Malvern and Prince Gavin Crisdean.

Yea, he was responsible for Gavin's behavior and disappearance. He would do anything necessary to protect Alysa and all that was dear to her, even deceive her and let her suffer for a short time. With the aid of potent herbs, secret potions, and mind-controlling powers, the Hawk of Cumbria had become the Viking warrior Eirik.

For weeks before Gavin left the castle, Trosdan had trained him without his knowledge or suspicion. He had instructed and compelled Gavin to behave as he had. He had furnished the unfamiliar horse, garments, and weapons. He had hidden Gavin's Trojan and possessions. He had darkened the prince's hair, removed the royal tattoo, and created the clever scar. He had made up the lineage and stories which Eirik related. In his last message to Damnonia, he had instructed Weylin to add those last two lines in his message to Alysa. On a walk which Eirik could not remember, he had compelled Gavin to write the note which had been meant to help her resist Eirik, the note he had delivered to Bath when he had claimed illness and left Rolf's band.

Gavin Crisdean had doubted Alysa's abilities and her destiny. When his memory was returned after the quest, Gavin would recall everything that had happened here, and he would finally be convinced for all time of Alysa's skills and fate. Never again would Gavin be fearful of letting her be herself or of losing her.

Trosdan smiled peacefully. *Gavin will know her needs and wants, and be happy to provide them. He will be stimulated and overjoyed by the strong and confident woman and ruler at his side. He will know she is worthy and capable of ruling her land and joint-ruling his one day.*

It did not matter to the old man if Alysa, or Gavin, never forgave him, or even slew him for his daring deceit. All that mattered to him were Alysa's survival and happiness, and that of her children.

He could not tell Alysa the truth at this point. She would demand to break the spell over Gavin, and that was too dangerous. If she knew the truth, she could make a careless slip or be enticed to take dangerous risks to have her love again. For her to continue to behave as necessary in this ruse, she could not be told until later.

Nor could he break the spell over her husband at this time. Gavin had to be completely like Eirik, be a Viking warrior. If they were allowed to reunite too early, they and this ruse would be imperiled. They were too close to victory to take a chance of discovery. It was only a while longer before all would be righted as he had promised.

Trosdan recognized one happy side to this dilemma. Alysa was attracted to Eirik. That was good, because Eirik was just like Gavin in nearly all ways—actions, deeds, feelings, and words. Yea, the two men were nearly matched in character and personality. When Alysa discovered she could and would have both men in one, she would be thrilled.

The only peril in waiting to reveal the truth to Alysa and Gavin lay in their irresistible attraction to each other. It could cause trouble if anyone suspected it, and definitely would if anyone witnessed it. For that reason, he had to force Alysa to avoid Eirik for the remainder of this task. Gavin was in no danger. He was a powerful and cunning warrior, and Trosdan was guarding Alysa's love. Gavin would win the quest, and win Alysa a second time.

Trosdan sighed in relief in knowing Alysa would avoid Eirik now that she had heard from Gavin. Surely she would obey him now! He shuddered in alarm. If she but once in

313

the throes of uncontrollable passion said, "I love you, Hawk of Cumbria," the spell would be broken and his deceit would be exposed to both.

Eighteen

After Alysa had eaten, bathed, and dressed for the next adventure, she asked Trosdan, "Who drugged the men, Wise One?"

After a soft chuckle and sly grin, he answered casually, "Surely you know it was me, Princess Alysa."

"How did you perpetuate such a ruse? Why did you not tell me?"

"I slipped slow-working herbs into the cooking pots in Eirik's and Rolf's camps. I had to give you time to reach the bath to recover the message from Weylin. Since it was so close, all would have raced straight there and back. You would not have been given a chance to be alone. I needed your surprise and doubts to look convincing, so I did not enlighten you. Ulf is wary and alert and watches you closely, as do Rolf and Eirik. It is best you do not know some things in advance or you might make an error in judgment or response."

"Ulf knows it was not him, and should suspect it was neither Rolf nor Eirik. Will such a deed not make him more wary of us?"

"It does not matter what Ulf thinks. The others did not believe him. If they should suspect another, it will be Einar, not us."

"But that will include and endanger Rolf," she protested.

315

"Rolf is a Norseman, our foe, one of those who must die," he reminded her. "Would it not be best if he is slain by his own forces?"

Alysa considered his words. "You are right, but it still pains me. He is a good and kind man. I wish he did not have to die."

"There is no other way, Alysa. Always remember they are foes."

"We remain here too long and get too close to them."

"We knew this ruse would require many weeks. It is only natural to make friends here. But all are future threats to you and must die."

"Why must I be spared at any price, Wise One?" she asked sadly.

Trosdan was a firm believer in his gods. He was also a firm believer in his powers as a wizard and in his sacred rank of Druid High Priest. He truly thought he was obeying his gods and doing what was best for Giselde's heir. "Because our gods will it," he replied simply. When she looked skeptical, he reminded her, "Do not forget, my warrior queen, your ruse will save not only all you love and rule but will also save all of Britain. As well as for Damnonia, you also battle for your grandfather's survival and that of Gavin's parents. This task is far bigger and more crucial than you realize."

Imagining the terrible battle which would soon take place, she murmured, "There will be great bloodshed."

"Better it be that of fierce barbarians than of yourself, your children, your beloved, and your people."

"Such is true," she admitted, feeling the weight of her heavy responsibilities. Why had the gods chosen her as Britain's champion? She knew why; she had a way to get to their foes and defeat them.

* * *

Loud noises suddenly seized their attention and when they rushed outside, they found a peasant girl surrounded by seven Vikings, who were shoving her about roughly and teasing her unmercifully.

Alysa hurried forward and demanded, "What cruel mischief do my brave warriors practice on a mere child?"

One man replied, "We found her sneaking around our camp, my queen. Surely she came here to give us pleasure and amusement. Perhaps she is a spy or a warrior in disguise. Perhaps she is Loki or another evil spirit," he teased mirthfully.

"Nay!" the frightened girl shrieked. "I came to see my mother. She is your captive. Please do not hurt me," she pleaded, dropping to her knees before Alysa and sobbing pitifully.

Alysa cast the sadistically mischievous men an admonishing glare. "Go about your tasks," the queen ordered sternly, "while I calm her and tend her injuries. She is but a child and should not be treated so badly by grown men. We have serious matters to handle."

As the Norsemen dispersed, Alysa told Trosdan she would join him soon, and led the trembling girl into her abode.

Inside, the girl laughed and clapped her hands! "I fooled them, easy as catching a worm after a rain," she boasted, confusing Alysa.

The beautiful ruler fetched some wine. "Drink this," the queen commanded softly, thinking the girl daft or in shock.

The peasant girl shook her head and grinned. "Do not let my tiny size and face of a baby fool you, too, Your Highness. I am twenty, a fully grown woman, and a clever one. I came to give you a message. The man you helped escape was my uncle. My family and others are preparing to aid your brave deed if you have need of us. How exciting it will be to watch these barbarians flee or die!"

Alysa wondered at the girl's behavior. She was annoyed

to learn that the smithy had shared such perilous and valuable information with this strange female who claimed to be older than she herself was. "I do not understand. Your uncle is dead and cannot aid me. One of the evil men here slew him when I was not present to halt him."

The overly confident female asserted, "Not before he begged us to help you battle these beasts if your forces fail you. If your victory does not come within two weeks, we will attack and rescue you. Then, you can lead us against them. With your skills and the wizard's magical powers, we shall chase them from our land."

Alysa was hesitant to believe or trust the cocky wench. "Time is short for me today. Return to your people and tell them all captives here have been slain, but against my orders. Tell them to be careful whom they trust with my secrets or all is lost. I will find a way to get a message to your people soon. Where is your village?"

The dreamy-eyed girl gave Alysa directions and they talked a while longer. Alysa urged, "Go quickly while the men are at the stone temple and before we are exposed. Do not risk another visit to me."

As the Vikings gathered at Stonehenge to begin the fourth quest, Rolf approached the area carrying a shield. He called out, "Ulf did not find the third treasure. I did. The shield he has is a false one. This is the prize of Freyja."

Startled, the red-haired leader stalked forward and examined the shield. "You seek to trick us, Rolf," he accused.

"Nay, Ulf, bring your shield forth and compare them," Rolf challenged, then laughed tauntingly. "I found this one in the old mud bath as the clue revealed. You hold nothing more than a Roman symbol."

All waited while Ulf fetched his shield. The two were compared. Trosdan said, "The image upon Ulf's is that of the Roman goddess Minerva. The shield of Rolf's bears Freyja's face and signs."

No one could dispute the wizard's words or the evidence. Rolf grinned mockingly. "Your evil deeds have defeated you, Ulf."

Ulf approached the altar and placed his hands upon it. He cried out, "Hear me, Great Odin. If I have lied or deceived my people, strike me dead. I swear upon your altar I am innocent."

All waited breathlessly, but nothing happened. Ulf removed his hands, turned, and lifted them skyward. He shouted, "See, my friends, I speak the truth. If there is evil amongst us, it is not mine."

Trosdan wished he could have struck down the offensive man, but he had need of Ulf later for a special task . . .

Rolf could not suppress a frown. He had hoped Odin would slay Ulf. No matter if the redhead still breathed and walked, Rolf did not trust him or believe him. When they were finished here, he would let Enid, who had washed and polished the shield, hide it for him as she had done with the amulet. No one would suspect he trusted a captive to assist him, and he had Enid totally enchanted with him!

The lots were drawn. Trosdan was to go with Ulf. Rolf was to travel alone. And Alysa was to journey with Eirik . . .

Trosdan stood upon the altar and gave the fourth clue. "The Roman Emperor Julius Caesar had conquered all of the known world, except this isle. He hungered for it. Hearing the Celts were fierce warriors, he knew he must use guile to obtain Britain. Learning of King Cassivelaunos's love for horses, the Great Caesar selected the best one in the world and had a fine harness made for the grey. A merchant delivered the animal to the Briton king, saying it was a gift from the Emperor of the World who wished to meet the only ruler who could compare with him. The prideful Cassivelaunos was fooled by such flattery. Thus, the sly conqueror was invited ashore. With his feet and men on land, Caesar announced his intention to conquer Britain."

Trosdan took a breath before continuing. "Too late Cassivelaunos realized his error in judgment. He was outraged by the command of a ruler who was also descended from the Trojans as they were. The challenge was given and accepted. The forces met on the battlefield. But all did not go well for the Celts, for Caesar possessed a powerful and magical sword called Yellow Death. Every blow with this sword caused death, even a small cut from it. The Britons were forced to withdraw for a time. Cassivelaunos's younger brother Nennios determined to steal the enchanted sword and save his king and people."

Trosdan kept his gaze on the three champions before him as he related his riddle. "Nennios charged the Romans and received many wounds. Yet he made his charioteer race toward the invader. Nennios battled feverishly with Caesar and seized the fearsome sword. Jumping into his chariot, he ordered his driver to carry Yellow Death to his brother, the king, as he had been wounded by the lethal weapon. The brave warrior died quickly, but the sword was delivered to Cassivelaunos, who wept and vowed vengeance. The Celtic king stabbed the sword into the ground and the earth bellowed with rage. Caesar knew he was beaten for the present, so he hastily withdrew his forces from this isle."

Trosdan's tone grew louder and clearer as he instructed, "You seek the place where Yellow Death was taken from the hand of the Roman emperor, the place where Nennios died, the place where Caesar battled King Cassivelaunos and lost. You seek the enchanted sword which can defeat the might and magic of all forces when it is empowered by Odin during our final ritual. You must travel for two days to find this prize. You must not catch the eye or ear of

Hengist, so travel stealthily. It is said the earth still bleeds red upon the spot where such evil took place. It is said Cassivelaunos's wizard performed a secret ceremony and tossed the deadly sword into a deep well so it would lose its evil powers, as only water and fire can triumph over magic. It is said that Celts fear this area and curse, and never go near it."

Ulf asked sullenly, "How will we know this sword, Wizard? I do not wish to be tricked with a false one as I was with the shield."

Rolf chuckled and taunted, "You tricked yourself, Ulf, and Odin punished you instead of slaying you."

Ulf glared at Rolf. "I have proven I did not cheat. From this day hence, I will be wary of guile from others. Any man who seeks to darken my name will be slain," he vowed coldly.

Trosdan responded to Ulf's question. "The sword bears the image of Caesar on its hilt and the sign of Odin on its blade."

The group dispersed. Ulf left camp to find someone who could reveal clues to him about the battle, sword, and cursed well. Trosdan rode with the redhead to make certain the man did not attract Hengist's attention, as the well was in the land claimed by the Jute chieftain.

Rolf went to question Enid, who supplied him with a few helpful hints. He asked where she had hidden the shield and amulet, and the smiling slave told him of her cunning. Pleased, Rolf departed.

Rolf did not notice that one of Ulf's most trusted friends had been left behind.

As Alysa journeyed with Eirik, they were both silent and pensive. They traveled the same path which they had used while seeking the first prize, for the fourth one was near it, in Hengist's territory. Alysa was amazed by Trosdan's cunning and foresight, as he had spread out the prizes across the large kingdom of Logris to require a long recovery period which allowed their forces to prepare and train.

Eirik watched his love from the corner of his eye. He wished he knew what was wrong between them, within her. She was tense and wary. She was distant and sad. Did she fear that Ulf was going to win the quest and somehow prevent them from being together? Was she angered because, after being tricked by Ulf twice, he had not challenged and slain the wicked man? Did she fear that he could not beat Ulf or that he was afraid of the redhead? Surely she knew he feared no man and would do anything necessary to win her!

Eirik's troubled mind continued to wander over his emotional domain, searching each area for answers. Perhaps she was scornful of his history and lineage. Perhaps his lack of challenge and revenge to his family's lethal rivals dismayed her. Perhaps she did not want his evil father's blood flowing in their children. Nay, she had not acted so.

Eirik had to admit he possessed no wealth, land, or high rank to offer her. But he could acquire them to please her.

Perhaps she was wary of his "wandering spirit," as she had mentioned it many times. She had teased about him becoming "bored and restless," about him growing weary of her and simple homelife. Did she not know he would never leave her or harm her? Did she not realize all he wanted and needed was to share a life with her, anywhere?

Something was tormenting her deeply. If only she would explain her feelings and problems to him and let him help her solve them.

Alysa's mind *was* in turmoil. She loved and desired the man riding beside her. Yet she could not have him, not if she returned to her life as it had been before this quest began. She could not imagine giving up her loved ones, home, crown, and people; but that would be the only way she could have Eirik, to flee somewhere with him. What if, as with Gavin, she had misjudged Eirik? What if things did not work out between them? What if, as with Gavin, his love and desire for her also waned and he grew restless? What would she do then, far from home, an outcast, a traitor?

She also had to consider Eirik's reaction to the truth about her. She had lied to him, used him, misled him, defied his gods, abused his laws and ways. Her forces were going to slay everyone in camp, including his friends. Would hatred and revenge then replace his love and desire?

There was no way she could halt this ruse or change it. The defeat was vital for all of Britain. She could not be selfish and think only of her desires. Yet somehow she had to save, spare, Eirik.

There was nothing she could do except carry out the daring plan for victory. Afterward, she must return home to rule her people, to one day rule Cambria and Damnonia. She had to return to Prince Gavin Crisdean; he was her husband and joint ruler, and she was pledged to him. She must find a way to make her life with him work. In a wicked sort of way, through Gavin, she would have a man like Eirik.

But he will not be Eirik, her mind cried out in anguish. Why must she choose between them? Why must she love two men, two men who were so alike? Why must one suffer and possibly die? Even if Eirik was allowed to escape, he would hate her; he would hunger for revenge and possibly become a future threat. *Or would he?* her heart argued. If he truly loved her, he would endure enormous torment over her treachery and betrayal. He would become angry, bitter, miserable, lonely. How could she hurt him so deeply?

Their passionate night in the secluded hut returned to plague her. Eirik had said, "Sometimes I fear you cannot be real and this is only a cruel dream." But they were both very real, and so was their problem. If only she could discuss it with him, could explain what she must do, could make him understand and agree, but she could not. It was too perilous. He had told her "soon, they would have all the time they desired." But there would be no time for them, no future for them; there could be none.

She wished there was some way she could sneak off to see Weylin. Soon, he would be awaiting her summons at Aquae Sulis. If only she could check with him about Gavin, learn why he left, where he had been, how he felt now . . . Nay, it was reckless to meet with Weylin this close to victory. It was also impossible to send a message to Weylin or Gavin, as there was only one bird left.

Each time they rested, Alysa was careful to avoid Eirik by always remaining with the other men. Yet she furtively watched his every move and listened to his every word. How could he be so like Gavin and not be Gavin? How was the old Druid so certain that . . .

Wild suspicions flooded her mind. What, Alysa wondered, if she had been tricked by both Trosdan and Gavin to force her to play her part convincingly? What if Gavin was also secretly working with Trosdan? What if the two men had decided this ruse would work better if she was not told Eirik was Gavin, had decided it would be more persuasive if she truly believe Eirik was Eirik?

Alysa considered the evidence in this startling conjecture. Trosdan had been preparing her for this task weeks before Gavin vanished, and then Eirik suddenly appeared. What if the old man had also been preparing Gavin to aid this ruse but had convinced her love that it was imperative for all that she not be informed? Would that not explain Gavin's insane behavior? Her husband had drugged her with potent herbs. Where had he gotten them and learned how to use them, if not from the wizard? If her love could trick her once, then he could do so again! Trosdan had supplied her with strange weapons and garments, so why not do the same for Gavin as Eirik? Too, Trosdan possessed the powers and skills to have effected the minor differences in the two men!

Alysa was staggered by her speculations. She knew that the old wizard had done many things without telling her first, always claiming her responses had to appear convincing. What other secrets and surprises did the Druid have in store for her? Trosdan had known Gavin was going to vanish; he had known Eirik was going to be here. Trosdan had left Rolf's group in time to reach Aquae Sulis to hide Gavin's message and return! If Eirik was Gavin and those two were partnered secretly, Eirik could have written that message from Gavin for Trosdan to deliver. But why continue their ruse so long?

Was Gavin disobeying Trosdan's warnings by romancing her? Was that why the Druid was so desperate for her to believe he was not Gavin, to make her avoid "Eirik" since he refused to avoid her?

Alysa tried to recall each of Trosdan's words to seek clues in them. The old man was clever and daring, but how far would he go to obtain victory for them? And why would Gavin comply?

Suddenly a horrible suspicion filled her mind. What if Gavin was truly enspelled and honestly believed he was Eirik? What if that was how Trosdan was forcing her husband to comply with her destiny? To not interfere? Yea, Trosdan possessed the power and skills to bewitch Gavin.

That would explain everything: Gavin's strange behavior, Eirik's presence, her attraction to the "Viking" foe, and Trosdan's vow that they would be reunited and their bond would be stronger than ever. If Gavin recalled everything that had happened while he was living as Eirik, he would be convinced of her prowess, wits, and success. Her husband would never doubt her again, or leave her again! He would have the honor of having assisted in this daring ruse which he had opposed.

If her conclusions were right, that explained why Trosdan was always defending her "traitorous" husband! It also explained why the Druid had bewitched Gavin to force him to aid them and their cause! Once the spell was broken, how could Gavin be angry at his victory? The people would praise them for their joint success. Yea, it was a cunning and daring ruse for Trosdan to include the reluctant Gavin!

When she returned to camp, she would force the old wizard to tell her the truth! Trosdan had tormented her into avoiding Eirik when it was unnecessary. Alysa's spinning mind shouted, *Nay*.

Nay, she agreed, it had been necessary. If she did not avoid Eirik, she could expose all of them! If she had been told the truth, would she have obeyed those cautions? Nay, she decided shamefully.

Trosdan had been right to keep the truth from them. Gavin had to live, breathe, act, think, and feel as Eirik. She had to treat him as Eirik. If they had known the truth, they would have made a slip, because Gavin would have behaved differently with her and with the Norsemen, and because she would have done the same. Yea, their private quarrel and feelings would have exposed them and their ruse.

Alysa's heart surged with joy and pride. Her love was working with her. She would not have to slay Eirik or betray him. She would not have to give up anything or anyone. She could have both men.

She glanced at Eirik who was tending his unfamilar horse. Her body trembled with happiness and desire. He was her love, her husband; he must be! There was no reason to feel guilty over her passionate actions; she had bedded her husband. There was no reason to suffer, as "Eirik" would not be slain or hurt or lost.

Unless someone guessed their secrets . . . Alysa realized Trosdan had been desperate to keep them apart, to protect their safety and ensure victory. Hard as it would be, sh had to keep her distance until Gavin was disenchanted. Yet she did not have to be so hard and cold with her love. Surely "Eirik" was confused over her curious behavior.

A cold chill swept over Alysa. How could she explain to Gavin her behavior with Eirik when she had not known he was her enspelled husband? Somehow she must convince Trosdan and Gavin that she had known the truth all along. In her heart, she had, had she not?

Eirik walked over to where she was sitting and resting. He asked, "How do you fare today, m'love?"

Alysa gazed into his troubled eyes. "I am fine, Eirik. I beg you, keep your distance from me until we decide how and when to be together for all time. We must not yield to our passions again until after the quest when it is safe. Do this for me, for us."

Eirik's expression registered surprise, then joy. He admitted, "I feared you no longer loved and desired me."

Perhaps it was rash, but she told him softly, "I love you and desire you with all my heart, my beloved. But until the quest and rituals are over, we cannot be together again. It is too dangerous. Trust me, for I have seen our future together in my dreams."

Eirik smiled and replied, "It will be as you say, m'love."

When they halted for the night, Alysa used the pallet which she had brought along and placed it near a small fire where Aidan and Saeric were camping. She dared not risk a more secluded spot where Gavin might be tempted to approach her. Now that she understood Trosdan's cautions, she agreed with them and would follow them.

In the Viking camp, Enid was being tortured by Sigurd, Ulf's friend, for information. When the ravished and bat-

tered slave could endure no more brutality, she told Sigur
where the shield was hidden, but did not reveal news o
the location of the amulet. None knew Rolf possessed i
and he might need it for survival and victory.

To prevent the Logris captive from aiding Rolf furthe
Ulf had ordered her death, and Sigurd obeyed. Sigur
sneaked the body from camp and buried it, after makir
sure the slave had told the truth about the shield's hidir
place. As Ulf surmised, Rolf would be led to believe th
woman had fled in terror of the blond warrior's wrath aft
leading Sigurd to the shield's hiding place.

They slept only a few hours before Eirik aroused ther
to continue their journey under the cover of darkness. The
traveled for hours, resting and napping as needed, befor
pushing farther into Hengist's territory with stealthful mov
ments. On the third day from camp, they reached the are
which Eirik said was the Jute chieftain's location. No oth
band was in sight yet, nor were any of the Jute's forces.

Eirik gazed across the landscape and grinned, delighte
that he knew this land so well. He pointed to where th
ground was covered with countless bloodred wildflower
"See there, the earth still bleeds where evil took place. Th
is where Caesar and Cassivelaunos first battled and Nenno
died. The Celtic king was a fool to discard the magic
sword. Look," he remarked, indicating a circle of rocks
the midst of the flowers. "It is the well where the Brito
king threw the sword of death. Come, we will fetch it."

Eirik was lowered by rope into the deep and dark we
Aidan and Saeric eagerly aided their friend. Time passe
and Alysa grew worried. What if her love had drowned
What if the lethal sword had nicked him and he had die
What if there was no sword here?

Eirik called out that he was ready to be withdrawn. Aida

328

and Saeric backed the horse and Eirik appeared. He climbed out and held up a sword. The hilt bore the image of the Roman conqueror and upon the blade was etched the hanged man, symbol of Odin. The band cheered their second success and clever leader.

Eirik called out, "Let us leave this place before we are discovered by Hengist's forces." The men agreed. Eirik placed his sword, Yellow Death, inside a large blanket to prevent anyone from being nicked by its lethal edges. They mounted and galloped from the site.

They camped at the edge of the Jute chieftain's domain. It was nearing midnight when the other two bands joined them. When Ulf and Rolf discovered that Eirik had already claimed the fourth prize and was on his way back to camp, they were displeased.

Ulf asked details of the victory, and Eirik's men cheerfully related their tale. Ulf remarked peevishly, "Eirik lived here with Hengist a long time and has an unfair advantage over us."

Eirik scoffed, "If I truly had an advantage, Ulf, I would be in possession of all the prizes. Then, I would not have to battle you and Rolf for the others after the quest is completed."

Ulf warned, "It does not matter how many you and Rolf find, as I will take them from you both in the battle ring. No man can defeat me."

"We shall see," Rolf and Eirik replied almost simultaneously.

A large camp was set up and food was prepared. Ulf was in a terrible mood, even though he knew he was in control of the second and third prizes and knew Rolf's Logris slave had been slain by now and could aid his rival no more. Rolf, though he thought he had the first and third treasures

safely hidden, was depressed by his rival's success. Eirik
believing he possessed two of the four prizes, was elated
as were his men.

Alysa did not question Trosdan about his duplicity; she
planned to discuss the serious matter with him when they
were back in camp and had total privacy. Until then, she
would observe him closely.

When the united bands awoke the next morning, Eirik
was missing. They searched for him in the area, but none
could find him.

Alysa wondered where he had gone and what he was
doing. She was glad he was safely out of Hengist's territory
as the Jute could unmask him. The Druid had taken a big
risk with Gavin's life by providing him with that particular
story! Surely Trosdan had no way of knowing if any of
Hengist's men or Isobail's past raiders had joined this group
and would know Eirik was lying. Yet, it had worked out
perfectly so far. When she talked with the wizard later, she
would ask him what precautions he was taking to protect
Gavin while he lived as Eirik.

Trosdan accurately surmised that Eirik had gone to hide
the sword near the Viking settlement. The Runes had
warned him of Rolf and Ulf's mischiefs, but he was here
to guard Alysa's love. Finally, the bands were compelled to
head for camp without him.

Two days later, the bands reached the Viking settlement
to make several unexpected and shocking discoveries.

Rolf learned that Enid was missing, as was the shield.
Quickly he checked the hiding place of the amulet, to find
it still safe.

Ulf smugly displayed the shield as he told everyone that

Sigurd had seen Rolf's slave hide it and that his friend had remained behind to steal it, fairly and by the rules. He ventured aloud that the careless slave must have fled in fear of the blond warrior's wrath.

Neither Eirik nor Rolf believed that Enid had been careless or was still alive. Both cautioned themselves to be more wary of Ulf.

As far as the people knew, Eirik had the amulet and sword, Ulf possessed the figurehead and shield, and Rolf had no treasure.

Eirik smiled at Alysa as she cast her worried gaze upon him. He had galloped near camp and hidden the sword by hanging it high in an oak tree in the distant woodland. When the time came, he would find the fifth and last prize, and he would defeat Ulf for the other two.

Alysa and Trosdan followed Rolf to his longhouse to check on the last bird, which Enid had been tending for them. Since the woman had been gone, surely dead, for days, they were alarmed. When they found the cage in Rolf's dwelling, the poor creature was lying upon the bottom, having had no water or food for four days.

"He is dying!" Alysa gasped in panic, wondering how they would get their final message to Weylin. Trosdan would have to find a way during the fifth quest to sneak to Aquae Sulis to alert Weylin of their problem and schedule. Within six days, the last adventure would be completed. She would order them to rest on the seventh day, have the final matches for the prizes on the eighth, and hold the ceremonies and rituals on the ninth. She trembled as she thought of the magical number for the Vikings. Nine days hence, this daring ruse would be finished and the battle would take place. She hoped this number was a good omen for her side and that the blood *hault* following the ritual would be furnished by the Norsemen.

Trosdan withdrew the limp bird from its cage and studied

it. Sadly he murmured, "Yea, my queen, he is at death's gate."

Alysa and Trosdan returned to their borrowed dwelling, with the Druid carrying the wooden cage. He placed it on the table and withdrew the white bird. He gathered his supplies and began to tend the pitiful creature.

"This is not a good omen, my princess," he murmured.

"He will survive, Wise One. If he does not, you will find a way to get a message to Weylin, as you found a cunning way to get Gavin's message to me." When the old man's head jerked upward and light-blue eyes fused with dark-blue ones, Alysa smiled and said, "Yea, Wise One, I have guessed your ruse with me and Gavin. Explain it."

Nineteen

Alysa related her suspicions to Trosdan. "It is time for the truth, Wise One. I will not be angry or disobedient."

The snowy-haired man smiled affectionately. He revealed what he had done, how he had done it, and why. "Even if you never understand or forgive me, Alysa, I did what I must to save you and your land from certain destruction. The sacred Runes commanded it, and I was compelled to obey. I love you as if you were my own child. I would never endanger or imperil you if there was any other way to win."

Alysa embraced the wizard. "I know your words are true, Wise One, and I agree with all you have done. You were right to keep your second ruse a secret from me, for your caution has protected us all."

Trosdan's eyes teared with happiness and love as he gazed at the girl who so favored Giselde. If Alysa's grandmother was not wed to King Bardwyn, when this matter was over, *he* would wed the only woman he had ever loved. "My old heart sings with joy and relief to hear such words."

Alysa sighed heavily. "Gavin's will not when he discovers how we deceived him and used him."

Trosdan asserted confidently, "He will be angry for a while, but not for long. He, too, will understand and accept what I have done. He will have no reason to blame you."

Even though her cheeks glowed with modesty, Alysa refuted, "Yea, Wise One, he will, unless you tell him I was a part of your ruse. If you do not, he will never forgive me for what I have done here."

"I do not understand," Trosdan murmured in confusion. There was no way anything could have happened between her and Rolf.

Alysa revealed her secret relationship with Eirik and her motives behind it. She admitted she loved Eirik, even if he was not Gavin.

"Nay," the old man argued. "You love and desire him only because he is your fated love and the bond between you was too great to resist. I am not disappointed in you, for you were compelled to follow your heart and destiny, as was I. Have you done or said anything to arouse Eirik's suspicions about us? He truly lives as Eirik, and this is not the time to break the spell over him."

"Nay, and I will be even more careful henceforth. I have told him we must keep our distance until after the quest, and he has agreed."

"That is good, Alysa, for we cannot awaken him until the last moment. When the spell is broken, he will know and remember all things both as Gavin and as Eirik."

"What if he is endangered by Ulf in the final match?" she fretted.

"I will keep no more secrets from you, Alysa. Ulf will battle Rolf and slay him, so your friend's death will not be at your hands or command." When Alysa looked dismayed and about to protest, Trosdan entreated, "It must be this way, my queen; it is their destinies and cannot be changed. Eirik will defeat Ulf and become the last champion. You will wed Eirik in a Viking ceremony. When you return to this dwelling as man and wife to spend the night before the empowering ritual and celebration, you will say the word to break his spell. That night, you will explain our deception

334

to him. The next day, he will help us battle these foes as himself."

Alysa mused on those exciting plans. She was eagerly looking forward to marrying "Eirik" and to spending a passionate night with him. Perhaps she should wait a while before spoiling their blissful wedding night. Yea, she decided, she would make rapturous love to "Eirik" all night, then, early the next morning she would break Gavin's spell! They would have too much to do then for her husband to take time quarreling with her over her past actions! By the time that glorious day was over, Gavin would be too elated by his two victories to remain annoyed with her and Trosdan!

The wizard returned to his task with the messenger bird. He forced special herbs and water into its beak. After replacing it in the cage, he said, "That is all I can do for now. Surely he will survive to aid us, for I was not warned by the Runes of this peril."

To distract the man from his worry, she said, "I wish I could have saved Enid's life. I am certain Ulf had her slain. I warned her about him. Was it a premonition?" she asked.

"I am sure of it, Alysa, but the warning was in vain. It was her fate to die at Ulf's order. If she had survived, her life would have ended in misery, for she loved a man who was deceiving her."

"What do you mean, Wise One?" she inquired.

Trosdan clarified. "Enid was helping Rolf solve the riddles and was hiding the prizes for him. He used her because of her love for him. If he had won you, he would have gotten rid of her. She was a lowly slave to him, nothing more. As with Ulf, to prevent Enid from causing trouble for him, he would have slain her without regret or hesitation. It is their way to remove threats to avoid future problems; they are barbarians. You only see the sunny side which Rolf wishes you to see. There are other sides to him, dark sides you would despise and fear."

Alysa knew that the Druid was not lying or exaggerating to make her feel better about Rolf's sacrifice. "I am glad I have not seen them and will not do so. Soon, Wise One, Good will triumph over Evil. There is something I must tell you," she began, then revealed what had happened with the blacksmith and peasant woman. "If the messenger bird dies or our forces fail us, the people of Logris will come to our aid, if the girl's words can be trusted. I fear she spoke too cockily to suit me. I am not certain she did not make up the tale for an adventure. I trusted the smithy and I am disappointed in how he misused my faith in him. Loose tongues and boastful natures can lead to trouble. I will be more careful in the future when obtaining helpers for our cause."

Trosdan did not want to make her feel worse by scolding her, so he held silent. He also did not want to dishearten or frighten her by telling her she could expect no help from the terrified peasants. When he finally spoke, his words were soothing ones. "It is late and you must rest. Sleep peacefully, Alysa."

Alysa smiled happily, knowing she could do so tonight

In Ulf's longhouse, many men were enjoying a game of gambling. Ulf excused himself to go to the privy at the rear of his dwelling. He then barred the door, lifted the loosened corner of the turf roof, and heaved himself outside. Stealthily the redhead made his way to where Aidan and Seari lived in a *shieling,* a small house. He sneaked inside and found both men asleep. With his knife, he slew them, and wished Eirik was there to join their lethal fate. Ulf slipped outside to the shed then which was attached to the house and killed the slave slumbering there, killed him with cooking knife and in a manner which would appear to b self-inflicted. Quickly, he returned to his dwelling and rejoined the men.

As the games continued long into the night, Ulf drank a great deal of ale and pretended to pass out. The men placed him on his bed and departed, passing Eirik on a pallet. The green-eyed Viking had chosen to sleep under the stars tonight rather than in Aidan's *shieling* with his friends.

When the murders were discovered the next morning, Eirik questioned Ulf coldly. "Who did this wicked thing to my friends?"

Ulf shouted back, "Probably the slave who slew himself in fear!"

"These wounds are the work of a skilled warrior, not a captive who had joined our side! And the dark deed was done with cunning stealth!" Eirik wondered if *he* had been the real target.

The unsuspecting men who had been with Ulf last night related their side, vowing that Ulf could not be guilty.

Ulf shouted at Eirik, "If you doubt their word and mine, challenge me and we will prove who lies in the battle ring!"

Eirik chuckled mockingly. "We will settle our differences in the battle ring, Ulf, but *after* the quest. This is but an evil trick to lure me there so you can rid yourself of one rival, since you failed to slay me last night," Eirik accused, his rage enormous but controlled.

Ulf sneered. "It is not my doing, Eirik. Look elsewhere for your foe. Perhaps Rolf wishes us to battle and slay each other so only he is left, for he has no prizes to keep him in the competition."

Rolf's face grew red with fury and his hazel eyes enlarged with it. "You insult me, Ulf, and you shall pay. But in the ring after the quest as Eirik said. You will not trick us again."

Before they headed to Stonehenge for the final clue, Rolf ordered his closest friend, "Remain here, Sweyn, and watch

337

his men sharply. I do not trust Ulf. If you can, steal back my shield. I have need of a prize to qualify for the final contest."

Alysa watched Eirik as the three champions approached the pale-green sandstone altar. The flakes of mica in it caused it to glitter in the sunlight, making it appear mystical. She knew "Eirik" must be feeling grief over the deaths of his "friends," hatred for their killer, and anger over the dark deed. As Trosdan had told her, it was best this way, as she would not be compelled to order their deaths soon.

The drawing of stones took place. Trosdan was to ride with Eirik. Ulf was to travel alone. Alysa was to journey with Rolf. She and Trosdan would help the blond warrior locate the fifth prize to keep him in the competition, as he was destined to die in the ring.

Trosdan stepped upon the Altar Stone and gave out the last clues. "You seek a place which was there before the Romans came, a place the invaders used as a garrison. Once it was a walled city, but no more. It is in an area which has passed from hand to hand between conquerors and Celts. It was viewed a wedge between the north and south, a stronghold which was vital to defense. You must travel over two days, but do not enter Cumbria or Albany. If you reach the first hall of Hengist, you have gone too far. A great fortress stands in ruins there. It reminds all of a time of weakness and defeat. It will lend its magic to a warrior who is not dumb. It offers a prize which will guard his mind, ruler of the body and deeds. Frey will guide her chosen champion to her treasure."

Before they left the settlement, Alysa whispered to Rolf, "Do not worry, my handsome champion, for you shall obtain this prize. It is a helmet which is hidden in the fortress ruins. I shall help you find it. But we must keep our distance

338

prevent suspicion," she cautioned, needing and wanting im to remain distant.

For two days, they traveled over beautiful terrain which vas surrounded by cotswolds, a hilly range where numerous heep roamed. The grasses were a yellowy green this time f year, and the trees were beginning to change colors. From ome rolling downs, the land spread out before them like painted picture of exquisite talent. It appeared a world olored in gold and green.

They swept through the serene Midlands at a rapid pace nd bypassed the Fens, marshy lands to their right. The oad they journeyed, called the Fosse, was a good one, uilt by the Romans and stretching between Aquae Sulis nd Lindum.

At their last rest stop on the morning of the third day way from camp, Alysa revealed, "The area which lends its nagic to a warrior who is not dumb is Lindum. The fortress ; near there and stands in ruins today. There is a pile of ocks near a back wall. The helmet is buried beneath them. rey's symbols are upon it."

In the Viking camp far away, those present were building funeral pyre for Sweyn, who had been killed in an acci- ental fall.

Rolf located the pile of rocks and flung them aside to xpose the coveted helmet. He placed it on his head and ave forth a cry of joy. Quickly, he ordered his men to head or home to give him time to relax and to practice before e final contest. With luck, he mused, Sweyn would have covered his stolen shield by now.

* * *

They traveled swiftly, staying off the main road to avoi
the other two bands. When they camped the first night, Rol
confided, "Now I have two prizes with which to challeng
for you, my queen."

"Have you forgotten, Ulf stole the shield from you?"

Rolf chuckled, but decided to keep news of the amule
a secret. He wanted no one, not even his trusted love, t
be in a position to drop a careless hint. With a sly grin, h
confessed, "Yea, but it will not matter. I shall win you. Eiri
and Ulf will die."

Fear chewed upon Alysa's nerves. Both men were eage
to slay her love! What if something went wrong with thei
plan? What if something happened to Trosdan? Without hi
skills, she was helpless! Nay, without him, all was lost. I
the bird died, she had no way of sending word to Weylir
She had no way to drug the Vikings into vulnerability. Sh
had no way to disenchant Gavin!

By the next evening, the forces of Cambria, Damnoni;
and Cumbria were poised at their Logris borders. The mes
senger line was set up, and Weylin headed for Aquae Suli
to await the final summons.

Tuesday before dusk, Rolf's band reached the settlemen
Einar hid the helmet for Rolf. The camp was quiet, as th
other two bands had not returned. Alysa hurried to he
house, telling Rolf they must be careful not to arouse any
one's suspicion against them.

Within a few minutes of her departure, Rolf learned c
Sweyn's death. He suspected Ulf's friend was behind it, bu

knew he could not prove his charge. He vowed revenge against his wicked foe.

After dark, Ulf sneaked into camp and slew his friends Leikn and Sigurd to throw suspicion off himself. Now, his rivals' helpers were dead and could not thwart his victory. In addition, all who knew of his mischief were dead and could never expose him. Afterward, he galloped back to where his band was camped for the night.

Shortly after midnight, Eirik's band arrived. Trosdan entered the dwelling which he shared with Alysa, and they compared tales.

"You did well, my queen. When we reached the fortress and we found the pile of stones moved, I knew you had succeeded."

Alysa looked worried. "Not all goes well, Wise One. Sweyn is dead, by accident they say. I do not believe it. I suspect Ulf had him slain. Now, all who shared my friendship are gone, save the cunning Rolf. This saddens my heart, but makes my duty easier. That is good."

"Yea, it is good. All is coming true as the Runes predicted."

"There is one matter which troubles me, Wise One. If anything happened to you, how would I succeed? I do not know how to drug the Vikings, and I do not know how to break Gavin's spell."

Trosdan revealed such things to her. "The bird has recovered and will take our message to Lord Weylin."

"What of my love, Wise One? How does he fare?"

"He asked many questions about you and about me. I revealed nothing more than he already knew as Eirik. He was vexed to discover Rolf had beaten him to the fortress. He did not expect his rival to do so well without Enid's aid."

341

"Do you think he suspects I helped Rolf?" she inquired worriedly.

"Nay, as his love and desire for you are great. He trusts you; I read it in his eyes and voice."

Alysa wanted to go to the village to plan backup strategy with the peasants. Because of the many strange deaths, the Vikings were alert and wary. She could not risk exposure this close to the attack date. She also wanted to visit Horsa to bargain for the release of Lord Daron's family. She could not bear for Lady Gweneth and her girls to be slaves any longer than necessary. That action, too, was reckless, as the Jute would surely rush to his brother's stronghold to tell Hengist all about her, and she must not draw their attention and interest to her.

Weylin sat in the Roman bath in pensive study. He had found Alysa's message. All was going according to plan. Yet something was not right. He had found his last message to her, the one with the added lines which the wizard had requested. But the letter from Gavin to Alysa bewildered him. He had pieced it together and read it. How had the false message gotten here? Where was Gavin? What was he doing? If Gavin knew about their message system and ruse, then he had to be in on it! But why dupe his friends and wife? He must be nearby, but where? Doing what? He and the wizard had to be partnered, which meant the old man had deceived Alysa, him, and the others back at the castle. That was unlike Gavin Crisdean.

From the condition of the note from Gavin, Alysa had not taken his news well. Weylin could not blame her, but he could envision her reaction when she discovered it was another lie from her husband. "I hope you know what you are doing, my friend." Whatever it was, there had to be a good reason, or so Lord Weylin hoped for all their sakes

Weylin decided there was nothing he could do except wait here for the summons from Alysa. Perhaps Gavin would appear and enlighten him on this mystery. No matter, for as soon as Alysa's final message arrived, he would send for the combined forces. They would unite here until they sneaked to the Viking camp in three days. On the fourth day, they would attack, at the wizard's fiery signal. All he could do now was wait, and pray to the gods that nothing went wrong.

Wednesday morning, Ulf returned to camp with his band. The bodies of Leikn and Sigurd were discovered. Ulf shouted in feigned rage, "Who did this evil thing while I was gone?"

"Many have died strangely, Ulf," Einar remarked. The *attiba* listed the odd deaths: "Rolf's slave, Aidan, Saeric, the male captive, Sweyn, and now Leikn and Sigurd. It makes no sense. We have sent their souls to Odin in Valhalla. He will punish the guilty one."

Ulf glared at Trosdan. "Why do our best friends die? If this quest is sacred, who takes the lives of our companions?"

"There is much evil here," the wizard replied. "Loki does not wish us to succeed with this quest and victory. We must defeat him. We must not quarrel amongst ourselves. Odin will triumph."

"But how will we triumph when so many of us are dying? Soon we will not have enough warriors to conquer this isle," Ulf reasoned. "Since your arrival, wizard, we have lost over a hundred men."

Keeping her eyes on the redhead, Alysa asserted, "Yea, Ulf, but the strongest have survived, and most were slain by *friends* during the contests. When we are ready to begin our conquest, we will use many tricks which will not endanger more lives. As Princess Alysa, I can worm my way into castles of kings and noblemen pretending I have come to visit. At night, I can unlock the gates for my forces to attack while they are sleeping and vulnerable. We can sneak into villages after dark and do the same. Few lives will be at risk with such cunning. I can lure their bands of knights and warriors into traps by pretending I am being chased by brigands. Trosdan and Einar can use their powers and skills to weaken them. We will ride from area to area, and they will not know where we will strike next. They cannot defend against such seemingly aimless tactics. We will break their spirits. We will terrorize them with our prowess and might. They will cower before us. We will slay the men and soldiers, but keep the women and children alive to serve us. When we leave one area for another, there will be no force left behind to recover it."

Rolf declared, "It is a clever plan, my queen!"

"But will it work? Can you fool them?" Ulf inquired skeptically.

"You have witnessed my prowess and powers, and know I can lead my people into battle. With my warriors behind me, I have no fear of these Celts. Why do you question your queen and this strategy?"

The redhead replied boldly, "I am wary because so many strange things are happening. This quest is demanding a high price from us."

"Did you think such a vital quest would be easy or without dangers? Did you think no person or evil power would try to halt us? What prize or rank truly has value if won without skills and cunning?"

"She is right," Eirik stated, pride and amazement filling him. While trying to conceal his love and desire for Alysa, he insisted, "If any leader can travel a path to victory with us, it is our warrior queen. We must not allow Loki's mischief to sway us."

As Eirik was speaking, Trosdan saw the white bird take ight from the open window of his dwelling. It pleased the ruid that the bird had regained enough strength to carry e last message to Weylin. His light-blue eyes scanned the eavens. Having studied the stars and skies for many years, e knew the signs which warned of a violent storm about) break, the kind which gave no prior warning.

Ulf scoffed, "It is not Loki's mischief which worries me. here is another evil one amongst us." Ulf had gotten rid f Eirik and Rolf's strongest supporters. Now he needed to d the queen of hers! Then, once Eirik and Rolf were slain, o one would challenge him for any reason. The kingship ould be his, and Alysa would be under his control!

Trosdan shouted above the grumblings to be heard. Gather at Stonehenge and the gods will unmask any evil ne amongst us!"

Alysa walked to the stone temple with Rolf and Einar. he told him how sorry she was about Sweyn's death. She elt Eirik's potent gaze upon them, but she did not look his ay.

The wizard gathered supplies from his dwelling and led e Vikings to the stone temple. He ordered a fire to be uilt before the altar and he climbed upon the stone. He ooked skyward and prayed, "Oh, Great Odin, there is doubt mongst your people. Send your message to us." He cast owder into the fire and colorful flames burst forth. "Hear e, Great Thor, send down your thunderbolts to slay any e here. Winds of the gods, blow away all doubts and evil." rosdan cast more powder into the air, and the wind hanged.

As Trosdan continued to pray and to use his magic, the ind grew stronger and the sky grew darker. An ominous ura filled the area. The superstitious Vikings looked about wonder and fear.

Large black clouds swept across the sky, seeming to

hover over Stonehenge. Brilliant lightning zigzagged above the towering stones. The wind wailed like a crying woman. Trosdan continued his clever ruse. With mesmeric voice and gaze, he had an hypnotic effect over the crowd. More glittering powder was flung into the air, and the storm's violent core moved closer and increased in strength. Roaring thunder boomed loudly and fiercely. Lightning slashed like a radiant sword which was cutting open the heaven.

Eirik watched Alysa as she reverently observed the wizard. The wind blew her unbound hair across her lovely face, nearly obscuring it from his view. She made no attempt to push the dark-brown curls aside. Her thin garments whipped in the strong air. She appeared caught up in the wonder of this moment, aware only of the wizard.

Trosdan lifted his arms in supplication as he pretended to earnestly and humbly entreat the Viking gods to answer his pleas. "Hear me, Great Odin, Great Thor. Prove to these warriors that I am your servant and do your will. If there is evil amongst us, destroy it with your powers."

Almost immediately a silvery bolt of lightning shot from heaven to earth, striking down one man: Einar. The crowd shrieked in panic and fell back, their eyes wide with astonishment and fear. The Viking *attiba*'s body jerked about on the ground, then ceased its spastic movement. His chest was charred by fire, and smoke rose from the burned flesh and black robe. No man approached the body.

Trosdan stared at the lifeless form of Einar. The timing of the storm and the false wizard's death were perfect. He mentally thanked his true gods for aiding his ruse in the startling manner. "Hear me, Norsemen, the gods have spoken. The evil amongst us has been destroyed by Thor's thunderbolt, for Einar was a false wizard. But there is more. Odin has placed his thoughts in my head. Our god knows Ulf has been misled, but he has chosen to give him another chance to prove himself worthy of life and forgiveness

346

din says to you, Ulf, go and question your true *attiba* no
ore. Obey your queen, or you will become Thor's next
ictim."

The winds howled around the stone temple. The thunder
nd lightning increased. Rain began to fall.

Ulf shouted to be heard over the combined noises of na-
ire. "What of Rolf? Einar was his friend and helper. Why
he spared?"

Rolf's head jerked in Ulf's direction. He was about to
rotest his innocence, but Trosdan replied loudly and
learly, "Rolf was not aware of Einar's deceit and wicked-
ess. He cannot be blamed for them." The blond warrior
rinned tauntingly at his rival.

Ulf inquired, "You are saying Einar is responsible for all
vil which has taken place here?"

Trosdan shook his head. "Odin has not yet revealed that
uth to me. He ordered Thor to destroy Einar for his false
laims and deeds. When the time comes, Odin will judge
olf, Eirik, and you in the final battle ring. Only the man
ho deserves to become king and Alysa's husband will sur-
ive that last test."

"Let the final contests begin tonight," Ulf urged.

"Nay, Odin has instructed us to rest for another day. His
orm will keep us inside tonight and tomorrow. The fol-
wing day, the sun will shine brightly for the final matches.
o to your dwellings, for the storm will become more pow-
rful as Odin conquers his rage."

Within moments of that warning, the storm's fury broke
ver them. Rain poured from the blackened sky and doused
e fire at the altar. Lightning flashed dangerously. Thunder
ared with a deafening volume. Powerful winds yanked at
arments and hair. The crowd, except for Eirik, quickly
ushed back to camp and sought protection in their dwell-
gs.

Eirik stood in the downpour and gazed at Einar's body.

347

He wondered if the wizard had truly called down the wra
of Odin, or had he only used powerful skills to make
seem so? There was something about the old man whic
troubled him, so he did not fully trust him, if at all. Eir
did not like the powerful influence and control which Tro
dan had over his love. And he did not believe Einar wa
the evil one in camp. Why would the gods, if they had do
so, deceive them? How had Rolf found the last prize s
quickly and easily? Who had killed his friends, Sweyn, ar
Ulf's friends? Why? Perhaps what he wanted to know mo
of all was why the wizard and Briton princess had sudden
appeared and laid claims to high ranks. Why were they wil
ing to turn against everyone in their land and in other
How could such a gentle creature speak so calmly of slayir
so many Celts when she was one? Something strange ar
perilous was taking place.

Alysa was drenched. She closed the curtain and pull
on dry garments. She bound her hair in a thick cloth
blot it. When it no longer dripped, she brushed and braid
the brown locks.

Trosdan also changed garments. Then he poured the
both wine to take away their chill. He smiled when Alya
pushed aside the curtain and joined him. "All is safe agai
my princess."

"How did you control the weather?" she asked in awe

Trosdan laughed softly. "I did not. I read its signs in th
sky and used the storm to fool them. Yet the mighty Zer
did strike down Einar to aid us. I had planned to use trich
to frighten them, but it was unnecessary. We must rest un
the final matches begin."

"Do you think Ulf was frightened into obeying us ar
dropping his suspicions?" she inquired as she sipped th
heady liquid.

"Nay. He only believes I have great powers and tricked everyone today. Yet it will make him fear to challenge me again. He is the one responsible for the deaths. He wishes to be rid of his rival's support. He plotted to have me doubted and slain, but I halted him."

"He wishes to kill you?" she questioned frantically.

"He desires to have no one left to protect you from his evil. Do not worry or fear. Nothing will happen to me or to your love."

"Three more days, Wise One," she hinted with relief. "I will be happy to return home and to seek no more daring adventures."

Trosdan laughed again. "That cannot be, my princess, for another great adventure awaits you."

Alysa did not look pleased. "Explain your words."

"The adventure of raising children," he teased. "Do you not realize that you carry the son and daughter of your love within you?"

Alysa's hands flew to her barely rounded stomach. Her blue eyes were wide with astonishment. "How do you know such things when I do not? How can this magic be true?"

The Druid jested, "Bearing twins has nothing to do with magic, my princess, only with love. The Runes told me of our secret. Your husband will have more than his victories to make him happy and settled. Your son will sit upon the throne of Cumbria, your daughter on that of Damnonia. You and your love shall rule from your grandfather's land."

Alysa's hands lovingly caressed her abdomen as she pondered Trosdan's unexpected revelation. "I guess I know little of such matters, as I did not suspect it."

"The Runes told me while I traveled with Eirik. I waited until you could have time alone before telling you. Rest while we await the contest and attack. During the battle, we must take great care to protect you and your unborn."

"I have endangered them with this demanding ruse. I

349

must be very careful until I return home." Alysa was annoyed with her gods for keeping this secret from them, as she would never have attempted such a perilous task if . . . That was the answer to their silence!

As if reading her mind, Trosdan concurred, "Yea, that is why we were not told. I would not have brought you here with child, and you would not have agreed. The deed is nearly complete, and we are all safe. You must be easy with yourself during the contest and rituals. And you must not join in the battle."

Alysa nodded agreement. "I will obey, Wise One, but you must use all your powers and skills to protect my love and his children."

"No harm will befall any of you, my princess," he vowed.

"In only two more days I can break the spell over my love and reveal all things to him. I pray you are right about his understanding and acceptance of what we have done."

Trosdan shivered as a curious and intimidating chill passed over him. He tried to clear his mind and concentrate so the warning could form there. He was deeply concerned over an unknown dark threat which nibbled at his body. Something was wrong somewhere . . .

The last messenger bird reached Weylin at Aquae Sulis. Gavin's closest friend read it with delight. The short letter told Weylin of Gavin's presence in the Viking camp, of their successes, of their plans. Weylin sent word along the messenger line for all forces to gather at his location. Friday they would sneak close to the battle area and camp nearby. Saturday, under the cover of darkness, they would encircle the Norse settlement—not Stonehenge, as previously planned—and attack the drunken warriors as they celebrated their alleged victory.

The signal to prepare would come from the stone temple.

During the so-called "empowering ritual," Trosdan would use special powder to create colorful flashes of fire and smoke to alert the joint forces. Afterward, they were to wait for several hours while the Vikings consumed large amounts of drugged ale and food. When their foes were helpless, the joint forces would swoop down and destroy them.

Weylin smiled in contentment. Soon victory would be theirs. Gavin was there to lead them, to be with his wife. Lady Kordel was awaiting him back home. Everything was going well.

It was late and the storm's violence had not ceased when the door opened and someone rushed inside, dripping wet. Alysa and Trosdan awakened instantly, realizing they had forgotten to bar the door, and seized weapons to defend themselves against this noctural intruder.

The peasant girl flung off her cape and shrieked, "Do not attack!"

Alysa questioned, "What are you doing out in this storm? Why have you risked another visit here? You will be slain if caught again."

The petite female sighed heavily, exposing her turmoil. Her forehead was etched with anger lines and irritation filled her eyes. "I have come with bad news, Your Highness. I spoke too quickly and bravely last time. The villagers refuse to fight our king and his wicked warriors. They are frightened children, cowards! I have argued and pled your cause; I have shamed them. But they will not listen to me and my father. I am not afraid. I will side with you."

This news did not come unexpectedly, but still it vexed Alysa. She was risking her life to defeat the Norsemen who had a stranglehold on this kingdom. The least its inhibitants could do was assist her! "How can they refuse to help halt the tyranny which oppresses them? Your king does nothing to protect your people from being robbed and slain or enthralled to barbarians. The women here are captured and abused, forced to serve evil masters. How can the men of Logris let such evil things continue?"

"They are weak and frightened, Your Highness, but I am not. They give many excuses for their lack of courage. They say the raids and captures have stopped. I told them it was because of your orders, because of your power here as their false queen. They say they have no weapons to match those of the Vikings or any battle skills. It is true our enemies are strong and many, but there are more of us than them. My people fear they will call down the wraths of the Jutes and King Vortigern upon us if we rise up against them. But they have promised to keep your secret and will find a way to rescue you if your attack fails. Please do not think evil of me for their weaknesses."

If nothing more, at least the peasants would try to save her life! Now she knew help from them was unobtainable. She had to gain some control of this overly zealous female. "Please return to your village and continue to work on your people. Perhaps your courage will inspire bravery in them. Try to be patient and understanding, and perhaps you can change their minds. Whatever happens, you must not approach this camp again, else you will endanger both of us. If I get into peril, I will escape and come to your village. Unless your people become willing to aid me, the best help you can offer is to remain at home and hold silent about me. That is what I need most. Can I depend on you and trust you to carry out my royal command?"

The girl smiled and nodded. "I will obey, Your Highness." She pulled on her cape and left, considering herself the queen's helper.

Alysa sighed wearily. "I hope she heeds my words or she could endanger us and our mission, Wise One."

Twenty

The storm continued to rage all night and most of the following day. One of the remaining slaves brought Alysa and Trosdan their meals. They went over every aspect of their plans, making sure each knew exactly what to do and when. Alysa rested after Trosdan left to check on the healing men.

Alysa responded to the knocks on her door to find a wet Eirik standing there. She stepped backward and invited him inside out of the rain. When he closed the door, she cautioned, "You should not be here. Victory is too close to endanger it. You must go quickly."

"Is the old man here?" the handsome warrior asked.

Alysa watched him push his dripping hair from his face. "Nay, he went to tend the wounded. But he will return shortly."

"Do you fear him?" Eirik inquired, noting her look and mood.

"Nay, I have no fear of Trosdan. Why do you ask such strange question? He is my friend and teacher, my adviser, my protector."

"That is good, for he is a powerful man. Did he tell you

to stay away from me? Is that why you have done s
lately?"

"I have explained my reasons, and you agreed with then
He does not know about us, as it would hurt and disappoi
him to learn of my wanton deeds," she lied out of necessit
"You must leave me. Only two more days of separatic
remain."

He lifted his hand to caress her cheek and he felt he
tremble. "Afterward, will we be together for all time as yo
vowed?"

To calm him and to get him to leave swiftly, she confide
"Do not worry, Eirik, for you will win me and the ques
We shall marry and rule our people side by side."

He gazed into her entreating eyes. "Did the wizard rea
this in the Runes and tell you?"

Alysa smiled as she wiped beads of water from his fac
"I am a *volva,* and I saw it in my dreams. Trust me. W
will be together soon."

He pulled her into his arms and kissed her passionatel
As his lips seared over hers, he held her tightly against h
hard body. Alysa responded feverishly and helplessly. It fe
so wonderful to be in his arms and to taste his sweet lip
But if Trosdan returned, an untimely confrontation woul
surely occur. Worse trouble would take place if either Ro
or Ulf came to visit. She gently pushed him away, the
glanced at her wet garments and warned, "Do not be s
reckless, my love. If someone came, how would I explai
this? Or your presence? Be patient and cautious a whil
longer," she urged.

Eirik tenderly relented to her fears. "I came to fetc
something from my chest. I will get it and leave." He wei
to the chest, knelt, and opened it. He noticed how the cor
tents had been shifted about recently. He lifted several iten
and frowned. He removed every item and shook each on
Dread washed over his wet body. The amulet was gone.

354

"What do you seek?" Alysa inquired as she witnessed is reaction.

His tone was sullen and wary as he replied, "There was sacred talisman here which I wished to wear in the final ontest. It is gone. Did you borrow it?"

Alysa was glad he had not asked if she had stolen it. Nay, I have not troubled your possessions. Someone must ave taken it while we were out of camp on the quests."

Eirik tossed his belongings back into the chest and lammed the lid. A scowl lined his handsome face. He eaded for the door.

Alysa rushed after him. "You go without a farewell kiss r word? What troubles you over the talisman? You do not eed it."

"It was a gift from my mother before her death. It is old nd valuable, and special to me. I wished to wear it for ood luck. I will find and slay the one who stole it."

Alysa realized how upset he was. She ventured, "Perhaps nid took it. She is the one who cleaned and cooked for le. She is the only one who had permission to enter this welling while I was gone."

Eirik turned and gazed at her. She looked so beautiful nd concerned. Enid . . . Rolf . . . His green eyes narrowed a suspicion. "I will question Rolf about it," he remarked, ien left.

Alysa watched him run through the mud to Rolf's dwell- ig and go inside without knocking. She closed the door, s rain was blowing into the room and her face. She did ot want to become chilled. Happiness made her smile. She as eager to tell Gavin her news.

The door opened and Alysa whirled to see if Eirik had eturned. It was Trosdan. She related her love's visit to the ld man.

Trosdan looked befuddled. "I gave him no talisman or ich tale."

"But he was angry and annoyed to find it gone," she reasoned.

Both faces shone with enlightenment at the same time. Alysa ventured, "He must have hidden the amulet here where he thought no one would find it. How very clever he is." Then panic assailed her. "You do not think both the amulet and sword were in the chest and were stolen, do you, Wise One? If so, he is out of the quest! I cannot marry either Rolf or Ulf tomorrow night. And there is no way to inform Weylin of a change in plans. What shall we do?"

"Calm yourself, my princess," the old man coaxed. "I am sure he would not hide both treasures in the same place."

Alysa glanced at the chest. "I should have known Eirik and Rolf could not be trusted! I must know if he still has the sword. Where is my mantle? I will go and question both men."

Trosdan captured her arm and halted her. "You cannot go out in the storm! If you are seen with Rolf, Eirik will also get suspicious of you. We cannot let that problem arise."

"He would never doubt me," she argued. "He loves me and knows I love him. He would never believe I would aid another."

"Remain here and I will see what I can learn. I warn you, Alysa, for the safety of all, including what you carry, remain here."

Trosdan searched for Eirik in Aidan's *shieling,* but he was not there. He hurried around the settlement and saw Eirik galloping from the corral and surmised that the warrior was going to check on or recover the sword from its hiding place. He headed for Rolf's longhouse, but Rolf was not there. He waited around for a time, but the blond warrior did not return. No doubt Rolf was also fetching his prizes. Tomorrow, the three champions would be compelled

356

o present their treasures before drawing lots for the final matches, as only those involved could fight. The Druid decided to make a final deceitful check on the wounded before returning to Alysa's side. He would seek out Eirik and Rolf later.

As the old man was leaving the longhouse where most of the injured were being tended, Ulf called to Trosdan and summoned him to his dwelling. The wizard responded, and the two men went inside.

In the heavy rain, Eirik paced beneath the large tree with the sword in his grasp. Finally, he sheathed it and leaned against the trunk. He did not care if he was being drenched or sheltered from the storm, as a greater one raged within him. A flurry of thoughts plagued his mind. Was he wrong to have these tormenting doubts about his love?

In the beginning, he had mistrusted the half-blooded princess, but her surrender and vows had dispelled all doubts. She had yielded to him, seduced him, taken him, on three occasions. Yet she had known a man before, so there was no way of telling if he was the only other man in her life. She had said she saw him that day in the forest, but had she? Was Rolf the man she truly wanted? She had been with Rolf when he had made his quick and easy find of the helmet, giving the blond Viking a way to remain in the quest for her! She had whispered to Rolf at Bath. About the shield? The amulet had been in her dwelling; now Rolf had it. A coincidence? Or disarming guile?

She had vowed to him that she was duping Rolf, but was it actually *him* who was being duped? Once she had him enchanted by her, she had pulled away. But to protect them or herself from discovery? Or because he was no longer a problem to her?

Who had slain Aidan and Searic, and why? To keep him

357

from having strong supporters if something went wrong. Who had drugged their cooking pots? Surely not Ulf, who had also lost his two closest friends. The powerful wizard. With or without the Briton princess's help and knowledge. She, too, could do magic. Had she worked her enchantment upon him for a wicked reason?

What if he was being tricked and deceived? What if she was trying to help Rolf? What if they found a way to make him lose? Make Ulf lose so only Rolf remained? What better way to win his confidence and aid than by pretending to confide in him, to love him?

Another speculation filled his troubled mind. What if the wizard was behind all the tricks? What if Alysa was inno cent? Being used and controlled like he and others were. Not once had she tried to entice the hiding places of his prizes from him so she could tell Rolf. He had suspected that she feared the old man, but she had denied it. Was she afraid of the powerful wizard? Afraid for them? For him? Was that why she had pulled away from him?

Eirik turned and beat the trunk with a balled fist until his anger and tension melted. If only he knew the truth. He cautioned himself to be careful of everything he ate and drank, everything he did and said.

He could not get to Alysa again with the wizard living there. He needed to ask her questions and determine her part, if any, in this grave matter. A woman, that was what he needed! He mounted his horse to head for the closest village to abduct one.

Time passed as Alysa's fears increased. She paced the house, wondering where Trosdan and Eirik were. At least Rolf did not have the sword. But what about Ulf? Had he or his men found a way to steal it, to eliminate Eirik from the final contest? What if Eirik was suspicious of her? After all, he had seen her dallying with Rolf. What would he do? She needed to see him and convince him of her innocence and love. But how? When? Where?

More tormenting time crawled by, and someone knocked at the door. Her heart leapt with intermingled hope and dread. Rolf entered Alysa's dwelling. He was grinning broadly, and wearing the helmet which she had helped him locate. If she had known about the stolen amulet, she would not have done so! She scolded him about such perilous behavior and warned him to leave.

As he withdrew the sacred dagger and held it up for her to view, he confessed, "Eirik knows I have his amulet and he is furious. Enid saw him hide it in your dwelling. She took it for me. When he sought it just now, he found it gone. I possess two prizes, but Eirik only has one and Ulf the other two. First, I will slay Eirik, then Ulf in the battle ring. Then you will be mine, Alysa."

"Eirik came to fetch something from his chest," she related, pointing to it. "He was angry when he found it missing. He did not reveal it was the amulet. He questioned me, but I told him I had not bothered his possessions. He shouted, 'Enid!' and hurriedly left. This explains his odd behavior."

Rolf boasted, "He guessed accurately, but it does not matter. Enid is dead by Ulf's command; I am certain of it. It is good, for she would have been trouble for us. She was a weak and foolish slave. She loved me and desired me to choose her over you, my queen," he stated with a devilish laugh.

Alysa chided softly, "Be kind, Rolf, for she was not responsible for her feelings or enslavement. She helped you in many ways and was very good to me. You must go quickly before others wonder why you remain here so long when we are alone. Someone might suspect I helped you win unfairly, especially Eirik, since you took his prize from my dwelling and I was with you on your victorious quest."

"I hope he does believe such things, as hatred and anger will make him careless in the battle ring." Rolf seized her and kissed her soundly. He smiled and left. He had decided it was best not to tell Alysa that he had slyly led Eirik to believe they were in love and she had indeed aided the theft and his last victory.

It was dusk by now. Alysa was frightened. Trosdan had been gone for hours. Eirik had not returned to question her. She could not help but suspect that he doubted her. Maybe she should find him and break the spell over him to prevent trouble. She flung her mantle over her head and shoulders and opened the door, and bumped into Trosdan.

She backed up and demanded, "Where have you been, Wise One? I was so worried." She related details of Rolf's visit and revelation. "Where is Eirik? What did he say?"

"He left camp before I could speak with him. He has not returned yet. Surely he has gone to recover the sword. Do not fear, for neither Ulf nor Rolf have it. Ulf summoned me to question me about the contest and rituals. I slipped a potion into his ale and bewitched him. He will defeat Rolf, but he will die by Eirik's sword."

"Are you certain, Wise One?" she persisted worriedly.

"It will go as the Runes predicted long ago. Beneath conqueror's moon, you will be reunited with Prince Gavin. This I swear."

"Are you certain I cannot summon him tonight and break his spell? I fear he doubts us and will cause trouble."

With unwavering confidence, the wizard replied, "Yes, he mistrusts us, but all will go according to what has been planned and predicted. You shall have him tomorrow night.

"I wish it were tonight, for I fear something is going wrong."

He must keep one last secret from Alysa; he had ordered Ulf to take Eirik and others in the morning to gather supplies for their impending feast. By having Eirik out of camp until the matches, Alysa would not be given a chance to yield to temptation—physical or emotional. "Nay, all is as it should be," Trosdan refuted.

Still, Alysa worried.

Rolf took a walk to exercise his body and to distract his restless mind. He wished it had not rained all day and prevented him from practicing his skills. Since the quest began, he had hardly lifted a sword except to place it in his sheath. Dulled instincts and rapidly tiring arms led to defeat.

Rolf halted in the shadows and observed the curious sight which greeted his disbelieving eyes. Eirik was pulling a lovely young woman toward Aidan's dwelling. The captive female was gagged and her hands were bound. As she slipped and slid in the mud during her struggles, Eirik grabbed her and tossed her over his shoulder, and vanished inside with her. Rolf knew, with Aidan's and Saeric's deaths, that Eirik was alone with the slave. Rolf grinned. In the morning, he would take great delight in revealing Eirik's disobedience and wanton behavior to their queen. If Alysa had any desire for his rival, this news would destroy it.

As the wizard had said, the sun came out the next morning. It beamed down on the land and joined the earth in sucking up the abundant rain. The final contests were scheduled for midafternoon.

Eirik took the sullen captive to one of the trusted slaves and said, "Guard her and train her while I am gone. I ab-

ducted her to serve our queen, as the other woman is gon
and our queen has no servant to tend her. Until her stron
will is broken and she will obey, she cannot be gifted t
our ruler. See that she learns her place and duties. If sh
remains stubborn, punish her."

Eirik had wanted to use the gift as a means to see Alys
this morning, but the captive was too troublesome at thi
time to burden his love. With luck and persistence, th
woman would be ready to serve them after their marriag
He joined Ulf and others at the corral. "Where is Rolf
Are we not all to ride together to fetch supplies?"

The redhead informed him he could not find Rolf. "Per
haps he has gone to retrieve his prize. We have no time t
wait for him. We must gather food for our feast. Do yo
fear to leave camp with me?" Ulf taunted, eyeing th
sheathed sword at Eirik's side.

"Nay, I fear nothing and no one, save Odin and the gods.

The band mounted and rode off at a swift gallop.

Alysa prepared herself carefully, wondering why Eiri
had not come to see her. In a few hours, he would face a
awesome challenge: Ulf. She longed to speak with him, t
make certain he trusted her.

Rolf arrived, and Alysa frowned at him. "Why do yo
continue to ignore the peril of such actions?" she scolde
him.

Undaunted, Rolf suggested, "We will stand here in sigt
while we talk. There is something I must tell you. Eirik ha
disobeyed your command. Last night, he returned to cam
with a female captive. I saw him drag her into his dwellin,
bound and gagged. He is unworthy of you, queen of m
heart. If he desired you as I do, he would need and wal
no other female to sate his hungers. I swear it is true, fc
I witnessed the wicked deed myself. She is still there now.

The blond warrior's revelation struck Alysa hard and deep, for she knew Rolf would not lie about something which could be checked easily. She could not prevent shock from showing on her face. Last night, Eirik—nay, Gavin—had betrayed her with another woman, a helpless captive! Why would Eirik do such a thing against my command?" she asked to stall for time to recover and to think.

"He has been here many weeks and has taken no woman that I know of. Perhaps he had need of one last night to dispel his tension and anger. Men cannot go very long without . . . having a woman."

"But I forbade the taking of any more captives until the quest was over," she stated angrily.

"The quest is over, my queen," Rolf reminded her.

"I meant, until the matches and rituals were completed!"

"Perhaps Eirik did not understand your meaning, or wish to do so. Perhaps he thinks he will win and this was his last chance to have another woman. The law forbids a king to have but one wife, the queen."

"It does not forbid him from taking concubines and slaves, if his lusts are greater than his wife can sate!" she scoffed too boldly.

"I will have need of no other—"

Alysa interrupted before the conversation became lewd and immodest, "Nay, we must not speak of such private things. I am vexed with Eirik for disobeying me and not thinking clearly. This is a bad omen, Rolf. Send him here to be scolded."

"That is impossible. He has gone araiding with Ulf for supplies for the feast—our wedding feast," he asserted confidently.

"Gone with Ulf? Alone?" she inquired anxiously. "Is that not unwise and dangerous? What if Ulf plots another accident as with Enid?"

"Then I will have one less rival to battle for you."

"Your jest is not amusing, Rolf. If the contest is wo
unfairly, great havoc will occur. If Eirik is not here to batt
Ulf, that means you must do so. Have you forgotten ho
wickedly he fights? These matches are to the death, as w
can have but one champion left."

"Do not worry, my lovely enchantress. I will not b
harmed. I will use this sacred dagger to slay my rivals with,
he said, holding it up and kissing its shiny blade. "I mu
leave you for now. I wish to practice while they are gon
Then I will have the advantage."

"Where is this female slave which Eirik took?" she qu
ried.

Convinced she wanted him, Rolf did not suspect Alysa
feelings. "He placed her in another's care while he is gone.

"Why did you not go with them this morning?"

"I needed to remain here to reveal Eirik's treachery t
you, and to exercise with my sword. It has been too lon
from my grasp."

"Find the girl and take her back to her village," she con
manded.

"You wish me to release Eirik's slave? He will be fur
ous."

"Not *release* her, safely escort her home. I do not ca
if your rival is filled with wrath. I am the queen and mu
be obeyed. This will shame him for his disobedience. Soo
Eirik will be no more, but I want him punished for suc
treachery behind my back!"

Rolf left to carry out Alysa's order. He related it to t
captive in charge of the lovely woman. When the blon
warrior told the female herself that the queen had con
manded her release and that he was taking her home, sh
smiled with joy and relief, causing her beauty to increas
Rolf eyed the captive with burning loins and wicked plan

Alysa, concealed nearby, studied the earthy beauty ar

364

pain knifed her heart. Dejected, she returned to her dwelling to be alone.

She raged against cruel fate for doing this evil thing to them. It was not fair. In a few hours, everything would have been righted again! Now her husband had sinned against her and their love. There was no excuse. Even if Eirik mistrusted her and was angered against her, he should not have turned to another woman for solace.

Tears filled Alysa's eyes and rolled down her cheeks. How could she forgive Gavin or ignore this weakness? How could she ever forget that woman's face, knowing her love had lain with her all night? How could he do such a cruel thing as kidnap and ravish an innocent woman? Had he done it to hurt and punish her for his mistaken beliefs? If only she had followed her heart last night and broken Gavin's spell.

In a wooded area, Rolf flung the lovely slave to the ground and pinned her there. Amidst her futile struggles and curses, he ripped her garments from her body and eagerly ravished her. The slender woman stood no chance of thwarting the strong giant of a foe.

When he was sated, Rolf stared at the bewildering sight upon his manhood and between the girl's legs. He demanded, "How can this be when you were abed with Eirik all night?"

The young woman glared at the blond Viking and shouted, "Because he did not ravish me, Spawn of the Devil! He did not steal me for himself. He captured me to serve your queen. May the gods curse you forever, Droppings of a Cur!" she screamed at Rolf, clawing at him and spitting into his face.

Riled past thinking, Rolf yanked the dagger from his belt and stabbed the brave woman several times. He stood over her lifeless body and wiped the spittle from his face. "Curse you, wench! If you had not offended me, you would have lived and returned home."

Rolf concealed the body, washed himself in a nearby stream, mounted, and rode for camp.

When Trosdan reached Alysa's dwelling, she asked frantically, "Where have you been, Wise One? A terrible thing has happened."

"I have been at the stone temple praying and making sacrifices to our gods. What troubles you? Why do you weep?"

"Gavin has betrayed me and our love with another woman," she related painfully, then told him the plaguing tale.

"Rolf lies," Trosdan declared confidently. He placed his arm around her shoulder. "He is innocent, my princess."

She refuted, "I saw her myself. He kept her with him all night."

Trosdan argued gently, "Nay, it cannot be. I forbade him to touch another woman while he was enchanted."

Alysa accused angrily, "The spell was not strong enough, for I have witnessed his dark deed myself. I ordered her from camp. I could not bear to look at her, or slay her for tempting my husband. I should have gone to him last night and prevented this evil from coming between us."

The Druid protested, "Prince Gavin would not do such a thing."

Alysa reminded him, "He is not Prince Gavin. He is Eirik, a Viking warrior. Your spell has made him too much like them."

"Nay, the spell is too strong. He could not take another woman to his bed. It is impossible. There is another pre

ention: Eirik loves and desires you. He would not risk
estroying your feelings."

"Not even if Eirik no longer loves me or trusts me? Not
en if he thinks I favor Rolf, and secretly aid his rival?
ot even to punish me or to prove I have not hurt him with
y lies and deceits?"

Trosdan shook his head. "That, too, is impossible, Alysa.
alm yourself and think. You are wrong. If you had not
nt the girl home, we could have questioned her and proven
s innocence. Why do you not speak with Eirik about her?
ut be certain not to drop any careless hints about his iden-
ty and our ruse," he cautioned.

"Eirik is away with Ulf, raiding for feast supplies. What
Ulf harms him? What if I never learn the truth?"

"Ulf will not harm Eirik, for I enspelled him not to do
)."

"What if Ulf's spell is no stronger than Gavin's about
omen?"

Sadness filled Trosdan's eyes. "Why do you doubt me
w? Has all not gone as we planned? Why lose faith the
st day?"

Alysa retorted, "We did not plan for my husband to bed
other woman, but he has done so. Is this my payment for
ing my duty?"

"Nay, my cherished princess. They will return soon and
u will see for yourself."

Trosdan left to see if the band was back, but it was not.
e returned to the dwelling. "I must prepare the herbs for
morrow."

"And I must go for a walk. I need fresh air and exercise."
lysa left the old Druid sitting and working at the table.

As she strolled around the settlement, she realized that
l of this would be destroyed within two days. Their Viking
es would be dead. The threat to Britain, to herself, to the
ildren whom she carried, would be vanquished. She

touched her abdomen and raged at fate's cruelty again. Pe haps by now another woman carried her love's— Alysa turmoil was interrupted by the returning band.

She could not face her traitorous love right now. She wa too distraught, too infuriated, too filled with anguish. Sl turned and headed for her dwelling. She had seen Eiri and he had seen her.

He caught up with Alysa and asked, "What is wron m'love? Why did you look at me that way? I have the swor so do not worry about the stolen amulet. I will defeat the and win you. Trust me."

Alysa glared into his entreating eyes. "Trust you?" sl scoffed. "Why should I trust you when you do not tru me? If you loved me, you would not seek to hurt me you have done. Leave me be," she commanded and walke away from the befuddled man.

Eirik wondered what she had meant by her icy wor and why she was so cold to him, today of all days. If anyo should have reason to doubt another, he did! Yet he did n He had tried to doubt her, but could not deny her love a commitment to him. He had concluded, if any mischief w afoot, it was not Alysa's.

The supplies were unpacked for use in the celebrator feast. As Eirik was leaving the storehouse, the Logris ca tive told him of the queen's anger toward him and of h order to release Eirik's slave.

Enlightenment flooded him immediately. Then he smil in pleasure and relief. He went to Alysa's dwelling a knocked on the door.

"Who is there?" Alysa asked without opening it.

"It is Eirik. I must speak with you. Now," he add sternly.

"There is nothing to say. I am occupied," she respond

Eirik vowed, "I shall remain here until you see me."

Trosdan coaxed, "Speak with him outside. You must n

t him enter, for my work is upon the table. Go, before he
izes the eyes and curiosities of others. Let him prove he
innocent."

"Bar the door, Wise One. I shall not be long." Alysa
pened the door and stepped into the fresh air. "What do
ou want, Eirik?"

"To spank you, for one thing," he teased. When Alysa
oked at him as if he were crazy, he chuckled. "The slave
as a gift for you, a servant to take Enid's place. Lorne
as to train her to obey, but he says you have commanded
er release and Rolf has returned her to her village. I could
ot bring her to you last night or this morning because she
as too defiant and disrespectful. Is that why you are angry
ith me, because you thought I took her for myself? I did
ot."

"Last night, you did not . . ." Alysa halted, and blushed.

Eirik chuckled and shook his head. "Nay, for I only de-
re you, Alysa, and love only you. I have not taken another
oman since leaving Hengist's hall. Forever it will be only
ou next to me."

Alysa did not know why she felt so strange, even shy
nd nervous, with her own husband. She could not recall
ver blushing before; and they were not strangers. She felt
s if suddenly she was again the virgin whom this myste-
ous adventurer had met and wooed long ago.

"Does my boldness in words and feelings embarrass or
ighten you? How can that be when we have . . ." He went
lent as he watched a radiant smile cross her face and fill
er eyes. "You believe me."

Their gazes fused. "Yea, my love, I believe you. Are you
ngry because I doubted you?" she inquired.

"If you did not love me, the slave would not have upset
ou."

"It was what Rolf said that distressed me most." She

369

related her visit from the blond Viking. "He was mistaken and he misled me."

"As he misled me about you," Eirik replied. He watched the astonishment seize her face as he revealed what Rolf had told him.

"Nay, I did not give him the amulet. I did not know was there. He seeks to make us enemies. Do you think h suspects us?"

"In a few hours it will not matter, for Rolf will be dead as will Ulf. Tonight, we shall become man and wife, queen and king."

Alysa's body enflamed, causing her eyes and cheeks t glow. "Tonight," she murmured dreamily. "Soon you wi be mine again."

Eirik did not catch the true meaning of her word "again. He smiled and said, "I must go before our eyes expose us.

"Tonight we shall begin a new life together. I love yo Eirik."

"As I love you, Alysa. If I do not go quickly, I shall bur into flames and be consumed upon this spot. Until tonigh m'love." Alysa turned and knocked on the door.

Within moments, Trosdan let her inside. Noting he happy expression, he chuckled and hinted, "So, he is inn cent as I vowed?"

Alysa embraced the old man. "Yea, Wise One, he is ir nocent of all wrongs. Tonight we shall be together again.

At the old Roman baths, the combined forces of Cambri Damnonia, and Cumbria united and camped. Tomorrov they would sneak to the Viking location and surround i When Trosdan gave his fiery signal, they would prepare t attack.

Weylin revealed the news about Gavin, and all wer pleased. With their king present to lead them, the Damnon

...s were no longer anxious about the absences of Princess
...lysa and Prince Gavin. As for Weylin, he was hoping for
swift victory and return home, where Lady Kordel was
waiting him. He could hardly wait to share his good news
with Gavin and Alysa.

King Bardwyn of Cambria and Damnonia sat at his
campfire thinking about his granddaughter and wife. He
would be happy and relieved to see Alysa. Within a few
days, they would all be reunited and peace would rule their
lands, thanks to his granddaughter.

King Briac sat at his campfire with Gavin's friends. He
was eager to see his son, to hear about this stirring tale, to
have Gavin's mysterious disappearance explained. His beloved wife Brenna was waiting for them at Malvern Castle
with Queen Giselde. It would be good to spend time there
getting to know the valiant woman his son had wed.

Everyone was confident about their imminent victory, as
the plan was a clever one and nothing had gone wrong, so
far.

Twenty-one

The Vikings gathered in the center of camp where a new battle ring had been marked upon the ground. Trosda chanted reverently, deceitfully, as he sanctified the circle. The three questors were called inside the ring, where only one champion would depart after the competition. The instructions were given for the matches.

"You must battle your rival with all your might and wit. You can use any weapon, or many weapons. The only restriction is to remain inside the ring. If you step out, you must be slain by those nearby. If you are thrown out, you must reenter and continue your battle. But if you cast out your rival, you must finish the battle with one hand bound behind you. You are not the winner until your opponent dead. After you draw lots, numbers one and two will battle. The winner will be given a short rest, then he must battle number three. When the final victor is chosen by Odin, Queen Alysa will wed him this night. Tomorrow at noon we will meet at Stonehenge for the empowering ceremony of the sacred objects from the five quests. Then we will have a great feast. The following day, our conquest will begin. Place your prizes at the queen's feet, then let Odin will be done."

Ulf called to friends to lay his figurehead and stolen

shield upon the ground near Alysa. Trosdan examined them and nodded. Rolf did the same with his helmet and stolen amulet, and Trosdan nodded acceptance again. Eirik placed the sword in his right hand before her. Trosdan checked it and nodded.

Alysa was glad her bewitched husband did not look at her, for surely love and apprehension were written in her eyes. He looked splendid in his dark-brown warrior's apron. His chest was bare and his feet were clad in furry boots, held in place by encircling leather straps. His wrists were covered by bronze armlets. Around his waist was a wide leather belt which held two sheathed knives of varying sizes. In his left hand was a sharp sword which glittered in the sunlight.

Ulf was attired in a short tunic, but Rolf was clad much like Eirik. She noticed scratches on Rolf's chest and arms, and sadly surmised the reason for them. She eyed the two Norsemen, knowing these evil foes would be dead soon.

Trosdan held out a leather pouch and the men reached inside to select their opponents. Each glanced at his stone but did not speak. The crowd was silent and alert. The wizard, clad in a black robe with sleeves which flowed over his hands, asked for Eirik's stone.

The deft magician clasped his hands within the concealing sleeves and said as he cleverly switched stones, "These battles are to the death. We can have but one champion in camp. If the other rivals are allowed to live, they would seek ways to slay our new king to take his place."

Alysa hoped that no one caught the contradictory error in the Druid's words. If the empowering ritual was to make their new king invincible, no rival should be a threat to him. Thankfully, no Viking appeared to notice that oversight in the wizard's speech and planning.

Trosdan glanced at the stone and called out, "Number three."

373

Eirik was surprised, for he was certain he had read "1" on its surface. He risked a glance at Alysa, who smiled playfully. He wondered if she had convinced the wizard to help him win so she could have him over Ulf or Rolf. Surely the victor of the first battle would be fatigued and sore during the second one, as they had gone for weeks without fighting anyone or practicing. However, he had secretly exercised every day to keep in shape, to keep his body agile and limber.

Before the redhead had time to look at his stone again, Trosdan took it from Ulf's sweaty grasp and slowly turned as he surreptitiously exchanged it with Eirik's first one. If Eirik had chosen "3," no switch would have been necessary. Trosdan had placed an extra "3" in a hidden pocket inside his abundant sleeve, with the plan to exchange Eirik's "1" or "2" with it, then give his number to the rival who possessed the real "3." The exchange had to be done quickly before the man with the same number questioned and challenged the drawing.

Trosdan glanced at the cunningly exchanged stone and called out, "Number one." He retrieved the marked stone from Rolf's hand and called out, "Number two." Trosdan dropped the three stones into the bag, pulled the strings tightly, and hung it on his waist cord. "The first contest will be between Rolf and Ulf. The winner will fight Eirik for the queen's hand and kingship. Gather your weapons and ready yourselves," he told them, and left the ring to join Alysa, with the false stone safely hidden in his sleeve pocket.

Ulf shouted, "My stone was marked with a three! You cheat! We shall draw again and another will handle the stones this time, wizard."

The crowd reacted with astonishment to Ulf's insulting charges. Jeers were heard, as were disgruntled murmurings.

"What manner of wickedness is this, Ulf?" Alysa de

manded. "All witnessed the drawing and revealing of numbers. How could our *attiba* switch stones before so many eyes? You dishonor yourself."

"I do not know how he did this trick, but he has done so!"

Alysa trembled in fear, but it was masked from all eyes except Eirik's. He observed her closely and prayed their ruse would not be exposed, for surely it was done to aid him.

Trosdan glared at the redhead. "Have I not proven at the stone temple I am Odin's servant and mouthpiece? See for yourself. There are only three stones in the bag. Your evil eyes deceived you, or Loki blinds you." Trosdan shook the stones into his palm and waved them beneath the redhead's nose and beneath the gazes of many other warriors. He held up his arms and ordered one of the bystanders to feel along his waist and hips. "I have no pockets in which to conceal a false stone."

The man reluctantly examined the sides of the black robe and said, "He speaks the truth, Ulf; I find nothing."

Alysa held out her hands, palms upward. "And he passed none to me, as there was no false stone, only your wickedness."

Rolf taunted, "They say, 1, 2, 3, Ulf. Do you fear to battle me first? Do you seek for Eirik to tire me in the first match? It does not matter, for I shall win both battles and become champion."

Ulf stared at the three stones. He was *certain* his had said "3." No matter, he would slay both Rolf and Eirik! And when he was king, he would find a way to get rid of that guileful wizard!

As Ulf and Rolf gathered their weapons, Eirik glanced at Alysa again. Once more that sly smile was sent to him. He was certain now that the wizard had exchanged the stones. He was certain now that all he had to do was defeat

Ulf and lay claim to his dreams. His gaze walked over he
from dark-brown head to booted feet. Her long thick man
was unbound today and held in place with her golde
crown. She was wearing a sea-blue gown which flowed ove
her body like sensuous water. The wrist-length sleeves wer
sheer, exposing her lovely arms, arms which would soo
be wrapped around him. The neckline of her beautiful gar
ment began just above her supple breasts, evincing a spa
of flesh which begged his lips to travel its downy-soft sur
face. He could not wait to get his hands around her slende
waist, and to allow them to wander over her inviting skir
She was exquisite, a prize more valuable than all five treas
ures put together!

Ulf and Rolf began their match with waving swords an
insulting words. Knowing this competition was to the deatl
the men battled fiercely and brutally. Weapons slashe
through the air. Bodies shoved against each other, o
swerved to miss a charging blade. The wet earth mad
squishing sounds as the rivals stomped upon it.

The weapons slammed together with deafening nois
echoing the men's grunts of exertion. Attacks were parrie
and thrusts were made. Blows were given and receive
Sweat beaded on their faces and bodies and blood fror
cuts trickled down their arms and chests.

Ulf made a deep slash across Rolf's cheek. The blon
warrior howled in rage and viciously attacked his foe. H
blade missed its mark, and Ulf's greedy weapon chewe
into Rolf's arm above his elbow. Rolf's sword went for Ulf
middle, but the redhead avoided it. Ulf entangled Rolf
feet and left arm and flipped Rolf to the ground. U
dropped his knee into Rolf's back and twisted it back an
forth, then his large hand shot to Rolf's head and presse
his face into the soaked earth. Quickly tossing aside h
sword, Ulf drew his long knife and jabbed it forcefully be

ween Rolf's shoulder blades into his heart. Rolf's struggles
halted.

Ulf lifted his arms skyward and howled as if a malicious
wolf dwelled within him. He kicked at Rolf's body before
walking to where Eirik was standing several men away from
Alysa. He placed his bloody tip at Eirik's heart and vowed,
"You die next, so prepare yourself. I shall return shortly to
finish this matter quickly. I do not want to use all my
strength playing with you, as this is my wedding night."
Ulf had looked at Alysa during his last statement, and
grinned lewdly.

Eirik's hand slapped the blade from his chest and scoffed,
"You shall die by my hand before gloam arrives. Take as
much time as you need for rest, as years of practice would
not change the outcome of our match." He wiped Rolf's
blood from his flesh and smeared it on Ulf's already spotted
tunic.

Ulf laughed wildly. He parted the crowd with his husky
frame and strong hands and returned to his longhouse. He
wanted to rub on the special ointment which prevented sore-
ness and muscle fatigue. He quaffed an ale and mentally
readied himself.

Alysa wished she could speak with her love, but she
dared not draw attention to them. She ordered no one to
touch the sacred objects, but told several men to carry
Rolf's body to where two funeral pyres had already been
constructed. "He was a valiant warrior, and he has yielded
to his destiny, for Odin has summoned him to Valhalla.
Place his body there with his weapon. We will light the
sacred flames tonight to call forth Odin's Valkyries to guide
them heavenward."

She and Trosdan returned to their dwelling for a short
time. She smiled and embraced him. "Are you sure all will
go well with Eirik's match? Ulf is strong and violent."

Thinking of the post-trance command he had given Ulf,

the wizard replied, "At this moment, Ulf is smearing th magical ointment on his flesh. His sweat and heat from hi body will make it work. Gradually he will grow weary an Eirik will slay him."

As Alysa passed Eirik on her return to the ring, sh pressed an amulet into his hand. With lowered head to pre vent anyone from seeing her lips move, she whispered "Wear it and Ulf will weaken as you battle him. I lov you."

Alysa took her place at the edge of the circle. She waite while Trosdan consecrated the ring again. She watched Eiri step inside with his sword drawn and wearing the amule about his neck. His tawny body was magnificent, sleek an hard and strong. His expression exposed confidence an serenity. His stance and movements evinced self-assuranc and agility. How wonderful their reunion would be!

A curious aura of suspense and anticipation hung heav in the air. Every Norseman was silent and alert, eager t watch this final match for their king. The sky was clea but an odd shade of blue. The sun was warm and brigl and timeless. An eerie quiet surrounded them. No bird san; No insect buzzed. No horse neighed. No animal spoke i tongue. All living things seemed frozen. No wind coole flesh or tugged at garments. The potent aura felt strang mystical, intimidating. Many destinies were at hand.

In Hengist's Great Hall, King Vortigern of Logris wa ranting. "I pay you to guard me against invaders! My peop are frightened and displeased with their raids. Go there ar drive them from my land."

The sly Jute chieftain replied calmly, "They only re before pushing into other kingdoms to raid. They take on supplies they need for survival. They have not terrorized plundered your kingdom, and do not plan to do so. I ha ent spies to observe them. They reported no danger to you nd your subjects. They have vowed not to attack here. 'here is no need to challenge them and turn them against is."

Vortigern shrieked, "I do not want them here! Leave to-lay and you can defeat them tomorrow. I demand it, Iengist. They are strong and many, and no doubt wait for others to join them. Attack now while you are stronger. Slay hem or drive them out of Logris."

Hengist shrugged. "I will send them a warning to depart. f they do not do so within a week, I will attack them and ou will owe—"

"Nay!" Vortigern shouted anxiously. "Leave within the our. By gloam tomorrow, the problem can be solved. Do o, and you shall be rewarded with the land between your erritory and Horsa's."

Eirik and Ulf faced each other, and the signal was given. 'he two men slowly and purposefully moved sideways in circle as each assessed the other's skills. Their eyes locked nd spoke, mutely giving and receiving challenges. Their novements halted simultaneously. They stared at each other riefly, then attacked.

Thrusting sword was met by parrying sword. Charging ody was halted by a defensive one which was just as hard nd strong. The blades clanked together, to their right, to neir left, overhead, and before their legs. Ulf's long red ock swayed wildly with his movements. Eirik's dark-blond air soon became mussed. Perspiration beaded on their aces and bodies and raced down their sleek flesh like fall-ng rain.

Loud exhalations of air were heard from both warriors. quishy earth sucked at booted feet, and mud splattered gs and shoes. Ulf's blade zinged off Eirik's thick metal

armband. Eirik balled his fist and slammed it into Ulf
heart area. The man laughed wildly. Eirik flexed his finger
several times, as striking Ulf's chest had been like hittin
solid oak.

Flickers of sunlight danced off their crossed steel. Spark
flashed each time the weapons touched forcefully. Ul
shoved Eirik backward, but the handsome warrior did no
lose his balance. He quickly ducked his head and ramme
it into Ulf's unprotected belly. The man staggered, but di
not fall. Again the redhead laughed tauntingly.

As the two rivals grappled inside the ring, Eirik seize
Ulf's free wrist and tried to fling the man backward. Ulf
hand twisted and banded Eirik's as he tried the same plo
Their blades seemed interlocked as they struggled fiercel
Boots dug into the slippery ground as each sought to contro
his stance and to shove against his foe.

They grunted from expended energy, and gasped fo
more air to fill their greedy lungs. Eirik lifted his foot t
stomp into the front of Ulf's leg. The redhead jerked it asid
just as Eirik's boot landed heavily in the spot he had va
cated. Ulf chuckled mockingly.

Eirik jerked to free his arm, as Ulf's grip was slick wit
sweat and his armband prevented a good hold on him. Bu
the pugnacious foe hung on like a starving dog to a hun
of meat. Eirik wriggled and writhed as he attempted to ge
his right leg behind Ulf's to trip him. That ploy failed, to
Still each rival imprisoned the free wrist of the other ar
kept the other's blade from moving forward and downwar

Eirik noticed something in Ulf's eyes, a curious pani
The warrior was sweating profusely and laboring to breath
It was obvious that Ulf was weakening, and fear was re
placing his confidence. Eirik knew he could win this matc
but must remain alert and cautious.

Sighting that advantage spurred the green-eyed warri
to boldness. Eirik called upon all his strength and energ

to break Ulf's hold on his arm and blade. Ulf yielded just enough for Eirik to free both. Instantly Eirik whirled halfway around and sent his booted foot backward into Ulf's sensitive groin.

Ulf yelled in agony and doubled over, fighting his nausea and pain to defend himself. The ferocious Norseman growled at his opponent, and his dark eyes glared with hatred and coldness. He knew he was in trouble. He was tiring too quickly and easily, too strangely. His mouth had never been so dry; his throat ached and pleaded for water. His muscles raged against movement. His head throbbed and tormented him. What was ailing him? Even his wits were dulling. He felt as if he were fighting in a dream. Was this what it was like to die? To feel destiny calling?

Eirik tossed aside his sword and raced behind Ulf. He locked his arms around Ulf's shoulders and yanked upon them as his knee jabbed painfully into Ulf's spine. He shook his foe, flinging him side to side as if he were a limp cloth doll. Ulf's sword fell from his grasp. Eirik threw the man to the ground and withdrew his longest knife.

Desperately, Ulf rolled aside and tried to draw his own dagger. He could not seem to rise or clear his wits. He felt a searing pain wrack his chest. He groaned and thrashed weakly against the soaked earth. The agony spread over his body and into his head. Blackness was engulfing him. At that moment, Ulf guessed the truth. With all the strength and volume he could muster, he shouted, "Trosdan!" and died, causing the crowd to wonder why his last word had not been "Odin."

Eirik gazed down at Ulf's bloody form, his knife still buried deeply within his opponent's chest. For a time, he was too exhausted to realize he had won this awesome battle; had won his love; had won the kingship of these people.

A roar of cheers went up, startling Eirik from his dreamy daze. He looked around as comprehension set in. His gaze went to Alysa's smiling face. Never had she looked more beautiful than she did this moment with her loving gaze locked on him. He left his weapons where they lay and approached her. Kneeling before his special prize, he said "I am honored to accept my destiny with you and our people."

Alysa's quivering fingers touched his bare shoulder "Rise, Eirik, for a Viking king kneels to no mortal. Truly you are a worthy champion and you will be a matchless ruler. Soon, Odin will make you invincible. Go, rest, and await our marriage at dusk."

Eirik stood, smiled at Alysa, and departed. As he passed through the crowd, the Norsemen slapped him on the back and praised his prowess. He gathered fresh garments and headed for the river to bathe and change. Within hours Alysa would be his forever.

Alysa commanded, "Take Ulf's body and weapons to his pyre. Trosdan will entreat Odin to open the gates of Valhalla for them."

The Last Viking Queen was obeyed. After Trosdan's false prayers, the wooden beds were kindled with difficulty. The branches were damp from the recent storm, so they burned slowly at first. As the heat dried them, the flames increased and enwrapped Ulf's and Rolf's bodies.

Alysa eyed the two burning forms and reflected briefly on how both had touched her life and aided her destiny "May Odin's will be done, my people," she murmured, and took her leave of them to prepare for her second wedding to Gavin Crisdean.

Alysa's love washed the mud, sweat, and blood from his body. His heart was pounding in excitement and joy. He had come here, joined this band, and won more than he had ever dreamed possible. No longer would he be alone and miserable. No longer would he have to go from place to place seeking adventure or peace of mind. No longer would he have to obey the orders of others. He had won the enchantress who had stolen his heart and mind. He was the ruler of this fierce and greedy band. They would travel together making legendary conquests. They would share everything in their lives and hearts.

Then, he asked himself, why was he not bursting with total joy? He knew why. He no longer wanted to roam, to raid, to reek havoc on helpless lands and victims. Killing, plundering, ravishing, and destroying no longer gave him pleasure. He no longer cared about seeking wealth and recognition. All he wanted was to settle down in a safe and tranquil place with his wife. He wanted children, a home, peace.

As he pulled on a short tunic in dark green, and a loincloth, he wondered how he could convince his love to think as he did. How could he persuade her to let them give up their high ranks? If he succeeded, how could they escape her people? Where would they go?

Alysa had completed her bath and donned a gown of bronze whose interwoven gold threads glittered in the light, as did the precious gems which decorated its neckline. She brushed her hair and placed her jewel-encrusted crown upon her head. She fastened a shiny golden medallion around her neck and a matching chain about her waist. Having cleaned the mud from her boots, she was compelled to wear them outside tonight to prevent ruining her matching slippers.

She was more than pleased with how she looked. It was vital that these Vikings were not given a chance to forget who and what she was, and what her love had become. By tomorrow night, this ruse would be over, and victory would be theirs.

Alysa poured a pouch of dried flower petals over the bedcovers. She rubbed their lingering scents into the material. Afterward she shook the covers to cast the petals to the floor around the bed where their heady fragrance would linger for hours. She placed candles on the floor, to be lit before they went to bed, to cast their seductive glow around them tonight. She laid out no sleeping kirtle, for she would have need of none tonight. How glorious to spend hours together without fear of a perilous discovery or an untimely interruption.

Trosdan, who was to take over Aidan's *shieling* in Eirik's place, knocked on the door to summon her for the long-awaited ceremony. "It is time," he said with a broad smile and gentle gaze. "I will leave you alone tonight. I will return in the morning to make plans with you two. Tomorrow our destinies will be fulfilled, as the Runes predicted."

Alysa followed the Druid High Priest to the center of the settlement. Eirik was waiting for her with an appreciative gaze and smiling lips. She eyed the muscled arms and legs which were exposed by his chosen garment. Brown boots snugly traveled to his knees and his waist was belted with brown leather, but he wore no weapon. The amulet which she had given to him was around his neck. Her gaze roamed to his sleek and shiny dark-blond hair, and she was glad its sunny streaks would soon return. He was so splendid, and her heart beat rapidly in desire.

Alysa and her love stood before Trosdan and followed his instructions to clasp the wrists of their right hands. The wizard removed the golden cord about his waist and wrapped it around their hands and wrists, the symbol which bound them together for all time, even beyond death. The wizard chanted the ancient wedding words which sealed their fates as one and blessed their union. From a slain lamb, he put a dot of sanctified blood upon their foreheads.

placing a small torch in the left hand of each, he told them to walk in a circle to the right.

Trosdan's mellow voice entreated Odin to bless this union of Sacred Champion with Viking Queen, to protect it and them from all harm, to light their paths to victory and to obedience of his will.

Alysa's sea-blue gaze never left Eirik's grass-green one. Their grip on each other was gentle but firm. Their shoulders touched as they made the nine circles with the torches. Desire blazed between them more brightly and hotly than the flames they held.

Trosdan unbound their wrists and took the torches from their hands. "Forever walk and rule as one, for it is Odin's command. Go to your dwelling and seal your vows as you unite your bodies."

Alysa blushed, and wished those words had not been a part of the Viking ritual, for she could imagine the men's reaction to them. But Trosdan was compelled to perform it according to Norse law and custom. Eirik grasped her hand and guided her through the parted crowd which was cheering them, and envying him.

Inside his old dwelling, Eirik barred the door and turned to her. For a time, he was content simply to gaze at her, to engulf her presence and beauty, her close proximity, her entreating aura. Without touching her, he confessed, "My head is spinning as swiftly as my heart is beating. I cannot believe this is not a dream."

Alysa felt her heart race with anticipation and joy. They had all night to love, to arouse their desires and to blissfully sate them. Eirik was hers; Gavin was hers; and soon victory would be theirs and they could return home together for all time. She remained where she was, a few feet away, and replied, "It is not a dream, m'lord. Command me and I will obey."

Surprise filled his eyes and he trembled with love and

385

passion's hunger. She appeared so willing, so eager, to hav
him. Her love and desire for him could not be hidden o
denied, as her gaze revealed them. "Nay, it is not my plac
to order my queen about. It is your right and duty to com
mand me and I will obey."

Alysa laughed softly and seductively. "That is no longe
true, Eirik. You are my king, my husband; it is my plac
my duty, my destiny, to let you lead and command. Speal
m'lord, my love; what is your heart's desire and I will fulfi
it?"

He did not have to give her query any thought. "You ar
my heart's desire, Alysa, only you," he responded huskil
He closed the distance between them, halting before he
His hand lifted, but then slowly lowered. He looked hesitan
unsure of himself.

As she caressed his cheek, she inquired playfully, "Wh
do you fear to take what is yours by right and conquest?
am not a dream, my love. I will not vanish or disobey. An
this is not our first union."

Eirik grinned and calmed. "The wizard helped me wi
you by magic. Will Odin not punish us?" he questione
unexpectedly.

Alysa reminded herself that Gavin was a Viking in min
and she smiled. She surmised that he would be vexed wit
her in the morning for not disenchanting him at this mo
ment, but she wanted to spend these next hours loving him
not battling him. "Nay, it was Odin's will. He commande
our *attiba* to aid you; I did not, though I wished for it an
made it known to him. I have loved you since first sightin
you, and could not resist you. It is you who is the enchante
my love, not I. You captured my heart, and I did not wis
to free it. Now you are mine for all time."

"As you are mine, Alysa. I never wish to leave your sid
even for an hour or a day. My heart no longer craves

roam wildly and freely. All it desires is to spend my life with you."

Alysa hoped and prayed he would still feel that way after he was awakened from his spell. "We shall share a long and happy life together," she vowed, slipping into his embrace as she could no longer resist touching him. Her arms went around his waist and her hands caressed his back. How wonderful this moment was! She nestled her cheek against his chest and listened to his rapidly beating heart.

"There is something I must confess before we join our bodies again," he hinted, then related his thoughts at the river.

Alysa lifted her head and gazed into his eyes. They were shiny with happy moisture. "I, too, feel the same, Eirik. Tomorrow we shall go through with the ritual and make you invincible. While the others are celebrating, we will slip away to safety."

He smiled and hugged her tightly. "Surely this is a dream, for I cannot be so fortunate."

"I came here to find and claim my destiny. That is you, my love. I do not wish to be a warrior queen, only your wife, mother of your children. The summons of Odin no longer rings in my head. Rolf and Ulf have been destroyed. We have been united. Once we are gone, these people will think it a bad omen and sail for home. We will be safe."

"And happy," he added.

"Yea, my love, happy, very happy," she concurred.

His lips sought and found hers. Their mouths fused with an urgent need to explore this powerful bond and attraction between them. He kissed her closed eyes, her unlined forehead, her rosy cheeks, the tip of her nose. Alysa laughed softly and snuggled against him.

For what seemed a long time, their lips worked to increase already heightened desires. "Shall we try your bed together, m'lord?" she hinted enticingly. "We cannot make love standing here, and my body burns to join with yours. It seems ages since the last time."

He smiled and nodded, feeling almost as if this was their first night together. In a way, it *would* be the first time, the first time they could love fully and freely, without fears or restraints.

Alysa lit the candles on the floor and started to remove her garment. Eirik halted her. "Nay, my queen, grant me that pleasant task," he urged. "I only wish to give you great pleasure tonight."

She went to him and lifted her arms. "Do as you wish with your treasure, m'lord," she coaxed. "You have found it, claimed it, and won it. I hope you will cherish it as long as I shall cherish mine."

Her husband chuckled. He removed the medallion and crown and placed them aside. He worked with her chain and discarded it. He knelt to remove her boots and tossed them to the floor. He stood and lifted the gown over her head. When her chemise and lower garment were gone, his smoldering gaze roamed her bare flesh hungrily. Her beauty and sensuality overwhelmed him and he shuddered with desire.

Alysa unfastened his belt and playfully tossed it behind her. She knelt and removed his boots. Very slowly and sensuously she pulled the short tunic over his head, exposing a hard chest which would soon bear the royal crest of Cumbria again. She grinned mischievously as she boldly removed his loincloth and flung it to the floor. He was virile and compelling, all male in appearance and manner. He flesh tingled with suspense. "You are more splendid than all the golden treasures in the world. Even the Roman statues must surely envy you this face and body. Nay, even the gods themselves."

Eirik smiled with pleasure and refuted, "Nay, you are the

ne the gods desire and the goddesses envy. But you are
nine for all time."

"As it was destined before our births when our fa-
ers . . . chose our mothers," she responded, removing the
pace between them. She was glad his father had not wed
er mother, though Briac had hurt Catriona deeply with his
etrayal of their love. Destiny had forced their parents apart
o this special and crucial moment could occur.

Eirik's mouth covered hers and his arms banded her, pull-
ng her more tightly against his nakedness. Their bodies
lamed and trembled at their contact. He lay her on the
ragrant bed and joined her. As her fingers teased over his
ps, the candlelight reflected upon the large purple stone
f her wedding ring. Eirik gazed at it, then asked, "What
f your husband back home?"

"You are my only husband, my only love," she vowed
onestly.

He knew she was being truthful, but had she considered
hose sacrifices atop the ones she would make here? She
ad a home there, a crown there, friends and loved ones
here. He ventured in a grave tone, "You will be unable to
eturn home with a Viking husband, or to put a Celtic prince
side for one. Your people will consider your marriage to
im binding, and will view ours as sinful. Can you give up
ll things and people to have only me?"

"With you, I have all things, my love," she answered
yly. "We shall discuss such matters in the morning. For
onight, only our love needs attention. Now that we are to-
ether as one, destiny will settle all else for us. Have faith.
ou will see."

Eirik nodded agreement. They were strong and brave.
hey would find a way to live, a place to live. No woman
vas more suited to him than Alysa Malvern. He sealed their
ps once more. His fingers drifted lightly over her skin like
ummer sunshine. Every spot he touched warmed and re-

389

sponded. One hand cupped a supple breast and fondled
His fingertips rubbed back and forth over the hardened bu
stimulating it.

Alysa closed her eyes and allowed her love free rein ov
her body and senses. He smelled so fresh and clean. H
skin had a taste all its own, which she savored as she sprea
kisses over his face. She loved the way he caressed her, an
the way her body responded and pleaded for more. For suc
a strong man, his touch was so gentle. For a man who ha
suffered and lived as he had, he was so sensitive, so tende
Suddenly she realized she was thinking of him as Eiri
with that man's alleged past. But Gavin was much the sam
she reminded herself. He had been an adventurer, an aimle
wanderer, a restless spirit, a hired warrior.

Eirik's mouth journeyed, slowly, seductively, down h
throat. It nibbled at her ears, her neck, her collarbone.
pressed against her pulse point. His hands traveled dov
her body, tantalizing each area they crossed. His wild, swe
caresses were whetting her appetite for more delectab
treats, which he gladly provided.

Eirik's tongue circled the rosy peaks of her breasts wi
skill, causing her to moan in delight. His hand trailed ov
her abdomen, making her squirm at the tickling sensatio
and teased over her inner thighs. He rested it over her wor
anhood and absorbed its heat, heat which exposed the heig
of her desire. Deftly, his exploring fingers entered that sti
ring area and pleasured the small bud which they foun
there. She writhed upon the bed and sighed with raptur
encouraging him to continue. He loved and craved an
needed this woman more than he had anything in his lif
Her spirit matched his, as did her passions and dreams. H
ached to fuse their bodies into one, but he was too impa
sioned to take her too quickly. In his state of arousal, sure
he could not restrain himself very long within her.

Alysa's mind was dazed by the ecstasy which encor

assed her. Her love knew her body and moods well, though e did not realize it. He knew where and how to touch her,) kiss her, to stimulate her, to sate her. He was in no rush night, though she sensed how difficult his control was to aaintain. Her fingers wrapped around his manhood and ca-essed its silky length. Her other hand wandered through is mussed hair, enjoying its feel and smell. Her body was flame; her hunger for him was enormous. Her voice hoarse vith emotion, Alysa urged, "You have examined your treas-re long enough, my love. Plunder your domain or I shall erish from need of your conquest."

Eirik slipped between her welcoming thighs and entered er. Both gasped with exquisite delight. Their mouths neshed feverishly as their bodies worked to seek bliss. As is hands cupped her head, hers traveled down his sleek ack, over rippling muscles and indented spine, to grasp is moving buttocks. They were firm and soft, and she neaded them passionately. She thrilled to the way his hips noved skillfully, driving her wild. She pressed her fingers gainst his bottom to urge him to fill her completely with is manhood. Locking her legs around him, she coaxed him) ride her swiftly and urgently.

Eirik yielded to her eager pleas. United as one, passion's ourney was completed within moments.

As she lay cuddled in his embrace, she murmured, "This me you will not have to sneak from my side."

He pressed his lips to her forehead and stroked her tan-led hair. "There can be no greater pleasure than loving ou fiercely, then remaining in your arms all night. I shall ot release you until we are compelled to leave this house a the morning."

Alysa looked up into his serene and loving gaze. Her ingers trailed over his lips as she teased, "I shall never let ou release me. I will only allow you to be apart from me or a short time. Did I forget to tell you, my husband? I

am a greedy and selfish wench. If you dare to leave my
side for more than a few hours, I will hunt you down and
enchant you. I shall work hard to make you think of nothing
and no one except me and our love."

He kissed the tips of her fingers and grinned. His green
eyes sparkled with life and love, with playful mischief. "If
I was forced to leave our home for any reason, I would
take you with me. I could not endure the loss of this lus-
cious body for even a day."

She feigned peevishness as she retorted, "Is that all you
need from me, m'lord? A body to keep you warm in winter
and to sate you?"

He stared into her twinkling eyes. "Nay, my wife, I need
you for all things. I need you every day and night. You are
more than a treasure to keep in bed. Though I am tempted
to do so. You are a woman who must be at my side at all
times. No matter where I go or what I do, I want you near
me."

Alysa traced the scar on his cheek and argued seductively,
"When the time comes, if danger does assail us, you will
change your mind. You will forget I can defend myself and
battle beside you. You will order me to remain behind." She
sighed dramatically and jested, "Nay, my husband and ruler,
you will soon view me as nothing more than a woman, a
wife to serve you, a female to bear your children."

Eirik rolled her to her back and lay atop her. Fusing his
gaze to hers, he vowed, "Never, m'love. I have watched you
here and on the trail. You are far more than an ordinary
woman, far more than a simple ruler. You are skilled with
weapons, with wits, with words. You inspire men to obey
you and follow you, and they would be fools not to do so.
You have courage and stamina and strength, as much as
any highly trained and experienced warrior. Never would I
be so selfish or fearful as to doubt or deny what I know is
true about Alysa Malvern."

Her expression and tone were serious when she responded. "I hope and pray you shall always remember these words. You cannot know what it means to me to hear you say them."

"I say them and feel them because they are true," he vowed.

"You have no fear of us challenging these people together?"

"I do not want to place you in peril, but it cannot be avoided. We no longer wish to live this way, and I know you can fight at my side."

"Are you certain you will not miss your adventurous life?"

"Nay, m'love. I am no longer restless in heart, mind, or body."

She reasoned, "What of the friends and sacrifices you must make to share this quiet life with me?"

He replied as Eirik. "I have no friends or family. My sacrifices are small and few compared to yours. It stirs my heart to know what you have done and will continue to do for our love and survival."

Alysa probed, "What if Aidan and Saeric were still alive? What if your family was still alive? Would you feel the same?"

Eirik gave her queries deep thought so he could reply honestly. "You are the most important thing to me. Without you, I would have no joy or meaningful existence. Whatever had to do to remain with you and keep you happy, I would do it. I have changed much since meeting you, and I can change more if need be."

Alysa smiled. "Each person must change when his or her life alters, as ours have done. We have lived so differently, but we have chosen to live as one. It is easier for some to adapt to a new life than it is for others. For this commitment to work between us, we must share all things,

including dangers. We must think, breathe, and love as one
I have lived a sheltered and settled life with others control
ling my behavior. Now, I rule my life and make the deci
sions. I was raised to accept my duty to others withou
thought to my own wishes. I was taught to put my peopl
first. Then my life changed drastically. The same is true o
yours, Eirik. You have lived for your own pleasures an
desires. You have come and gone as you pleased. Now
am half of you, and you must think of us first. If you eve
get restless again, you must ask yourself which you desir
and need most, our life and love or brief excitement."

"How could I get restless with you at my side?" h
teased.

"You have lived your life traveling, seeking adventure
taking risks. You have challenged many perils, constant
testing and proving your prowess to others and to yoursel
These past weeks, we have shared an exciting quest. Ther
have been pains and joys, defeats and victories, contest
and journeys. What happens when all is quiet and du
around you? What happens when there are no friend
around to distract you? What happens when you have mor
time than work upon your hands? What happens when tha
work does not stimulate you or challenge you?"

"Do not worry about me or doubt me, m'love. I will d
what I must to make our life a good one. I am ready an
eager to settle down. Work and duties, even if they are bor
ing, must be done. If we get restless, we will find ways
prevent boredom."

Alysa eyed his sensual grin and returned it. "Yea, m
husband, that is exactly what we shall do. We are cleve
so no problem can outwit us or destroy our love. I am ce
tain we can find things to stimulate, challenge, and sa
you."

"My wife stimulates, challenges, and sates me. Wha
more could I desire or seek?"

"What more indeed?" she asked merrily, climbing atop im.

Eirik pulled her head downward so he could kiss her. When their lips parted, he jested, "I have won a bold and wanton wench."

"Nay, my husband, you have won a constant challenge. shall prove I can pleasure you more swiftly and feverishly an you can pleasure me. I shall . . . love you forever, my usband, m'lord."

"And I shall accept your dare, my queen. We shall see who begs for sweet mercy first." His mouth claimed hers nd the heady game began, to last for blissful hours before umber captured them.

They awoke the next morning and made love again. Afterward, Alysa told him, "Trosdan is coming soon to discuss that we are to do today. We must get dressed and be ready or his visit. There are many things we must tell you."

Eirik sat up on the edge of the bed. Alysa knelt at his ack and leaned against him, draping her arms over his moulders and locking her fingers at his chest. It was time disenchant Gavin Crisdean, and she dreaded his reaction. he nuzzled his head with her cheek, then murmured the words to break the spell: "No matter what happens today r later, always remember that I love you, Hawk of Cumria."

Her husband stiffened as countless memories and realities ooded his mind. Time passed as Alysa remained silent and antic. Finally he grasped her hands and pushed them behind him. Turning, he stared at her in disbelief and anger. Why did you do this to me? To us?"

Twenty-two

Alysa responded with confidence, "To save the lives an lands of all we love and rule. To save our lives, Gavin, th lives of our unborn children, the lives of our families an friends, our land, Cumbria and Cambria, and all of Britai This was the only safe way to remove the Viking threa but you refused to understand and accept it. Every time tried to reason with you, my husband, you closed your min and excluded me."

She sighed dejectedly when he frowned in skepticis "Remember what I told you last night about the difficul some people experience in adapting easily to rapid and u expected changes in their lives? That is true of you, Gavi For our union to work, we must share all things, includi perils. We must live and love as one person, as one rul You were a wandering adventurer who thrived on cha lenges, dangers, excitements. After we wed, you viewed r as nothing more than a female to serve your needs, a wom to fulfill your desires, and a wife to bear your children could not convince you I was so much more. You had faith in me and my skills, in Trosdan's powers, or in o fates. When your life with me became too quiet and settl and there were no friends around to distract you, you we miserable. A ruler's work did not stimulate you as your pa xistence had. You left us no choice but to compel your ssistance through magic. The sacred Runes predicted it, nd our destinies revealed it. Have you forgotten the times vhen you have used deceit, even upon me, to solve prob-ems?"

Despite his nakedness and hers, Prince Gavin Crisdean ose and paced the floor around the bed as he argued, "But ve are in a Viking camp, surrounded by enemy warriors! Iow could you place us in such peril? What madness pos-esses you and that old man? Now that you have appeared o them and duped them, how can we escape their wrath? hey will never let you go or forget about you. You have alled down their vengeance upon all of us. When you van-sh, they will raid without mercy while seeking your recov-ry."

Alysa remained in her kneeling position upon the bed, ut her eyes followed him and remained locked on him. Dead men cannot raid our lands or threaten me again. At ais moment, our forces stand ready to attack this camp onight. We shall defeat them, slay each one. Victory will e ours and we shall never fear them again."

Gavin halted his movements and stared at her. "What ash plan is this? Our forces cannot defeat these Norsemen. Ll will be slain. For what, Alysa? A dream? An old man's oolish words?"

"I beg you, Gavin, sit and hear me," she pleaded.

"Hear what? More reckless plans?" he scoffed. "I must ind a way to get us out of here safely and to warn off our orces."

"Nay!" she stated sternly. "All has gone according to lanned and predicted. You must not interfere with fate." he related their ruse and actions to the shocked male, re-ealing the motive behind the false contest and treasure unts. She told him of the preparations in their lands and f the messages which had been passed back and forth. She

397

briefly went over the impending ritual, feast, and attack "Recall what you have witnessed me do here and on th trail. As Eirik, you admitted I am not an ordinary womar a simple ruler. You have seen how I can inspire men t obey me and follow me. You said I have courage and stam ina and strength, as much as any trained and experience warrior. Becoming Gavin again should not alter your opin ion. If you remain Eirik today, the Vikings will be daze with ale and potions tonight and our combined forces ca defeat them."

Gavin considered her words and recalled all he knew a Eirik. Still, his pride was rankled by the daring deceit, an he had to appease his anger with an enlightening argumen "My father and King Bardwyn have agreed with this wil plan and joined your side?"

"Our side," she corrected. "All is prepared. You cannc change things now; you must not or all is lost forever. Ou message told them you are here aiding this cause, but the do not know you did it because of Trosdan's enchantmen There is no need for them to ever know that secret, Gavir You will lead the attack, not me. I will hide and remai safe. The glory will be yours."

"I do not care of glory. I care of your safety and that our loved ones. Look what you have done here! You hav taken great risks by traveling alone with strange men. Pei ilous foes! Wicked barbarians! During your impulsiv game, you challenged Ulf to destroy you, and you dallie in the forest with Rolf. And what of your wanton behavic with Eirik?" he asked suddenly, his mind in a turmoil.

Alysa stared at him. "But you are . . . were Eirik! I di nothing wrong by yielding to my own husband. I love yo and needed you. And you know I did nothing wicked wit Rolf or with any man here! I explained my behavior 1 you."

Irrationally he accused, "To make this Eirik jealous!"

"Nay, to protect my enspelled husband! Rolf was jealous
f you and I had to beguile him to prevent suspicion. As
irik, you understood my actions and agreed with them."

"What other mischief have you done that I do not know
out? You constantly enticed Eirik and repelled him. You
ept him in a dangerous state of confusion. He was ready
 kidnap you just to have you. What of your wild scheme's
uccess then?"

"That is why I had to threaten Eirik and keep him off
 lance. I could not resist you, Gavin, even though I knew
ur relationship was perilous. I could not help weakening
 times, for you are my husband. I needed your comfort
 d aid. I needed your strength and courage. I had to mis-
ad Eirik to keep from arousing his suspicions about us."
 nger flooded Alysa. "You are being unfair and cruel,
avin!"

He looked surprised by her charge. "After what you and
at wizard have have done to me, you speak of fairness
 d cruelty? What of that message Trosdan compelled me
 write? If you knew I was Eirik, why was it necessary?"

Alysa sank to her seat and sighed heavily. She was as
 nest as she dared to be, "When you drugged me and
 nished, I was pained deeply. At that time, I did not know
 out Trosdan's spell over you. I was hurt, frightened,
 nely. I thought you were trying to punish me, to control
 e. I did not know if you would ever return home to me,
 t after the strange way you had been behaving and what
 ur note said. Yea, I was also angry and bitter! With you
 ne and the Viking threat drawing closer, I did what I
 ew I must."

Alysa licked dry lips and continued rapidly. "I did not
 ow you were Eirik until we were here for a time and the
 se was in motion. At first, I almost believed you were
 rik, perhaps a trick by Evil to entrap me, or a ruse by
 u and Trosdan to force me to play my role convincingly.

But our bond is so powerful that I was drawn irresistibl to you. And there were many clues to your true identit You called me 'M'love,' and I recognized your kisses an caresses, and the way you moved and spoke. Eirik appeare right after you vanished. I caught your friends here in lie about Eirik, about your past and that scar. I knew the wizar had the skills to enchant you and alter you. I knew yc must have gotten the drugged wine from him. He supplie me with strange garments and tales, so why could he n do the same for Eirik? I honestly believed you were n love and I forced the truth from Trosdan after he tried fool me with that false letter to keep us apart. I am sorr if you are hurt and angry, but I agreed with his actions ar went along with them. As Eirik, you trusted me and allowe me to do my duty. You believed all such things were a pa of me, and accepted me as I was. Eirik did not want change me, control me, suppress me, as Gavin does. / Eirik, you had no doubts in me or my prowess. Eirik need and wanted me when as Gavin you did not. As Eirik, yc wanted me at your side at all times and believed I cou face and conquer any peril beside you. As Gavin, we qua reled, and I was excluded. With Eirik, we loved and worke together. Knowing such things, can you blame me for war ing you to remain Eirik a while longer? You were never any danger, for Trosdan was protecting you with his magic

"As with when I defeated Ulf?" he demanded.

Alysa wanted to cry, but controlled that weakness. Sl blamed it on her condition, something she could not te Gavin until the danger was passed. "You would have wc that match on your own prowess, as you did with all tl others without Trosdan's help, but we could not take chance on him wounding you."

Wondering and dreading what others would think of hi when the shocking truth was exposed, he accused resen fully, "You and the wizard have made a fool of me, Alysa

400

Alysa quelled her fury and gently refuted, "Nay, my love, we have made a *hero* of you, a legend for the bards to tell of for centuries."

Gavin looked at her, this stranger who was his wife. He had witnessed her fight with Thorkel, her many clever speeches, her easy guile. Yea, she had played her role with alarming conviction! Just as she had beguiled him as Thisbe not long ago! How could he tell when she spoke the truth and her behavior was real? Did he know this artful pretender at all? "Why, Alysa?" he asked again, as if he did not understand, as if he were intentionally shutting out the truth.

Tears welled in her blue eyes, but did not spill forth down her flushed cheeks. "Because challenging adventures are what you seemed to need and want more than what I and our life together could offer," she replied, sadness tinging her voice and expression. "Because you could be here with me at this special moment, but only as Eirik. Because I could prove myself to you and open your eyes to the truth about yourself and about us. You needed to understand for yourself your tangled feelings and confusion before you could relent to your new existence, which this task has helped you do. You have lived for your own pleasures and desires. You have come and gone as you pleased. Now, I am half of you, and you must learn to think of us and our and first. I was compelled to do this task. What more can say to make you comprehend?"

When Gavin simply stared at her, she added, "Trosdan will be here soon to go over the plan, so I must bathe and dress." She reminded him of what was in store for them ater. "The ruse will work, Gavin, even if you do not agree with what we have done. For the survival of everyone and ll of Britain, please aid us. While I am gone, think on this crucial matter and what is at stake. I beg you, release your nger and pride. You are a prince, a ruler, a future king. Do what is best for everyone concerned. When I return, we will discuss it further." Alysa gathered her garments, the Viking Valkyrie outfit which Trosdan had given to her, and headed for the *eldhus*.

Trosdan knocked upon the door and called out his name, stalling her bath with his arrival. She quickly pulled on a kirtle as her husband yanked on a tunic. Gavin let the Druid inside and barred the door behind him for privacy. The two men looked at each other.

Trosdan stated, "So, she has told you of my deeds."

At the old man's nonchalance, Gavin's eyes narrowed. "Yea, she told me everything. Now I wish to hear your explanation. For what you have done to a ruler, you could be put to death, Wizard. Convince me why I should not slay you for this wickedness."

Trosdan took a seat at the table and calmly revealed why he had deceived Alysa and why he had enspelled Gavin. "Since your memories have returned, Prince Gavin, surely you realize what a great task we have performed here. And surely you realize such desperate and daring actions were necessary. Yet victory over the Norsemen was not my only motive. There were things which you needed to discover and accept, things about Alysa and about yourself. You needed one last great adventure to calm your restless spirit so you can be content with your new life. Damnonians needed for you and your friends to become great heroes to them. Surely you know that many there are disgruntled by your takeover of their land and queen. You have not hidden your childish feelings from them; your misbehavior spoke loudly to them and to your wife. I changed nothing in your character and personality. I simply commanded you to expose your innermost feelings, for I was aware of them. They needed to be brought forth and resolved for all time. What you did and said in Damnonia was not of my doing. It lived within the dark recesses of your mind and needed to b xcised; I have helped you do that. You will be a stronger, iser, better man and ruler for your personal victory. This lorious deed which you have aided, however unknowingly, ill evoke the Damnonians' acceptance, fealty, and admition forever."

Prince Gavin Crisdean did not want to believe such terble things were true about him. "If not for your intrusion, Vizard, I would never have left Alysa and home for any eason, no matter how bored or restless I became. I am not man without honor and strength. Why enspell me so I as a helpless slave to your plans?"

"Otherwise you would not have agreed and joined us. In ear of her safety and doubts of her skills, you would have alted Alysa's participation. You would have prevented this unning plan because you would not have believed in it. Io prowess, not even the superior skills that you possess, ould have defeated the Norsemen so quickly and easily, ithout great bloodshed and sufferings. Has Alysa not roven herself and her destiny to you? Recall what you have arned and witnessed here as Eirik," Trosdan urged. "Has ll not gone as the Runes predicted, as they commanded? Lysa is a queen and must live as one, but you have prevented it. You did not understand and believe in the forces f destiny. In your blindness, you would have found a way o thwart us. I had to intercede and change your mind, the nly way I knew how, with potions and magic. Admit it, rince Gavin would not have played a pagan Viking as convincingly as Eirik has. Without Gavin's fears and worries nd doubts, you have carried off your role perfectly. What re your pride and anger compared to survival and peace? Ve are here now, so you must aid us to the end."

"Do you realize what enormous danger you have placed er in?"

"None, for I am here to protect her and you."

"From over seven hundred savage foes!"

403

"Seven hundred or seven thousand, it makes no diffe
ence while fate is guiding and defending us. Do not blar
Alysa for my daring deeds. I did not tell her of them un
we were here and it was too late for her to resist."

"She went along with you, even after learning the truth

"She had no choice. The ruse was under way and su
ceeding. She is wise. She knew that to flee or to risk di
covery would have imperiled all lives and lands. If she h
awakened you, you would have made a slip and expos
us. She knew she could trust Eirik here, but not Gavin Cr
dean, for you had made that clear to her many times. S
knew I would let nothing happen to you, for she has fai
in me, in our gods, in our fates." Again the Druid urge
"Do not blame her for what I forced her to do."

Alysa refuted, "You did not force me to do anythin
Wise One. I agreed and acted of my own free will. I a
sorry if Gavin does not understand or believe us, but
would take the same path again. What he does from n
on is of his own free will."

Trosdan told Gavin that her dreams tell her what to d
that she is compelled to obey them.

"Dreams which you create and control with your bre
and skills!"

Incensed, Trosdan scoffed, "Nay! I have not enchant
her! She is truly a Seer. She was chosen and guarded
the gods. In a way, she was as much enthralled by th
matter as you were."

Gavin focused his gaze on his beautiful wife. "Why d
you not awaken me last night to give us more time to talk

"You mean, time to *quarrel*. I needed you, needed o
closeness, before this matter was revealed and this argume
took place. I love you, Gavin, and I never wanted to h
you or deceive you or embarrass you. Back home I tri
to explain everything to you, but you refused to listen,
discuss our peril with me. You excluded me at every tu

as if my words and thoughts had no value, as if our threat was not partly my fault. You have lived as a warrior; you saw this threat through a warrior's eyes; you believed only a warrior's prowesses could defeat it. Your mind was closed to other solutions. Trosdan knew we could defeat our foes in a safe and cunning manner, and I believed in his plan. Once we were here, there was no turning back."

Her troubled blue gaze fused with his troubled green one. "I know you have been miserable and doubtful as Gavin. But as Eirik, you believed in me. You accepted me. You wanted only me and our happiness. As Eirik, you had returned to the man I first met, and I wanted to spend time with him before my restless husband was returned. As Eirik and in the beginning as Gavin, you claimed I was the most important thing to you, that I gave you joy and meaningful existence, that I disspelled your restlessness. You vowed you would do anything for our happiness, that you would change as neccessary to share a quiet life with me. Last night, you were ready and eager to settle down, to carry out even monotonous work. You said that if we needed adventure and stimulation, we would seek it side by side. As Gavin, why can you not feel and think the same way? If you wish to leave me forever after we defeat these Norsemen, I will understand, and accept your decision. When this challenge is met, if you get restless and bored again, you must ask yourself which you desire and need most, our life and love or brief adventure. If you cannot be happy and content there . . . Do as you must, as I did," she finished.

Trosdan and Alysa looked at Gavin and awaited his decision.

Prince Gavin Crisdean of Cumbria paced the room again as numerous thoughts and feelings plagued him. He remembered everything of his life before coming here, everything about his life as Eirik, and everything about last night. He bravely searched his mind, heart, and soul for the truth. He had to admit, though it was painful, that Alysa was right, about everything. He reflected on her words last night, and comprehended their meanings. He had been selfish and fearful, but she had proven herself to be more than a woman, more than his wife. He had doubted her destiny and Trosdan's words, but all had come true. He had wanted his new existence to be a certain way, perfect, but had resisted the only path which led in that direction! *Eirik* had been right; she was no ordinary woman. If not for the spell, impending victory would not be in sight. Before them would still loom a vicious war with bloody and bitter consequences.

The ruse was cunning and effective. There was no reason why it would not work in their favor. But what if something went wrong; she would be in peril today. *Nay,* his keen mind argued, *she has proven she is a warrior queen.* He recalled how she had behaved here and with Eirik. Now he grasped the strain she had been under for weeks. She had been clever and brave and steadfast, and loyal. And, despite her courage and strength and resolve, she had turned to him as Eirik because she had loved and needed him. She had agreed to the ruse because he had left her no choice except to dupe him. Truthfully, their life as Eirik and Queen Alysa had been wonderful. They had shared all things, as she had craved to do with Gavin. Yea, there was no time or place in which she could not stand at his side.

Gavin's moody silence tormented Alysa. If he did not understand all things by now and accept them . . . She sighed heavily. "While you two talk further, I will go for a walk. I need fresh air and quiet."

Gavin commanded softly, "You cannot leave this dwelling. Your expression and mood would give us away. You are a new bride and should not look so sad or be out wandering alone the morning after our wedding. What you said to Eirik last night is true. And what you have said this morning true. Perhaps I have been too proud and stubborn to admit to such flaws and weaknesses." He confessed uneasily, "I *was* feeling bored and restless, but only because my entire existence had changed so swiftly and completely. Suddenly I was responsible for many lives, for the prosperity of our land, for your happiness. I was used to being free, wild, adventurous. Suddenly I was a husband, a ruler, and one day certainly a father. I was compelled to remain in one place with too much leisure time. There were many confusing and intimidating things which plagued me, Alysa."

He lifted his hand to caress her pale cheek. "I understand what you two did, and I agree. You are wise and correct; if I had known, I would have tried to stop you. I love you, Alysa, and I cannot bear the thought of losing you. I am sorry you had to handle matters this way, but that was my fault. What I said to you as Eirik last night is true. You are more than an ordinary woman. It has been hard to comprehend my good fortune, but I do now. Truly you were destined for greatness, and you have achieved it. I am glad we have shared this last adventure together. It has taught me many things about you and myself. When we return home, all will be fine. Whatever happens in the future, you will be at my side in all times and places."

Alysa glowed with happiness and relief. She rushed into his beckoning arms and hugged him tightly. "Trosdan vowed we would be reunited beneath a conqueror's moon, and one will rise tonight."

Trosdan stood, smiling. "I will leave you two alone to talk. But you must hurry. Time for the ritual approaches."

Gavin inquired, "One thing I do not understand, Wizard; why did you place two of the treasures in Hengist's area, especially when I had allegedly come from his camp? What if he had approached us?"

The old man grinned, his light-blue eyes shining brightly.

407

"I *knew* the Jute would not intrude on our ruse or expo
you."

Alysa and Gavin smiled, too, and it was unnecessary f
the wizard to clarify his meaning. Obviously he had p
pared well for this ruse.

Gavin asked, "Who killed Eirik's friends and the other
Why? And what am I to do at this ritual?"

The wizard said, "Come, sit, and we shall go over c
last ruse for today, and I shall answer all your questions

Alysa and Gavin followed Trosdan into the *eldhus,* ho
ing hands. After their hasty talk, the old man left to he
for Stonehenge to prepare for the upcoming ritual.

Gavin teased, "You fooled me, Eirik, another tin
m'love. When you were praying to Odin about the fi
quest, you knew I was spying at the window and you sl
gave me those clues. You did not know Trosdan had plac
clues within my mind for most of the quest sites. He ma
certain all went well. You will never know how har
worked to win you and the kingship of these barbaria
You were smart to let Eirik know how much you loved h
and wanted him."

Alysa and Gavin discussed the quest for a short tin
then embraced and kissed. They vowed their love to ea
other and reaffirmed their commitment.

"I must bathe and dress, my love," she murmured rel
tantly.

Just as reluctantly, Gavin released her to do the sam
"Must you wear those garments?" he asked, eyeing the p
vocative outfit.

"I know it is revealing and immodest, but it distracts f
men while Trosdan does his tricks. I will cast it away wh
this task is done."

Gavin's smoldering gaze wandered over his ravishi
wife from head to foot. "Nay, m'love. Save it for use
our private chamber. It stirs my blood and enflames r

ody. It will remind us of this exciting time together. In ur own world, you can become Alysa again, the Last Viking Queen, and I can be your Eirik."

She stroked the scar on his cheek. "You are my Eirik, r he is parts of you, sides which I had not met until we ame here."

"When we return home, you shall discover all things out me, just as I shall learn all things about my beloved ife."

Alysa seductively jested, "If you do not grow silent and ease looking at me like that, we shall be late for the ritual."

The anticipatory crowd gathered amongst the towering ones at the Druid temple. Trosdan, Alysa, and Gavin stood the center, near the pale green Altar Stone. All eyes were pon them.

"We have come to do Odin's will," Trosdan called out the suspenseful Norsemen. "We must crown our High ing and empower his weapons so we can begin a legenary conquest. Eirik, our glorious champion, stand forth d receive the god's gifts to you."

Gavin, clad in only a warrior's apron and boots, faced e old man, reminding himself to play Eirik perfectly. His ance was tall and proud and reverent. He waited while rosdan chanted prayers to the Viking gods as the old man rinkled blue water—which was supposedly sanctified— ver his entire body. The colorful beads eased down his lden flesh and made visible streaks to match the heavens.

Next, Trosdan prayed and chanted indistinguishable ords over the five objects from the quest and flicked blue ly water on them. He called Alysa to stand on the altar d enchant the prizes for her husband with her magical ng.

Eirik helped her mount the stone. The queen lifted her

hands skyward and implored, "Hear me, Great Odin, se
down your power to make these weapons invincible." S
positioned her hand with the false ring and wiggled it. T
brilliant sun passed through the cleverly cut stone and se
purple flashes upon the prizes. With the wizard's skill
preparations, sparkles were seen dancing off them a
"zings" were heard as the slender purple lightning bo
struck them.

The crowd was awed and amazed by this display of pow
and magic. Superstitious and susceptible, they believ
what they viewed. Excitement and joy flowed through
stimulated Norsemen.

Gavin was filled with pride and delight as he observ
his wife's enormous wits and skills at work. Truly Aly
was an amazing and unique woman, more than a wort
and capable ruler. Yea, he ruefully admitted, he had und
estimated her as a ruler, as a warrior, as a woman. He w
glad his eyes had been opened to the truth. All men he
craved her, but she was his, his for all time and for
purposes.

Trosdan evoked, "Great Njord, god of wealth and seaf
ing, hear our summons and answer us. Empower this pr
for our new king. Let its all-seeing eye guide him to rich
and victory for his people." He heated water over a sacr
flame and tossed it over the ship's figurehead. With spec
powder inside the dragon's wooden mouth, the water unit
with it and caused it to activate. Sizzling sounds were hea
like hisses. Curious smoke left the creature's mouth. Foa
formed and ran over the sides and down the beast's nec

The crowd drew back in trepidation, as if the dragon h
come to life and was about to devour them. Trosdan co
manded two men, "Come forward and see if you can tou
him."

The two men obeyed, placing their hands on the carv
neckline and making contact with the strong chemical. Th

410

reamed and jerked away their burned hands. Trosdan told
avin, "Touch it, King Eirik, for Njord will protect you
om all harm on land and sea."

Gavin knew to make no contact with the liquid. He
uched the dragon's neck and head anywhere the chemical
as not. He lifted his hands and slowly turned to show
eryone he was not burned or pained. A cheer arose for
m and that blessing.

Trosdan lifted the helmet and called out, "Our goddess
ey, we summon you to hear our plea and respond. Grant
ir king peace, plenty, fertility. Use your powers to enchant
is helmet to protect his mind, the ruler of his body. Touch
" he commanded two others.

The Norsemen fearfully obeyed, then yelled in agony. He
ld Gavin, "Take it, for Frey will protect you from harm."

The Cumbrian prince carefully took the helmet as Tros-
n had instructed and placed it on his head. He turned
veral times to evince his power, then removed the helmet.

The same trick was performed with the shield, calling
on Freyja—Viking goddess of love—to protect his heart.
ie Norsemen did not realize that Gavin knew the only
fe spots to touch each item and were fooled by his guile.

Trosdan held up the quest dagger. "Odin's blade is deadly
all except our enchanted king. Great Odin, ruler and crea-
r of all things and people, hear our prayer. Protect your
osen champion from all harm. Reveal your will to him
d he will obey it and lead your people as you desire."
 slew a lamb with it and drained its blood into a sacri-
ial bowl. The Druid placed one dot in the center of
avin's forehead and a handprint over his heart. He put the
gger in Gavin's hand and told him to clasp his hands and
ld it over his head. When Gavin obeyed, the wizard with-
ew his trick knife and pretended to stab Gavin in the
art, in the center of the bloody symbol.

The crowd shouted in dismay and surged forward to at-

tack the treacherous *attiba*. Trosdan held up the blade. "
calm. He lives. He cannot be slain. See, he does not bl
or reveal a wound."

The crowd gaped on in ever-increasing astonishment. T
had never seen an indestructible mortal. Surely their g
had a hand in this matter and were hovering over this sac
place. To think of an invincible ruler with invincible weap
stirred their minds to a near frenzy. The dagger was pla
on the altar with the other prizes.

Trosdan lifted the last treasure, the legendary sword
Julius Caesar. "Hear us, Great Thor, guardian of law, just
victory, and power; grant such gifts to Odin's chosen c
The sword Yellow Death kills with only a minor cut, but
our champion, even if it is taken from his hand as it was w
the Emperor. It is Thor's gift to our king." Trosdan gras
Gavin's hand and sliced across his forefinger. Blood ran fo
and Trosdan captured it in a small metal dish.

The Vikings, recalling the legendary tale of Caesar's
perous sword, looked on in fear and dread for their ki
but nothing happened to him. Tension mounted, as did s
pense and awe.

The wizard took a rabbit from a cage and knicked its
with the sword. The creature kicked and writhed upon
altar and died. "See, Yellow Death is lethal to all forms
life except our king."

As the people whispered in wonder, Trosdan poure
healing potion over Gavin's finger. The bleeding halted
the injury sealed itself. "We must leave these weapons h
all night for our gods to come and touch. No one m
come near this temple or he will be struck dead. At da
our king will reclaim them. We shall make a sacrificial
and then begin our feast."

Trosdan glanced at the rapidly setting sun. Dusk
near, so the signal could be seen by their spies not far av
While word was being passed to all three forces, the

uspecting Norsemen would be drinking ale laced with a low-acting sleeping potion. The Druid could not let their oes drop too swiftly or suspicion would arise. It had to ppear to the other Vikings as if their friends were passing ut because of too much ale. The wizard placed the lamb's ody and the rabbit's on a wooden altar and set it ablaze. Ie tossed Gavin's blood upon it, then cast another liquid here. Colorful flames leaped skyward like a magical fire vhich was trying to reach the heavens and warm the gods.

Weylin smiled with relief and pride. He could hardly wait o see Gavin and Alysa. He told the five men with him, There is the signal to prepare. We must return to our amps with this good news. Soon our pagan foes will be runk and helpless. We will surround their camp under the over of darkness, and attack in force at the next signal. his battle will be won quickly and easily."

In their dwelling, Alysa and Gavin were in the tub he ad stolen for her as Eirik. She was playfully scrubbing the lue streaks and bloody marks from his virile body. She vas surprised that his cut finger needed no tending or ban-aging. "The signal has been sent to our united forces, my ove, and the deadly feast has begun. Soon this task will e over and we can return home."

"Yea, *home*," he echoed contentedly. "This time, I am ooking forward to a quiet existence with you. You have iven me more than enough fear and excitement and chal-enges for a lifetime."

As she rubbed the cloth over his chest, she teased, "You ay that now while you are sitting in the midst of your reatest adventure. But what of two months from now? A ear from now? Three years?"

413

"Nay," he vowed honestly, confidently. "As Eirik tol[d] you, my restless spirit lives no more. Our new challeng[e] will be to make our land the most prosperous and happie[st] in Britain. Perhaps soon we shall have children to offer [us] other challenges and pleasures."

"That is so," she informed him with a sly smile. "Yo[u] are a very virile force, my lusty liege, and my body is ferti[le] ground. Already your wonderful seeds grow within m[e] where you planted them."

"What do you say?" he questioned, staring at her.

Alysa smiled serenely. "That I carry your children. I d[id] not know until the night of the storm. Trosdan told me. H[e] read it in the sacred Runes, for they know all things. H[e] says we are expecting twins, a son to sit upon the thron[e] of Cumbria, a daughter to take the crown of Damnonia, an[d] we shall rule from Cambria. Will that be enough stimulatio[n] for you, my wandering rogue?"

"Why did you not tell me this morning?"

"There were other things to reveal and discuss first. Yo[u] were angry and distressed. You had the ritual. I did not wis[h] to spoil such a special announcement. I was going to wa[it] until after the battle to tell you so you would not worr[y] about me, but I could not contain my happy secret an[y] longer. The danger to us is passed. At this moment the V[iking] kings are celebrating their good fortunes and getting drun[k] on ale laced with Trosdan's potions. I will lock myself [in] here during the attack, though it will hardly be a difficu[lt] battle, which is good. I want none of our friends, familie[s] or subjects harmed. I will be safe; I promise you."

Gavin's wet hand went to her abdomen, dampening h[er] kirtle. He gently rubbed it and grinned broadly. "This [is] wonderful news, m'love. A glorious victory, peace, hom[e,] our children . . ." he murmured ecstatically. "Surely I a[m] blessed by the day we met." He pulled her head forwa[rd] and kissed her passionately.

Alysa gazed deeply into his eyes and knew, this time, all would be wonderful between them. As Trosdan and the runes had predicted and vowed, Gavin had been changed for the better by this joint task. "We were both blessed, my husband, for it is our destiny."

On the far side of the Viking camp, two Jute spies were watching the celebration. One said, "We must return and report to Hengist." They slipped from their positions and mounted their horses.

Attired in the bronze gown and with her Viking circlet in place, Alysa strolled about the camp arm in arm with her husband, who was clad in a short tunic of blue and also wearing a gold crown. They were both delighted to see the Norsemen drinking heavily as they feasted and toasted their queen and king. The happy couple sipped nothing but the wine which Trosdan had given to them and nibbled on the food prepared by Logris slaves. They chatted falsely with their beguiled foes while mischievously alleging a great victory was at hand.

It was dark, and many torches lit the center of the settlement. A few men were lying about, near a debilitating state, while others were staggering as they resisted that same condition.

Trosdan, Alysa, and Gavin knew, from the original number of foes, that around six hundred and sixty Norsemen remained alive. Some were still suffering from contest injuries, but were joining in on the celebration from their pallets. What they did not know was that a few men had left camp this morning during their private talk to fetch more casks of ale for that night. Those taken by force from Logris village had been placed in the storehouse with the

415

already treated casks. With all barrels taken out for th[e] feast, many Norsemen were drinking from untainted one[s] or drinking little from the heavily drugged casks.

Alysa and Gavin joined the Druid near Ulf's deserte[d] longhouse. Gavin smiled broadly and said. "All is goin[g] according to plan, Wise One. Soon these fierce barbarian[s] will be too weakened by your special brew to defend them[-] selves. When our forces respond to our signal, they will b[e] slain and all of Britain will be saved."

"Yea, Prince Gavin, our ruse has worked perfectly. The[y] are all duped. I will give them a little more time to drin[k] more of the tainted ale, then I will light the fire to sign[al] our forces. The Norsemen will be defeated tonight. Tomo[r]row you and Princess Alysa can return home to Damnoni[a.] All kingdoms will praise your daring deed."

Gavin hinted, "I want none to escape, Trosdan. I nev[er] want my wife threatened by them again. They were fools t[o] believe Alysa Malvern Crisdean would become their quee[n.] The contest was a cunning way to rid ourselves of many [of] them, and this drugging feast will finish them off for us. D[o] not wait too long before giving the fiery signal, Wise On[e.] We want our forces to enjoy at least a small battle with ther[m.] Else they will feel cheated during this glorious victory."

The wizard nodded understanding. "Take the princess t[o] her dwelling, where she will be safe during the attack. T[oo] many of these foes are still alert. I will wait a while long[er] to summon our warriors."

Gavin looked at Alysa and grasped her hand. He escorte[d] her to the stone house, then said, "Go inside and bar th[e] door. Open it for no one except me. Protect yourself an[d] our children."

She teased, "I thought you did not believe in the wizard['s] powers and foresight. What if he is mistaken about my co[n]dition?"

Gavin met her playful gaze and said without a doubt, "[

trust Trosdan and the Runes. They have proven themselves to me. I shall never doubt such forces and powers again. When we return home, we shall make him our adviser. Does that please you, my beautiful wife?"

"Yea, it pleases me. When a man is strong enough and confident enough to recognize his limitations and strengths, that is when he is truly invincible. Be careful," she urged and kissed him.

Prince Gavin Crisdean watched his beloved wife, Princess Alysa Malvern Crisdean, enter the abode he had won as Eirik in a gamble and battle with a Viking foe. He headed back to join Trosdan.

The Logris captive who had been standing in the shadows near Ulf's longhouse to relieve himself of spent ale had overheard the shocking talk. Having sided with the powerful Norsemen, he knew what must be done. He hurried to the spot where several Vikings were chatting and drinking, and he related the incredible news to them.

The Druid High Priest said a silent prayer to his gods and lit the large signal fire. He had kept one last secret from Alysa and Gavin; his death as a result of the attack. He had told them he was willing to give up his life for them; now he would be compelled to prove it. To save Gavin from a lethal sword blow, he must die.

Trosdan gazed into the colorful flames and awaited his fate. As he did so, he thought of Giselde, Alysa's grandmother, now the wife of King Bardwyn of Cambria. *I love you, Giselde. I always have. But to achieve this great moment in destiny, I could not claim you.*

* * *

Far away in Malvern Castle in Damnonia, Giselde stiffened and chills raced over her body. Within her mystical mind, she heard the words of her teacher and friend, as Trosdan had neglected to recall her special powers. Giselde quickly fetched her belongings and prayed.

Gavin whirled as he heard many Vikings shouting and running toward him and Trosdan near the signal fire. He heard the angry Norsemen yelling, "Put out the fire quickly!" "Arouse our men and warn them!" "Ulf was right about the wizard! He is evil and treacherous!" "The quest was only a trick to fool us and weaken us!" "Slay them!" "Fetch our traitorous queen and she will die with them!"

Gavin hastily drew his sword, placing his vulnerable back to the large fire. He was vastly outnumbered by foes who were still alert and agile, men who seemed to have no fear of him being invincible. Amidst their hatred and rage, the Norsemen seemed to have forgotten all they had witnessed earlier and in days past. "Something has gone wrong, Wizard! Our forces will not reach us in time! Pray for the gods to save Alysa and our children!" He mentally and physically prepared himself to battle the approaching men to the death.

Alysa had felt the supernatural stirrings between the wizard and her grandmother. She, too, possessed a mystical mind, and she had seen and heard the contact between them. Nay, her mind shouted. She could not allow Trosdan to be slain! *I will save him, Granmannie.*

Despite Gavin's prior warning, Alysa unbarred the door, grabbed her sword, and rushed forward on her sacred mission to save Trosdan from certain death. She never imagined what was occurring outside.

Twenty-three

Trosdan tossed a pouch of highly flammable liquid into the signal fire, causing its flames to reach greater brilliance and heights. The wizard grabbed a handful of tiny balls from his pocket and flung them toward the approaching foes. The chemical balls burst upon forceful contact with the hard ground, giving off loud bangs and heavy clouds of smoke which briefly frightened and halted the Norsemen.

"It is only a wizard's tricks! Attack them!" one enemy shouted.

The magician tried another ruse to stall for time. Trosdan seized a handful of powder and tossed it before them. Colorful stars seemed to dance in midair, temporarily mesmerizing the Vikings. He whispered to Gavin, "We must flee to the house and hold them off from there until our forces arrive. Come quickly while they are blinded."

The prince and the wizard raced in that direction, to see Alysa hurrying toward them with her sword. Gavin shouted, "Get back inside! They are on to our ruse!"

Before the startled princess could obey, she heard a Norseman yell, "There they go! After them!"

Then another Norsemen yelled, "We are under attack!"

From all sides of the settlement, loud voices and running feet were heard. Swords clashed as the siege got under way just in time. The Vikings spread out to defend themselves, all except five who continued their vengeful pursuit of Trosdan, Gavin, and Alysa.

The first Norsemen reached them and fought with Gavin. As a second joined his friend, Trosdan rushed to the prince's rescue. Just as the warrior was about to bury his blade in Gavin's back, the wizard bravely and unselfishly stepped between them.

Alysa realized what was happening and charged the foe. Her shout and attack was enough to cause the Viking to jerk aside and only wound Trosdan. Alysa shoved her blade through the man's body.

The other Norsemen reached them. Alysa and Gavin stood back to back in the circle of enemies which formed around them. "I love you, Hawk of Cumbria," she murmured.

"As I love you," he replied, his sword clashing loudly with the first man's blade.

The settlement was overrun by warriors—knights, peasants, noblemen, kings—from the three united lands. Assistance arrived for Gavin and Alysa, who were fiercely struggling for survival. The Norsemen were forced to break off their attack on the royal couple to battle countless other men, who included Lord Weylin and Sheriff Dal.

Gavin said, "We must get you and Trosdan to the house until this matter is settled." With Alysa on one side of the wounded wizard and Gavin on the other, they helped Trosdan inside and placed him on the bed. "Bar the door and do not open it again until I call out."

Alysa closed and locked the door. She went to tend Trosdan. As she examined the wound, she was relieved to see that she had acted in time to prevent a fatal injury. "I must bandage it, Wise One."

Trosdan could not believe he was alive. "You should not have risked your life to save me. I saw my death in the

Runes. How can this be? The Sacred Runes are never wrong."

Alysa reasoned, "You saw yourself stabbed by an enemy sword and assumed you would be slain. Your troubled thoughts traveled to Granmannie and hers traveled to mine. I had to rescue you, Wise One. I love you and depend upon you."

Suddenly, Alysa was grasped from behind. A Viking had slipped inside while the door was open and had hidden himself in the *eldhus* when he saw them approaching the house. His strong arm banded her throat and yanked her against his body.

Alysa tried to free herself, but could not. "Release me! I am your queen! Odin will strike you dead for this offense!"

The infuriated warrior shouted, "You are the one who will die, false queen! You tricked us with your beauty and lies. One of the slaves overheard your talk outside and warned us of your evil. Your Celtic forces are attacking us. You shall become my shield to escape. I will gather help from Hengist and return to attack them. Our vengeance will make your lands run red with your people's blood." He roughly jerked her more tightly against his hard and smelly body. "You are the ones who drugged us during the third quest and blamed it on Ulf. His charges against you were true, but your clever wizard duped us with his magic. Your cunning ruses got many of us killed and wounded. No doubt you slew Saeric, Aidan, Sigurd, Leikn, and Sweyn!"

Alysa shouted back, "Nay! It is Loki's mischief which blinds you and dupes you. The slave lied about us. We are not foes. Release me so we can help our people defend themselves," she commanded.

The irate, unconvinced Norseman shook her. "Einar must have guessed your evil, so you killed him with magic so he could not expose you. You were only stalling us with the contests and quests while your forces gathered and traveled here. Your rank will not save you, witch-woman! You are as traitorous as Astrid and Rurik, for their evil bloods flow within you. The legend and curse will end with your death."

The Norseman was so focused on Alysa that he failed to notice the wizard rising from the bed with Alysa's discarded sword. Trosdan jabbed it into the man's side. The Viking screamed in pain and fury. But it was too late, for Trosdan yanked out the blade and quickly ran it through the man's chest.

The foe staggered and collapsed. The weakened Trosdan nearly did the same. Alysa caught him and helped him back to the bed. She fetched the healing herbs and clean cloths. After washing the area, she sprinkled the mixture on the wound and bound it. With the old man's instructions, she began to brew an herbal tea to prevent shock.

Outside the longhouse, the battle between the Norsemen and Celts raged on for a time. But the Vikings were vastly outnumbered, and many were drunk on untainted ale or dazed by drugged ale. Every structure and shed was searched to make certain no foe survived.

The Celts had been warned not to sip any of the ale to quench their thirsts. Gavin ordered all casks to be dumped and he was obeyed. Soon, only Celts were alive, and victory was obtained.

King Bardwyn asked Gavin, "Where is my granddaughter?"

The prince replied, "She is safe in that house. I will get her."

When Alysa opened the door, Gavin saw the dead Norseman on the floor. "What happened here?"

Alysa explained the episode to the men who were crowded at the door and revealed how their ruse had been exposed. When her grandfather—her king—made his way inside, Bardwyn and Alysa embraced affectionately.

The elderly king of Cambria and Damnonia smiled as his gaze roamed over her to make certain she was all right. "You have done a great and daring deed, Alysa. All is saved because of you and your husband and the wizard. This ruse and victory will become a timeless legend."

Alysa hugged him again. "I am happy you allowed us to carry it out, Grandfather, for we feared you might halt us. It was an exciting, but often frightening, adventure. I am glad it is over. At last, we can have peace. Where is Granmannie? How is she?"

"Giselde and Queen Brenna await us at your castle. When all are rested and tended, we shall journey there and celebrate." Catching sight of King Briac nearby, Bardwyn hinted, "You have not met Gavin's father, King Briac. He is as proud of you two as I am."

Briac stepped forward and clasped Alysa's hand within his. He and Alysa looked at each other. In his mind, he saw so much of Catriona—his first love—in his son's wife: that same indomitable pride, courage, spirit, beauty. He was pleased with Gavin's choice.

Alysa eyed the man who had given up his love for her mother for his duty to his land. Briac appeared a strong man, not one easily swayed by the opinions and dictates of others. She had been willing to go against Gavin to perform her duty, so she could understand how Briac had made a similar decision long ago. Gavin favored his handsome and virile father, and Alysa saw why her mother would have been drawn to such a man. She smiled at King Briac. "It is good to finally meet you, father of my valiant husband."

The Cumbrian king replied, "Brenna and I have heard much about you, Princess Alysa. We look forward to learning more in Damnonia. We are proud and happy that our son chose such a unique woman to be his wife and joint ruler. When the time comes for me and Brenna to leave this life, we shall depart knowing you are a worthy wife and a superior ruler."

Alysa smiled again and thanked him for his confidence in her. Briac's expressions and personality were so like Gavin's. Yea, she decided, she liked and respected this king. She glanced past him and greeted Gavin's friends: Weylin, Dal, Tragan, Lann, and Keegan. How she wished Sir Bevan were here with them at this glorious moment, and perhaps he *was* in spirit.

To all the men near the doorway, she said, "Your timing was perfect. Together we have won a marvelous victory."

Sir Lann entreated eagerly, "Tell us about the ruse and quest. How did Gavin get here? Why did you vanish so secretively?"

Trosdan, who was sitting on the edge of the bed, responded to those queries. "Prince Gavin is wise and brave. He allowed me to enchant him into becoming a Viking warrior named Eirik. He realized he could play his vital role more convincingly if he truly believed he was Eirik. To save all, he took a great risk to dupe the Vikings. Until this morning, he did not know he was Prince Gavin. We broke his spell and all worked together to complete the ruse. I was the one who compelled him to act so strangely back home. It was necessary that no one knew where he had gone or why, so no slips could be made. When I approached Prince Gavin with this plan, he knew it was the only way to obtain victory and peace, so he agreed to allow me to enspell him. He is truly a great man, a matchless warrior and ruler."

Gavin was pleased by the Druid's cunning explanation and let it stand unchallenged. He briefly related what they had done here, then suggested, "It has been a long and hard day for everyone. Let us finish our tasks outside and re-

424

so we can leave this place in the morning. I am eager to get home with my wife."

Briac embraced his son. "I am proud of you, Gavin. Your mother will be happy and pleased to hear this news."

"In a few months, there will be more to make you proud and happy. Alysa carries our children. Twins, the wizard has predicted."

All eyes glanced at the beaming Alysa, who smiled and blushed. Bardwyn hugged her. "More than one victory has been won."

Gavin snuggled in the bed with Alysa. He sighed in fatigue, releasing all lingering tension. "You and Trosdan were right about everything, m'love. The plan was cunning and successful."

"And we were reunited on this conqueror's moon as he vowed. I am so happy, Gavin. I can hardly wait to get home to see Granmannie and to meet your mother."

"You two will like each other; I am certain of it. I love you, my beautiful enchantress," he murmured, closing his mouth over hers.

A few day's ride from there, the Jute chieftain was saying to his closest friends, "When our spies return with news, we will know if the Norsemen have kept their word to depart soon. If they are still there, we must ride against them to appease Vortigern. If they leave peacefully as promised, we shall do nothing to challenge them."

The following morning, the Viking bodies were burned and their camp was destroyed, leaving only stone shells of their longhouses. As they worked, numerous Logris peasants arrived with homemade weapons to join a battle whic[h] had been won last night. Alysa was delighted by the change of heart and courage, and was surprised to lear[n] the peasant girl was responsible for it.

After the news had been shared from both sides, th[e] leader of the peasants confessed ruefully, "She forced u[s] to realize you were right, Your Highness. We can no long[er] live in such terror and pain. Villagers and noblemen hav[e] agreed to join forces to drive all Norsemen and Jutes fro[m] our land. If King Vortigern resists our demands for peac[e] we will replace him. Logris belongs to us, and all barbaria[ns] must be sent fleeing or be slain. You have given us th[e] courage to unite and move against them."

After a short talk, Alysa observed their departure, wavin[g] a final time to the petite young woman who had done f[ar] more than keep her promise to the Damnonia princess.

The Celts separated into three bands to return to the[ir] homelands, except for Bardwyn and his retinue and Bria[n] with his, who were to journey to Damnonia for a visit be[-]fore returning to their kingdoms.

Along the way, Weylin revealed his love for Lady Kord[e] and his intention to wed her. Gavin and Alysa were happ[y] for their friend and eager to give the wedding at Malve[rn] Castle.

The few who were injured, including Trosdan, heale[d] steadily. The group was a joyous one, repeating stirring tale[s] over and over. The Damnonians were thrilled by Princ[e] Gavin and his friends' aid and roles in this enormous vi[c]tory, and vowed never to go against them again.

Alysa's heart leapt with joy to see all of Trosdan's pr[e]dictions coming true. Yea, this was a multiple victory, s[he] decided.

On their way home, Gavin recovered his horse Troj[an] and all of his possessions from the old man who lived [in] a secluded glen. Trojan was as happy to see his master [as]

Gavin was to reclaim his loyal steed. The man who had been safeguarding the animal and belongings was thanked and rewarded for his help and kindness. Prancing with excitement, Trojan was eager to race the wind with his beloved master upon his back. Gavin chuckled and mounted, and off they galloped to rejoin the others and continue their journey to Damnonia.

At the castle, Giselde, Brenna, Teague, Thisbe, Leitis, Piaras, and all others hurried out to greet the returning party. Again, the splendid tales were repeated and everyone cheered.

Alysa and Giselde looked deeply into each other's eyes and smiled knowingly. "It is over, Granmannie, and we have won."

The gray-haired woman replied softly, "Yea, my precious child, the evil past is over, and a beautiful future is only beginning."

Brenna joined the two women. Alysa embraced Gavin's mother, and was not surprised by her immense beauty and gentility. "We shall have many days to get acquainted. I am very proud of you, Alysa, and very happy my wandering son discovered such a treasure on his adventure here. It warms my heart to see him so content."

Alysa and Thisbe exchanged news of their pregnancies, and both rejoiced for each other. Soon, Teague and Thisbe would be returning to their feudal estate to run it for Lord Daron's heirs. She recalled the peasants' promise to rescue Lady Gweneth and her girls during their defeat of Horsa and Hengist and to send them home. This time, Teague and Thisbe would be safe and happy there. In the years to come, Teague would inherit his father Lord Orin's title and estate.

Lord Keegan's wife had arrived with Queen Brenna and would go to live at Land's End with her husband. Alysa could imagine how happy both would be there and together again.

Also with Brenna was Sheriff Dal's betrothed, so another wedding of one of Gavin's close friends would take place soon.

That left only Tragan and Lann unmarried, but surely she and Gavin and their friends could help them find good wives.

Alysa eyed the five quest treasures which would be hung in the Great Hall as trophies of their stunning victory over the Norsemen. From this day forth, every time she looked at them she would recall her exciting days and nights in Logris with a Viking named Eirik.

In her chambers, Alysa glanced around the large room. It looked so different from when Prince Alric had occupied it, and had died in a dark and dank chamber months ago. But her father was with her mother now, and both were at peace, a wonderful peace which they had savored so rarely during their turbulent existences.

The nights were getting cooler as winter approached the land. To chase away a damp chill, a small fire was burning in a braiser and casting warmth and a sensual glow about the room. Alysa removed the false ring and slipped the ancient wedding band on her finger. Many Norse queens had worn it. From her own Viking bloodline, Astrid, Gisel, and Catriona had worn it. One day she would pass it on to the daughter she now carried within her body. The legendary ring was back where it belonged, as were she and husband.

As if she had mentally summoned him, Gavin entered the room and locked the door. He went to his wife and took her in his arms. "I love you, woman, and cannot wait a moment longer to have you."

428

He lavished kisses over her face and lips, and she laughed merrily. The feast was still continuing downstairs, but they did not care. They needed to be alone, totally alone, for a time.

Princess Alysa Malvern and Prince Gavin Crisdean removed their garments and entwined on their bed. Trosdan had told them he would remove the scar and replace the royal Cumbrian crest tomorrow. But for tonight, they only wanted to cuddle in their own bed and to share wild, sweet caresses.

Author's Note

I hope you enjoyed reading THE LAST VIKING QUEEN, Book II in my medieval fantasy series that began with WILD IS MY LOVE. It was fun working with those special and exciting characters again, and they "insisted" I allow them to finish their story. I want to thank all my faithful readers and the many booksellers who requested this continuation of Alysa and Gavin's adventures. I want to thank Zebra Books for reprinting WILD IS MY LOVE and, most of all, for publishing the original/unabridged edition of this book as I wrote it years ago. Who knows? Perhaps there'll be saga #3 one day . . .

A Janelle Taylor Newsletter, bookmark, and booklist are available with a self-addressed, stamped envelope (long/legal size) from:

Janelle Taylor
P. O. Box 211646
Martinez, GA 30917-1646

Please print your name and address clearly on the inside and out to prevent letters from getting lost in the mail. I wish I could respond personally to every letter I receive but time and expense don't permit me to answer thousands of letters and still have time to write exciting novels for you to enjoy. Please know that I appreciate each letter and comment. Most reader questions are answered in my bi-rly newsletter.

I want to thank Joy Chant for the historical information learned from her Celtic novel THE HIGH KINGS (Bantam Books, 11/83) and Bantam Books for permission to use those facts.

Books are prized possessions. Always keep Love in your heart, Romance in your life, and a book in your hands. Support literacy by reading something every day or teaching others to do so.